Double Take

David R. Smat

Double Take is a work of fiction. Names, places, characters and incidents are products of my imagination or modified renditions of personal travels and experiences.

The bottom line is that I made all of this up, and I hope you enjoy the adventure.

(David R. Smat)

ISBN 978-0-9904132-1-9

Printed in the United States of America

Acknowledgements

I want to thank my wife, Laurie, and sons Rob, James, Michael and Joey, and my editor Mary Venturella for their support of my writing endeavors. You are my true inspiration.

Prologue

We've all dreamed about having a twin; physically identical in every way so that no one could tell you apart.

My life has been exactly this; I am John Stone, the geeky MIT-grad now military intelligence officer (the "brain") and my identical twin brother Joe, who boasts a 25-year U.S. Special Forces career (the "brawn").

Our co-development of a TOP-SECRET DoD remote sensing technology unexpectedly catapulted us into a world in which we must secretly swap identities, requiring every bit of our ingenuity and training, to stay one step ahead of our captors just to stay alive.

This is my story.

Chapter 1

Its Monday morning ... just another day, driving the same road, the same 25 miles, the same trip I've followed almost daily for the past 10 years. I peer at the other cars and those driving them. We are all like a school of fish, all going the same direction, heading to our final destination--that being our place of employment, or simply "work."

To relieve the boredom of my drive, I've made a habit of watching the other drivers in their cars. Today I happened to notice the woman in the car next to me, texting on the cell phone as she drives--I've always hated that habit, and always turn off my cell phone whenever driving, to the chagrin of my friends who constantly complain when they cannot reach me, as if I would answer anyway even if my cell was on.

So, back to the woman driver texting in the car next to me. She was so intent in the texting process that she undoubtedly was following the taillights of the pickup ahead of her just to stay in her lane. If the pickup ahead of her was to drive off the road, she would follow. Looking to my left, there was yet another distracted driver talking on his cell phone and to my rear was a woman applying her make-up in her rear-view mirror. It's amazing that I ever make it work with these crazies surrounding me. I continued to notice this repeating pattern of distracted drivers for the next two miles. Same picture ... different car. And then, I noticed a noticeable difference in the school of fish.

To my left I noticed that the driver, a middle aged man, short dark hair, dark complexion, nicely dressed in a dark suit and tie, was not distracted by his cell phone, and was apparently paying close attention to me, staring straight at me as I drove next to him. Maybe he was wondering why I was staring at him. No matter, I took the next exit--game over, time for work.

Turning into EXos Incorporated, my car approached one of the nameless security guards that monitor employees entering the main guard gate. As I have many times after people watching on my drive in, I had forgotten to hang the security pass behind my rear view mirror, which of course became the highlight of the guard's day when he noticed my non-compliance. I slowed down to a stop in response to the madly waving guard who no longer was the normally friendly greeter present upon my distant approach.

"Can I help you?" the guard asked with obvious concern in his voice.

I quickly located my tag and flashed it to the guard, whose day was plainly ruined now that his apparent felon was just another employee. As he waved me in, I wondered what the guard would do if I had been a terrorist or intruder. My guess is that he would do absolutely nothing, as our guards are all unarmed and would probably run and hide - what else could he do? No wonder they make minimum wage.

I parked in my assigned parking spot, adjacent to the front entry to the headquarters tower--seniority has its privileges. As I exited my car, my colleague, Jim Davis, parked his black Mercedes to the right of my car. Jim is actually the one who hired me ten years ago, and has been a close friend of mine since we were in high school. Ironically, we both relocated to Texas from our hometown in Wilmington, Delaware after attending Graduate School where we specialized in Electrical Engineering. Jim arrived at EXos a few years ahead of me, and I still find it amazing that we're both here now. Predestination maybe, but then again, maybe not.

"Hey Jim, I've been waiting for you to get here," I exclaimed. "Yeah, right. This is the one day of the year that you arrive before me, so don't be so proud," Jim says. He's right, by the way. Same banter between us two . . . just a different day.

"How was your weekend?" Jim asked, as we walked up the stairs towards the stately entry way.

"Was wonderful, but too short," I replied. Same reply ... different day. I placed my I.D. badge near the proximity reader and received the familiar green light and door latch click allowing entry. Jim did the same after me. Back inside again, safe and sound.

We both greeted Cindy at the office reception desk. She was in earlier than normal, which equates to any time before 8:00 a.m. Cindy always appeared to be in a good mood, even when she wasn't, which was seldom. Her favorable looks also had the same effect on whoever entered the reception area. "Favorable," meaning long blond hair, steel blue eyes and all of the accompanying attributes that make most men stare a bit too long before turning back to their business. The bottom line is that Cindy was our office gate keeper, and could cut you down with a look of her eyes, if the need arose. OK, to put it plainly, Cindy could be a real pain in the butt when deemed necessary, which is apparently why Jim and I hired her two months after I joined EXos. Luckily, she likes me, or at least tolerates me, probably more so the latter than the former.

Why the guard, the elaborate access control system and the blond gate keeper, one might ask. Pretty simple. EXos Incorporated is a specialty electronics manufacturer. "Specialty" meaning that we work for the government; not just the U.S. Government, but literally any government (or private individual) willing to pay for our products. "Specialty" also refers to the type of products that we design, which include electronic surveillance, recording, and associated encryption devices of all types ... what some people might refer to as "spy equipment."

The interesting thing is that the equipment that people consider "spy equipment" such as that seen on television spy shows is actually 20-year old technology. The Top Secret technology that EXos secretly sells to the military today will appear to be state-of-the-art during our children's generation, similar to classified military aircraft guidance systems from the 1980s that are now commonplace on today's commercial aircraft.

What makes EXos "systems" unique from our competitors is the integral design that Jim and I designed while in Graduate school at the University of Delaware, working for the now infamous Dr. Liimus, who died recently of old age (he must have been 100, because he was old when we worked with him over 20 years ago). The surveillance system that Jim and I perfected is in the form of a 0.83 millimeter thick transparent wafer, completely flexible, with a diameter of 13/16th of an inch. The "femto wafer," as we call it, is capable of recording and transmitting high resolution video with the added capability of infrared and night vision. In other words, due to its concave shape and small size, our femto is the ultimate video system that can be worn as a contact in a soldier's eye, providing him perfect night vision, or infrared capability, if the need arises. In layman's terms, the user can see in the dark or can track the body heat of personnel through building walls, all of which can be immediately processed by the user and saved on video. The fact that the femto can also receive video means that any image can be projected directly into the user's field of vision, equivalent to wearing a GPS on your eye. The entire femto, including the Tech Pack, is no larger than the size of an iPhone, and only requires a 12-volt power supply that can last up to 14 days without recharge. No too shabby for a mere $250,000 per unit.

Our femto is the next generation of the Pentagon's Darpa research branch's SCENICC system unveiled publicly in late 2010. The SCENICC, short for "Soldier Centric Imaging via Computational Cameras" is similar in its ability to provide a 360-degree, 1 kilometer radius, 3-D video image to the user's eyepiece. SCENICC utilizes a stereoscopic-binocular system that weighs 700 grams, or about a pound and a half, most of the weight of which is the battery which lasts a maximum of 24 hours.

Completely insufficient for most battle situations, in my opinion, which apparently is the same opinion of the Pentagon, since they're our primary investor for the femto.

Someday, when the military is done with their application, we may be able to use the femto to enable the blind to see, once we figure out how to transmit the video output directly to the brain. Another project for another day. For now, we strive to assure our current customers stay happy, which is easier said than done.

Chapter **2**

This particular Monday was a pivotal day for EXos, and particularly exciting for both Jim and me. At 10:00 a.m. we had scheduled the first demo of our femto prototype ... a long awaited milestone after five exhausting and increasingly costly years of design and system assembly. Since Jim and I knew the most about the unit, we eagerly agreed to become the primary beta testers ... although we wouldn't have it any other way. Again, seniority has its privileges.

The test chamber that we would be using today was an artifact of an earlier electromagnetic interference study, that being our million cubic foot anechoic chamber. This anechoic chamber was simply a 100 by 100-foot cube that was lined on all sides with radar absorbing material, in the shape of cones of varying shapes and sizes. For our femto beta test, we simply needed the darkest environment we could muster and this chamber fit the bill. Jim and I flipped a coin to see who would wear the femto and I was the lucky winner for this inaugural test.

The test today was simple enough, as we desired a successful first test vs. an initial failure. My task was to enter the pitch black chamber, locate six pre-located markers and return to the entry door with them. The markers were colored black to match the floor with each being a different temperature ranging from 10 degrees below ambient room temperature to 10 degrees above room temperature.

Our expectation was that the femto would be unable to locate the ambient temperature markers or those below ambient, with those markers above ambient standing out like red beacons on a runway.

As Jim and I prepared to venture to our Process Development lab to retrieve the femto prototype, Cindy paged in on my telephone intercom noting that I had a call from an individual who did not want to provide his name. As I am never one to turn down a potential client, I replied that I would take the call so Cindy forwarded the call to my direct line.

I picked up the receiver and said, "This is John Stone, how can I help you." After approximately 10 seconds of silence, the person on the other end of the line queried, in a monotone voice,

"Are you the same John Stone that grew up in Wilmington and attended Archmere Academy?"

I replied, "Yes, but that was at least forty years ago ... How can I help you?"

The person on the other end noted, "You just have," and hung up.

Great - another weirdo. Just what I needed to start the day. I called to Cindy and asked, "What did the caller ID say his number or area code was?"

She replied, "Oddly enough, the number was blocked--even the area code didn't display. That's what you get for picking up when I tell you not to do so."

I replied, "I guess I missed the 'not to' part."

Cindy replied, "Not the first time you've used that line. You need some new material."

"Thanks, Cindy," I said. "I'll work on my new material after lunch." Enough banter, time to work. Nevertheless, I've never liked prank phone calls ... they've bothered me ever since I was a child. I guess weird memories ring true, even decades later.

10:00 came and went, as we continued to experience interference between the femto lens transmitter and infrared receiver. They were in effect competing against each other, as the communication cycle called for a two pico-second pause between the transmission and receive signals. Ironically, this timing technology is easy to implement ... but apparently not today. After a readjustment of the timing rheostat, we were in business.

Time to suit up. Although Jim and I have both donned the femto and associated power and tech pack many times, the lenses always bring a tear to my eye, literally that is, as the femto lens is similar to the hard contact lenses first introduced in the 1970s. Not unlike having a grain of sand in your eye, at least initially. We considered a soft monomer-based version of the femto, but found that the lack of rigidity promoted less long term durability due to the saline content of human tears. So, a little discomfort serves the femto, and the the user, well.

The right and left lenses inserted without difficulty, or extended discomfort. By now, you would think that I would be used to the feel of having pieces of plastic in my eye--not the case, but my excitement overcame the slight discomfort. Next, I reached to the tech pack to activate the voice control, and stated "System On Right, System On Left." Immediately, my vision was enhanced by the addition of a cross hatched pattern across my field of vision. "Night Vision On - Right" instantly changed my right eye's vision to a light green field. This is would be the mode that I would trial inside the chamber.

After entering the chamber, Rodney, our Tech Assistant, closed the door behind me enclosing me in pitch black. The vision in my left eye was now completely dark and the right eye continued its green hue of the entire chamber.

I spoke the command "Night Vision Left" and I could immediately see the entire chamber disguised by the familiar glowing green scene, but in both eyes now, allowing much greater depth perception than the single eye by itself. I searched for the markers and couldn't identify any. I spoke the command "Infrared Right" and my right field of vision turned to a grayish hue with now easily identifiable bright white glowing circles located on the floor ... that being the "warmer" markers randomly placed across the room. A quick first success, as we had hoped.

Just for fun, I wanted to test the capability of the satellite imaging of the femto before exiting the building. With a "Satellite active" command, then "Self-locate," I was instantly viewing the building in which I was located, from the perspective of the EXos satellite suspended approximately 8.35 miles above the earth's surface. One of four EXos satellites capable of this function, to enable redundancy and the ability for full 24-hour coverage considering the continuous rotation of the earth. Next, "Zoom 100 feet" enabled a field of view approximately 100 feet above my current location. "Infrared on" then enabled the ability to detect heat sources throughout the building, which at this time indicated six glowing forms inside the building, five close together near the operations lab directly outside the chamber, and the sixth in the middle of the building (i.e., me). The clarity was amazingly sharp. Another success.

After removing the femto lenses and the power and tech pack, downloading the operations data, and a two-hour debriefing session with the Team, our Monday was done. Before heading out for the day, I have the internal need to completely clean out my email box at the end of each day. Call me OC, but it's my way to keep control of my hectic work environment--purely a psychological exercise, but effective nonetheless. After 15 minutes of performing the 4-Ds of email etiquette, "Do-Delete-Delegate-Defer," I came across an email flagged by our Spam Filter from a unrecognized sender "Abrams@yahoo.com." I released the email simply for the reason that I was getting tired and wanted to leave.

The email was redirected to my In-Box with a subject line simply stating "Project Update." Upon opening the email, the message simply stated "We know who you are." This email fell under the "Delete" category of the 4-D, and away it went. My In-Box was now empty and my life was once again back in control. I grabbed my jacket from the hanger on the back of my office door, assured my desk and files were locked, closed my door and wished Cindy a good night. I then proceeded out the secured entry door into the parking lot, via yet another requisite swipe of my badge to exit.

Chapter 3

As I walked to my car I thought about the evening ahead. I had been asked to meet up with Jim and a few folks from the Team at the local bar to celebrate the positive results of the trial run this morning. The bar du jour was a dive we nick-named "EXos West", only because we've seemingly solved more issues there than we do at the office. As odd as this seems, there was truth to this. Clearly beer has a positive effect of relaxing the engineering mind, at least the first few drafts. After that point, the theory of diminishing returns kicks in.

The truth was that I was totally exhausted. The success of today's test was essential to the schedule and success of EXos overall, and I had lost many nights of sleep in anticipation. I reluctantly agreed to meet the Team anyway, despite my preference to go home and relax. Social events take too much personal effort lately, especially with the folks from work because inevitably we always discuss our work.

I hopped into my car and started the engine. My Audi A6 hummed to life after a single push of the "Start" button. I've always marveled at the simplicity of proximity starters in cars. The premise is that as long as the driver has the key FOB in their pocket, the car can be started with the push of a button. Proximity starters will surely be the demise of car keys in this decade. This is a perfect example of Top-Secret technology that originated in the military, and made it's way to commercial use two decades later.

As I pulled out of the parking lot, the security guard gave me a half-hearted wave, probably remembering me as the unbadged rebel from the morning commute. Or maybe he didn't and just waved at everyone, which would be the more plausible explanation. I took a quick left to head towards "EXos West" which was approximately 10 miles away. My guess is that I would be the last of our group to arrive, as usual.

As I merged onto the interstate, thoughts of the day's success flooded my mind. We were clearly a long way from completing the validation of the femto, which was exciting yet stressful at the same time. Oh well, I thought, what would my life be without stress. Strangely enough, I actually craved it. As I continued my self-distraction, I noticed a flash of sunlight reflecting off of an unknown item in the vehicle to my left. To my amazement, when I turned my head to the left, I was confronted with what appeared to be the individual that was staring at me on my drive to work this morning. This time though, he was not staring at me as he did this morning (assuming this was the same guy). What alerted me to this driver was the reflection of the setting sun off of his ring. He then turned to his right and noticed my gaze, which I quickly averted to the road.

I thought to myself, what's the chance that I would notice a driver next to me two times in one day? Actually, the odds are reasonably good that this could occur, and has probably occurred numerous times in the past considering the route that we collectively follow every day. I'm just being paranoid, I thought. It wouldn't be the first time. Just to ease my mind though, I noted to memory his license plate viewed from my side-view mirror as I pulled ahead of the White Chevy Malibu, Texas plate AV09 012.

I exited at Bethany Street, and shortly after was entering the parking lot at EXos West, a.k.a. Slade's to the local folk. As I entered the parking lot I recognized a few of my colleagues' vehicles near the back of the lot. Typical engineers, who would rather walk than park close to the entrance and have their car scratched. My sentiments exactly, so I pulled alongside, exited my car and began the trek to the front door.

On the way, I noted Jim talking on his iPhone just outside the entrance, which is no surprise. When Jim is not at work, he's continually talking on his iPhone. He motioned to me to stick around, so I assume he had a work question that he needed my assistance with, which was close but not the case. Apparently, Cindy had just called Jim in a tizzy asking for advice since his wife was on the other line asking where he was. Apparently, Jim had neglected to remember that he and his wife, Corrine, were to have met for dinner 30 minutes ago. So now Jim wanted me to tell Corrine that we've been working late and he was on his way. What are friends for? Of course, I covered for him, spent about 5 minutes chatting with Corrine until Jim got "ready," and then Jim hit the road. This is the prime reason why I'm not married, mostly because of my unpredictable work schedule, and second, because no sane woman would put up with me.

Upon entering Slade's, I immediately saw our Team at our usual spot, adjacent to the billiard tables in the back of the room. The hard part is getting to the back of the room considering the large crowd surrounding the television screens at the front of the bar ... a bad design in my opinion. Shuffling through the thick crowd, I saw Tom, our electro-optics guru motioning to me from the back to buy another round. Best to do so before I left the bar area as the waitresses in Slade's are practically non-existent when you want to order a drink. Certainly they must not work on tips alone, otherwise they would go hungry. I ordered a round of the usual, a selection of beers ranging from Rolling Rock for Tom to Blue Moon for the rest, with an orange on the side, of course. The bartender noted, "That will be twenty dollars even, or do you want to put it on the EXos Tab." Yes, it's sad when the bartender knows you well.

I noted, "I'll do cash today," and reached for my wallet which was to my dismay, noticeably absent from my right rear pocket. "Crap," I said. "Appears I've lost my wallet so let's put it on my tab. Also, please have the waitress cart these to my friends playing billiards in the back." I can't imagine where I would have left my wallet, which bothered me more than the fact that I lost it. I'm not the type to lose things and even more so the type to stress until I find the item.

After pushing through the crowd, I made my way to the billiard tables where I alerted all that another round was on its way. I was a hero yet again. I also noted that I needed to run back to my car to locate my wallet, which I now assumed fell from my pocket while driving just as my security badge has done many times in the past. Janet asked if I needed an escort to my car, not for protection, but to assure I returned and covered the tab tonight, as I always did. Again, what are friends for?

Back pedaling through the crowd was beginning to get old, for me as well as the patrons as I continued through to reach the door. After about 3 minutes, I was back outside of the bar and walking towards my car. Just to be sure I had not simply dropped my wallet, I was slowly back-tracking my earlier steps, carefully looking around each car.

Then I saw it. It was not my wallet that caught my eye, it was the parked car with Texas plate AV09 012. The same white Malibu that I saw before I exited on Bethany Street was parked mid-way between my car and the bar entrance. Other than a few water bottles and cups, the vehicle appeared empty. It was a rental, as indicated by the bar code sticker located on the side windows. Enterprise, to be exact. There were no indications of occupants, so I assumed they went inside. Out of curiosity, I tried the doors which were all locked. I needed to find my wallet so I continued to my car. After 5 minutes of thoroughly searching my car, no luck--no wallet.

As I passed the Malibu on the way back inside, my mind began to play tricks on me as I considered the repercussions of this coincidence. What if the driver was waiting for me behind the next car, or if there was really more to this than I realized. I decided at this point to continue back towards Slade's. I also had a plan, as I'm not a believer of coincidences.

As you can imagine, since Jim and I were the inventors of the femto, we took the liberty to use our toys for our own purposes. This was one of those instances. I returned to my vehicle, opened the trunk, and accessed the femto unit stored in a compartment above the wheel well.

I popped the lenses into my eyes, placed the cigarette-sized tech pack into my pocket, locked my car and headed back to the middle of the parking lot.

Via command "System On Right, System On Left," the units jumped to life. "Satellite active" and "Self-locate" drew the system to local coordinates, followed by "Infrared on" and "Zoom to 100" and I saw myself in the center of the parking lot in which I was standing. With the IR activated, I could also locate any warm objects in the lot with me, which at this time included the still warm engines of the parked vehicles. No other human-shaped emitters were present in the lot. Comforting as this may seem, it did not answer the questions I had running through my mind. Now, it was time to find my unknown friend or foe in the bar.

As I entered Slade's I deactivated the left femto via "Left System Off" so I could function somewhat normally in the crowd with one un-enhanced eye. I waited near the entrance for a few minutes to intentionally attract the attention of my follower. I then relocated myself to the most visible wall of the bar room to enable my personal view of the entire room. As I stood there, I feigned the largest and longest yawn that I could muster. I then activated the "Night Vision On" command and panned the crowd looking for patrons with "contagious" yawns.

The premise behind the yawn reflex has long been observed to be contagious. If one person yawns, this may cause another person to yawn. The cause for contagious yawning may lie with mirror neurons in the frontal cortex of certain vertebrates, which upon being exposed to a stimulus from similar organisms, activates the same regions in the brain. Mirror neurons have been proposed as a driving force for imitation which lies at the root of much human learning, such as with language acquisition. Yawning may be an offshoot of the same imitative impulse. Or least that's what I've heard.

It only took me a few seconds to identify the contagious yawners in the crowd. For the most part, I assumed that no one was looking directly at me in such a large room, so inevitably, it would be just be my unknown friends watching my every move with contagious yawns. There they stood, approximately 40 feet across the room, yawning in unison. Two men, both well dressed in sport coats and jeans, still staring directly at me. Switching to the femto's infra-red mode, the two men's faces lit up on my field of view, indicating elevated body temperature commonly attributed to nervousness or excitement. Two men instead of the original premise of one . . . just wonderful.

I zoomed in until I could just see their faces. Both men appeared to be middle-eastern, my guess being Israeli or Serbian. Neither appeared to be above six-feet tall, but reflected the tell-tale signs of well-trained operatives, due to their attentive stares, their now visible neck microphones and ear pieces. Both were quietly conversing with each other using these systems while continuing to stare at me.

Another feature of the femto which we added as a nice-to-have option was the lip reading capability, which was currently being assessed by the Tech Pack located in my pocket. It was a new addition, so there were still a few bugs to be worked out, but effective enough to decipher the language of Arabic. Unfortunately, their distance and the occasional passer-by, prevented full translation, which would have been extremely helpful at this point.

I shifted approximately 15 feet around the outer wall, and glanced back at my apparent followers. No surprise. Their gaze was fixed on my new location. Now for my dilemma, do I meet my followers head-on, or do I escape and wait until they find me again. No contest, as I've never been the type to give up a personal advantage, especially one which is so strongly in my favor.

Chapter 4

The first objective is to separate your opponents, which I must assume might not just consist of two men. Luckily, they did not know that I had spotted them, so they were already at a disadvantage. I walked over to the bar and ordered two 20-ounce mugs of beer, and headed towards the bathroom. I had a 50/50 chance that only one of the men would follow me, which was my preference versus having to deal with both at once. My peripheral vision indicated that this is exactly what occurred, with one man remaining in his original location and the other circling through the crowd in my direction.

I entered the men's bathroom and proceeded to the sink farthest away from the entry, dumped out my beers, kept the empty glass mugs and turned on the faucet full blast. I then returned to the stall immediately adjacent to the entry door, closed it, and hopped up onto the commode in attempts to hide my feet. "Night Vision On - Right" activated my right femto. Then I waited.

Not more than 3 minutes later the bathroom door opened and my opponent slowly walked in. He neglected to check the stalls and immediately proceeded towards the sound of the running faucet. As soon as he turned the corner, I quietly exited my stall, reached towards the entry, and switched the bathroom lights out. Pitch black. Lights out for him, but a well-lit greenish tinted room for me. I could see my opponent reach under his jacket for what I expected was a weapon of some type.

I acted quickly and approached the man and swiftly struck the right rear side of his skull with the empty glass beer mug. An expertly placed strike with the intended result of temporary unconsciousness versus permanent injury. The strike was effective as the man dropped face down onto the bathroom floor. His gun rattled to the floor as well, about four feet away, where it came to a stop.

Not knowing if his partner was following, I picked up his Glock, dragged the man into one of the stalls and searched his pockets as quickly as possible. No surprise, no identification and every pocket was empty with the exception of his rear pocket, which contained a familiar item, my wallet, which he apparently obtained when we were squeezing through the crowd to enter Slade's, and a cell phone. His weapon, a late model Glock 45, was placed in my belt for safe keeping, along with the cell phone.

Now for his partner, who was either directly outside the door or still at a safe distance from the bathroom, watching for his partner to exit. No windows in the bathroom prevented my easy escape, so the options were two-fold. Stay put and wait for him to enter or take advantage of the unexpected, that being a quick exit and frontal attack. Thinking as my opponent, he would place himself 10 feet from the door, away from the opening side of the door, hands out of pockets, awaiting the exit of his partner, or the assailant. He would not chance displaying his Glock in such a crowd. He also would not enter the bathroom, for at least five minutes or earlier only if summoned by his partner.

Fortunately, his cell phone was not locked, and displayed recent placed calls and text messages. This could be easier than expected. Assuming that my friend was nearby and possibly blocking anyone from entering the bathroom, his ringing cell phone should be easily recognizable. Better yet, texting may be more effective, considering my voice would not be recognized.

Before executing the plan, I turned the bathroom lighting back on and retuned to my stall in hiding, along with my first victim, who I managed to balance over the toilet so his partner could not see him slumped on the floor under the stall door.

Activating the cell phone, I replied to the first, and most frequent, text, which was apparently sent by "Assan." Entered "Subject apprehended--All clear. You need to see this. You coming in? I'm in the back near the sink."

45 seconds passed -- No response. Crap. Think. Quickly.

After looking up Assan in the cell directory, I quickly identified that the most recently sent call was also to Assan, pressed the call button and listened for a ring. As is now common knowledge for most, the first ring that you hear on a cell phone is not actually the recipient's phone, but a 'fake' ring that is automatically transmitted to the earpiece until the actual connection is made via numerous microwave cell towers in between. The second ring is usually the real deal, occurring at the cell phone that you are calling.

No ring outside the door, but a voice in the phone stating "Coming", then a hang-up. Change of plans--no time for option 1. Option 2 about to be implemented. Within 20 seconds, the door opened and Assan walked in.

No time to waste, as the same lights-out trick would not work twice. As soon as Assan passed the stall, I raised myself above the door just enough to forcefully thrust the second beer mug down upon the rear lobe of his head, expertly placed, maim but not kill.

Assan dropped in his tracks, just as his friend began to stir, mumbling something in Arabic, I assume. Time to go, but first, I needed to find their car keys, which hopefully Assan had in his pocket. Seventeen seconds later, and I was leaving the bathroom with a new key FOB, two Glocks hidden in my belt, and two new cell phones. I could only hope that there was not a third friend.

I walked past the EXos Team and noted that I had to run unexpectedly, thanked them for a successful test, reminded them that the tab was covered and rushed for the front door. As I squeezed through the crowd, I grabbed a fork from the hamburger bar and managed a call to 911 using Assan's cell phone and told them that I saw two guys fighting in the bathroom at Slade's.

Chances are the police wouldn't make it in time, but still worth a shot. The fork was for a different purpose.

On the way through the parking lot, a quick stop by the Malibu was in order. The parking lights flashed with one push of the key FOB. The fork is a very useful tool, whenever one wanted to temporarily disable a car. Simply jam one tine into the valve stem, twist, and the entire stem comes out, along with all the air in the tire within 15 seconds.

A quick look inside turned up nothing other than a few half-full coffee cups, three empty Ozarka water bottles, and food wrappers. The glove compartment was locked, which popped open after another click of the FOB. Inside was the obligatory Rental Car rental papers, which was apparently rented by a Mr. John Smith--go figure. The other object was a one-half inch thick legal sized folder, containing documents stamped "Confidential" in red at the top and bottom of each page. All reviewing the life and military record and activities of a man named "Joseph Stone." A name that I think about my every waking day. The individual that they were chasing was not me, but was my twin brother, Joe.

Chapter 5

September 4, 1977. Another first day at another new school.
John Stone was poised for the inevitable that being the first exposure
to the myriad 8th Grade personalities that inhabited the halls of Mt.
Pleasant Middle School. Ironic, but the school's name was not an
indication of the general student population, as the school was a mid-
city public school which was known to have budgeting troubles,
among others, for the past five years. It was expected that this year
would be the last year that Mt. Pleasant would remain open.

John had survived the walk into the crowded halls, filled with
excited teens, glad to see each other again after the long summer.
Other students clearly did not have this enthusiasm, and were just
biding their time until they made it through the system or until the
local truancy officer lost them from his radar, whichever came first.

Within five minutes, John located his homeroom classroom,
entered the room and slipped into the chair near the window to the
right rear of the room. He was intentionally a few minutes early
allowing him to claim a seat before the remaining classmates
entered. He had learned that it was always beneficial to
anonymously grab an early seat than to walk into a full classroom
and become noticed. Plus, the remaining open seat was never a good
place to sit as the new guy.

John had been in this situation many times before, due to his military family's frequent global moves. He could not remember how many times he had moved or how many schools he had attended. Typically, a new school every year, sometimes two per year. At least this school was located in the United States, Pennsylvania to be exact. Even though John was now fluent in French and German, it was always easier to return to the culture and language of his upbringing. Plus, with his brown hair, dark complexion and tall mesomorphic build, he mixed in well with the Americans surrounding him, more so than he did with Europeans or Asians.

As the 8:00 bell was about to chime, a rowdy group of students strutted into the classroom, high-fiving a few of their friends in the class and thumping others who were clearly not. Their leader was a rather large chubby boy with spiked hair that they reverently called Sid. Sid bounced past the teacher's desk and headed towards the right side of the classroom, making a bee-line for John Stone, who had for some unknown reason caught Sid's attention.

"Hey you!" speaking directly to John, as he quickly approached John's desk. "Didn't I tell you this morning that if I saw you again I would kick your ass?"

John now stood to face the on-coming bully, meeting him eye-to-eye. John was the taller of the two, and clearly the more physically fit, but he was outnumbered four-to-one by Sid and his entourage of three similarly menacing teens.

"You must be mistaken, as I would have remembered a guy as ugly as you," John boldly stated. "I don't have time for your garbage, as this is the sixth school I've been to in the past two years. Take a guess how many dumb-shits like you that I've had to take out and then ask yourself if you want to be next?"

Sid seemed stunned for a few seconds by John's bold retort, but calling the bluff, replied with scorn that he looked forward to playing together at lunch. John sneered back, with an air of confidence on the outside but concern on the inside.

He had learned to never underestimate your opponent, especially when in unknown territory. Besides, why did every first day of school turn out this way?

As the teacher entered and introduced herself, John thought to himself that he knew exactly why Sid recognized him, and would use this to his advantage just as he had done in the past. Same story, just another first day at another school.

Class continued uneventfully until 10:00 a.m., short of a few hard stares received from Sid and his three henchmen. Lunch may be more interesting than originally planned, or maybe it was par for the course. Specifically, these actions were typical protocol for John, who believed that a new player to any environment must make his mark early in the game. Waiting to be chosen or excluded by the local powers should never be left to chance. Either take the bull(y) by the horns or suffer the consequences of personal inaction.

The end-of-period bell rang at 10:00 with all students rushing out the door for their next class. John intentionally hung back and allowed the class to exit, expecting that Sid would wait for him. Interestingly enough, Sid and his crew had already departed by the time John was ready to leave. No bother, John expected that Sid would surely save him a seat at lunch.

John made his way to the next class, noting a few of the same students from his previous class nodding at John when he entered. It was evident via their hushed conversations and furtive glances that he had already caused a stir, which was how he liked it. Reputation was the key to success, whether it be a positive or a negative reputation, the former of which was John's preferred choice.

11:30 came quickly, since the current class was pre-algebra, a subject that John enjoyed with a passion, plus the teacher, Ms. Wood, was hot, so two reasons to enjoy class. After the chime of the end-of-period bell, John returned to reality and the realization that the time had come to deal with Sid and his buddies. He leaned over to the student next to him, named Tim, and asked where the cafeteria was located.

Tim appeared startled but stammered, "Out the door, take a left, go to the end of the hall."

"By the way," Tim noted, "Sid does much of his work on the playground, which is where we are forced to wait after lunch is over, from noon to 12:30." "Good luck," Tim said.

"Thanks," John noted in reply and headed out the door, taking an immediate left.

The lunchroom was easy to find, just as Tim described. The wall-to wall tables and chairs were half filled with students, with the other half in a line that crept around the inside wall of the room. As John waited in line, he witnessed the many groups of students quickly gathering in their peer groups. There were the jocks, the nerds, the cheerleaders, the goths, the techies, the divas, and way in the back, the Sid entourage. Apparently, Sid's group had more than the three goons noted this morning. There appeared to be a total of six goons now, all with their feet propped up on the table while they ate.

John grabbed his lunch and sat by himself at an empty table diagonal to the Sid entourage but close to the door to the playground. A few sandwich bites later washed down by a pint of milk, John headed for the door to the playground, intentionally in direct view of Sid's table, the occupants of which scurried to their feet as John exited.

Always take the offensive was John's motto, and have other tricks up your sleeve. He positioned himself toward the end of the bleachers adjacent to the football field--a location where he could see the entire playground, but also could be hidden in a matter of a single step if he needed to retreat.

It took about 20 seconds for Sid and his crew to exit the cafeteria, with half of the student body, who apparently had all heard of John's earlier antics. Perfect--the more, the merrier, and the better the spread of reputation.

Sid and two of his friends came around the bleachers, with the other three goons unaccounted for. As Sid approached, he screamed, "This is your chance to run away, chicken shit!"

"Not going to happen, you ugly bastard," John replied. "In fact, I would like you alone to come behind the bleachers with me, to make this a fair fight. One on one, Mano to Mano."

Sid stated, "I don't think so, so how about us three against you?"

"That works for me," John stated, "As long as you don't mind getting embarrassed in front of your friends," and with that, John proceeded to run behind the bleachers, hidden from Sid and the entire student body who had collected to watch the scene.

Sid and his two goons ducked behind the bleachers from the opposite end, about 30 feet from where John had entered.

From the vantage point of Sid and his friends, once they ran behind the bleachers they were confronted by John on the far side, and raced towards him. Once half-way across the length of the bleachers, they heard a voice from the location where they entered, and as they turned, were amazed to see John himself standing where they entered, running at them at full trot. Similarly, from the original location, the second John, or was it the first, was running at them at the same time. They froze in their tracks, more so in amazement than fear, but were nonetheless completely at the mercy of the two John's, or whatever their names were. It took a few round houses and expertly placed knife hand strikes by John and his twin to incapacitate the three bullies. John and his twin, whose name was Joe, came out from behind the bleachers, each from opposite ends, as their victorious introduction to the awaiting student body. The students gasped, were quiet for 5 seconds, then cheered. John and Joe specifically searched through the crowd for Sid's other three cronies, to assure they understood the lesson they had just witnessed, and the pecking order that had just been established.

This ploy had worked many a time for John and Joe in the past, which was why the first day of school was always an eventful one. It is one of many experiences with Joe that flashed through John's mind every day. Joe was his partner, his brethren, his protector.

Chapter 6

Joe and John were fraternal twins and were surprisingly similar visually, physically, and mentally. As was the case during their youthful escapades, as adults they still looked incredibly similar, except now at six-foot-four, approximately 250 pounds, with short cropped brown hair, brown eyes and dark olive complexion. The biggest difference between the two brothers was that John was the intellectual and Joe the athlete, or more simply John was the brains and Joe the brawn. Not to say that John couldn't hold his own in a fight, but Joe could achieve the needed result in quicker fashion. Joe could likewise match most intellectuals in a battle of the minds, just not as effortlessly as John.

In 1982, it was no surprise that Joe was accepted into West Point and John into MIT. Both kept in touch as much as possible, despite their busy college lifestyles, and knowingly maintained parallel lives with both following the path of their military upbringing.

Specifically, Joe joined the Army's Green Berets shortly after graduating from West Point, Summa Cum Laude, with a specialty in Electronic Counter Countermeasures, or ECCM. ECCM was an acronym that didn't directly describe his so-called specialty, which was what the U.S. Army preferred for one of their most highly trained combat specialists. For ten years after joining the Green Berets, Joe served in Operation Just Cause in Panama, the Persian Gulf War, and Operation Enduring Freedom, inclusive of tours in Afghanistan, Spain, and Pankisi Gorge.

In early 1995, Joe was removed from the battlefield and transferred state-side to the Special Activities Division (SAD) of the Central Intelligence Agency's National Clandestine Service (CIA-NCS) responsible for covert operations, black ops and other "special activities."

John, on the other hand, graduated from MIT in a record three years earning a Bachelor of Electrical Engineering and transferred to the University of Delaware for his Master's Degree, with a specialty in Electro-Optics and Digital Design. Due to a particularly innovative remote sensing design that John developed as a graduate student, he was courted by the Darpa research branch of the Pentagon and was hired upon graduation as a design engineer in their Advanced Warfare Surveillance Systems Unit. In fact, John's graduate and post graduate work directly resulted in advances that enabled the development of the SCENICC system, first tested by the U.S. Army in the early 1990s.

Ironically, John and Joe ultimately partnered in the co-development and co-testing of the SCENICC system, one from a development, design and pilot perspective and the other from field testing and integration. Joe had extensively used the SCENICC unit real-time during Operation Enduring Freedom in Afghanistan, almost 15 years before the notion of its existence was communicated to the general public. Consequently, both brothers knew the system inside and out, and became renowned in the Pentagon community as a result.

Their reputation was also well known by numerous International Secret Forces across the world, most notably the Israeli Homad, known as the equivalent of the United States' Central Intelligence Agency. Unknown to U.S. Intelligence, or at least not outwardly communicated, the Israeli's believed that the SCENICC technology was stolen from them during allegedly co-operative efforts between the U.S. and Israeli forces following the Gulf War, with Joe being one of the primary targets for their dismay, due to his direct involvement during that time.

The U.S. military soon thereafter released SCENICC for covert use by their Green Berets, resulting in significant casualties for their opponents, the Israelis included. It was not the mere number of soldiers lost, but the principle of the betrayal that infuriated the Israelis. It may also have been a result of the coincident loss of the Israeli General's only son in a related battle gone wrong. Despite the direct reasoning, the Israelis remained relentless in their pursuit of related U.S. advances, via internal and external operatives planted inside numerous U.S. agencies, the CIA included.

This intense vengeance and remnant distrust was about to change the lives of John and Joe Stone forever.

Chapter 7

June 7, 1995 - John sat thinking in front of his computer, in his zero-window office connected to his personal test lab located on the third floor of the Pentagon. It always amazed him that Joe now worked in the office down the hall, instead of on an unknown battlefield somewhere on the other side of the globe. Comforting as it was, John felt that their close working relationship would not last if they remained employed by CIA/NCS, since he knew Joe was too valuable in the field, and would soon be sent back to some unknown hell hole.

John was also recently displeased with the Agency as they were not as aggressively allowing him to pursue the next generation SCENICC device that he had proposed to the current CIA Head. John was confident that he could design a much smaller and effective system that could be worn directly in the eye, similar to a contact that would be more useful than the almost two-pound goggle that comprised the current SCENICC. The SCENICC's 24-hour battery was a joke as well, as had been directly communicated by Joe during numerous battle debriefs. John was beginning to lose faith in the CIA/NCS with each passing day.

Just then, Joe popped his head into the office.

"You got a second, bro?" he asked.

"For you--always. What's up?"

Joe walked in and sat down across from John's desk.

"I've got an odd problem and would like to get your read."

"OK--shoot."

"Since I've been stateside for the past few months, my instincts tell me that I'm being watched. Sounds stupid, and I know we're always under 24/7 surveillance just because we're in NCS, but this is different."

"Different how?" John asked

"You and I know surveillance and know when and how we're being watched by our employer, but the techniques that I'm seeing aren't the typical stateside methods."

"Not stateside, interesting. Do you have any proof?"

"Yes. For example, as you know, our landline phones are bugged by the Agency and monitored electronically for key-words that match the NCS watch list. 20-year-old technology but effective for those who don't have a clue. You and I, on the other hand, know the bug is there and are careful what we say, even if speaking in jest. Just not worth the hassle of explaining in front of the General."

"Keep going, as I don't see the odd part yet."

"Wait for it, Brainiac."

"Waiting", John replied.

Joe continued, "Just last week, my paranoia was getting the best of me, so I went looking for the Agency phone bug which, to my complete surprise, was apparently replaced . . . by this gadget." John slid his iPhone out of his pocket and pulled up a number of photos of the apparent bug. "Of course, I left it there, but have yet been unable to define the make or origin."

John looked closely at the photos and did not recognize the unit either, which was troubling from a personal perspective.

"Can you email me these pics?"

After a few clicks, Joe replied, "Done."

"John, we need to talk about something I've not fully disclosed to anyone. Can we meet at the La Gastronomique after work tonight? This isn't the right place or time for this discussion, if you know what I mean."

Joe was referring to the internal surveillance systems integral to the Pentagon, which were comprised of continuous video and audio taping of practically every room throughout the facility, as if the bio-readers and proximity card readers were not enough. Additional systems were implemented to detect excessive employee body temperature and rapid heartbeat to define those who may be under stress. They had yet to define the difference between stress and an illness accompanied by a fever, with the kinks yet to be worked out.

Joe stood up and said, "I need you to look at something real quick in my office. Can you escape for 20 minutes?"

"Sure," replied John.

The two brothers completed the quarter mile hike down three floors and through the Pentagon's maze of concentric rings and spoke-like corridors, interspersed with bio-readers and access controlled doors, down to the Human Factors and Testing Lab where SCENICC was originally developed prior to external issue to the Army.

"I still get lost every time I come down here," noted Joe.

"No kidding," said John. "If it wasn't for the Pentagon map I found on www.hqda.army.mil and saved to my iPhone, I wouldn't be able to get around. It still amazes me that this depth of info is available to the general public. If they only knew how close to reality Internet info really is."

"No kidding. By the way, send me that map link when you get a chance."

"Will have it to you if I find my way back upstairs," John joked.

Upon arriving at Joe's sparsely decorated basement office, room BD126, Joe motioned for John to sit down, and proceeded to walk behind his desk. He then quietly pointed towards his computer and motioned for John to look towards the rear of the unit, specifically pointing at the USB ports at the rear. When John looked closely, there was a practically unnoticeable object connected to the one of the USB ports, well out of sight of the user. John peered at the object closely, with a quizzical look on his face.

"Want some coffee?" Joe asked. "The break room is right down the corridor, about 600 yards away." and walked out of the office. John followed without a word spoken between the two until they were a few steps down the hall.

"OK - What was that?" John asked.

"That, my friend, is a keystroke reader."

"How do you know that and more importantly, how did you know it was there?"

Joe replied, "Every morning, I run a tracer on my system to see what's happened since my last login. It's just a practice that I adopted while I was a cadet in West Point, when we had some hackers provide fake login screens in the computer labs, which would emulate a complete login sequence, record your username and password, then pass you seamlessly to the actual system. The hackers were actually targeting the professors, and would steal their login info and access tests before they were issued, or change their own grades. It would have worked except that scanning systems in the labs located the duplicate login screens in the hackers' personal files--boom, kicked out of West Point and probably work for the National Security Agency by now. So, my morning scan has become a daily ritual, even when I'm working on a non-networked computer."

"So you found it when you ran your trace?" John inquired.

"Yes. Once I knew it was there as "New Hardware," I was able to access what it was. To put it simply, it records every keystroke I make, as a single lengthy ASCII string. "

"Do you know when it showed up?" John asked.

"No, but I know how frequently it is accessed, or should I say, replaced."

"Replaced?" John asked. "How would you know that?"

"Simple . . . you remember the SCENICC goggles I have on the shelf behind my desk?"

"Of course, and I assume you activated them to video the room, then you watched the video."

"Bingo"

"So that means you know who it is."

Joe nodded, "Yes, I do, and now I do not plan to ask her out."

"Her?"

"Yes, it was Gwen Herrera."

"Really?"

"Really really."

"Have you told the Chief about any of this yet?" asked John.

"Not yet, I need to confirm something first, as you know I'm a cautious type. Let's plan to discuss the specifics tonight after work, as I have much more to tell you."

"10-4," replied John, "How about 6:00?"

"OK--I'll meet you there."

As John walked back to his office, this conversation with Joe again reminded him how paranoid his brother had become since his return from active duty. It was an issue he had discussed with Joe a number of times over the past few months. Joe's response to him was the same: With the exception of John, there was no longer anyone he could trust. The truth was that everyone he openly confided in while serving as a Green Beret, ended up missing or dead. It bothered John that he was about to enter this inner circle.

Chapter 8

John arrived at La Gastronomique fifteen minutes after Joe, who was already seated. The maitre d' led John to Joe's table, which was located in a remote corner of the room.

"Sorry I'm late," John said, as he sat down.

"No worries," Joe replied. "I'm just glad to be away from the 24/7 surveillance for a second."

"Same here . . . so what is going on?"

"It's a long story, occurring during my stint during Enduring Freedom, specific to the death of the Israeli General's only son."

Joe proceeded to describe the situation, in which he was assigned to prevent the release of SCENICC design plans to the Serbs, since it was the ultimate advantage for ground troops. It was known at the time that numerous operatives where vying for the same Top Secret design information to gain this advantage. The U.S. actually orchestrated the release of bogus design information, with Joe assigned as the controller of the information, and those who were to receive it. The competing operatives were manipulated by Joe to the point that they literally killed each other off, with the final pre-planned winner being the Israelis. It was a means to identify and eliminate the operatives with one fell swoop.

Joe was unaware that the Israeli General's son, Rhajib, wanted to impress his father by obtaining the SCENICC design information at any cost and had, unbeknownst to Joe and his father, made arrangements with numerous operatives to buy the information. In the end, the son's secret became common knowledge among the competition, which led to his disappearance and later, tortuous death. The General was completely mortified by the loss of his only son, and blamed himself and, presumably, Joe for not foreseeing and preventing the outcome.

Joe noted, "The last time I saw the General was at Rhajib's funeral. I attended out of respect thinking I was doing the proper thing. I also wanted to explain how Rhajib had caused the predicament, which I was never able to do as I could not get the General alone. The General personally told me to leave and to never show my face again, else he would personally execute me."

"Do you still feel personally responsible?" John asked.

"Yes, even though it wasn't solely my fault. I would have preferred to inform the General of what Rhajib had actually done to cause his own death, as I doubt he really knows. Either way, I'm sure I'm still on his radar for execution, as he put it. I also heard after the fact that his son's wife was pregnant at the time."

"I would tend to agree that you're on his radar," John replied. "So, what is the plan you told me about earlier?"

"That's the second part of the story, which hinges on the keystroke recorder I showed you that was hidden in my desktop USB port. My plan is simple. Give whoever is monitoring me some personal information and see if they take the bait."

"What type of personal information?" asked John.

"If they want me dead, then I give them the chance."

"OK--you lost me on that one, as that sounds like a bad idea."

"Calm down . . . hear me out. My plan is to alert Gwen, or whomever, via the keystroke recorder that I'm planning a weekend by myself at the cabin on the lake."

"But you don't own a cabin on the lake."

"I do as of last week. So, the deal is, I leak the weekend vacation info via my desktop and see if they come after me."

"And if they do?"

"I'll be ready for them."

"And I'll be with you?"

"Not directly, but solely from the viewpoint of SCENICC. If I am right, they will come for me, and only then will I alert the Chief. I need to have proof."

"I don't like this. There are too many unknowns," noted John.

"Yes, but I control the game, since they don't suspect that I know their plan."

"True. How soon will you initiate this personally hazardous 'game'?" asked John.

"I already have. I've communicated my vacation plans via email yesterday."

"For this upcoming weekend, meaning tomorrow?" John asked.

"Yup."

"So, has Gwen been by to swap out the USB recording device?"

"Yes, she came by and swapped it out late last night. I assume they have my info by now, so we see if they take action. Let's order dinner--I'm hungry."

"Are you serious? How can you be hungry after all of this?" John asked.

"John, I've been living with this issue since the day I left Rahjib's funeral and even more so since I've returned to the States. I'm actually relieved that I may be ahead of the game on this one. You've got to trust me on this . . . this is what I am trained to do, and I'm damn good at it."

"I'm still not completely on-board, but agree that this is a rare opportunity, with success strongly in your favor. I'll go along under one condition . . . that you involve me."

After a full 30 seconds in thought, Joe noted, "Deal. We've always been a good team, and I can use all the help I can get. OK-- now let's order dinner."

Chapter 9

June 8, 1995 - Joe noted in his baited email that he had planned to arrive at the cabin on Saturday morning, at 10:00 a.m., giving his opponents ample time to prepare their approach the evening before. Joe had planned for this by placing myriad monitoring devices across the property, the week before. All of which were continuously monitoring the property and providing real time alarming and video feed via his laptop and iPhone.

The cabin itself was located approximately one hour outside of Washington D.C. on a unpopulated shore of Lake Whitney. It was a single story one-bedroom cube, stacked log construction, constructed on a concrete slab. The nearest residence was over a mile away, and was as remote a location that Joe could find on short notice.

The cabin was located on a two acre pseudo-peninsula that seemingly floated out 200 feet onto the lake. This site was carefully selected by John, as it solely allowed land access via the entry road that snaked to the cabin's front porch. If the intruders decided to approach via the lake, which was highly unlikely, they would be sitting ducks. Even Joe's colleagues who were Navy Seals would find this a challenge, especially in daylight. For this reason alone, Joe expected that the fun would begin after dark, which is when he was at his best. That is to say, if they came at all.

Joe and John met at John's home the morning prior to drive to the Lake. Surveillance video from the property indicated zero intruders, with the exception of a few raccoons and an occasional deer.

John had expected to have seen some activity by now, which meant that the visitors were either not coming, or planned their approach that evening.

The plan was reviewed once, twice and a third time, by the two brothers. It had been developed by Joe, replicating a safeguarding operation that he had managed in Spain five years earlier for a local diplomat. It worked well that day and would work now, considering similar site characteristics and the expected number of intruders, conservatively estimated at less than ten. Joe and John walked to Joe's pickup, a late model four-wheel drive Toyota Tundra with oversized mud tires and a roll-bar with retro KC-Daylighters peering forward above the bed. The back seat of the Tundra had been loaded with a variety of armaments, showcased by two Colt M-4s, sufficient ammunition to support a small army and other nondescript weapons that Joe had collected over the years. Two pairs of SCENICC goggles completed the ensemble.

Neither brother spoke during the drive to the cabin, as they both considered the next 24 hours and ran and re-ran the possible scenarios through their heads. John continued to check the electronic surveillance of the property while Joe drove. The surveillance remained clear of any movement at the property, not even animals. Consequently, their approach should be uneventful as apparently no others had arrived. Joe performed a thorough reconnaissance of the neighboring lake properties, before cautiously proceeding to the cabin entry. No out of the ordinary vehicles or related personnel were noted. Safe to proceed to the cabin.

Twenty feet after entering the drive that led to the cabin, Joe stopped the truck. The brothers took one long look at each other. Not for any particular reason, but one look nonetheless. Joe slowly steered his Tundra down the 200 foot gravel drive, closely followed by a trail of brown dust that dissolved into the trees that blanketed the entry. John instinctively checked the surveillance screen on his iPhone to assure the truck they were in appeared on the screen. The truck was clearly visible, with Joe and his himself clearly identifiable via the truck windshield. Joe parked the truck end-first adjacent to the cabin's porch. John checked the surveillance systems one last time and hopped out.

No intruders, no strange noises, nothing. Just the wind rustling through the pine trees, and the occasional chirping bird. Locals could be heard playing on the lake, which included the sound of a small motor boat or possibly a jet ski.

Joe and John unloaded the arsenal from the back seat of the Tundra and transferred it into the cabin. The cabin interior was rustic and mostly clear of furnishings with the exception of a 6-foot diameter circular wooden table and four matching chairs located near the kitchen, and a sofa bed which probably converted to a queen-sized bed, since there was not significant room for a bed. The kitchen was sparsely furnished as well, short of a faded lime green refrigerator, a four-burner gas stove and an automatic dishwasher. In Joe's previous visits to the cabin he had stocked the refrigerator with a few staples. The exit door to the cabin's back porch was located in the center of the rear cabin wall, which offered a clear view of the lake. The back door was thus the only exit from the cabin, with the exception of the windows, one per wall. A six-foot wide dock extended at least 75 feet onto the lake, from an enclosed boathouse located adjacent to the shore.

After approximately three hours of final preparation, occurring inside and outside the cabin, the brothers were ready. They sat at the kitchen table with the lights off discussing previous escapades they had as teens, while waiting for the external surveillance systems to alert them of activity.

Joe noted, "Do you remember when we did the switch at school where you attended my classes and I attended yours? It worked great until the Principal got smart and included us in the same classroom."

John noted, "Yes, it still surprised me that no one figured it out, not even our closest friends. We could have kept it going indefinitely if we wanted to."

"Very possibly." Joe agreed.

"Our classic switch was when we swapped dates at the Homecoming Dance in 10th Grade. God, was Mary Stuart pissed off when she found out," John said.

"Only because you kissed her." Joe said. "She knew it wasn't me, either because you were outwardly nervous or you did some weird tongue thing."

"Or it could have been the fact that I couldn't keep a straight face afterwards." John laughed. "I guess I kind of messed up that relationship for you. Sorry, Joe."

"No worries." replied Joe. "I think she was fooling around with little shit, Jimmy Reid. Besides, Mary probably has a full mustache by now as she had a pretty good one going even as a teenager."

John looked at Joe and asked, "Do you frequently think about Mom and Dad?"

"All the time." replied Joe. "Especially when I was on assignment overseas, where I would be waiting in hiding for hours at a time. I remembered how they both taught us about patience and about always being the best we could be."

"I miss them a lot too." John replied. "We're both who we are today because of their positive, and negative, influence. They may not have done everything perfectly as parents, but in the end, I guess it worked."

"Have you been to their burial plots in Arlington recently?" asked John.

"No, not since their accident and the funeral two years ago." noted Joe. "It was too hard for me to think that I spent the last ten years prior to their passing in another country, and wasn't here with them."

"Don't beat yourself up. Neither of us knew they would die so young. It wasn't like they were sick and we weren't here for them. It was an unforeseen accident."

"I know, but the last time I saw them alive was the Christmas before I left for Afghanistan. I still feel I let them down." noted Joe.

"I understand, and sympathize. I was here and I still didn't see them as much as I should have. Just during the Holidays or birthdays, or if it was convenient." noted John. "The only positive I fall back on is that they would be proud of both of us, and that they would not want us to dwell on the negatives."

"I use the same reasoning when I start going down the same path. I know that's the way they would have wanted it." Joe replied.

Their silent thought-filled stares through the back door towards the lake were suddenly interrupted by the vibration alarm of the motion detectors placed 150 feet outside the property boundary. Unsure if the alarm was due to a human or animal, they quickly accessed the video feed from the same direction. A small nondescript black Jeep Wrangler with a black hardtop had approached from the west and had stopped 100 feet short of the road that led to the cabin's entry road. The Jeep remained parked near the edge of the road, the engine apparently still running. Despite the angle of the vehicle, the video indicated two occupants in the front seat.

Approximately four minutes later, a second motion alarm was activated from the opposite end of the same road, approaching from the east. Panning out, the video indicated a similar Jeep, with an unknown number of occupants. Two similar vehicles appearing at the same time is never a good sign. The plan would be activated, if and only if the vehicles or their occupants entered the property boundary. Currently, both vehicles remained at their current position. At this point, John and Joe considered they may be outnumbered four to two . . . acceptable and favorable odds.

The third alarm was a complete surprise, indicating a small water craft entering lakeside from the south, originating from the widest part of the lake. John had placed laser sighting across the surface of the lake which defined the craft's distance as well as its presence. The unidentified craft was well outside of their zone of concern.

Via a quick visual check via binoculars, the single occupant of the boat was a woman wearing shorts and a bikini top, reading a book. Still, good to be aware.

"Now we wait," Joe noted. "They must first assess if I'm actually in the cabin, via drawing fire-- typical protocol. They will do this by sending in a recon team on foot, to assess how close they can get. If they drive off of the gravel drive, it will be an easy answer."

"Easy, how?" John asked.

"Easy as a field of assorted pressure sensitive and proximity land mines," Joe replied.

"Crap!" John shrieked. "Are you saying that I could have walked or driven off the gravel drive into a mine field?"

"But you didn't, so not an issue." Joe smirked. "Besides, I was driving, for that reason alone."

"Thanks--that's really reassuring," John noted.

"So, if we eliminate their on-foot team, what will be their next course of action?" asked John.

"Once their team confirms an occupant is in the cabin, they will hold their distance but open fire with all barrels," replied Joe.

"What constitutes 'all barrels'?" queried John.

"That depends upon who 'they' are. I suspect they'll keep their distance and fire RPGs, or rocket propelled grenades. This way they will further limit their losses. This is why we will relocate to the boat house down by the lake immediately after we eliminate their on-foot entry team. We might have 30 seconds at best after their team goes down, if we're lucky."

"But our weapons are here in the cabin, plus the boat house construction appears a bit flimsy," noted John.

"Not exactly," Joe replied. "I assured the boat house is very well stocked with an assortment of toys plus I've slightly reinforced the north, east and south walls with half-inch steel plating."

"So how will we get down to the now steel-plated boathouse?"

"Run, of course." replied Joe.

"Genius. But really, how will we make the run without being seen or picked-off by our friends?"

"Let's just say that they will be rather distracted, plus the path to the lake slopes away from the cabin, so they will not have a direct line of sight once we leave the porch nor will they know there are two of us. Besides, as I noted, they will be dealing with other issues at the time. Trust me on this one."

Just then, the motion detection system began to alarm, indicating the entry onto the property. Via video, it was now apparent that both Jeeps had approached the gravel drive, and had driven side by side down the center of the drive, which was an odd turn of events. They continued to creep down the drive and stopped 100 feet from the cabin. As John predicted, one occupant exited each of the Jeeps, and proceeded outward towards the cover of the trees located on each side of the drive. Video quickly lost sight of both individuals, which was not an issue as the screen quickly erupted in a flash of flame and dust from the east side of the Jeeps. A similar explosion occurred from the opposite side of the other Jeep.

"30 seconds and counting . . . out through the porch and don't look back." John had already crossed the cabin and was opening the back door. "Take this M-4 and run like your life depends on it, because it does. I'm right behind you."

Almost immediately after the mines exploded, both Jeeps had removed their hardtops each revealing a tripod with a .50 caliber machine gun.

Twenty seconds later, both Jeeps opened fire on the cabin, splintering the cabin walls into sawdust. The barrage continued uninterrupted for a full 30 seconds, until both guns had fully exhausted their supply of bullets. The cabin walls remained standing, despite their almost non-existent, now transparent structure. All was quiet.

The Jeeps slowly inched forward single-file down the gravel drive to assess the damage. As they were within 50 feet of the rubble, the "distraction" that Joe referred to earlier began in the form of rolling explosions occurring above the second Jeep. Joe had suspended C-4 explosives on a 2-foot grid below the tree limbs above the gravel drive. The ignition of each was activated by slow-response proximity detectors also suspended in the trees. Slowly moving vehicles passing below the detectors for more than 5 seconds would initiate the ignition process.

The second Jeep was decimated in a matter of seconds. The lead Jeep, which had passed more quickly, received minimal damage and proceeded towards the cabin. Three men cautiously exited the lone vehicle, with weapons drawn.

By this time, both John and Joe had reached the boat house undetected and quickly ducked inside. The inside of the now reinforced structure resembled a rusted metal safe, with sheets of steel covering all walls with the exception of the south wall facing the lake. Numerous weapons were stacked along the inside of the metal shell along with large green ammo cases stationed in all four corners. The sound of the water slapping up against the piers below the boat house echoed loudly. A five-inch hole in the north wall was the only aperture allowing a view of the cabin. The pile of rubble which was originally the cabin was barely visible to the north, up-hill from the boathouse. Voices could be heard at the cabin as the intruders combed through the rubble.

"OK Joe, what will they do once they're unable to locate a body in the rubble?" asked John.

"First of all, I expected my C-4 would have taken out both Jeeps. But I guess that wasn't in the cards so it's onto Plan B," noted Joe.

As Joe was about to continue his response, a completely unexpected turn of events occurred. Specifically, a woman wearing blue jean shorts, a bikini top, with a high pressure scuba tank on her back, climbed into the boat house through a hinged door in the floor boards.

"Hi guys," she said. John couldn't speak, his jaw open in complete shock.

"Hey Brenda," Joe replied. "Long time no see. How's the family?"

"Great, Joe, thanks for asking. Would love to chat but I'm on the clock and have a hair appointment so let's get you two the hell out of here."

"Next time, knock, so my brother here doesn't shoot your head off. Don't be so rude, John, say hello to one of my partners from a secret mission I cannot tell you about."

John just stared, incredulously.

"John, you OK?" asked Joe.

"Um, yes. I'm OK--uh no, I'm not," stammered John. "Where the hell did you come from?"

"Who, me?" asked Brenda, with an ear-to-ear smile.

"Yes, you!" exclaimed John.

"I was the woman in the boat on the lake that you saw earlier. Didn't you wonder why Joe wasn't concerned about the boat on the lake? Didn't it seem a bit odd?"

"OK kids, enough chitchat," noted Joe. "Brenda is here to get us out of here. There is a rope that is attached to the piers below us and stretches to a location just below Brenda's boat. We have two Life-Air 10 Respirators that we can use as we follow the rope to the boat . . . do not under any circumstances break the surface of the water until you are behind the boat, otherwise assume you're dead. Brenda will go first, then you, then me. The boat has an in-hull entry port to allow boarding from beneath the boat. Go now, as our friends will soon define there's no corpse in the rubble on the hill."

Brenda donned her scuba tank, popped back through the floor hatch and was gone in seconds.

"I like your Plan B." noted John with a smile. "How much time do you think we have?"

"None. Brenda is far enough ahead. It's time."

The exit through the hatch and ensuing entry into the water was more difficult than expected, as was locating the rope through the murky brown water. Once under the water, the rope was the only lifeline providing solace, with each hand-over-hand motion moving towards certain freedom. Although the entire trip took less than a few minutes, it seemed like an eternity, until the rope actually stopped. About 15 feet above was the hull of the boat, with the port opening visible. Entry towards the opening was hampered by the constant motion of the boat, but achievable. A hand extended down through the entry port . . . Brenda's hand. Mission accomplished.

From the edge of the boat, the cabin was barely visible. Using binoculars, it was clear that the Jeep Team had confirmed the lack of a body in the rubble and had zeroed in on the boat house. Two of the soldiers entered the Jeep with one remaining on foot. As they drove closer, something appeared to move inside the exposed side of the boat house, followed by an unexpected round of gunshots originating from inside the structure. The approaching Team retreated to the rear of the Jeep, assembled an unknown weapon and fired a single projectile, which appeared to be RPG, towards the boat house.

It was a direct hit. The heat from the ensuing explosion could be felt all the way to the boat. The blast was so intense that even the soldiers were thrown unexpectedly to the ground. Additional explosions followed as the stored ammunition was activated along with numerous grenades and miscellaneous explosives.

No sign of Joe. No movement on the rope. Nothing.

Brenda stated, "We need to go. I don't know why Joe stayed to fight but we need to get our asses out of here--NOW!"

"But what if Joe is still on the rope?"

"The rope is attached to the boat that we will drag away when we leave. There is no tension on the rope, so no Joe." Brenda replied. "He made the choice to save his only brother. He told me you were his first priority and he was expendable," Brenda added.

Silence. Brenda started the motor and eased to the south.

That was the last mission for Joe Stone. Mission accomplished.

Chapter 10

Washington Star-Times--June 10, 1995

On June 8, 1995, Joe Stone went to be with the Lord. He was 46 years old, a decorated Green Beret, a hero and a friend of many. His multiple tours in various wars across the globe saved the lives of many a soldier. He is survived only by his brother, John Stone. His funeral will occur on Saturday, June 12, at Arlington Memorial Cemetery where he will be buried adjacent to his Mother and Father. Joe . . . Rest in Peace. We will see you in heaven.

Chapter 11

John sat in the rental car, staring blankly at the thick "Confidential" folder that contained the Top Secret military history of the late Joe Stone. The memories of childhood experiences, teenage escapades, college graduation, partnering in the CIA, all preceding the day of their tragic separation, flashed through his mind as if it were yesterday.

The possibility of this scenario was an issue that John and Joe had discussed at length, years ago. John knew what had to be done, the first of which was to get to safety, which certainly did not include reminiscing in the rental car.

John placed the "Confidential" folder and its contents under his arm, closed the glove compartment and exited from the rental car. He then used his handkerchief to wipe down any surfaces he had intentionally or inadvertently touched, to remove his fingerprints. John then loosely twisted the handkerchief and inserted it into the gas filling inlet. Gasoline fumes were quickly detectable and began to invisibly saturate the handkerchief. John removed a cardboard matchbook he had taken off the bar in Slade's, bent one match outside of the pack and placed the make-shift fuse on the exposed edge of the handkerchief, outside the influence of the fumes. Via his femto, he checked the parking lot for bystanders, using Infrared at a 100-foot vantage point. None noted. Equally important, the absence of bystanders also meant no evidence of colleagues associated with his new found friends that he left on the floor of Slade's bathroom.

John lit the single exposed match, watched the flame slowly extend along the length of the match towards the full matchbook, then casually walked out of the parking lot. Seventeen seconds was all he needed to remove himself from harm's way ... closed matchbooks offer at least 25 seconds, considering the waxed cardboard that manufacturers now use.

The explosion and ensuing fire projected an orange flickering glow on the buildings that surrounded Slade's parking lot. Screams could be heard from the patrons quickly exiting the bar, amongst sirens in the distance either due to John's earlier 911 call or the blazing inferno. John would return for his vehicle at a later date. An urgent telephone call was next on his list.

Chapter 12

John chose to walk perpendicularly away from Slade's, not necessarily in any particular direction, but just away from the mayhem that had developed as a result of his handiwork. The femto had been built for the military, and had a variety of modes built-in for convenience, one of which was sat-phone capability, which was the purpose it was providing John at the moment. The mere mention of "call Mick" was all that was required, similar to the Bluetooth capability of current-day cell phones when you activate them in one's car ... which again was already 10-year-old technology that has been in use via Special Ops teams for years.

Mick, short for Mickael, was a longtime partner of Joe's when he was in the Special Forces. They fought side-by-side together in many missions, and owed each other their lives, many times over. Mick had been assigned to protect John and his family after Joe's death, and they had become very good friends as a result. Mick had an uncanny ability to appear when things got tough, which always made John wonder how much surveillance time Mick spent watching him to assure things stayed under control. Mick's background and experience equaled or maybe exceeded that of Joe, with numerous accolades to his name, none of which were ever communicated to the outside world, which assured his anonymity. Now, as a retired Ops Specialist, Mick spent his days, and apparently nights, doing what he enjoyed most, which included watching Joe's brethren, plus "making right" where he believed things were wrong.

John instructed his femto, "Call Mick."

The femto responded with a female voice into the earpiece in his left ear, "Call Mick. Is this correct?"

John stated, "Yes."

The femto voice replied, "Calling Mick."

Two rings, then a man answered, immediately asking, "Why did you meticulously wipe off the fingerprints from the inside of the car before you lit it up, John? Very colorful, by the way."

Clearly, Mick had been remotely viewing John's heroics, through his direct link to the femto he had activated before heading into Slade's. Similar to the modern day Facebook, John could establish "Friends" that were alerted whenever his system was activated. The system also alerts specific contacts, such as Mick, whenever the wearer's vital signs or actions indicate non-typical behavior, such as John's increased heartbeat just a short hour ago. This accessory mimics that of the newer model Mercedes sedans, which monitor erratic driving response to assess if the driver is sleeping, in order to prevent crashes. Not rocket science, but a useful mode specifically designed for this particular type of instance.

John chuckled in response to Mick's comment, and replied, "Mick, don't you have anything better to do than watch my daily activities?"

"Nothing good on the tube tonight, but back to my question--why waste the time for the fingerprint wipe down? Are you doubting your clandestine abilities, specifically the matchbook trick, which I taught you myself?"

"Right now, I'm doubting many things," replied John. "Too many coincidences have occurred to me today. Don't tell me that you didn't expect contact to occur at some point."

"Yes, I suspected," replied Mick. "Just not this soon."

John nodded to himself as he walked, and replied, "The timing surprised me as well, but I always like a challenge."

"As do I," replied Mick. "So, what's your next move?"

"I plan to make this easy for them," replied John.

"Hmmmm," replied Mick. "Did you read the paper today about the drug dealer who was shot dead over in the Hills area, from an unknown sniper located almost 200 yards away? It was a head shot, by the way, expertly piercing the frontal lobe at a 35-degree angle ... a single .308 caliber round from a long rifle, or so I've heard."

"Yes, I saw the article in the Star this morning before I left for work. Appears the guy was the leader for the Middletown drug ring, and was directly responsible for the deaths of a handful of local youth due to intentional arsenic poisoning of the pheds they distributed. A real scum bag."

"Yes, that's him," replied Mick.

"Why do you ask? Am I correct in assuming you had something to do with the expertly placed 35-degree .308?"

No answer. None needed, as this was typical of Mick's handiwork--taking one more scumbag off the streets, as a personal vendetta against those who continually evaded the law on the taxpayer's dime and were deserving of punishment.

Then Mick replied, "All I recommend is, don't be "that guy" ... and I don't mean the drug part, but the dead part. As you and I know, the Hamad are not to be fooled with, assuming that's who we're dealing with considering the two Glocks that you borrowed from your friends in the bathroom at Slade's. They are a proud and ruthless team and don't like to be made fools of, as you've accomplished nicely in less than 30 minutes. You've poked the bear, and can now expect to get bitten. In other words, carefully consider the consequences of what you're suggesting."

"No worries. My head's on straight. I just need to find out what's going on, and will need your help to not become 'that guy'."

"You have it. So, what exactly did you mean when you stated you would 'make it easy for them'?"

"I'm simply going to go home now, where I expect they will be waiting," replied John.

"Wow, you're a dumb ass," replied Mick. "Please tell me something that gives me comfort that you're not completely plastered or just trying to get killed."

"My guess is that they need me alive, so they can retrieve past info on Joe, given his military personnel file that I recovered from their rental car."

"Maybe, or on the other hand, they didn't like Joe and now your head is to be the next trophy on their wall. Are you willing to take that risk?"

"If they wanted me dead, they could have easily done that a number of times today. They began following me this morning on the way to work."

"OK, suppose you're right," replied Mick. "If we correctly assume they are on an info search, they might just pop you 25 cc's of Pentothal and ask you their questions when they 'easily' find you, at home. Then they'll follow it with an injection of 50 cc's of air bubbles into your vein ... end of story."

"Mick, this is my brother that we're dealing with here. I've never been one to walk away, and cannot this time. We knew this day would come. I just need to see what they know, or need to know."

"Are you in on this, or am I going this alone?"

"As I noted before, yes, I'm in. Are you heading home right now?"

"Not yet. I need to get a few thallium pills from the office."

"Yes, now that will make my job easier."

"And will keep me from being 'that guy' that you noted earlier?" John asked.

"That's the intent", replied Mick. "Plus there's nothing on television, so I've got nothing better to do tonight."

"I recommend that you never subscribe to the 300 channel deal with Direct TV, as I assume it would negatively affect my ability to stay alive," kidded John.

"That it might, my friend, that it might," agreed Mick.

The thallium pills that John was referring to took advantage of yet another identification friend-or-foe (a.k.a. IFF) capability of the femto. Specifically, thallium pills, when ingested, allowed the user to glow like a beacon when viewed from any femto, due to their radioactive content, which lasted about three hours. Unlike the thallium injections commonly used in nuclear imaging of heart patients to define artery blockage, a chelate was added to the pills to minimize the radioactive effects on the user, allowing it to be excreted or urinated out of the body.

Of course, the femto unit itself offered IFF capability, but the thallium was a foolproof method used in the event the femto had been removed from the user. The inception of these thallium pills was necessitated by an unfortunate incident in Afghanistan where a self-guided HAWK (i.e., Homing All the Way Killer) missile was directed away from a known (femto-like) unit, which had smartly been taken from the user by his captor, and worn as protection. The HAWK missile redirected itself way from the desired target (the captor), and instead eliminated the entire entry team. The thallium pills would minimize the possibility of such a reoccurrence.

John walked four more blocks and hailed a taxi to transport him back to the EXos offices, where he was met by the friendly guard from earlier in the day. Since John's badge was still in his car that was still in the Slade's parking lot, he was presented with a dilemma, easily solved since Jim was still in the office. One quick call and John was driving through the gate.

Jim met him at the front entrance to provide initial access into the building, along with a temporary badge to enable access past the front lobby.

"OK, John," Jim noted when he saw him. "You have that look in your eye. So what's going on?"

"If I told you, I would have to kill you," replied John. "Seriously though, I lost my car keys somewhere inside Slade's tonight, so I'm back here to get my spare set."

"That almost sounds believable," replied Jim. "It doesn't explain the look in your eyes, so I'm guessing it also has something to do with a female acquaintance that you met there. I'm right, aren't I?"

"Yep, you're a mind reader. I ran into this hot blonde and my brain went right out the window."

"Along with your keys, I assume?" queried Jim.

"I assume so, or she's a spy from another country who wants me for my secrets." Truth in jest.

"Well, John. Are you heading back there?" asked Jim.

"Yes, as soon as I can, as once I realized I had lost my keys, I told her that I was only going to be gone for a short time."

"Well, I was on my way out, so lock up when you leave," Jim noted with a smile.

"You know I will", replied John.

John watched Jim to the point of his car exiting from the parking lot. Much needed to be done to fully prepare for the upcoming 24 hours. These preparatory activities would consume a few hours, so it was clear that early morning would be the best time to become easy prey.

Step one was to activate the newest model femto, via upload of the 16-bit configuration software. The new unit, known only to John's closest team members as project "Eye-Phone" (a.k.a. the femto EP, or fEP for short), was a mostly cosmetic rendition of the existing femto, adapted to the look and feel of Apple's iPhone. Ironically, the larger size of the fEP's battery pack mandated use of the thicker iPhone 3G shell, which ironically was also the Apple iPhone model that did not have video capability (introduced with the newer model iPhone 3G-S). John still chuckled every time he thought of the related irony, as the result was completely unplanned.

In addition to the numerous capabilities of the original femto, the fEP's added capability included a countermeasure option, whereby the user could jam the transmission and reception abilities of any older model femto, located within an approximate 100 foot radius. Similarly, the fEP could simultaneously superimpose any video onto that same earlier model femto. The fact that there was currently only one fEP in existence, made this feature unique and very advantageous to the fEP owner, John Stone.

Although John knew there was risk to using the fEP, its benefit outweighed any potential drawbacks, plus he had the original femto as back-up.

Second, was to get a few hours of much needed sleep while the system uploaded. John's current location at EXos was at this moment the only safe haven that he could be assured of. John set his watch for 0600 and relaxed for the last time.

Chapter 13

0600 hours - John awoke with the plan of approach fully in his mind just as if it was yesterday that he and Joe conspired in the cabin 10 years ago.

The underlying objective was simple. Become visible with the intent of capture, define who his assailants where, what they knew, and then get out. The plan from that point was yet to be determined, and would depend upon what was gleaned from the earlier steps.

John validated the fEP software load, successfully ran through the simplex diagnostics program, and was ready to go. One swallow of the chelated thallium pill and all preparatory activities were complete. A quick call to Orange Taxi and fifteen minutes later, John found himself returning to Slade's to retrieve his car. So as not to surprise any followers watching his car, he asked to be let out two blocks south of Slade's and would walk the rest of the way. A $25 fee to the taxi driver, and John was afoot by 0640, heading towards Slade's. The sun had not yet risen, although crimson streaks in the clouds were becoming visible to the east. As John turned the corner, he entered an alley that connected to Slade's parking lot where his car remained parked. He instinctively felt that something was wrong once he was half-way through the alley. Apparently animals have that same sense of danger, and John had always professed that he possessed the same sense.

The sound of shuffling feet came from both sides of the dimly lit alley, as John passed in between two parallel rows of dingy green garbage dumpsters. There were three of them. Not large, or appreciably menacing looking, but wide eyed and clearly hyped up due to excitement, drugs, or a combination of both. John suspected the latter.

Keep walking, John thought to himself. Appear unnaturally calm. No sudden movement. Just like he learned from his brother years ago. They might decide to stand down.

No such luck, as the three men surrounded John radially at a five foot distance. John kept his gaze focused on the largest of the three, watching closely for weapons, which appeared to be knives--three switch blades, to be exact. Comforting, but only slightly, as the bearing of a knife in a fight typically precludes the presence of a gun. The reason being that guns are always presented proudly within the first few seconds, and if not, then they are typically a non-issue. John hoped this was the case.

There was clearly no option for avoidance . . . time for more aggressive tactics. John continued to address the largest man, who slowly branded his switchblade at eye level for effect, reflecting light from a nearby incandescent lamp located on the left alley wall.

"Where do you think you're going?" asked the largest man whom John continued to stare down, all the while aware of the other two men's position and movement.

"None of your business," replied John. "I've got no issue with you. I suggest that we keep it this way."

All three men laughed, with the second stating. "We will decide what business you have with us."

"No, I don't see it that way," replied John.

"Really, so how do you see it then?" the third man asked.

"I see an ambulance, and hospital stay for one of you, the second running back to your mommy, and the condition of the third yet to be determined," quipped John. "You see, you have no idea who I am, or what my capabilities are. I could be one of the most lethal fighters in the area, or I could just be an engineer searching for my car. Are you willing to take the risk that I am the former?"

"We don't care who you are, replied the largest. We just want you to shut up and give us your wallet and cell phone, otherwise we'll kick your ass."

"Not going to happen guys. I've already exceeded the allotted free minutes on my cell phone this month, so I do not plan to have you guys rack up my monthly bill at 30-cents per minute."

"Wow--you're a funny guy," noted man number one.

"Not so much," replied John. "I don't have time for this."

John had already calculated his next move, and was waiting for the break that would allow its initiation. Then it happened as he had predicted. Instinct immediately took over.

The largest man thrust his knife in an overhead but downward arching motion, his right arm fully extended, originating from two feet above John's head. Similar to the motion of hitting a nail with a hammer, with the switchblade being the hammer and the top of John's head being the nail. Clearly an amateur move, as knives are best used in short-range forward-striking repetitive motions, which conserve and concentrate power instead of a wildly arcing blow that is easily deflected.

John fully extended both arms and crossed them above his head into an X configuration, immediately stopping the downward thrust and trapping the man's wrist in the base of the formed X.

John's lower arm slipped from the X-block position, down below the elbow of the man's fully extended arm, slightly under the base of his upper arm. In one fluid motion, John then rotated both of his arms in a circular counterclockwise motion and squeezed them together, which immediately drove the knife backwards over the man/s right shoulder blade, into a position that partially dislocated the shoulder from its socket. The switchblade dropped from his hand, and fell with a metallic clang to the concrete. This entire process spanned a full 1.5 seconds, with the other two men barely able to move from their original positions, their mouths gaped open in shock.

The large man immediately dropped to his knees, with John still standing above him, continuing to pin his shoulder in the backwards position. The finishing touch included a simple release followed by a downward elbow thrust to the same dislocated shoulder. The characteristic pop of the ligaments fully releasing the shoulder from its socket could be heard a block away, and certainly was heard by the other two men. The large man shrieked in pain, looking down at his arm which literally hung from the shoulder socket, completely immobilized and uncontrolled. The man quickly passed out due to the pain, lying on the ground with his arm unnaturally tucked backwards, behind his back.

John looked at the other two men, and stated "OK guys, who's next?"

The two men glanced at each other, then back at their friend piled in a heap on the ground, and left as quickly as they appeared. John exited the alley and continued the one block walk to Slade's, checking his front pants pocket to assure the fEP was still intact, which it was. John made a personal note to not take that particular alley again.

Upon arrival at Slade's parking lot, John noticed that the burned out car had been removed from the lot, but the ashes and visible remnants of the fire remained. Only three other cars remained in the lot, considering that the bar had closed almost 5 hours before. No other people or patrons were visible. John's car remained at the far corner, sitting by itself.

John was confident that his assailants had posted a sentry to watch for his return to retrieve his car, probably one of the original folks he dealt with last night who could identify him. This was a key to John's plan to his own abduction and keyed into his strategy.

Unlike television portrayals, it is very easy to spot sentries, despite the number of cars parked along the street. It all revolves around the use of simple science. Specifically, due to the moisture that exists in the pre-dawn air, condensation collects on every surface, to very visibly include windshields, rear windows and potentially side windows of a parked car. This process takes approximately three hours, give or take 30 minutes, so those vehicles that had not been parked during the pre-dawn hours, would have no condensation, and are easily identified from a distance due to their completely clear windows.

From John's position in the empty parking lot, he scanned the parked rows of cars as far as he could see. Within 30 seconds, he zeroed in on two cars with clear windows, one of which contained a lone figure. Science wins every time. John knew that the sentry's orders would be to watch and follow, and not to engage, so he was safe to continue his plan.

John approached his car, and unlocked it remotely with his key. As an additional precaution, he kept his distance, and while behind one of the lone cars in the lot, remotely started his car, in the event it triggered an explosion or other surprise. His vehicle started, with no surprise explosions.

John entered his vehicle, backed out of his parking spot, and stated, "On my way, Mick. No boom."

"How boring. Appears our opponent doesn't have any creativity," Mick replied through John's ear piece.

"Or they're just not pyros, like you," John replied. "What color boom would you have used, if you had been in their shoes?"

"It's all about color to you non-pyros", Mick laughed. "It's the surprise that makes the grade. So, in response to your question, I would have wired your car's speedometer output to the explosive starter input, with a go-setting of 45 miles per hour. When the car reached 45, then the boom. And yes, I would have used a sodium additive in the powder packet, for an attractive greenish-orange tinted explosion."

"Nice, so you couldn't ignore the color after all," John noted.

"Just icing on the cake, my boy," replied Mick. "By the way, how fast are you driving now? Are you above 45 miles per hour yet?"

"Not yet. 40 as a maximum. I'm taking back roads, just because," replied John.

"Not because of anything you've heard?" queried Mick.

"The speed limit is 35 on these roads, so just playing it safe."

"OK ... truthfully, I actually would have used 15 miles per hour, so the boom would have occurred as you were exiting the parking lot. I knew that if I told you that, you would take 30 minutes to get to your house," laughed Mick.

"So you would have let me enter a rigged car?" asked John.

"Not a chance. I've been watching your car since you first entered Slade's. I just like to see you sweat," replied Mick.

"Nice," replied John.

"Enough of the chitchat. You've got one trail on you, about one block behind you," noted Mick.

"I assume it was the lone guy in the car parked to the west?"

"That's the one."

"Saw him when I came into the lot," noted John. "Just one guy."

"Yes," noted Mick.

"Good to know, thanks."

"Are you ready for this?" asked Mick.

"Absolutely, but will need your help."

"I'm all over it. Let's just get in and get out," replied Mick. "Remember, don't be that guy."

"I'm not planning on it," replied John.

Chapter 14

John maintained his 40 mile per hour speed, just because. His mind circled through the scenarios that would soon occur. He suspected that his opponent needed information on his brother, which was the sole reason why they had left John live this long. The primary question was, did John have the information they were searching for, and would they believe him if he did not. On the other hand, if John did have the information they needed, would they believe him if he did not divulge it. Neither of the two scenarios would result in a positive outcome. A clear lose-lose situation for John either way. The only saving grace in the whole equation was Mick. Only Mick could even the score.

Per plan, John drove the familiar route back to his neighborhood, where he knew he would find his soon-to-be captors. To break the tension, John closely observed the details of the quiet suburban community, awakening in the early sun-lit hours of the morning: The familiar joggers, the early walkers, the cyclists, others pulling their green rectangular garbage cans and blue recycling bins to the street, and those retrieving their newspaper from the curb. It was the same every morning. We were all creatures of habit. John flashed back to leadership training he had just initiated at EXos, which emphasized embracing change, as a means to change behavior and increase self-awareness. The thought of brushing one's teeth with the opposite hand, or crossing one's arms with the other hand over the top, felt so uncomfortable. The simple experience of these changes made employees self-aware of how they reacted or treated others in the work environment, promoting a simple yet effective transition towards Team cohesion and collaboration. Sometimes the simplest changes make the most impact.

Driving within three blocks of his house, the practice of self-awareness, coupled with observation of well-known surroundings, was keen on John's mind. The familiar morning scenes he witnessed just two blocks ago were littered with the un-familiar.

John slowed down slightly to better observe these outliers.

First, John noted two women jogging side-by-side, both brunettes, wearing skin tight black lycra shorts and tops. The larger of the two had a red top, with her partner in blue. Not uncommon, except that neither appeared sweat stained nor did they seem to even have a glisten of sweat on their faces. The giveaway though, was their gaze, which was simultaneously directed at John's Audi. Mistake number one, whereby only one observer is to target the prey ... never both. Furthermore, John had yet to see any joggers who had any interest in the countless cars and drivers that passed them, once they were fully into their running high, especially women joggers who had little desire to attract attention from unknown, potentially psycho, drivers.

As the pair of women approached, their gazes simultaneously averted towards the passing row of houses. At this close range, which was now no more than 20 feet from John's car, the twisted white ear pieces were self-evident, stretching uncharacteristically from the ear canal, along the top of their ears, along the side of their necks, through their tops, to the hidden receiver that John assumed was attached to their belts.

"Watcha think, Mick," John noted.

"36-28-32 for the right, 32-26-30 for the left," Mick's voice responded through John's earpiece.

"No, you know what I mean," John replied.

"Two hot ex-CIA, is my guess. I assume our opponent pays better than our U.S. Agency does. Plus they have that slightly olive-colored skin and brunette hair, which makes me think they're eastern European. Probably speak six or seven languages including Arabic."

"My thoughts as well. It's a pity," replied John. "Watch them for me, and let me know where they end up or if they circle around."

"Roger Will-co." replied Mick.

"You realize that those two aren't used anymore--Roger Will-co, that is."

"I'm just testing you to see if you are listening", replied Mick. "I know that "Roger" represents "received," and "Will-co" means "will comply," but that the combo was a movie thing. I just like to test your patience because that kind of stuff bugs you."

"Thanks for that. Glad to see you're focused on keeping me annoyed instead of alive," replied John.

"No worries. Whatever it takes to keep you focused, and not staring at two joggers boobs," replied Mick. "Did you copy that?"

"Roger that," replied John.

The next anomaly that John observed was a middle-aged man pulling his single garbage can with recycling box to the street approximately one block from John's house. Again, this would not seem odd, except that this particular house had three sports flags flapping from the front porch, each representing a different local high school sport (football, volleyball and what John believed was a running sport of some type, such as cross country). What this projected was that there were three high schoolers living there, who would easily contribute to much more than a single garbage can and mostly empty recycle bin. Every other family with three teenage children typically generated a plethora of waste each week, to include a mound of plastic water and Gatorade bottles to boot. Not the case in this instance, unless the kids were all visiting grandparents this past week. Doubtful, but possible.

As John's car passed within ten feet of the man, he too gave John an initial stare, which he quickly averted upon receiving John's gaze. The real giveaway sign was the tattoo that the man sported on his left forearm, which John quickly recognized as the Kanfei Shayetet. Specifically, the tattoo was a sword, shield and batwings, identifying the wearer as a member of the Israeli Shayetet 13, or S-13. The Batwing tattoo illustrated the unit's reputation for stealth, speed and valor, representing one of Israel's most prestigious combat units, equivalent to the U.S. Navy SEALS. One of the most notable S-13 operations included the Spring of Youth, whereby the S-13 hunted down members of the Black September in Beirut, in revenge for the 1972 Munich massacre.

It surprised John that a soldier would brand his body in such as visible location, easily giving away his identity. Most soldiers had a variety of body markings, just not as visible a location as this one. It was this type of arrogance that led to the demise of many a soldier, which was not in the cards for this man, at least not today.

The man quickly turned and began walking back towards the house, exiting from view. John continued to drive slowly, looking for other out of the ordinary signs.

"Nice tat," noted Mick, via John's earpiece.

"Good eyes," replied John.

"I haven't seen that one for a while, at least since my last tour near the Gaza Strip."

"Bring back any memories?" asked John.

"None that I care to resurrect," stated Mick. "Time heals, as does a bad memory. Oh, by the way, your girlfriends stopped after they turned the corner, and are circling back through the backyards parallel to your location."

"Yeah, I have that effect on women," kidded John. "Do you think they want my telephone number?"

"That's not my first guess, but I've been wrong before," replied Mick. "Heads up, but our S-13 friend has just exited the rear of the house and is meeting up with your girlfriends."

"Wonderful," replied John. "I'm almost to my house. I think I'll just pull into my driveway, just to be creative."

"Aren't you clever," joked Mick. "Seriously though, be careful."

"No worries, just keep an eye on me, especially once I get inside, assuming I get that far."

"Roger that."

John crept past his next door neighbor's home, a two story brick Victorian, with the typical spires from the rooftops and a front porch with a chain link supported three-person swing. Brown trim, white outline--a color that John never cared for. He activated his right-hand turn signal, and slowly spun the wheel to align his tires parallel to the drive and drove into his driveway. He parked half way up the drive, and stalled in his car, pretending to look for something in his glove compartment.

"Any activity yet, Mick?" John asked.

"Yes, two cars coming to you, from opposite ends of the street. Both containing two occupants, both seated in the front seat. Only one has a rider in the back. The front seat passengers of each vehicle are cradling a cold object in their hands, which I assume to be short range automatic weapons."

"Which one has the rider in the back?" asked John.

"The vehicle coming from the same direction as you did."

"Great, I'm going inside now."

"Make me a sandwich, no mayo."

"Toasted or not?" asked John.

"You decide."

"I doubt I'll have time. My fEP is showing two intruders coming approaching my front door, so cancel the sandwich."

"Yes, I see them. The one in the rear is yielding a handgun of to-be-determined type."

"By the way, the two cars are almost to the front of your house."

Just as Mick advised, John could see one of the vehicles in his peripheral vision, approaching the front of his house from the same direction he had just taken. He recognized the wide silver grill of a Crown Vic, black exterior with tinted windows. Looking towards the other end of the street, an almost mirror image crept down the street, also slowing to a stop in front of his home. Drivers were evident in both vehicles with another passenger in the front.

The vehicle approaching from the direction he had just come pulled directly in front of his yard, and stopped. The other entered the driveway, parking one foot behind his Audi.

John knew that if the key contact was in this group, he would be the last to show his or her identity, and would only do so once the scene was secure. "Secure" meaning that the goon squad would first nullify any threats, which John planned to facilitate. The key was to act surprised, to not give away his personal knowledge of what was really going on.

John cautiously walked to the left door of the vehicle which had just boxed him into the driveway. He shrugged his shoulders and assumed a quizzical expression. As he approached he could see the MPK supported in the arms of the passenger of the vehicle, as the driver opened his car door and stood to exit.

The driver was male, about 6 foot 2, and about 210 pounds, dark complexed with wiry short cropped hair. He was not an overly large man but had the cold eyes and unfazed look that identified him as a soldier of some type.

John's senses peaked, and if he had been playing a different strategy, he would never have placed himself in such a vulnerable position. He hoped the information that he needed was worth this personal risk.

John also knew how this process would work. Weapons would be branded, words would be spoken, and they would either bring him inside his home, or take him away in one of the vehicles. He suspected the latter, considering the need for neutral turf, which his home was not.

Mick was now practically within earshot, as he had circled towards John's backyard, in search of the two joggers, which he expertly came upon without their knowledge. Always nice to maintain the element of surprise. Mick had left his car parked just around the corner, within easy reach in a matter of a 30 second run.

Next the second passenger exited the vehicle, propping an Uzi on the roof of the Crown Vic, pointed towards John. He too sported similar black and white attire but was a clear mesomorph build, yielding 20 inch biceps and the 52 inch chest to match.

His expression mirrored that of the driver, with a slight smirk that suggested he was enjoying his role in this shakedown.

"This appears a bit excessive for me not paying my parking tickets, guys," John noted to the two men. "You both dress like Tommy Lee Jones and Will Smith from Men in Black. I assume you've seen the movie? You must be Tommy Lee," looking towards the larger of the two men.

"Nope, I must have missed that one," noted the driver, the mountainous passenger maintaining his smirky grin. "Please, get in the car, Mr. Stone."

"Wow, the "please" really makes this easier," replied John. "Politeness will get you everywhere."

"Shut-up, Mr. Stone, and keep your hands out where we can see them," replied the driver. "We need you to get in the car."

"And why would I want to do that?" asked John.

"We're not asking. We're telling you," replied the driver.

"Again, why do I care what you are 'telling' me?"

"Because if you don't, we'll execute you in your front yard."

"No, you won't. Clearly you need something from me, and if that wasn't the case, you would have already popped me," John retorted.

"We may have information that will interest you," offered the driver.

"It certainly does peak my interest, but then again, it really doesn't. Why don't you tell me what this is about, and then I will consider if it's worth my time."

The driver reached his wrist to his mouth, and spoke into a concealed microphone. He mumbled a few words, which John assumed were directed to the individual in the back seat of the vehicle still parked motionless in front of his house.

Then the driver stated, "This is about your brother Joe."

This statement hit John like a ton of bricks. It was his original expectation, but he was still shocked, and certainly now more intrigued.

In John's earpiece, Mick noted "Bingo. I'm good to go if you decide to get in the Crown Vic."

"What about my brother? He died 20 years ago," stated John. "It's all summarized on the Internet. Case closed."

"True, and believe me, we've checked. But we still have questions. Questions that are not publicly available, questions that we know only you could answer", replied the driver. "This conversation is done. Get in the car, Mr. Stone."

"Not that I don't trust you, oh, and I don't by the way, but I still do not see how this benefits me," replied John.

"You will understand, Mr. Stone. You will understand very soon." the driver repeated.

As John considered his options, he knew that he had no choice but to enter the waiting vehicle. More than anything was his curiosity that drove him this far. Time to play along.

"Alright, but I want your buddies out of my house. I'm a real private guy and strangers roaming through my kitchen and looking through my refrigerator really bothers me. You guys get out and I'll get get in."

"Consider it done, Mr. Stone."

"OK, let's get this over with, as I have a date tonight and don't care to be late."

"The driver sauntered back to the rear right door of the still running Crown Victoria, grabbed the door handle with his right hand, opened it, and beckoned John towards the opening.

As John approached, the driver reached for John's right shoulder, stopping him rather abruptly, noting "I just need to pat you down as a precaution."

"No worries, just be nice as I'm ticklish", replied John. John's reflexes had almost kicked as a result of the unexpected battery from the driver. Would have made for a short meeting, and a mess in the front yard.

The driver patted John down from head to toe, and using a hand-held metal detector, quickly located the original larger femto in John's right front pocket along with the fEP unit that fully resembled an iPhone. The driver removed the femto, looking at it strangely, but amazingly let John maintain possession of the fEP, to John's surprise. Unknowingly, this slip would enable Mick to hear the entire conversation, in addition to seeing the exchange through John's eyepiece. EXos had yet to develop a means to incorporate a microphone in the eyepiece. Just add one more item to the list of performance improvements.

John peered into the dimly lit rear seat of the Crown Vic, inside of which was seated a wiry middle-eastern man smartly dressed in an all-black ensemble of jeans and a black button down shirt. He also donned black wing tip shoes, visible below the pant leg of his crossed legs. His socks were a charcoal grey with a single thin red stripe running up ankle and disappearing under the pant leg. He appeared to be in his mid- to late- 50s, although always hard to tell.

The man silently gestured for John to enter, pointing to the empty seat across from him. John lowered his head and sipped his tall frame into the seat as directed, sitting a mere 3 feet across from the curious man.

There was a window dividing the front and rear seats, so the driver and front seat passenger could not easily hear their conversation, assuming the rear microphone was not activated. John hated to be enclosed in such tight quarters, and his instincts told him that this may not be the best choice but knew he had passed the point of no return. Assuming that any or all of the vehicle occupants were armed, he concentrated on compartmentalizing his nervousness, appearing relaxed.

The man snapped his fingers at his driver who was still standing outside the car door John had just entered. He swiftly closed the door behind John, making a solid thud. The driver circled to the rear of the car, remotely opening the trunk of the vehicle as he passed with the key FOB. John could hear him fumbling through the truck space, and detected a sound that appeared to be the double snap associated with opening a brief case. He fumbled some more, and audibly closed what John assumed was the brief case. He then remotely closed the trunk as he circled to re-enter the driver's seat, lowered the window between the seats and handed the man a familiar folder, raised the window, and slowly drove off down the street.

"What, no blindfold or hood to prevent me from detecting the location of your secret lair?" John smartly asked the man.

The man ignored the comment and began with, "We have information that I believe would interest you." He continued to hold the folder in his right hand. "I want to show you something first."

The man opened the folder, showing John the front page. John knew exactly what the folder was a soon as it was passed from the driver and it was identical to the one he had seen in the rental car earlier that evening. Specifically, it was the service file, or jacket, that summarized the military career of many a soldier. On page one was the obligatory photograph of the owner that John knew as his twin brother, Joe.

"We knew you had a twin, but now in person, I am surprised how closely you resemble each other. Same facial features, body build, color of skin, eyes and hair style.

"So you're here to discuss my facial features? If so, I want out of the car."

"No, not the topic or question I had in mind", replied the man. "As I'm sure you have guessed, I am not from around here."

"Yup, your socks were a dead giveaway," replied John.

Again the man ignored John's comment and continued with, "We need information on your brother."

"You have more information in your hand than you would find anywhere in the world, much of which is classified. That's what that big red stamp means on the front."

"Yes, I am very aware of this, and am tiring with your side comments," the man quipped. "How about you just tell me what you know about your brother's most recent outings."

"Not hard to do, as he's been buried for almost two decades," replied John. "The cemetery is down the street if you want to see his burial plot. I expect that this is not the answer you were looking for?"

"No, it is not. In fact, we are more interested in Joe's whereabouts from a living perspective," noted the man.

"What the hell does that mean, from a living perspective?" asked John.

"To cut to the chase, Mr. Stone. We believe Joe is alive, and wanted you to know. You are well aware of the unfortunate incidents that he orchestrated in the Middle East two decades ago. We have never and will never forget the impact on our family that occurred from his actions."

John knew exactly the events that the man was resurrecting. He knew that this day would come, and wondered if he was about to be collateral damage for events that his brother affected.

John looked straight into the man's eyes, and asked, "I'm losing interest in this conversation, as you are incorrect. As much as I would like my brother to be alive, it is just not true. Every day he is in my memory and further discussion will make me very angry. I suggest that you let me out of this vehicle or risk further damage to you, in addition to your family. By the way, I'm sure you are aware that kidnapping is a felony."

"Mr. Stone, you willingly accepted to ride with me this evening. That in itself eliminates the kidnapping charge, per United States Law. Every first year law student learns this."

"So you're an attorney too. Wow, thanks for the free legal advice," replied John. "Let me the hell out of the car."

"Mr. Stone, I will do so, but I am not here to inflict damages on you or your family. I am also not here to harass you. In fact, my boss is a fair man, who also believes in legalities, just as you do. Instead, I am here to alert you that we know where your brother is, we are closing in on him as we speak, and will execute him within the next 7 days. This I can promise you."

John had to keep himself from outwardly showing how shocked he was. Again he compartmentalized and internalized his anxiety. Now was not the time to sweat or show any indication of weakness.

"This is an odd meeting. First you tell me you need information, but I've not provided any. Then you tell me my brother is alive, and then you top it off with a death threat against him. Don't you realize that you are wasting your time?"

"We realize many things, but my boss is a man of character, who believes in a fair chance. I have just given you and your brother that fair chance, and now you must go. Good-bye Mr. Stone."

The man switched on the intercom and alerted the driver to pullover.

Chapter 15

John found himself standing alone on the asphalt street as the limo sped away. The engine of the Crown Vic still surging as it accelerated north down the center of Green Avenue, until it was a just a silent blurred gray dot in his distant vision.

The thought of the conversation he had just experienced inside the limo weighed heavily on his mind, in between past memories of his brother Joe and personal indecision of next steps.

Throughout John's life, worries would cloud his waking moments, especially during instances with seemingly impossible odds. John had always justified this as an indication of intelligence. John knew that these were the times that differentiated him and his brother from the normal population, via their learned ability to compartmentalize and quell these errant thoughts. Specifically, when stressors increased, they learned to counter the situation, with an opposing outward display of apathy, despite the chaotic thoughts racing inside their minds. It was a trait that they had mastered as they grew older, which in many instances, served to save their lives.

This inner calm was a technique that John and Joe learned from their father, which he aptly labeled "winding the clock," first introduced to them when they were in middle school. The memory of the first time they heard their Dad's story, was etched in John's mind as if it had occurred yesterday.

"Boys, there will be times in your lives when you will be faced with decisions that will hit you like a ton of bricks," noted their Father. "Most of these will occur when you least expect, and it is the control of your knee-jerk reaction and body language that will make or break your success," he continued.

"A very dear friend of mine who was a C-130 Hercules pilot introduced me to the idea of 'winding the clock' when these stressors occur. Specifically, whenever a pilot is flying, and he faced with an emergency situation, he is immediately taught to reach down and wind the clock on his instrument panel to calm his thoughts and fully assess the situation, before taking action. This dates back to the early T-37 trainer aircraft, that had a spring loaded clock that required occasional winding, but it still applies today for modern aircraft that clearly don't have clocks that require winding."

Their father continued, "This idea stems from the story of a young fighter pilot flying a two-engine, P-41 War Hawk, on a sortie over Germany during World War II. While the pilot was flying at low altitude to avoid anti-aircraft radar, he experienced a bird strike to his right engine, which caused a flame-out that necessitated the pilot to manually shut down the aircraft engine. Later on that same flight, and still running on the single right engine, an ENGINE FIRE emergency indicator light appeared on his instrument panel. He immediately reacted by manually shutting down the engine, without looking to see if there was in fact a fire. It wasn't clear if the pilot just assumed the FIRE indicator was on the same shutdown engine damaged earlier, or if he failed to look at the left engine to confirm there truly was an engine fire. Luckily, the P-41s were an agile platform, much more stable than the quad-redundant aircraft controls of modern day (without which current day aircraft without engine power would auger to the ground like a flying log). The young pilot had enough altitude to regain control, re-start the engine and recover without harm."

"So boys, remind yourselves in these tough situations to first stop and wind the clock, then think it through, then take action. The few seconds that you spend doing this will pay off."

John had considered numerous scenarios while entering and sitting inside the limo, all of which could have shut down the only remaining engine that he had running; fully eliminating a successful recovery, or understanding of the purpose of his brief (and still illegal in his mind) kidnapping.

So John wound the clock, delaying any rash actions, and now remained standing in the street, still considering his options. Mick's voice came through his ear piece.

"Israeli Hamas, no doubt."

"Yes, my guess as well, considering the S13 tattoo on the bystander in the drive and P45 auto-mag the driver was wielding."

"What are you thinking?" asked Mick.

"Not much, still winding the clock," replied John.

"And thinking of your Dad, I assume."

"Yup, and Joe, of course. Can you swing by and pick me up in about five minutes, once you assure our friends all exit the area."

"Good plan. I've already noted that your two girlfriends immediately hightailed it back to their car, as soon as you exited the limo."

"That's good. Better yet, meet me at Red's Diner on East 5th in about 30 minutes. I need the quiet time to think, and then we can talk."

"Sounds good. See you then," replied Mick. "I'll monitor your approach to assure no followers. Napkins on my table meaning the coast is clear, otherwise walk on by. Our back-up is the Pour House on West 7th an hour later if you've been followed."

"Roger that," replied John.

Chapter 16

John took an indirect route down 4th Street, to 3rd, then doubling back to 4th and finally returning to 5th, where he noted Mick's black Dodge Charger parked in the half-filled parking lot. Red's had always been a popular eatery for the locals, with a 1960s motif that included an authentic juke box and decor to match. The walls contained hundreds of 45-records, and black and white photographs of singers from that age, such as Frankie Vallie, etc. The food wasn't spectacular, but it was consistently good every time, without surprises. It was the kind of place that didn't require menus, as each customer knew their order beforehand, or could be reminded of the daily specials on the black chalk boards displayed over the kitchen.

John entered Red's with a cautious eye for anyone paying more attention to him than any other customer. Any stare more than two seconds would have tipped him off. Normally, he would have utilized a more conservative entry method, but he knew that Mick had taken care of the recon prior to his arrival. Mick was seated at the left rear booth, close to the restrooms, with a full view of the entire diner, especially the front door. From Mick's vantage point, the entire parking lot was also in view through the plate glass window that circled the entire diner. John also knew that a door exiting from behind the restrooms allowed an easy getaway, if needed. Good 'ol Mick, always thought things through, leaving no mistakes to chance, or at least as few as possible.

As John made his way through the booths, he scanned the crowd, just out of curiosity, more so than concern. As he approached the booth in which Mick was seated, his eyes were focused for napkins left on the table which indicated that the coast was clear. No napkins meant John would exit past the bathrooms and double back one-half hour after at the Pour house.

Two sets of napkins with protruding fork and knife were present on the table in front of Mick, as a sign that the coast was clear. John passed the table anyway, to go check out the bathroom, for personal reasons more so than concern. In his fEP earpiece he heard Mick's voice.

"What, too good for me now, or is there someone I missed that looks menacing?"

"No worries," replied John, "You are the only menacing character in the diner. Just dropping by the restroom and scoping out the exit in the event anyone enters while we're here."

"You know I already did that."

"You took a pee too?"

"Yeah, that's it, I took a pee too. Nice. Hurry up so I don't look stupid sitting here talking to myself," replied Mick.

"10-4. Peeing now, so I need to concentrate."

Once finished, John washed his hands and exited the restroom, using the paper towel to grab the door handle so as to not dirty his clean hands. Oddly enough, John's tendencies bordered on obsessive compulsive, which especially flared when he was nervous. It was times like these that worsened these habits, which even winding the clock could not help.

The rear exit past the restrooms offered immediate entry to the vast parking lot that surrounded the diner. Not much cover was available with the exception of a few cars that were parked out back and a four cubic yard metal dumpster partially hidden behind a three sided wooden fence, which appeared to be a favorite eating establishment for termites. A propane tank was located to the left of the fence. Oddly enough, that particular fence reminded John of the many times he and Joe had been contracted by neighbors to install and stain wooden fences in their neighborhood as young teenagers. They became experts at the process, with many a summer evening spent building continuous rows of fencing between and around backyards, like castle courtyards that demarcated the ownership lines between properties. Looking at the three-sided dumpster fence, he thought how only one application of oil-based stain would have saved the wood from termites, when Mick's voice broke this thought.

"You OK?" asked Mick.

"Yeah, just looking at the fence out back."

"Ah, ok, now that makes perfect sense," replied Mick. "You sure you're ok?"

"Yes, coming back in now. Coast still clear?"

"Crystal", replied Mick.

John wandered back through the exit door, passed the bathrooms and slid in the seat across from Mick. The seat was made of a smooth kind of vinyl that he assumed had that distinct smell when it was first installed, rather strong but yet strangely appealing, just like the ink from the mimeograph paper that he remembered as a small child in First Grade. The kind of smell that made everyone place the still moist paper in front of their face, and take a big breath. Odd that memories like these seem as if they occurred yesterday.

"We have a dilemma," John said.

"Yes, we do," replied Mick. "One we can handle, though."

"If we choose to do so, and at this point, I do not see an option."

"I'm all in," replied Mick. "You know how I like a challenge."

Chapter 17

The brothers sat at the small wooden table in the kitchen, both in silence, the plan of approach fully discussed and agreed upon. After about five minutes, Joe broke the silence.

"So, what are you thinking, bro?"

"That you still have the uncanny ability to strategize, at a level far above my capabilities."

"It's a learned talent, but realize that the plan has faults, as you've just corrected."

"Minor changes, that simply add more icing to the cake," replied John.

"A few years in Afghanistan and you would learn a few tricks too."

"True, but one weak link in my mind is the boathouse. It is crucial to the plan's success. It fails, and we fail," noted John.

"Then I suggest we walk down there to alleviate your concern."

Joe rose from his seat, pushing up with his hands on the edge of the table. He grabbed the 45 from the table top, checked the clip, and inserted it into the shoulder holster below his left underarm. John grabbed a 44-Magnum from the mini-armory that John had assembled, and placed a 6-shot speed load into the chamber, and pocketed it in a similar shoulder holster as Joe's.

They checked the SCENICC for any visitors within a one-mile radius, with nothing noted other than a few resident squirrels and rabbits. Joe led the way through the rear door of the cabin, across the back porch and cambered down the slope that led to the boathouse.

From the distant perspective of the cabin, the boathouse seemed small, but upon their approach, that was not the case. John estimated that the boathouse could easily hold three to four ski boats, which could enter from the lake-side opening. From the north side there was no apparent openings, with the exception of a very small aperture, no more than six-inches square, located in the approximate ten-foot high north wall. To the west side, there was a six-foot wide dock the spanned the length of the structure, and appeared to wrap around the south side. A door was visible half-way down the dock, which enabled entry into the boathouse.

"Looks sturdy, with no apparent north entry," John said.

"Sturdy, to say the least. Considering my improvements that I described to you, it is an impenetrable mini-fortress, from the north, west and east."

"I like your confidence but I need to validate that myself," replied John.

"But, of course. I would expect nothing less from my always skeptical twin. Knowing your OC tendencies, I did not want to let you down."

The brothers walked to the dock that bordered the boathouse on its west side, walking on the planks that sported nails strategically located above the supporting stringers below. As they walked, John remembered the fences that he and his brother had constructed in their youth; each nail meticulously piercing the centers of the horizontal supports.

Joe stopped at the door, looked at John and said, "Ready for this?", and threw open the door and stepped inside the darkness of the large wooden cube.

As John entered the boathouse, his eyes not yet adjusting to the dark room, there was the oddest sound as the waves struck the shore below the structure. The waves were oddly amplified somehow, but he could not put his finger on how this could occur inside a fully wooden cube with one southern open wall. John reached to the right of the door and switched on the light. Immediately John saw the answer, noting that every wall glistened with the blurry reflection of metal sheeting. It was if they had walked into an empty industrial size freezer, the type with brushed stainless steel walls. Two jet skis remained suspended about 4 feet above them.

"What exactly did you do, or better yet, how did you construct this?" asked John in disbelief.

"That's my secret. Welcome to my metal lined box, just like I told you," laughed Joe. "Is it what you expected?"

"Yes, but no. I do feel better about the imperviousness of this mini fortress though. Let me guess--steel plating, right?" asked John.

"Exactly, with no less than one-quarter inch thickness, with each four by eight sheet weighing over 150 pounds apiece."

"Nice collection of FS 2000s as well," noted John, as his eyes locked onto the strategically placed row of automatic machine guns spanning the base of the north inner wall.

"They've always been a personal favorite of mine. You can never have too many."

"In this case though, I think you do have too many."

"That's a matter of opinion, as I considered bringing more," replied Joe.

"So, do you understand the game plan now?" asked Joe.

"Absolutely," replied John, thinking back to their original discussion occurring two hours before as they sat at the round table in the cabin.

"The gist of the plan is that once we hole ourselves away in this mini fortress, your protégée will arrive and whisk me away to safety while you hold off the bad guys."

"That's it in a nutshell," replied Joe.

"So where is the rope that is supposed to be underwater, and leads towards the speed boat somewhere on the lake?" asked John.

"I've attached it just below the water line, at the rear of the entry door. Also, the 'speedboat,' as you call it, won't be just somewhere on the lake, it will be exactly right there," with John pointing approximately 50 yards from the boat house.

Joe then walked over towards the open side of the boathouse and gestured towards the floor. A faint irregularity in the wood slats was visible, making a rectangle about three-foot square.

"That's the door where you will clandestinely escape," noted Joe. "Then you will follow the rope, hand over hand, and keep your butt low so you don't get it shot off. No pressure. My accomplice will make this easy."

"And then?" asked John.

"Then I remotely ignite the boat house," replied Joe.

"What color explosion do you want?" asked Joe.

"What?" replied John.

"What color explosion should I use for the boathouse?"

"Are you serious?" asked John. "Don't you have any better things to plan for, than to design the color of the explosion?" asked John in amazement.

"As usual, you're not thinking, and need to get with the program," replied Joe. "If you select a color, and the boathouse explosion produces that color, it will be an indication that I caused the event. If it is just a normal boom, with non-orange smoke, you will immediately know that I failed, and am dead. Does this make sense?"

"Surprisingly, yes it does. I choose orange, so as not to look overly suspicious, as would purple or other."

"Orange it is. A few blocks of sodium pellets in the water will cause a very vivid orange. Look for it, and it will confirm the plan worked."

"Or at least the fact that the plan was initiated," John replied. "There are so many next steps."

"To say the least", replied Joe.

Chapter 18

Orange smoke it was, visible from the small boat floating approximately 50 yards from the fully leveled boat shed. Joe's quote, "A few blocks of sodium dropping in the water will cause a very vivid orange. Look for it, and it will confirm the plan worked."
The plan worked. Step one of John's life changing future, was beginning exactly one explosion ago.

Brenda looked at John, and repeated, "He told me you were his first priority and he was expendable."

John remained still, watching the wisps of orange smoke rise into the darkness, the orange color quickly mixing with the dusk sky. Mission accomplished.

"John, time to go," Brenda stated. "Start pulling up the rope and place it in the boat."

John did so, hand over hand, until the entire coil was inside the boat. Brenda quietly started a trolling motor located on the rear hull of the boat and slowly steered them to the far side of the lake. The smoke blocked much of the view of the now obliterated cabin and boathouse, also providing cover as the smoke layered itself across the lake.

They reached the opposite side of the lake within 10 minutes, just as the sound of fire engines became audible in the distance. The firemen, unable to recover any of the property, would wait until the blaze subsided before attempting to extinguish the fire.

Undoubtedly, the assailants would have left long before the fireman's arrival, to assure their clandestine departure. They would assume that their primary target, Joe Stone, was now the late Joe Stone, and would report their success to their boss, whomever that may be.

As John exited the boat onto the shore, his mind raced at the overwhelming list of next steps. A new life, new continent, new language, new adventure. John began to miss the daily commonalities that he knew he may never see again.

"John, stop daydreaming and stay focused." Brenda scolded. "You are far from being out of the woods. We have much to do, so let's get going."

She was right. There were too many loose ends that could unravel at any minute. John had specific actions that had to be exercised exactly per plan, else jeopardize his entire future. Joe was always the strategist, correct to a T, which may have been his downfall.

"Good luck bro," John mumbled. "You'll need it."

"Grab the rope from the boat, and follow me," Brenda half-whispered, as she pulled the boat on shore. John did as he was told and followed her to a nondescript light gray pickup truck, with a camper top covering the bed. He raised the back window and threw the wet rope coil onto the rear bed of the truck.

After hoisting the boat onto the trailer behind the truck, John noticed that Brenda was already in the driver's seat, looking impatiently through the rear cab window. John took one more look across the lake, his eyes involuntarily drawn to the flashing lights of the fire truck squadron stationed a safe distance from the still raging inferno, and jumped in the passenger seat.

"He told me you were his first priority and he was expendable," still echoed loudly in his mind as Brenda accelerated up the road.

Chapter 19

Water is an excellent conductor of sound waves. A physical property that Joe was well aware of due to myriad underwater ordnance exercises while in the Gulf. The difference in this case being the minimal distance between the point of incendiary ignition, and Joe's current position, located merely 30 yards away at a depth of 10 feet below the water surface. Joe had planned for the resulting shock wave, and in an attempt to minimize the percussion, assured the bulk of the exploding C4 was located above the water line. He also afforded further protection by constructing an underwater steel coffin, into which he had entered seconds prior to the blast. Underwater hearing protection finished off his personal protective gear, to prevent an immediate blackout due to the deafening explosion and subsequent drowning.

Concerning the steel coffin, John objected to the name "coffin" the first time Joe described it. Either way, it was an appropriate name, despite the outcome, which originally was an unknown in Joe's mind due to the extremely close proximity to the blast zone. There was little choice though at the time, as his escape route distance could not be significantly increased.

As per plan, the outcome was a success. The fact that Joe heard the blast and the sustained orange glow from the explosion meant he was still alive, not unlike hearing a gunshot as proof that you had not been shot in the head -- gruesome, but logical. Joe hunkered down in his submerged steel coffin for another 5 minutes to regain his sense of equilibrium, using his Life-Air 10 as his oxygen source.

He could still see the eerie flickering orange glow above the surface of the water, along with pieces of wood, shards of twisted metal, and pieces of fiberglass potentially from the suspended jet skis in the boathouse that continued to settle through the water to the bottom of the lake. Everything was occurring in slow motion, as if Joe was at the center of a Christmas snow globe, with the only audible sound the continued ringing in his ears.

At T-minus 9 minutes, Joe cautiously emerged from his place of hiding, removed his Life-Air 10 to avoid a bubble trail, and swam underwater to the shoreline approximately 20 yards away. Upon arrival under a neighboring dock, he suspended his snorkel slightly above the water line, for a much needed breath of air. Joe had been taught to hold his breath for almost 5 minutes while in Navy Seal training. The difference this time being that the excitement and exertion quickly reduced his maximum to just under 3 minutes, which he estimated was surpassed over a minute ago.

Ten more minutes in hiding, and it would be time to move. Joe floated vertically, clinging to one of the dock beams, his arms and feet wrapped around the vertical structure, to assure he remained just below the water surface. The sound of sirens was conducted through, and amplified by the water, along with voices and the continual ebb and flow of the water surface striking the dock structure above him. All combined, there was enough commotion to allow his unnoticeable exit from the lake.

Joe slowly pushed his body away from the dock, fully exposing his head above the water and carefully making a full 360-degree review of his surroundings. The scene was just as expected, and even more chaotic. Lights of red, blue and white flashed and reflected in random patterns about 40 yards behind the explosion site, evidence that the fire trucks remained at bay as they watched the remaining wreckage burn. No need for extinguishing, at this point in the game.

Time to move. Joe lifted himself from the water and crept along the shore quickly making his way to a row of pine trees and shrubs leading towards an adjacent drive way.

In his preparations for escape, Joe had stationed a motorcycle behind the same tree line. He was not a fan of bikes, as they afforded zero protection from gun fire, but at this point, the vehicle provided a reasonably quick and stealthy getaway.

Joe grabbed the handle bars, tilted the bike to a vertical position, and released the kick-stand. Just in case there were onlookers that he had not seen, he donned a black helmet and pushed the bike 100 yards up the exit drive, clockwise around the lake towards the lot where John and Brenda had hopefully exited. Joe knew that the only remaining link to his presence was the steel coffin, still located near the explosion site. An underwater inspection by the local Police Department would easily locate the structure. Joe had purposefully placed a few steel plates alongside the coffin, so its presence might be construed as rough pieces of the plates originally lining the reinforced boathouse. The mere presence of these steel plates, no matter the location, would hopefully just add to the unknown artifacts of the event.

Joe hopped on the motorcycle, started it, and slowly putted to the parking lot where his brother was to have left with Brenda no more than 30 minutes ago. He was instantly comforted to see that this was the case, as the grey F-150 was no longer there. The only visible sign was the obvious path of distressed soil, created when the boat was pulled towards the trailer, and the still wet pavement, where Joe assumed John had moved the rope into the bed of the truck. John had wanted to leave a confirmatory sign for Joe, such as an empty Coke can at the edge of the parking lot, but both brothers knew that even this simple evidence could have negative ramifications.

Joe mounted the bike and rode away from the parking lot, taking the same clockwise path around the Lake as John and Brenda had, knowing that their paths would not likely ever cross again.

Chapter 20

"Brenda, your driving is going to kill us both," John exclaimed as they sped away from the lake.

"Get used to it, as I only drive two speeds, slow and wide-open, and I never drive slow," Brenda replied.

"I just don't want us to attract any attention, or get a ticket," noted John.

"No worries," quipped Brenda, "No worries."

Within 15 minutes, Brenda had navigated the truck back to a small motel near the airport, where John's clothes and a large plastic-shelled suitcase had been dropped off earlier that morning. This suitcase contained John's sole possessions, for the short term until arriving at his final place of hiding. Brenda stopped the truck immediately outside the motel room, within four feet of the door.

"Take your shower and get your stuff ready, then we're off to the airport," Brenda noted. "We have about three hours before your flight leaves. That enough time?"

"Absolutely," John said.

"Good," replied Brenda. "I'll wait in the truck."

Brenda reached above the sun visor and removed the motel room key card and handed it to John. He took it from her, noting for the first time a bloody gash above Brenda's wrist.

"You OK?" asked John.

"Just fine, but thanks for asking," she replied. "You are wasting time again."

"OK, OK -- I'll be out in 20 minutes tops."

John slipped out of the truck, traversed the four feet to the door and inserted the key. A very small rectangular green light came on, with an audible click of the door. John turned the handle, swung the door open and clicked on the light. The room was exactly as they had left it earlier that morning except it was more humid as the air conditioner had switched off due to the lack of occupants. He quickly shed his clothes, placing them in a plastic bag left just for this purpose, and jumped into the shower. Mud and sparkly grit was visible in the water, swirling clockwise down into the shower drain. John let the water pour on his head, in hopes of clearing his mind. It didn't work, as he knew Brenda was waiting outside for him, ready to deliver him to his new life and locale far from the motel room he was currently in.

Fifteen minutes later and John was closing the motel room door behind him, with his plastic bag of dirty clothes and towels and his suitcase in hand. He placed both items into the bed of the truck near the coiled rope, and hopped into the cab next to Brenda.

"Here are your tickets," she noted. "You're flying non-stop to Charles de Gaulle, where you will be on your own from there. Your new Passport is included, with your new identity and all. It sure helps having friends in all the wrong places."

John opened the passport, reading the name "Jean Pascual" aloud. "Rather common, as French names go -- nice work. Where is my apartment again?"

Brenda replied, "Do you remember the Paris Catacombs, where the French exhumed and relocated the dead bodies that were beneath the land where Notre Dame was to be built, among other parts of Paris?"

"I'm living in the Catacombs?" John asked.

"No, Genius," Brenda retorted. "Your apartment is located above the Cafe that faces the ground level entrance to the Catacombs. You've already discussed this with Joe, and chose this location, so don't sound so surprised."

"I know -- I was just yanking your chain," replied John. "I also was curious how much of the plan you were aware of."

"Don't test me and don't worry about it," Brenda snapped back. "I am actually impressed by your choice of locations, as that section of Paris is very populated and the Catacombs offer a very good escape route, assuming that one is looking for that sort of thing."

"Always nice to have an out -- I just hope that I will never need it," replied John.

Brenda continued driving in silence for the next five miles. She exited towards the International Terminal, at which point she said, "I wish you the best. Remember that you are not alone out there -- your enemies are ever present. Be sure to make a clean break from the life that you know, and start again -- it's your brother's gift to you, so don't waste it."

"I promise not to let him down, and I appreciate all that you've done for me, as well," John replied. "Were you guys close?" John asked.

"Extremely," Brenda replied. "When you trust someone with your life, and end up fighting side-by-side in foreign countries across the globe, you get comfortable with each other. Joe has taught me much of what I know, and I am indebted to him."

"As am I, and now to you," replied John.

Brenda pulled parallel to the curb below the entry to the Terminal entry, and stopped he truck.

"Get going, you barely have two hours. How much French do you know, Mr. Pascual?" asked Brenda.

"Enough to get out of the states," noted John. "I'll remember the rest once I get immersed in the culture."

"Good luck with that -- I know you'll be fine," stated Brenda. "Now go!"

John hopped out of the truck, grabbed his bag from the bed and walked into the Terminal, with Brenda screeching the truck tires as she sped away. Brenda's advice still fresh in his mind, "It's your brother's gift to you, so don't waste it."

I won't Joe -- I won't, thought John.

Chapter 21

Joe had already ditched the motorcycle in a location in which it would never be found by the authorities; in a dark deserted alley with the keys still in it, located in a sketchy part of town. Someone would feel very lucky tonight, as if Christmas had come early. Next, Joe walked five blocks north and caught a taxi directly to the Ardmore Mall, walked straight through the mall, then exited and flagged a second taxi which dropped him off at John's house.

Joe walked up the driveway, traversed the front walkway and ascended the six steps onto the Victorian style front porch. Grasping the ring of keys that John had provided to him, Joe searched for the gold-colored key with the word "Schlage" written on it, used it to unlock the front door and pushed it open. He took two steps across the threshold into the house -- his house.

Joe had succeeded through many military assignments, all with a risk seemingly worse than the prior, with no sure promise of return. Joe enjoyed a challenge and relished at insurmountable odds. This assignment was like no other though, not necessarily due to the associated danger, but due to its complexity and high chance for failure. At West Point, Joe was specially trained to understand the personality of his foe, in attempts to facilitate the prediction of their next steps. Now he was confronted with a different type of challenge. He was to assume the identity of his brother. To be more specific, he was to assume the life of his brother. Joe had many times considered stealing the identity of his assailants in past assignments, but never would have predicted that he would someday assume that of his own brother.

Even though Joe and John looked identical and knew just about everything about the development strategy for the SCENNIC program, there was still much room for error. Joe knew this from the start, but assured John that it would not be an issue. In actuality, Joe lied. He knew how difficult this life swap would be, but he needed to convince John to exit the country, after which time he would figure how to make it work. As Joe stood in the hallway, he thought to himself that he must have been very convincing to John, but now wasn't feeling so confident that he could pull this off.

First things first. Joe was by all evidence, fully departed. Preparations for the funeral were required, to include the scripting of his own Obituary. The Police would soon be made aware of the accident and the deceased, due to the presence of Joe's truck, or at least its remains, found at the scene of the explosion. The Police would first confirm that the vehicle had not been stolen, and then they would most probably stop by the house to assure Mr. Joe Stone was missing, leading to the worst case scenario that John and Joe had crafted. Joe was ready for their arrival, and was already walking up the stairs to shower and change into John's clothes.

It wasn't more than an hour when there was a knock on the front door. As Joe walked down the stairs, he could see two men through the stained glass door; one man in plain clothes, the other in full Police uniform. When Joe opened the door, he thought he detected the smell of smoke, which he assumed was from one or both Officers being at the scene of the explosion. Or it might have just been his imagination.

"I am Officer Johnston, and this is my partner Officer Mundst. Are you Mr. John Stone?" asked the uniformed officer. Both officers were probably assuming they knew the answer, as their facial expressions were intentionally blank.

"Yes, Officer, or should I say 'Officers.' I am Mr. Stone," replied Joe, being truthful in his reply. "What can I do for you?"

The plain clothes Officer spoke next, stating, "We have some bad news. It appears that your brother, Joe, is missing."

"Missing?" asked Joe inquisitively. "Missing how?"

"We found your brother's pickup truck near a cabin that he had just purchased on Lake Hubbard. The cabin appears to have exploded due to a natural gas leak. At least that is what the initial investigation points to," replied the uniformed Officer.

"When was the last time you heard from your brother?" asked the uniformed Officer.

Joe replied, "Joe noted to me that he was going to the lake -- but that was two days ago. Did you find a body? I mean, is there proof it was my brother?"

"We found a body, but it was burned beyond recognition, so badly in fact that CSI cannot even assess the molars," noted the plainclothes policeman.

"This is horrible," replied Joe. "Could you be mistaken?"

"If Joe doesn't show up, then we must assume the worst. We're here to alert you that this could be the case. We're extremely sorry. Is there anything we can do to help?"

"No --- I just need to think this through. Thank you for coming by," replied Joe.

"Again, we're very sorry for your loss, Mr. Stone."

Joe watched as the Officers returned to their squad car, and slowly backed out of the driveway. Convincing complete strangers that he was John would be easy enough. Convincing others that really knew John would be a whole different matter. Joe was dreading his first day in the office, and the funeral which he was about to schedule.

Joe sat down at the kitchen table, and began writing:

On June 8, 1995, Joe Stone went to be with the Lord. He was 46 years old, a decorated Green Beret, a hero and a friend of many. His multiple tours in various wars across the globe saved the lives of many a soldier. He is survived only by his brother, John Stone. His funeral will take place on Saturday, June 12, at Arlington Memorial Cemetery where he will be buried adjacent to his Mother and Father. Joe ... Rest in Peace. We will see you in heaven.

Chapter 22

John made his way to Gate 30 with ample time to spare; 90 minutes early, to be exact. Air France Flight 780 was on time, but much too early to board, so John went for a walk to clear his mind. Better to be distracted, than to sit at the gate.

After wasting 45 minutes shopping for a few toiletry items and exchanging $500 US Dollars for Euros, John had returned to his gate. Boarding followed within five minutes, at which time John boarded and sat in seat 15B, located in Business Class. Within 30 minutes, the remainder of the passengers boarded, the door to the plane was heaved closed, and Flight 780 was aloft.

John peered out the window, realizing that he may never again step foot onto the North American continent. This was the plan that he and Joe devised and one that made the most sense. John actually had the easier of the two roles, in his opinion. Certainly, Joe knew the projects John had been working on at the Pentagon, so this would not be a problem. Joe's difficulty would be trying to adopt John's personality, mannerisms and temperament. Unlike Joe, John wasn't one to bully others around. Joe's future disagreements could no longer end with a choke hold on his opponent -- doing so would immediately give away their secret, and could bring the wrath of the Hamas onto John, in whatever continent he was hiding.

"Voulez-vous un verre de vin?" (Would you like a glass of wine?) asked the stewardess, a tall attractive brunette with green eyes, wearing a short black dress.

John exited from his fog and involuntarily replied, "Oui, je voudrais un verre de vin rouge, si-vous-plait" (Yes, I would like a glass of red wine, please). Foreign languages had always come easy to John, especially French, which he had had four years of in high school.

"Bordeaux?" She asked, turning the bottle label towards John, awaiting his approval.

"Oui, c'est bon" (Yes, that's good), replied John.

The stewardess promptly poured a tall wine glass two-thirds full, tactfully reached across John and pulled out the retractable shelf from inside John's left armrest. She then placed a napkin on the shelf followed by the wine glass. John could smell her perfume when she did this, and muttered "Merci." She smiled politely, nodded, and turned 180-degrees to the passengers across the aisle in 15D and E. John could not help but instinctively read her name on her Air France name tag -- Jeannette.

This little encounter reminded John of the one issue that would have prohibited the life swap that Joe was now attempting -- that being, if John was involved in a serious relationship. The worst case being if John had been engaged or married, which would have made the swap impossible altogether. John knew that Joe would still have his hands full when it came to John's recent girlfriend Marion. The best recourse would be to break off the relationship, and avoid all contact with her. Joe was not always one to follow the easy path though, so who knows what he was in store for, or Marion, for that matter.

John took special care to listen to the stewardess and the passengers' conversations to try to regain his ear for the French language. One on one conversation would be much more difficult than ordering a glass of red wine. In retrospect, John had always found it odd that when an individual is first taught a foreign language, the question "Where is the library?" is always on the list of first phrases. During John's many travels, he had yet to ask for the location of the library. The police station maybe, but not the library.

Ironically, one of the best ways to learn a language is by watching children's cartoons. Cartoon characters have a tendency to talk slowly, and they maintain a very simple vocabulary and level of conversation, which is very easily followed. Even better yet are the cartoons that include subtitles at the bottom of the screen. John would search for these television channels once he was safely located in his Paris apartment. Until then, local sit-coms playing on the airplane video screen would have to suffice.

Within 25 minutes, John's adrenaline had subsided, and he was fast asleep. The stewardess, Jeanette, came by shortly thereafter and astutely removed John's still full wine glass, placed a blanket over him and switched off the video. Out of curiosity, and probably more so attraction, she returned to the stewardess station to check the passenger log to see the name of her client in seat 15B. Jean Pascual was the name listed on the log -- a name that would be hard to track down in the multitudes of Parisians. She would need to be creative if she was to coincidentally meet up with Mr. Pascual. Jeanette was up for the challenge, and planned to meet Mr. Pascual more formally when he woke up. They had 10 hours left in the flight, so this would not be an issue.

Chapter 23

The wake and funeral were combined into a single event, as is typical for empty casket funerals. Joe had many friends and acquaintances, every one of which seemed to attend the funeral. It was Joe's first real experience acting as John in a large group setting, all of whom knew them both very well. Joe had expected that the first day back at the Pentagon would have been difficult, and completely underestimated this evening.

Thus far, all was going well. To further his disguise, Joe added a very light shade of gray eye makeup under his eyes, didn't shave and mussed his hair. This changed his normal appearance ever so slightly to feign the exhaustion of a surviving family member. Numerous times, Joe involuntarily found himself turning his attention towards those mentioning his name, and had to force himself to ignore these discussions. On a few occasions he had ignored his guests' calls for John, but was able to use the excuse that he was unable to concentrate. This was going to be difficult -- Very difficult.

Despite the ongoing identity play, Joe could not help but scan the crowd for unknown faces. He didn't expect that any of the assailants would attend, but then again, surrogates couldn't be ruled out. Certainly, whoever was behind the recent slew of events would want to confirm the deceased. Joe also considered the remote possibility that they wanted John dead as well. This was a long shot though, due to fact that John's house was still standing.

This meant that the unknown foes ran out of explosives, or were truly not interested in John -- the latter being the most reasonable explanation.

"John?" asked Randy, an Intelligence Analyst from the Pentagon. "Are you listening to me?"

Joe refocused, and replied "I'm sorry Randy, I'm really having a tough time focusing. So many distant memories of Joe keep coming back to me -- almost as if they occurred yesterday. I really miss him."

"I'm so sorry," replied Randy, "I really miss him too. Is there anything I can do for you?"

"No thank you, Randy," replied Joe. It's like I don't even know who I am, without my brother. Our lives were so intertwined."

"Joe -- we're here to help you," Randy replied, then stared at Joe with an expressionless face.

For a second, Joe didn't know how to respond. Clearly Randy had made a mistake, by calling him Joe. Or was it really a mistake? Did she know something? Women are so observant -- Had Randy seen through Joe's disguise or was he just being paranoid?

Randy continued to stare at him, silently awaiting a response to her statement.

Joe held his composure, maintaining an equally blank facial expression, continuing to stare at Randy without saying a word or taking a breath. He knew that he had to allow her to make the next move, and hoped that she had just made a simple mistake. He wound-the-clock silently to himself, counting one -- two -- three -- four -- five -- six, when at last she broke the silence.

"Oh my word, John," she said, her face changing to a solemn look. "I am so sorry I called you Joe at this time of sadness. You resemble him so closely -- I can see him when I see you now."

You and me both, Joe silently thought to himself.

"No need for an apology, Randy," replied Joe. "I now see Joe every time I look into the mirror, so I completely understand."

This weird back and forth discussion had to end, and was really making Joe feel uncomfortable. He still had a very odd feeling that Randy had detected something out of order -- Intelligence Analysts were specifically trained to do exactly this. Any additional time spent in this discussion could become problematic.

Joe changed the subject. "Randy, let's please not talk about Joe right now. I cannot keep my composure otherwise. I hope you understand."

"Certainly, John," replied Randy.

"I need to continue to greet and thank my guests, so I must go," noted Joe, as he walked away from Randy.

As he walked away, Joe noted to himself that he needed to avoid another one of these encounters. Too many intelligence experts in one room, all with an eye-for-detail, is not a good population to begin chitchat with.

The wake and funeral service could not end soon enough. After a tedious hour, the service concluded and the pall bearers delivered the coffin to the hearse. Joe rode shotgun in the hearse as the procession continued to the cemetery. Joe guessed that approximately two-thirds of the guests attended the grave site ceremony. He was exhausted, and intentionally limited this portion of the service to the bare minimum. Not to be disrespectful, but he needed time to regroup and gather his thoughts.

At last, the ceremony concluded with lowering of the casket into the previously excavated grave, followed by one last handshake or hug from his colleagues and friends, as they left one by one.

Then it was just Joe and one other woman, standing under the temporary awning constructed above the grave.

"Glad that's over," Joe stated, once he assured all other attendees were well out of earshot.

Brenda replied, "You did extremely well, John," staring into Joe's eyes. "I am yet again impressed by your ability to partition and focus."

"Don't be -- I was sure I blew it more than a few times," replied Joe. "Randy from Intel saw right through me, I think. She tried the old name switch to see if she could catch me."

"She's always been a feisty one," replied Brenda. "What did you do?"

"I stared her down, and kept my mouth shut," replied Joe.

"So she gave up? That's not like her to give up on the first try."

"She didn't -- and started on a word game thing about how I look just like Joe."

"Let me guess. You couldn't help but play along, offering your counter-spin on hers?" questioned Brenda.

"Um -- yeah, kind of," replied Joe.

"So she's off the trail?" asked Brenda.

"I believe so, yes."

"Good," noted Brenda. "By the way, I've decided that from this point, I do not want to confuse you, or me, so I will begin calling you John. Joe is out of the picture, plus there's always the possibility of someone overhearing us. You OK with this, John?"

"Absolutely OK -- I need some simplicity in my life."

"So, did you see anyone that you did not recognize in the crowd?" asked Brenda.

"I was rather distracted, but I did not see any obvious perps. If I had planned better, I would have set up a camera."

"That's why you have me, as that is exactly what I did," boasted Brenda. "I placed a wide angle video camera at the entry to the funeral parlor. I can stream the video through the Pentagon's facial recognition software tomorrow. If anyone there today was not on our cleared list, or more importantly the Pentagon's Who's-Who, we'll know immediately."

"Unless they were smart, and looked down, or shadowed folks ahead of them. This would be easy to do as they entered," noted Joe.

"Yes, which is why I also posted a second video camera in the ceiling entering the greeting room. It's not a catch-all, but if they entered the building, we would have them."

"Thank you for that. I'm rather worked up and can't wait until tomorrow so how about we login from my laptop at John's house - I mean my house -- and see what we find?"

"I'll meet you there," noted Brenda.

"10-4," replied Joe.

Chapter 24

John was awakened by the pilot's voice blasting over the speaker located above his head.

The message occurred in French, which John easily translated as "This is Captain Anderson. We will be landing in approximately 30 minutes. The stewardesses will be entering the cabin to provide you with a small breakfast and will also be collecting the headsets from our Business and First Class members. Thank you for flying Air France."

The second message from the pilot was in English, and confirmed John's interpretation.

"Bonjour, Monsieur Pascual," noted a cheery Mademoiselle Jeannette, whose perfume smelled just as intoxicating as it did a few hours previous. "Parlez-vous Englaise?" (Do you speak English?) she asked, with a tilt of her head.

"Yes, I do," answered a still groggy John.

"Coming from the States, I assume you may be returning from business," she said. "I recognize many of the repeat fliers in Business Class, and I do not recall seeing you before. I hope you don't find me too forward, but do you live in Paris?"

"Actually, I am finally moving back to Paris after working in the states for the past ten years," replied John. He contemplated lying, and stating that he was just flying through Charles-de-Gaulle, but found Jeannette to be very appealing. Plus, she could serve as an excellent tour guide in this new City, assuming she also lived there. In the back of his mind, he was also wondering if he had made a mistake in divulging this information. It was too late now though.

"That is wonderful news, as I also live in Paris," replied Jeannette. "I was born in Nyons, and moved here when I started with Air France almost 10 years ago. Maybe we could get together one evening for dinner?"

"You don't waste any time, do you?" asked John.

"Je suis desole, Monsieur Pascual," (I am sorry Mr. Pascual), she replied, turning her gaze politely downward -- a noticeable blush forming in her cheeks.

"No apologies necessary, mademoiselle," John replied, smiling. "I am taken aback by your proactive attitude. I would very much enjoy having dejuener (dinner) with you. Please give me your contact number and I will call you once I get settled in my flat."

Jeannette looked up, her expression still bordering on embarrassment but quickly turning to delight. "I also look forward to our next meeting. I will be flying to Brussels tomorrow, and then to Frankfurt for a 3-day layover, but expect to return to Paris shortly thereafter."

"That should be enough time for me to get settled," replied John. "Where do you live?"

"My flat is actually outside the loop, in a northwestern suburb named Nuielly-Sur Seine." She removed an Air France pen from her left shirt pocket, along with a small pad on which she wrote her name and number on the top page, in loopy woman-like calligraphy, placing two eyes and a smile below it – "Jeannette Bouton, +34 139498039."

"Thank you, Jeannette," John replied, taking the single sheet of paper from Jeannette's hand. "I will call you once I get settled into my flat."

"Promise?" asked Jeannette, again tilting her head ever so slightly to the left.

"You have my word," replied John. Jeannette then walked down the aisle away from John to tend to her landing duties, still facing John until ducking into the next cabin.

John wasn't completely confident that he would be calling her, but hoped that their paths would meet again. Time to refocus on the task at hand -- getting through Customs and locating his flat, wherever it was. Jeannette would have to wait.

John readied his personal baggage located below his feet, tightened his seat belt and looked out the window. No more than a few hundred feet below the plane was the early morning view of the vast expanse of Paris. It appeared that they were approaching Charles-de-Gaulle from the south, which enabled a striking aerial view of the Eiffel Tower and the circular embarquements of Paris -- John's new home.

Welcome home, Monsieur Pascual, welcome home, John thought to himself. He hoped Joe was having as successful an experience as he was -- although he knew that he was not.

Chapter **25**

"Nous allons atterrir dans dix minutes. S'il vous plaît assurer votre siège est ramené à la position verticale. Tous les bagages personnels doivent être retournés au porte-bagages, ou placés sous le siège devant vous. Merci de voler Air France."

John interpreted the message as, "We will be landing in ten minutes. Please assure your seat is returned to the vertical position. All personal baggage shall be returned to the overhead bin, or placed below the seat in front of you. Thank you for flying Air France." -- or at least something similar to that.

The message was repeated in English immediately afterwards, followed by German, a language that John was familiar with due to German 101, 102, 201 and 301, taken in college. The Agency requested that each operative be familiar with at least three languages, as a minimum. Since Latin was not an acceptable language, which John mastered in high school, he was officially fluent in only three. Since he could converse most comfortably in French, then German and of course English, he would be well suited for Paris.

Latin, as the origin of many European languages, provided significant benefit in learning German, French and Spanish. John had initially appealed to his Executive Director at Langley to allow Latin as his fourth accepted language, which was quickly denied.

In his appeal, John suggested the benefit of understanding Roman Catholic Traditions, noting the success of Harrison Ford due to his substantive knowledge of Latin. His Executive Director, who John assumed had no sense of humor, smartly replied that this wasn't "Raiders of the lost Ark." This was followed by the only smile that John had ever seen on the man's face -- and then it was gone.

John could not see the stewardess providing the recent landing announcement, nor could he decipher if the voice was Jeannette's. He guessed it was not, due to the speaker's thick German accent, but then again most Europeans are multi-lingual due to the close proximity of neighboring countries. A stewardess in Business Class would certainly benefit from this ability as well - it may even be a requirement for employment. For this reason, John wondered if the CIA considered international flight stewards or stewardesses for global intelligence or espionage roles. They have the perfect cover since they are well travelled, and typically multi-lingual. Furthermore, as they are standing and constantly in motion while they work, they are typically in reasonable shape. At least the majority that John selectively remembered.

John tightened his seat belt, slipped a piece of wintergreen flavored chewing gum into his mouth, closed his eyes and placed his head back on the headrest. In his mind, he practiced his replies in anticipation of the questions from Passport Control and the Customs Agent. Most important was memorization of the information on his Passport, which included his birthdate, birthplace and address. He was Jean Claude Pascual, born in1964 in Colmar, France. He was a current resident of Paris who lived at 45 Rue Daguerre, 75014, in the 14th Arrondissement, near Montparnasse. The chip embedded inside the rear cover of his Passport included all of this information. Joe's associate Brenda had also assured enough trips between the U.S. and France had been logged into the chip to make the return trip, even though it was the first using this Passport, seemed commonplace. John knew that this was a reasonably simple process to pre-load this information onto the chip, but it was the one weak link that he did not have any control over, so he questioned if it was done correctly. Time would tell.

John also had to remember to pass through the returning EU resident line leading to Passport control, and not the "All Others" queue. Unlike Joe, John owned only one Passport, a U.S. military issue with a maroon cover, unlike the dark blue covers that U.S. citizens had on their Passports. Of course this passport was now in the possession of his brother Joe, who was now hopefully sound asleep in John's bed.

John removed his French Passport from his front pants pocket, just to assure he wasn't forgetting pertinent information. Similar to most passports, it sported the familiar thick fabric-like cover, but was a Bordeaux-red color, unlike the typical burgundy color of most other EU member states. The French Coat of Arms was in the center of the front cover with the word "PASSEPORT" underlined below the coat of arms. The words "Union Européenne" (European Union) and "République Française" (French Republic) were printed above the coat of arms. Since John had an electronic "e-passport," the cover also included a small microchip symbol at the bottom of the grot cover. The inside cover was very similar to U.S. Passports, with the unique inclusion of Jean Pascual's height and weight, which was listed as 225 pounds and 6-foot 2-inches -- very accurate. Thirty-one pages followed the cover, on which were printed a variety of stamps, mostly from multiple trips between the U.S. and Paris. Brenda's friend was a talented passport counterfeiter.

John's inspection of his passport was interrupted by a jolt, as the plane's rear wheels touched down onto the runway at Charles de Gaulle International Airport. After five minutes of taxiing, the plane entered the proper gate, connected to the walkway and relaxed its engines. The seat belt light extinguished, with the same stewardess repeating her welcome to Paris, along with a reminder to take all belongings. It was also apparently now safe to use your cell phones.

John unbuckled his seat belt, removed his carry-on bag from the overhead baggage storage and joined the exiting line of passengers. Upon exiting the walkway connected to the plane, he followed the signs indicating the exit, or "sortie," and followed the masses towards Passport Control.

After what seemed like a one-mile walk, he arrived at the division between "EU Citizens" and "All Others," and chose the former. Ahead of him were over 100 other recent arriving passengers, all looking as equally tired as he felt. John again readied his Passport, opening the booklet for one last look. In the distance, he noticed a familiar face, exiting through a much shorter line in between the two snaking lines of passengers. It was Jeannette, who had finally received eye contact with her new-found acquaintance. Once she realized that John had seen her, she placed her right thumb on her ear, and her pinky finger next to her mouth, as if she was on the telephone, making the universal "call me" signal. John nodded, and placed his hand telephone at his ear as well, then pointed back to her, acknowledging he would do so. She smiled, waved good-bye and turned through the Passport Agent's line, quickly disappearing from John's view. "If I make it through Passport Control, I will call you," John said aloud. First things first.

Ninety-five passengers later, John found himself standing behind the yellow line located on the carpet in front of the Passport Control Agent's booth -- making him the next one in line for Passport Inspection. The Agent silently motioned that John step forward with a wave of his hand. John already had his Passport ready and opened to the first page for the Agent, placing it into his outstretched hand.

"Bon matin, Monsieur" (Good morning, Sir), John said.

"Bonjour," replied the Agent, receiving John's Passport which was already open to John's picture and personal information. He looked closely at the picture, then back at John, then returned his gaze to the Passport as he flipped through a few pages. He also placed the passport near the electronic reader, to read the chip sealed inside the rear page.

Visible behind the Agent was a video camera that John knew was using face recognition software to analyze his facial features, comparing them to the numerous "BOLO" (Be On the Look-Out for) advisories.

With John's luck, he would resemble the latest French Charles Manson. Actually, he expected that Brenda's friend had already performed this search, just as a precaution, and would have altered John's features on his passport ever so slightly to avoid the Manson match.

The Customs Agent asked, "Retournez-vous à Paris après la conduite des affaires aux États-Unis?" (Are you returning to Paris after conducting business in the United States?)

"Oui" (Yes), replied John. One easy question--one easy answer.

"Where êtes-vous né?" (Where were you born?) asked the Agent.

"Je suis né à Colmar" (I was born in Colmar), replied John. Another easy question--another easy answer.

John's memory of the French language was quickly returning; his brain interpreting the conversation as if it was in English.

"I have been there many times," replied the Agent. "We have friends who live in the nearby town of Kaysersberg. Since you must know Colmar well, what is located in the round-about as you enter the town of Colmar from the north?" questioned the Agent, with a smirk.

John was taken aback by this off-the-wall question. Luckily, he had actually been to Colmar and knew of its once famous resident, Frédéric Auguste Bartholdi, better known for designing the Statue of Liberty in the early 1800s. In fact, as you drive into the town of Colmar, you will find a miniature replica of the Statue in the center of the first round-about. It is a mere 39 feet, in comparison to the actual 151 foot tall Statue of Liberty located on Liberty Island in New York City. Ironically, a second miniature replica of the Statue was located in Paris, on the river Seine near the Ile aux Cygnes, supposedly facing west in alignment with the Statue of Liberty in New York. John thought to himself that he would need to add this to his list of must-sees while living in Paris. He wondered if Jeannette was familiar with the history of the Statue. The silence was broken by the Agent asking, "Monsieur, Pascual?"

"Um, yes, I remember that a miniature replica of the Statue of Liberty exists in the center of the round-about as you enter Colmar from the north," replied John. Three for three, thought John.

"That is exactly correct," replied the Agent. "One last question -- How many times have you travelled to the United States this year?" asked the Agent.

John stopped breathing. This was the one thing he failed to review on his Passport. He had examined the myriad Customs stamps identifying his points of entry and departure, but he never considered the frequency of entry, or if he had even travelled outside of the U.S. this year at all.

Wind-the-clock, John thought to himself. He knew that the Passport Agent already had the requested information on his computer screen, and would not have to read John's passport to find this information. He also remembered seeing a number of entry stamps to Charles de Gaulle on his passport, but could not recall specificity in frequency or date of occurrence. He was stuck, in a very bad way. To guess was one option, or better yet, he could feign confusion.

"Can you be more specific in your request, please?" asked John.

The Agent repeated, "How many times have you travelled to the U.S.?"

John asked, "Do you mean in total, or just this year?" knowing that the question was just about this year.

"Just this year, please, Sir," answered the Agent.

"Should I count all of the connections through the U.S., or are you just concerned with those times I stayed overnight in the U.S.? I am not sure I can remember which ones included layovers and which ones were connections." replied John, stalling for more time. "I'm so tired after my flight, I cannot think straight." John adopted the silent approach, staring back at the Agent, maintaining a pensive look on his face.

The Agent stared at John, looked at his computer screen, and again at John. He hesitated, then stated, "No problem, sorry to bother you. Welcome home, Monsieur Pascual." He closed John's passport and slid it back to him.

"Thank you," replied John, grateful that he was not in the midst of further interrogation with the Agent. He reached down and grabbed his carry-on bag, turned and walked past the enclosure where the Agent was seated. He had to consciously tell himself to walk and not run towards the Customs exit; a red "Declaration" exit and a green "Nothing to Declare" exit -- he chose the latter.

John could not recall ever being stopped in a Customs line, and hoped for the same in this instance. Two Customs Agents were visible to his right, but seemed fully disinterested as he walked by. John continued past the Agents and exited through a double door into the throngs of people waiting in the passenger meeting area of Terminal A. He had made it -- the weak link chip in his passport worked, he answered all of the questions, and he was free. Free to live his new life as Jean Pascual. Mission accomplished.

Chapter 26

7:30 p.m. -- There was a knock on the front door. Joe rose from the couch, where he had sat for the last hour, poring over the wake and funeral, trying to remember the faces in the crowd, and hoping his true identity was still a secret. Randy's apparent mistake in calling him by his own name, still bothered him. She was too smart and attentive to make that kind of mistake. Something that he had said or done must have tipped her off. Not good. Joe would make a special effort to stay away from her when he returned to work tomorrow -- if she sought him out, it would confirm his suspicion that she was skeptical.

Another knock at the door. This time louder and more urgent.

Joe extracted himself from the couch, his right arm pushing against the armrest to release his body from the couch's grasp. John had been extremely frugal, so much so that he refused to replace the oldest known piece of furniture in his possession, that being said couch. It was a common argument between Joe and John, with Joe noting that it should be burned, as even the homeless wouldn't want it. John kept it to spite Joe, stating that it worked just fine, and was so comfy, most folks were unable to leave its drawing comfort -- Joe would reply that it was a matter of incapability to leave, more so than a personal desire. Sitting in that couch for fifteen minutes was the quickest way to get a backache.

He approached the door and saw Brenda already peering inside the window to the side of the door.

Joe guessed her hand was already clutching her 45 that she carried at all times, except when she slept, at which time it would be under her pillow. This was a custom that Joe personally understood, and lived by.

To hopefully entice Brenda to stand down and holster her weapon, Joe screamed "coming," just before he opened the door. He opened the door slowly, placing his finger to his lips, to assure she did not speak. He kept his finger there, as he fully opened the front door and gestured to her with his left hand to walk in. He established eye contact and maintained it as he reached down and grabbed a small white dry erase board from behind the door, about the size of an 8.5 X 11 inch pad of paper. On the board he had written, [The house is bugged - talk normally].

Brenda maintained eye contact, understanding the issue at hand, and nodded. Then she spoke. "John, I wasn't sure if I should have come by, but I was worried about you and wanted to check that you were doing ok." They continued to walk into the foyer, with Joe closing the door behind Brenda, looking out to the street before doing so -- no apparent followers.

"Thank you for coming by -- I can really use some company right now," replied Joe robotically, as he walked down the foyer to the living room. Brenda followed close behind, maintaining her grip on her .45. Joe erased the white board with his left forearm and wrote, [Put that away. No need. Keep talking.]

"Is there anything I can do? Have you eaten since the funeral?" asked Brenda.

"I have not," replied Joe.

"Are you interested in going out? I'll drive," Brenda offered.

"Yes, it would serve as a good distraction, as I am fully burned out from today. On one condition -- that it be somewhere that we will not run into people we know. I cannot take any more small talk," replied Joe.

"Get your jacket, and I will meet you in my car," noted Brenda.

"10-4," replied Joe, after which Brenda immediately shook her head, grabbed the dry erase board from Joe's hand and scribbled, [John doesn't say, "10-4." Play your part!].

Joe nodded, silently making the OK signal with his right hand.

Brenda stopped and wrote on her table, [Video cameras?]

[None], wrote Joe.

[How many bugs -- where?], scribbled Brenda.

[Three -- Kitchen, Living Room, Bedroom], wrote Joe.

[You do a full screen of house?], Brenda wrote.

Joe erased his board with his left hand and wrote, [Absolutely].

[What did you use to sweep with?]

[CS-Pro25, of course], wrote Joe.

Brenda shook her head silently up and down in approval, and walked out the front door towards her car.

John called, "I'll be right there. I need to stop by the rest room first." He actually needed to get his laptop, but used the facilities, flushed and washed his hands, before passing by his desk to grab his laptop.

He set the alarm on the way out and exited. He felt himself unconsciously running to Brenda's car, and forced himself to walk slowly once he reached the concrete driveway. He walked in front of the car, and entered via the right hand passenger door.

Once inside, his only word was "Drive," followed by a long deep sigh.

As Brenda pulled from the driveway, Joe noted "The bugs are military style, but surprisingly, not well hidden. My guess is that the individuals that placed them were either in a hurry or didn't suspect John would look for them. I was able to sweep the entire house and locate all three in less than 10 minutes."

"Seems rather amateurish," noted Brenda as she exited the neighborhood. "Why would they overlook such an important detail?"

"It's possible that they've been in place for quite some time -- I'm very curious, but of course, we'll never know. Where do you want to go?"

"Somewhere where we can talk and not have to worry about who's listening. The back booth of a Chili's would work well," replied Joe.

Brenda smiled and said, "Chili's it is," as she entered the I-20 entrance ramp, heading east. "I know there's one off of South Hulen."

Brenda drove as Joe spoke.

"The surveillance bugs must stay, as much as I cannot stand them. They may provide the break we need at some point, which makes them all worthwhile. At this point, they are the only link we have between the U.S. and the unknown entity that is causing this mess. Did you bring the video feed from the funeral parlor? "

"I did, but I cannot link to the Department's face recognition program without a direct Ethernet cable -- the bandwidth is too small otherwise. We'll need to wait until tomorrow at work," replied Brenda.

"I am not looking forward to playing John, tomorrow," noted Joe. "I just don't feel prepared."

"You are fully prepared," replied Brenda. "You did well tonight, and will do great tomorrow," reassured Brenda.

"You and John equally know more about SCENNIC than anyone. The technical side will be easy. It's adopting John's personality that will be difficult. That's what you need to concentrate on tomorrow."

Brenda turned the car into the parking lot and entered an open parking spot near the front entrance to Chili's.

"Thank you for your vote of confidence," replied Joe as he exited the car. "No more work talk. Let's eat."

Chapter **27**

John entered the masses of people awaiting arrival of relatives and friends outside of the International Terminal, a thin film of sweat still present on his brow. No one would be waiting for him, per plan.

The France Customs experience was more stressful than he had expected. Although John had been through similar experiences in his world travels, this one was particularly stressful due to his fake Passport. Clearly the embedded Passport chip worked, which was his biggest concern. It was the unexpected barrage of in-depth questions that he did not expect, but apparently handled well enough to satisfy the Agent.

Out of curiosity, John opened his Passport to assess how many entry and exit stamps were listed for the United States. Flipping through each page, he counted sixteen entry stamps and with the most recent trip, an equal amount exits, occurring primarily through JFK. John's Passport forger was clearly thinking ahead, as an equal number of United States entries and exits would have immediately alerted the Agent that something was awry. Thank you, whoever you are.

Passport stamps were also evident for myriad cities that he, i.e., Mr. Pascual, had frequented in the past 6 years including Istanbul, Prague, Sydney, São Paulo, Barcelona, Madrid, Dublin, and London. Despite John's love for travel, his goal was to limit near term excursions outside France, at least until his courage returned.

He immediately thought of Jeanne and the strong possibility that she might ask John to accompany her to a neighboring country, not necessarily because she had the perks of an airline stewardess, but because that is the norm for Europeans. Consider the benefit of easy travel between different countries simply due to close proximity, unlike the U.S. where one could drive hundreds of miles and never leave the same state. That was the beauty of Europe; a different culture, language and local cuisine, all within a 100-mile radius.

John continued to shuffle with the crowd towards the large green 'Sortie' (Exit) sign, which eventually exited the terminal to the outdoor sidewalk, and searched for the taxi queue. A line snaking through the guide rails was quickly evident, separating awaiting taxi customers from those waiting at an adjacent limousine service line. The limo service contained a lone customer, with a visible scowl on his face. No limousines were anywhere to be seen, hence the deduced cause of the scowl. John considered taking the train, but quickly reconsidered due to his unfamiliarity with the area in which he would soon call home. He also despised having to drag his luggage through the turnstiles and gates, not to mention the strong possibility he would require a taxi from the station to his apartment anyway.

John rolled his baggage into the taxi line and waited, staring at the personalities surrounding him. Ahead of him was a family of four, assumedly a father, mother and two daughters. It could have been a father with his three children, as French women in general tend to maintain their youthful appearance, or at least it seemed this way as John aged. Typical of most French natives, the family spoke very quietly and extremely fast, running their words into one endless string of monotone. Even though John was now less than two feet from the assumed parents, he had difficulty in understanding what they were saying. It didn't concern him though, as he was comfortable with the language, and wasn't too proud to ask that the speaker slow down, if the need arose.

A young couple filed in behind John, easily identifiable as Americans due to their lack of attention to the volume of their conversation, so typical of Americans but more obvious in Paris where the general population is more self-aware.

John could recall many times he would be enjoying a meal in a European restaurant, and be able to immediately pick out visiting Americans due to their outwardly loud discussions. It was no wonder Americans are easy targets for pick-pockets and thieves, as they inadvertently attract attention.

John realized that inevitably, he also exhibited these foreign characteristics, despite his frequent travels and associated etiquette. Assimilating oneself into a foreign culture was much the same as being an actor in a play, where the goal is to fool the audience into believing your role. Easier said than done in a foreign culture, where the language barrier complicates the process ten-fold.

John's thoughts were interrupted by a tap on his shoulder. It was the American man from the couple behind him.

"Parlez-vous Englaise?" ("Do you speak English?") the man asked, in Tarzan-French, staring patiently for a response.

"Yes, I do," replied John.

"Fantastic. My wife and I are visiting Paris for the first time, and do not know what to expect. We're staying near the Champs de-Lysee, at the Marriott. Do you know where that is?"

"I do," answered John, using his best French-English accent. Not too strong as to sound like Jacques Cousteau, but enough to appear like a native Parisian speaking English -- playing the part of the actor. "The Marriott is about mid-way from where all the streets come together, near the Arc du Triumph. The taxi driver will know it well, but be sure to first ask how much it will cost to drive you there, as they have a tendency to take advantage of tourists -- the round trip should be less than 30 Euro total, even with traffic."

"Very good," replied the man. His partner spoke up, "I've been reading Frommer's Guide to Paris, which recommends dinner cruises on the Seine. Have you ever done this?"

John realized that he was now playing the role of tour guide, but didn't mind, as it distracted him from the recent events in Customs, much the less the last 24 hours.

"Actually, you will find that most Parisians have never been on a river cruise, similar to how many New Yorkers have never been inside the Statue of Liberty. I suggest a walk along the Seine, followed by a quiet dinner in one of the many small cafes along the way. You could do this every evening you are here, for about the same cost of one river cruise, which will run no less than 200 Euro each."

"200 Euro; that seems extreme."

"Yes, it is, for the low quality of meal you are provided. Nevertheless, do not underestimate the cost of dining in Paris. The meals can be spectacular, but at a high cost. In fact, many of the well-known eateries require reservations months in advance."

"Months?" asked the wife.

"Not all, but the ones with the famous chefs. Also, never request an English menu, as the prices are always higher -- try to read the French menu and use French when possible to order," noted John. "Do you know any French?"

"En petite peu," ("A little bit"), replied the woman.

"Excellent -- this will help you more than you realize. Even though most Parisians know English, especially the younger generation who will most probably be your waiters or waitresses, they will begin in French to test you. Your attempt to speak French will show respect, which is huge in our culture. If you are doing well in your attempt, they will slow down and politely wait for you. If they see you are having trouble, they usually just switch to English. It's almost a game," (such as this one, John thought to himself).

"Thank you," replied the man. "This is not the type of thing that Frommer's describes. What else do you recommend seeing while we are here?"

"I always enjoy the museums such as the Louvre and the Musee D'Orsay, and of course, a visit to the top of the Eiffel Tower. Be sure to arrive early in the morning, and take the stairs to the first platform, otherwise you will waste precious time waiting for the elevator."

John noted that he was next in line for a taxi, the attendant motioning to him to move forward.

"Best of luck to you, and welcome to Paris. My taxi awaits." John noted.

"Thank you," replied the couple in unison.

John turned around, pulling his luggage towards the taxi that now had its rear trunk open.

"45 Rue Daguerre, near Montparnasse, S'il vous plait," instructed John to the driver.

The driver nodded, and walked around the Mercedes, jumping in the seat before John had a chance to get in the taxi.

Clearly, John's accent made the taxi driver comfortable, as the driver began a tirade of comments about the many tourists coming to visit Paris. This was a good sign, but one that also made John nervous, as he was ready to be away from the commotion of the airport and the extremely talkative French inhabitants. Interestingly enough, many people perceive the French as very quiet, and thus a non-communicative culture. This is completely the opposite, as although they may speak softly, they clearly enjoy the opportunity to relax and review the day's events with just about any acquaintance that is so inclined to listen. The hardest part for most non-French speaking natives, John thought, was being able to decipher the spoken words at such a low volume.

This taxi ride would not be this way, thank goodness, as the taxi driver was still perturbed at the latest riders that he had transported today. His comments drummed on, with rising intonation at the end of each sentence, indicating his excitement and disdain at the same time.

As they were rounding Paris' outer ring, approximately twenty minutes and 10,000 words into the taxi ride, an odd thing happened. The taxi driver stopped talking, paused, and noted a few indiscernible words under his breath, which John did not catch as he had stopped trying to interpret the driver's personal report at word 2,000. At this point, the driver was slowing down and pulling sharply to the right side of the highway, cutting off the rightmost two lanes of traffic. The taxi stopped with a lurch, making John's head jerk backwards due to the unexpected halt.

To John's complete surprise, and before he had the time to question the reason for this abrupt stop, the driver had opened his door, turned off the engine, removed the keys, exited the Mercedes, and was intently walking away from the car. John remained in the taxi, watching his driver circle the taxi, visible through the front windshield and then the passenger side windows. The driver walked up the grass embankment to the immediate right side of the highway where they were oddly parked, and disappeared out of sight behind the grassy hill.

OK, now what, John thought to himself. This was a first. Vehicles whizzed past outside his left window in a flurry of hardly discernible colors, all looking like gray after a while. At first, John assumed there was a physical problem with the vehicle, or that the driver needed to take a cell phone call; both of which were no longer logical choices considering the now absent driver.

Not wanting to venture from the vehicle, John "wound the clock," processing the situation, and immediate options of which there were typically three, ranging from the "Do nothing" (or no action) option, which was adverse to John's lifelong training, as an Engineer and an Intelligence Officer, to the most aggressive "Come out Shooting," that John assumed Joe would have adopted.

The middle of the road option to get out of harm's way, and exit the right side of the vehicle was John's chosen strategy, at which point he could define his next steps from the safer vantage point of the grassy hill. And then John's thought process was interrupted by a surprisingly loud tap on the glass, a mere 8 inches from his left ear. John's head turned 90 degrees counterclockwise in response to this noise, causing the cartilage to snap due to this involuntary motion.

Staring at John through the window, was a French Policeman of very thin build, wearing a dark blue uniform, still holding his 20-inch black police-issue Maglite flashlight, that he had just used to tap on John's window. His mouth was moving, completely inaudible to John, as he was simultaneously motioning for John to roll-down his window. John turned his gaze the remaining 90 degrees, to peer out the rear window. Parked to the rear of the taxi was a white French squad car, blue lights blazing, with the familiar "POLICE Municipal" emblazoned across the front of the curved hood. The policeman's female partner was positioned to the right rear side of the parked taxi, her right hand on her gun, which was strapped to her right side.

"Wind the clock," thought John, "wind the clock." Now was not the time for this unfortunate encounter. John knew that if he was to provide his Passport to the officers, his location, even though he had an alias, would again be on record, for the second time since his arrival in French Customs. Not commonly known to the public, but a person's location practically anywhere on the earth is available at any time to the National Security Agencies. One telephone call, one swipe of a credit card, or simple email login provides pinpoint accuracy of location. If it's not enough that cameras located on every street corner in practically every city can use face recognition to search for known criminals, having his name on recent Police reports would be devastating to John's needed secrecy.

The Policeman rapped his flashlight on the window for a second time, his facial expression looking a bit tenser than one minute prior, his eyes now darting to his partner, now moving counterclockwise towards the door to John's right.

Keep my hands in view, move slowly, smile, thought John. Following this process, he caught eye contact with his noticeably nervous officer through the window. John pointed down to the window handle, and slowly reached down towards it, grabbed the round plastic knob, and rotated the handle counterclockwise. The window retreated downward with a slight squeak, and stopped at the one-third point, which John assumed was for child protection purposes as in American made cars.

The Policeman, whose attention was locked on John's hands, moved cautiously closer to the window, looking down towards John's feet through the now open window.

"Hello Officer," said John in French, feigning his most pleasant smile. "How can I help you?"

The Officer replied, "What exactly is going on here?"

"That's my question as well, Officer," replied John. "I was on my way to my house and the taxi driver hops out of the car, runs behind that bluff, and leaves me on the side of the road."

"And why would your driver do that?" asked the Officer.

"I do not know," replied John. A few smart comments came to mind, but he refrained from using these.

"I will need to see your ID, please." noted the Officer.

This was not the answer that John wanted to hear, although it came as no surprise. John could feel his counterfeit Passport burning a hole in his left rear pants pocket. There had to be another alternative, and there was.

Neither Officer knew that John had just come from the airport, nor did they know that his luggage was in the truck of the taxi, or "boot" as the English call it.

"I have just returned from Charles de Gaulle," noted John. "Everything is in my suitcase, located in the trunk. Is it OK if I exit the taxi and open my baggage?" asked John.

The Police Officer was less interested in having John outside the vehicle during this odd exchange, than having an ID. John also knew that he would not go one-on-one with an unknown assailant without his back-up watching from the same side of the car.

In response to John's request, the Officer gazed back at his partner, giving her an upward nod of his chin, summoning her to his side of the vehicle. He retreated, meeting her at the left rear side of the taxi, obviously noting the conversation he had just had with John. John could see them in the rear view mirror, planning next steps. They appeared to come to a decision, approaching John's window, in tandem, with the female Officer hanging back about five feet from the male Officer.

"OK, let's see what you can find in your luggage," replied the Officer through John's window. "I will open the car door for you -- keep your hands where I can see them, and do not make any quick moves. Do you understand?"

"Yes," replied John.

The Officer looked back at his partner, turned back towards the taxi, and reached for the door handle. He grabbed the latch, lifted it, and with a click, the door opened. The Officer motioned with his hand for John to exit, his partner's hand still glued to her holstered gun.

John ducked down slightly, rotating his feet and body towards the door, so he could extricate himself from the cramped rear seat. As he stepped out, left foot first, both Officers quickly realized John's size, as evident in the slight gasp by the female Officer. Clearly these French Officers weren't used to corn-fed husky Americans, who outweighed their brethren by a factor of two.

John turned slowly, fully facing both Officers, and walked towards the back of the car. He reached for the latch below the trunk, and opened it. Both Officers peered nervously from his left side, intently looking from a distance into the abyss of the dark truck. At this point John knew they were inexperienced, as they broke the cardinal rule of law enforcement engagement, unintentionally giving control to their opponent. If John had been a criminal, he could have easily reached into the trunk for a hidden weapon, with negative consequences for the Officers. Instead, John backed away from the now open trunk, to allow an unobstructed view to his new acquaintances.

"Do you mind if I remove my suitcase, to find my ID?" John asked.

"That would be fine," replied the male Officer, still stationed to John's left.

John opened the suitcase, haphazardly throwing his clothes around, intentionally seeming more distraught as time passed. He did not plan to find his Passport, which was now sandwiched between the rear seat padding in the taxi, where John had placed it when the Officer conferred with his partner behind the taxi. John continued to search through his belongings, looking at both officers, and apparently coming to the realization that he must have left it in the bathroom at the airport.

"I cannot find it, and I distinctly remember having it in the bathroom at Charles de Gaulle. This is not good -- Not good at all," noted John.

Both officers watched intently for about two minutes, while John continued his display of discontent. Then the male officer noted, "This is no problem, but we'll need to get you a ride back to ..." He stopped mid-sentence as a man walked up from behind the hill -- it was the taxi driver. Unfortunately, the Officers did not realize this and both had drawn their pistols, at the fully surprised driver. John could have walked away at this instant and no one would have noticed.

"Down on your knees, with both hands behind your neck ... Do it, now!" screamed the male officer, his hands controlling his pistol visibly shaking.

"OK, I'm just a taxi driver. I'm not armed. Don't shoo ..." "Shut-up and get on the ground," interrupted the female officer, as she circled towards the opposing side of the driver.

"Officers, this is my taxi driver," noted John.

"Yes, I am his taxi driver," quickly stammered the driver. "That's a good thing, right? Because if it's not, then I'm just a guy coming over the hill from taking a pee."

That's when the male officers realized what had happened, asking, "So you left your taxi, and customer, because you had to go to the bathroom -- really?"

"Um, yes," replied the driver. "I knew the traffic was bad coming into the City, so knew this was my last chance."

"Do you do this often?" asked the female officer.

"Yes, I go to the bathroom when I wake up, four times during the day, and before I go to bed. Sometimes I get up in the middle of the night to go," the driver replied.

"Great, I have a wise-ass driver that will end both of us in a French jail," thought John. Not the right time, not the right place.

The female officer clearly took offense. "Answer my question, or take a drive with us to the station."

"I did answer your question, and unless you have a search warrant or reasonable cause to stop me, I'll take my fare and be on my way," the driver noted smartly.

John knew he was right. The officers knew he was right. There was no reasonable cause -- no reason for a trip to the station. Stalemate.

The three just stood there for a few minutes, waiting for the next move.

"OK, take your passenger and get out of here. Next time there is no stopping on the side of the highway. If we find your taxi on the side of the road, it's ours. Do you understand?"

"I understand," noted the driver, who knew he was wasting precious time and money because of this unproductive exchange.

Just then, another car pulled up behind the first police car. An unmarked police car, John assumed. Two plain-clothed officers exited, excited to join the ensuing melee.

"Let's get out of here, please," noted John to the driver. "It's worth another twenty Euro if you just walk away and get me to my apartment."

"Officers, it's been a pleasure to meet you -- enjoy the afternoon", the driver replied, as he circled to the front of the taxi, opened the door, and jumped in. John had already closed and secured his suitcase, sealed the trunk and had entered the back seat, closing the left rear passenger-side door behind him. The driver turned the engine on, placed the taxi in Drive, and sped off, throwing up gravel behind him as he entered the adjacent traffic path. John watched as the police cars quickly disappeared from view. Reaching between the seats, John retrieved his Passport, and repeated the address to the driver.

Then it occurred to John that he needed to go to the bathroom. It could wait.

Chapter **28**

On the drive to his first day as John at the Pentagon, Joe mentally considered the many differences between himself and his brother. He knew that it would be that one off-the-wall idiosyncrasy that would be his downfall. It wouldn't be an odd facial expression, a forgotten name, or an incorrect technical detail. It would instead be one of Joe's own traits, noticeable only by his closest friends. In other words, Joe needed to concentrate on not being himself, more so than trying to be like John. Joe's head began to throb, at this depth of thinking.

The first test would be getting past Pentagon security. The front-line guards, card-readers and entry passwords would not be the issue; it would be the bio-readers which could be problematic. Luckily, the government's bio-readers of choice were the iris scan and the fingerprint analyzer, both of which were easily circumvented. The SCENNIC, could easily replicate the complex visible structure of the iris, analogous to making a photocopy of John's iris and superimposing it over Joe's eye. Counterfeit fingerprinting was not much different, with a simple latex overlay attached to Joe's left thumb. Seemed elementary, but not personally tested, yet Joe remained cautiously optimistic.

Joe parked John's car in the underground parking garage, took a deep breath, stepped out and headed towards the elevator that would bring him to the ground floor where the Resource Protection Team controlled access into the massive structure.

Look relaxed, Joe thought, as he traversed the ground floor of the parking structure towards the southern employee entrance to the outermost ring. He knew there were video cameras at practically every turn, and had to consciously refrain from looking directly towards them.

Joe entered through one of the rectangular mirrored double doors, and approached the nearest line of Federal employees. After 3 to 5 minutes, he was standing in front of two burly, clean-cut guards, both wearing military garb typical of the Pentagon Resource Protection. Joe looked at them and forced a smile.

"Good morning, Mr. Stone," replied the larger of the two guards. "I am sorry to hear of your brother's passing--he was quite an amazing man, and always considerate towards our role as a gate sentry."

"Thank you," replied Joe. "I miss him greatly, and hope I can someday be like him." Today would be a great day to be like him, Joe thought to himself.

Joe reached down and placed his right thumb on the green light of the bio-reader, after successfully passing his (actually John's) badge near the proximity reader. The guard looked down at his display, his head tilting slightly to the left, similar to a dog that hears a high pitched noise.

"That's odd," replied the guard. "Your name came up as Joe Stone."

"What?" noted his partner, straining his neck to gaze upon the glowing screen. "Yes, that's what it says," he confirmed, the intonation in his voice rising. "This makes no sense," he stated.

Crap, Joe thought to himself, I used the wrong thumb. Messed up on my first try, and I'm not even in the building yet.

"That is odd," replied Joe, quickly switching to his other thumb. "Joe and I used to experience IT issue with our access, so this might be that same glitch."

He placed the left thumb on the reader. "Is it still messed up?"

"Ummm--No. Now it's OK," noted the guard with an inquisitive expression. "I guess it could have been a glitch."

Then his partner spoke up, "Could you please place your right finger back on the reader again, just to check?"

Wind the clock, thought Joe, while concocting his next action.

"I've never had confidence with the fingerprint reader," replied Joe, looking directly at each guard. "It's the eyes that don't lie--how about swinging the iris scanner towards me?"

The guard hesitated, looked at his partner in hopes of a sign of agreement, and then rotated the reader towards Joe's face. He knew the truth in Joe's statement, as the eyes were foolproof. Although this was not common protocol, he knew the Stone Brothers, and he was not going to be the guy who would prevent entry on John's first day back, especially considering recent events with Joe's passing.

"Blink once, blink again," noted the guard, as he zeroed the scanner onto Joe's right iris, a green laser tracking and quickly aligning with imperceptible movements of Joe's pupil.

As it was almost impossible to artificially replicate the intensely detailed structure of the iris, the SCENICC was only capable of taking a snapshot of John's iris. A recent snapshot had been taken just yesterday, and was now being displayed on the surface of Joe's eye, masking his real iris. Considering the fact that the human eye sheds and replaces cells at an incomprehensibly high rate each day, Joe knew that the scanner would quickly be confused by the SCENICC overlay. The system would check, and recheck a million bits of information each second, searching iris maps of all associates in the Pentagon's database, until it located the closest match--that being John's capillary structure. Unless, the batteries had drained, and then it would be over. Joe made an internal note to reduce the SCENICC's power draw at some point in the near future.

The guard stared at the data screen, while time stood still. The additional few seconds were clearly causing the guard heartburn, as he continually checked the screen, then the alignment of the scanner, and then the screen. Joe could see the man's irises enlarge, in the center of his hazel green pupils, in anticipation of another negative match.

"Is it out of batteries?" Joe noted, hoping the same wasn't the case for the SCENNIC.

"Ah, no. It doesn't use batteries," replied the guard, with a serious tone.

Brilliant, thought Joe, keeping a smile on his face, trying to display disinterest, so as not to attract attention or unintentionally display an odd look for the barrage of hidden cameras that surrounded the entrance.

In the planning stages, one problem area that had come to Joe's and John's minds were these access room cameras, and their facial recognition capability. Similar to the futuristic movies depicting the early 2000s, in the late 1980s the Pentagon had developed technology to search crowds of people and match facial features of a fugitive, a lost child, or other individuals of interest. The issue was never the search capability of the recognition system, but the match ability, requiring a very recent source scan of the person's face to enable a match. A recent photograph from the family picnic would not meet this need. Instead, high-resolution photographs from the left, front and right side of the face and head were preferred--three-dimensional laser scanning was even more accurate, which was uncommon at most family events.

As part of the background assessment of each new Pentagon employee, a three-dimensional laser scan was made of the face and head, to enable a precursory search of known databases. This scan was updated on each Pentagon employee's birthday, or after significant changes in facial appearance, resulting from injury, plastic surgery, or significant weight gain or loss.

Employees involved in CIA/NCS welcomed "face-day," as this simple scan might someday locate them while on assignment in a foreign country, when other location processes have failed. Joe did wonder how accurate the technology was for twins who had only very minute facial differences. Considering this, he had made an attempt to keep his face turned slightly down and away from the primary camera scanning the entry to the room.

"There we go," noted the guard, as his screen displayed a green bordered "CLEARED," with John's name and his "face-day" photo beside it. "Thank you for your patience, and have a nice day," said the guard.

Joe nodded, and passed through the turnstile next to the guard, relieved that this potential problem was now behind him. Access throughout the remainder of the Pentagon was not as well protected, with proximity card access and bio-readers at each entry to the facility's massive ring structure. There were only a few Top Secret locations in the basement that required special access, via Infra-red blood sampling, which Joe did not plan to enter.

Joe walked through the first anechoic chamber that wound through four alternating 90-degree turns in order to prohibit radio-frequency data from exiting the facility. The Pentagon itself was actually a fully shielded building or Faraday Cage, from an exiting data perspective. From a physical perspective, the external walls were a conglomeration of five-foot-thick concrete blocks, erected in Lego-fashion, similar to the Hoover Dam, except they were not poured in place. Only a direct strike from a hijacked large passenger aircraft could impact the edifice, assuming such a feat could occur considering the armory of ground-to-air missiles that lined the roof.

Joe made his way to John's office, almost on auto-pilot, counting each step as he walked. Four hundred seventy-five, or thereabouts. This morning's trip was a bit slower than normal, due to the many Pentagon associates stopping to offer their condolences. Joe would stop, say "thank you," and keep going. Be John, he would repeat to himself. Be John.

A few more steps, Joe thought, and I will be in the solace of John's office--just one more turn and I'm there.

And then, standing in front of him, was Randy, the Intelligence Analyst from the funeral parlor, who mistakenly called him Joe. Or at least that was what she alleged she had done.

Great, Joe thought. Just what I need--another test of the minds. He stared at Randy, and waited for the barrage of questions.

"Good morning, John," she stated, her wide blue eyes piercing through to Joe's soul. "Actually, my apologies, it is clearly not a good morning, and I am sorry for your loss."

"Apology accepted, Randy," Joe replied. "Thank you for coming last night. It meant a lot to me to have you there. Joe would have been impressed by the turnout."

"I'll bet," she said smugly. A response that caught Joe completely by surprise. "After all that we've been through, I expected that you would have at least allowed me to comfort you."

"Um, yes, I was, um, I was tired and not thinking straight," Joe replied. Randy's reaction made no sense. He had no idea what was going on here, or what John may have done to precipitate this suggestive behavior, in a woman that he never mentioned one word about.

"I hope that things between us will not be different, because of last night," Randy stated. "I mean, I hope we can still be friends, as a minimum," looking at Joe with an expression that asked for an answer.

"Friends, yes," said Joe. "I need all of the friends I can find right now, to help me through this."

"You can count on me," replied Randy. "It still amazes me how closely you resemble your brother. I see him in you."

Oh, not again, Joe thought. He just stared at Randy, intentionally speechless as he tried to read her expression and where she was going with this.

"No, really. You two have always looked identical to me. If not for the way you kiss, I assume I would be unable to tell you apart."

Joe's mind was sent spinning. He was not sure if this was a test, or if this was reality. Was Randy being truthful about a well guised romantic adventure with his brother John, or was she up to yet another psychological mind game; a primary weapon selected from her arsenal as a CIA Intelligence Agent.

Randy silently looked at Joe, her eyes peeled on his forced emotionless expression looking for that one twitch of confusion, which Joe was fighting to conceal.

Joe had a choice. Either go along with this seemingly crazy story, or push back, feigning indifference at the apparent advance. Joe knew that if he chose the former, and was wrong, duped by the juicy yet improbable account of their relationship, she would immediately know that something was up. Not necessarily giving away the secret that he was actually Joe, but shedding enough doubt to pique her instincts that something was wrong. The other option was to pursue the latter, and react in disgust that she would advance herself on him, especially within mere days of Joe's apparent passing. Joe chose the second option.

"What did you just say, Randy?" Joe questioned, watching Randy's eyes to detect even a hint of response. If she was to look away, whether that be up, down or past him, she was probably lying. On the other hand, if she continued to concentrate her gaze on him, then her report may be truthful.

Randy's eyes immediately darted left to right repeatedly, as she reached deep into her short term memory to extract what she had asked just a few seconds ago. This was the break Joe was looking for, and immediately stated, "Did you say, 'kiss'?" pausing for a second before saying the word "kiss," and turning his head slightly to one side.

"You know what I said," repeated Randy, rather curtly.

"And that's what surprised me. I've been so distracted for the past few days since Joe's passing, that I'm only partially processing people's words."

"I must assume then that you are talking about our kiss on New Year's Eve, two years ago, when we were both without dates? I must have made quite an impression on you that night, for you to reflect on that single distant kiss as a memory jogger."

Joe stopped talking, smiled, and looked deep into Randy's eyes, her black pupils quickly dilating inside the moat of blue around them. He knew he had found the right answer--she was lying, like the crafty little B that she was.

Randy's pursed lips broke into a smirk, her eyes rolled upwards slightly, silently expressing the "OK--you got me" look.

"As callous as that was, especially considering the events over the past few days, I had to try," replied Randy.

"Next time, don't try," scolded Joe. "This is the most inappropriate time for such ridiculousness. I need to trust you, and you need to trust me. OK?" Joe tilted his head slightly, signaling his need for an answer.

"Deal. I won't psychologically test you every time we meet," replied Randy.

"Much appreciated--and I won't analyze every question that you ask me," replied Joe, fully knowing that he was now lying and would continue this due diligence despite his statement. He knew that she could not be trusted, therefore his best bet was to stay away from Randy in the near term--starting right now.

"I need to get to my morning meetings. I'll see you later," noted Joe, turning and walking away from her down the hallway towards his office, before Randy could fire off another question. Note to self: Keep away from Randy.

Joe continued walking, almost turning towards his actual office, which was located next door to John's office. He wondered if Randy observed his hesitation, or if she was already walking in the other direction. He wasn't about to turn around to confirm.

Joe reached into his pocket and removed the slightly faded silver-colored key to John's office. As with typical Pentagon issued keys, there was a "Do Not Duplicate" stamped into the key, to alert any key maker not to do so. John wondered why they were still using keys at the Pentagon, which seemed archaic in his opinion, in comparison to the slew of proximity card readers that lined every entry. Oh well, it was still only 1995.

Joe inserted the key into the door handle and turned it counterclockwise, the tumblers rotating until a final click retracted the deadbolt and unlocked the office door. Joe walked three steps past the door frame, the overhead fluorescent light automatically turning on as a result of the motion activated sensor to the immediate right of the door. The office looked exactly as it did just a few days ago, sans John's briefcase, which he habitually would place to the left of the L-shaped desk, next to his recycle wastebasket. Recycling had always been a personal passion for John, as he believed each and every recycling effort made a difference in the world as a whole. Joe would always push back on John's recycling ethos, noting that each can was probably landfilled anyway by the Pentagon's cleaning crew. Now Joe would have to adopt this recycling mindset, as not to give away his new identity. This was not going to be easy.

John's L-shaped desk, and the office overall, was oriented exactly the opposite of Joe's adjacent office, with the phone to his left, and computer to the right. It was going to be odd to use his left hand to answer the phone, but luckily, both John and Joe were right handed so everything else was placed appropriately.
For the most part though, John's office was not much different than Joe's, with the obvious addition of the blue recycle bin, adorned with a white recycling symbol on the side. Joe laughed to himself, noting that it was empty, certainly because the cleaning crew had dumped the cans in the regular trash. Nevertheless, he would begin adding water bottles and cans to the container, just to play the part.

Joe slid into the chair behind the desk, immediately noting an odd setting of the lumbar support, which he would quickly adjust along with the seat height, which was too low for his preference. As he was making this finite adjustment, Jim stuck his head into the door stating, "5 minutes--Staff meeting in B2011. Don't be late, as it's about SCENICC."

"Ah--Okay," replied Joe, not really wanting to stray from the office so quickly. "I'll be there."

Going to a meeting without John's technical support had been an issue that concerned Joe when he first brought up the option of their role swap in the cabin just 48 hours ago. Joe could certainly hold his own, but he lacked the depth of engineering knowledge that John has developed over the past decade while working with SCENICC. He certainly could hold his own, but not if the discussion centered on MOS-FETs, OP-Amps and Flip-Flops. Joe grabbed John's tan leather DayTimer, and headed down the corridor towards B-wing, trying to keep any negative thoughts at bay. If all failed, he would use fall-back on the impact of grief as the reason for any obvious signs of confusion.

Joe reached Room B2011 quicker than expected, and was the third team member to arrive. He had to consider where John might sit, that being off to one side, versus his normal end of table location, which was now empty. Johnsen and Tim were already at the table, looking up at Joe when he entered. They looked a bit shocked, which was no surprise as Joe and John looked so similar, and were still visibly uncomfortable with the turn of events over the past two days.

Tim was the first to speak. "I'm sorry for your loss, John. Joe was an incredible man, and I am honored to have worked with him."

Next was Johnsen. "I also appreciated all that he did for me and the team--he taught me much of what I know about the inner workings of the system."

"Thank you, guys," noted Joe, looking at both men, as he slid into the seat across from them. "He was gifted, and we were all touched by his generosity in sharing his knowledge."

Others filed into the room, many softly patting Joe's shoulders as an outward means of comfort. Joe would acknowledge their intent, by eye contact and a slight nod of his head.

Within 45 seconds, the room was filled with 20 of Joe's associates, from all departments that supported SCENICC. From what Joe could overhear, few if any of those present knew the purpose of the meeting. There had been concern over the battery capability of the system, but this was not justification for assembling the entire design team.

Just then, Jim entered the conference room and seated himself in the intentionally-left empty chair at the head of the elongated oval table. He stared one-by-one at each person seated at the table. Those who were self-aware quickly stopped talking, with the few loud-mouths continuing their discussion with their neighbor. Jim loudly cleared his throat, and stared intently at the two still-talking associates, Rob and Ted.

Then Jim announced boldly, "Guys, anytime now. Just let me know when you're finished," with a scowl on his face, eyes concentrated in their general vicinity.

A muffled "Oh shit," could be heard from Ted, from across the table, followed by "Sorry, Jim, we were just discussing the tin whisker occurrence we're experiencing with some of our lead-free solder experiments." An issue that was a known dilemma amongst the team, as higher temperature rated electronic components presented a need for the latest version.

Both associates looked back at Jim, hoping Ted's explanation would suffice and quell Jim's well-known temper. Jim stared back at then, pausing for a full ten seconds before redirecting his gaze to the rest of the team.

"I appreciate that you are all here," stated Jim.

"I know how much time and effort you have each provided to get us to the SCENICC prototype that we have today.

As you are well aware, the system has its shortcomings, data glitches and battery load issues. Washington is well aware of these issues, and has provided us with an ultimatum to fix every issue, within the next six months."

Another "Oh shit," could be heard from someone in the room, followed by similar murmurs of disbelief.

Jim continued, "And before you all go off the deep end, here's the good news. As you know, John and the late Joe Stone, proposed a change to the SCENICC as we know it, specific to a next Gen device that is smaller, and is actually worn on the eye, to replace the two-pound goggles that now comprise the SCENICC visual sensor. CIA/NCS has provided full monetary support to enable us to make this happen."

Silence enveloped the room, although a spark of hope was ignited in Joe's brain. The new device that Jim alluded to would completely revolutionize the industry as they knew it. More so, it would in effect send the SCENICC design back to the proverbial drawing board. This was the best solution to Joe's limited depth of knowledge, which paled in comparison to John's ten years of design and systems test experience. The proposed system would require redesign, allowing Joe the time to achieve the expertise that John had developed. It would not be easy, but it was very feasible with a bit of self-study.

Randy was the first to speak. "Jim, thank you for informing us of this surprising turn of events. Am I to understand that the device will be implantable, such as an intraocular lens, or are we talking a surficial medical device, like a contact? We're also talking a one-to-five year window for design and testing, now that we're involving U.S. FDA as a new partner."

"Yes, you are very astute, Randy, as this device will require registration as a medical device, and will be surficial, not implantable. We also have been given a full five years for design and FDA registration, with a deliver date of year-end 2000."

"That's actually only four-and-one-half years," noted Scott, the Engineering Operations V.P.

"I can count," replied Jim, with an unimpressed stare focused on Scott. "So, is this feasible? Speak now or forever hold your peace, as I have to provide our decision by the top of the hour."

"It's not enough time," repeated Scott, fixating his gaze upon Jim.

"We have full support from up top, if we decide to take the challenge," reiterated Jim. "I have full confidence we can make the deadline."

"I disagree," noted Scott. "We're talking about developing an FDA approved medical device that is in effect a microelectronic version of our current two pound SCENICC goggles and battery pack. We're talking a year of R&D at a minimum, another year for bench testing, and a third for scale up to manufacturing. This does not even include clinical trials required by FDA, which have no firm timeline. The last I checked, we do not have any of these folks on staff."

"Not to be callous, but we also have a significant gap in field specialists considering Joe Stone's passing just 48 hours ago," chimed in Susan, the Human Factors Engineer. "Who in our ranks can bridge that gap?" she asked.

Joe smiled to himself, knowing that this would not be an issue, and then he spoke. "I agree with your concern, Susan. I've worked closer with Joe than anyone. What if I was to assume this role?"

"Really?" questioned Jim. "Not to insult your sense of initiative or capabilities, John, but you've never been in field ops or combat. How will you pull this off, and concurrently lead the design team?"

"You are right, Jim. Consider though that this opportunity will help me get past Joe's death and will fill the downtime. If I do not meet expectations, then take me off the project."

"I still don't like it--a medical device is too far outside of my comfort zone, especially considering the FDA unknowns," noted Scott.

"Okay. What if I told you that we would be partnering with an ophthalmic manufacturer, who knows 19 CFR requirements specific to device registration," offered Jim.

"And who might that be?" asked Scott.

"I cannot say yet, but it's a ophthalmic company that designs, manufactures and markets intraocular lenses."

"That certainly would help, but I'm still not sold. What other odds are in our favor?"

"300 million of them," noted Jim, after an intentional 10-second silence.

"What?" asked Scott.

"You heard me," replied Jim. "We're talking an R&D payment of $300 million, payable upon successful delivery of the prototype."

Scott hesitated, looking across the table to his colleagues, each of which nodded in succession, as their affirmed agreement to the terms.

"Well, that certainly makes a difference," noted Scott. "$60 million per year might just allow a reasonable design and prototype."

"So you're in?" asked Jim.

"Let's just call it job security," replied Scott.

"That's not an affirmative response," noted Jim.

After a 10-second pause, Scott looked back at Jim and said, "Okay. Yes, we're in."

Joe continued to watch this power play, and held his breath, so as not look anxious. Clearly he wanted the new design program to occur, which would give him precious time to gain the depth of knowledge that only John possessed. Joe knew that his intelligence trumped the majority of the common public, and even the educated public, but he also knew that his learning curve would not meet the design schedule that the Pentagon would require. So far, so good. Just hold tight, Joe told himself.

"Okay, then," replied Jim. "We're all in."

Then Jim turned to Joe and asked, "John, are you good with the plan of approach? This has been your project vision, with Joe, for quite a while now, so I expect nothing less than a 'yes'."

Joe looked back at Jim, and replied, "Then you have my 'Yes,' but on one condition."

"Which is?" asked Jim.

"That you have patience with me on the front end. My mind is still not crystal clear with Joe's passing just a day ago. I'll get past it, but give me some time."

"Absolutely." replied Jim. "You have a week."

Joe silently nodded his head up and down, in agreement. This was secondary to the summersaults that he was doing internally. This opportunity couldn't have come at a better time--but only he would know this, and someday, so would John.

Chapter 29

After a 15-minute drive in complete silence, the taxi driver turned his head 90 degrees in an effort to look at John and questioned, "Did you say 45 Rue Daguerre, near Montparnasse?"

"Yes, 45 Rue Daguerre, near Montparnasse, please," John replied to the driver.

"I have relatives that live down the street from there," noted the driver, looking at John through his rear view mirror. "You might know them, as Paris is a big, yet surprisingly connected town."

John had not ever heard that Paris was anything other than a city, much less a town, as the driver referred to it. He was also not interested in meeting any new friends, or old ones, yet he respectfully replied, "I may know them--what are their names?"

"Henri and Sabine Laroquet," replied the driver, who quieted in expectation of John's reply. He took a left turn onto Rue Daguerre, allowing the taxi to coast as John's stop neared in about 100 feet.

"I cannot say that the names sound familiar, but I look forward to someday meeting them, the next time I'm out grabbing my dinner baguette." Then John quickly changed the topic. "How much do I owe you?"

"I can give you their telephone numbers, as they're always interested in growing their group of friends," replied the driver. "Oh, sorry, umm, you owe me 70 Euros."

John wondered why this guy was so persistent, but was wary of accepting their names, which would open a reciprocal request for his contact info, which wasn't going to happen.

To divert the question, John asked, "Does the 70 Euros include your 10-minute bathroom break, because I'm not paying for your pee time?" John thought this rather snide question might reverse the driver's interests--which it did.

"Pee time. Really?" the driver replied with noted disgust in his voice.

"Really," replied John. "It's just a pet peeve I have."

John's rusty French translation might have been a bit off, with a few words out of order, as the driver replied, "You have a pet that pees? They do that, you know. It's really not out of the ordinary."

"Yeah, I know," John replied, realizing that this conversation was going nowhere. Either he should just pay the exorbitant 70 Euros or face this continued ridiculousness. John chose the former, and remained quiet counting the seconds before he could extricate himself from the taxi and this conversation. He began reaching for his wallet to remove a 50 Euro and a 20 Euro note, before the taxi slowed to a stop in front of his new apartment.

"Thank you again and have a good day," John said to the driver as he passed the payment over the front seat. "I can get my bag from the rear, if you can pop the trunk."

"Absolutely," replied the driver. "I hope your dog is OK."

"My what?" John asked.

"Your dog. The one that pees," replied the driver.

John stuttered. "Oh, yes, thank you."

John exited and walked to the rear of the taxi where the trunk was already opening as he approached. He reached the trunk at the same time that it fully opened, his bag stared at him from the loose articles of clothing and what appeared to be a collection of broken umbrellas strewn throughout the trunk. Why would anyone have this mess in their trunk, especially an individual whose occupation was based upon how much they can load into this space? Not John's concern, but his mind kept spinning, as it commonly did when he was under stress. Just get inside my apartment and I'll get some solitude, he told himself.

John closed the trunk, and the taxi sped off, without a look or a farewell from the driver. Thank goodness.

John turned 180 degrees towards the stairs leading up to his apartment building. That was when he realized that he did not know his apartment number. He had the key that Joe gave him, so at worst case, trial and error would prevail in finding the one matching lock. With his luck, it would be the last door that he tried.

John traversed the stairs towards the wooden door proudly located at the top. He peered through the nine-paned rectangular glass window into a dark hallway that appeared to have mailboxes on one side. Looking down at the doorknob, it became clear that there was no outer lock, which was troubling to say the least, compared to the fortress he was accustomed to at his previous home. Add that one to the list to recommend to his landlord.

John grabbed the doorknob, turned it clockwise and pulled the door towards him. Unlike a normal home, the French building codes required exit doors to open outwards, to allow safe egress in the event of a fire. Stairwells should be adequately sized to allow the downward flush of building inhabitants, so they do not get bottlenecked when they exit. Welcome to the world of Global Fire Codes.

John walked into the hallway, and closed the door behind him. It was surprisingly heavy, yet quiet in its closing motion thanks to five large brass hinges that bore the full weight of the door. To John's left, there was a wall of mailboxes--the kind that one might see in an antique store, approximately six-inches square, a clear glass front, a tumbler to dial in one's combination, and the apartment number on a small engraved plate located directly below the dial. John counted them--40 in total, with six of the mailboxes having mail inside them.

From his many military intelligence projects, John was taught to watch details, even the simplest of which can provide significant information if one knows what to look for. Mailboxes were one of those details, and one of the most common targets for identity thieves. Where else could one find so many details about a person, their habits, their family, their interests, in one box that provides confidential information six days per week, arriving at roughly the same hour each day. Unbeknownst to the general public, common thieves steal bank account information, holding it until the 1st or 15th of each month to steal monies or make charges, to align with payday when the accounts are full.

John took note of the six apartment numbers that had mail in them--008, 103, 208, 310, 402 and 404--as his first targets to try his key, knowing that the renters were either out of town, or had just not checked the boxes for quite a while. John suspected the former, considering the fact that the renters pass their mailboxes multiple times each day, and would collect the contents.

John also found apartment 310 an odd number, considering the assumption that each of the five floors had eight rooms. 310 was therefore an anomaly--one that may have been devised and planted by Joe, as an indicator for John. He decided to check apartment 310 first.

At the end of the hallway, past the mailboxes, were the stairs, that rotated upwards similar to an Escher drawing. He approached the stairs and looked up, the ceiling of the top floor visible through the winding stairway, almost 40 feet above him. It would be easy to see anyone climbing the stairwell, looking down from the top floor. Another positive, assuming the third floor was his floor.

John also knew that Joe would have chosen any of the middle floors, due to their exit ability. Specifically, the first floor was clearly a bad choice, given the easy entry from external intruders; whereas the fourth floor had the dilemma of only one direction to escape; downward into the waiting arms of whomever was chasing you. The middle floors, on the other hand, provided options for escape, more so than the top or ground floors.

John grabbed the round ball atop the end railing, and began the climb to floor three. Each floor looked exactly the same, with the walls adorned by the same tan paint and chocolate brown woodwork and molding. The dark colors made the hallways look dark, as they spread to the left and right of the stairway, which was placed in the center of the building. The first, second and third hallway were extremely quiet, with seemingly no sound coming from the rooms on either side of the hallway.

As John approached the third floor, he exited the stairway and took a left, expecting to see room numbers that started with the number three. Instead, all of the numbers began with the number two. John then remembered that in Europe, as in many parts of the world, that floor conventions were one number lower than what he was accustomed to in the States. In other words, the ground floor was floor zero, the second was floor one, and so on. Therefore, room 310 was located on the fourth floor--so there were actually five floors in the building, with eight rooms per floor.

As John returned to the stairs to ascend one more floor, he remembered a rather funny story that occurred to him upon return from a six-week assignment in Prague. He arrived at the Pentagon, and entered the elevator on the ground floor with four other Pentagon employees. As John was the last to enter the elevator, it was his job to press the button. The group he was with was going to the second floor, as was he, so John instinctively pressed the button to proceed to floor "one."

Nothing happened, so he pressed the button for floor "one" again. Oddly enough, the light on the round button with a number "1" on it did not even light up, as if it were broken.

"Second floor, please," noted one of the four employees, all of whom were oddly looking at John, and less interested in why the "1" button was broken.

"Yes, that is where I am headed, as well," John replied.

"Then hit the button for floor two," noted another of the employees.

"I just did," replied John. "Look, it's not working," very distinctly and slowly moving his finger towards the "1" button, and pressing it again.

Feeling justified, John said "See--not working," looking back at the four in the elevator, whose door had closed about 15 seconds earlier, but remained motionless.

"Are you ok?" questioned the third employee stepping back towards the corner of the elevator.

It was the fourth employee that figured out the problem, at about the same time that John had realized what the issue was.

The fourth employee moved towards the panel of buttons, and pressed the one with the "2" on it, smiled and stated, "My guess is you've been abroad for a few weeks. Right?"

John felt like an idiot, smiled grimly and said, "Yes, this is so embarrassing. Sorry about that. I'm still in European travel mode."

Just then, the other three employees caught the gist of what just happened, reflecting on their own experiences with their personal travels, and similar adjustment upon return to the U.S.

The "2" button lit upon the man's touch, and the elevator churned its way to the second floor, announcing its arrival with a chirpy "ding."

The door opened, and John and the four exited.

The last of the four employees noted as they walked away, "No worries my friend. Just do us all a favor and concentrate on your driving when we leave the parking lot tonight--I have no desire for a head-on collision."

"You got it," John replied, and continued to his meeting on the first, no, the second floor.

By this time, John had reached the fourth floor of the apartment, with eight doors numbered 301 through 310, with a not-so-obvious absence of apartment 308. John remembered that in the entry hallway to the building, he saw mail in the mailbox for 310. He was slowly becoming more assured that this was Joe's work and intention, simply because there would never be mail delivered to an apartment that did not exist in the building. The odd issue was where the mail for 308 was delivered, as 310 was actually the old 308. Don't think this too hard, thought John. Clearly Joe knew what he was doing, as the brother who left nothing to chance.

John walked from the stairway to the end of the hallway, towards a window that from a distance appeared to have an unobstructed view of the street below. He peered out the window upon arrival and was greeted with a spectacular and strategic view of the Rue Daguerre, and the intersection of streets below that radially connected into Daguerre. This will come in handy, he thought to himself.

John reached into his rear pocket, and removed his wallet which was 70 Euros lighter due to his recent taxi ride. He reached to the last credit card, and removed the Carte Blanche card, under which was the key that Joe had given him not even 24 hours ago. The key was completely void of any identifying symbols or lettering, and had a smoothed section that reminded him of a Master Key, that could open any lock. If it were the case, that would have been a bad choice, as he would enter the wrong apartment. Don't over think this, he again reminded himself.

The key entered the door handle, sliding easily into the key slot. A slight clockwise turn of the key, and the handle effortlessly followed, turning an equidistant rotation, and the door opened. Thank you Joe, you did well, he thought, as he slowly advanced the door, leeringly peeking inside as if he expected a family to be sitting on the coach, watching television, which luckily was not scenario. The apartment light was off, with furniture visible in the dim morning sunlight entering from two windows to the far right side of the room.

John looked for a light switch and found one immediately to the right of the door. He flicked the switch up, which made a barely audible pop, when a spark ignited upon contact with the throw of the switch.

One surface mounted lamp located on the ceiling in the center of the room provided a warm glow that illuminated the entire room. The room smelled a bit stale, but was very clean, with conventional styled furniture decorating the entry room. The essentials were all there, including a couch, a matching second chair with ottoman, and a coffee table. A small flat screen television faced the couch-- probably a 42-inch, which was small in U.S. terms but more than adequate for an individual who would rather read, pine away on his MacBook Air, or watch NETFLIX on Apple TV versus watch television commercials interspersed with mildly entertaining shows.

The living room opened to one side, revealing a small kitchen with a cooktop, refrigerator and a round clear glass breakfast table. Cupboards circled half of the room, providing needed storage space for essential staples and dishes. John walked into the kitchen, curious if there was food already stocked for his consumption. As predicted, the shelves were filled with an assortment of items including cereal, bread, canned goods, along with plates, bowls, and requisite utensils. The refrigerator was stocked as well, to include a few bottles of wine, more so local to the Bordeaux region, than Paris, which was relatively void of vineyards.

John proceeded to the bedroom, where a double bed was located, night stand and an odd shaped lamp that could extend similar to that which an Architect would use on a drafting table--this would suffice very well for bedtime reading. The bathroom was located to the left of a clothes armoire, with a stand-alone bathtub and two toilets. Actually, just one toilet and a separate bidet, which John would have zero use for. For the first time since leaving the airport, John thought of his stewardess acquaintance named Jeanette, but quickly and intentionally erased the thoughts from his mind. The last thing he needed now was a girlfriend.

John returned to the entry, locked the door using the deadbolt and second slide bolt which connected into the floor, and rolled his bag into the bedroom. He returned to the living room, turned on the television and flopped down onto the couch to think of his next steps. He remembered the conversation with Joe in the cabin, just 48 hours ago, going through the visual list of steps in his mind. Closing his eyes, it seemed like he was still there, plotting the strategy that was now reality and his soon to be daily routine. Before he realized it, he had fallen fast asleep, exhausted by the stress and the previous day's activities.

Chapter 30

Joe wandered back to his office, closed the door and sat down in his chair, still bewildered from the unforeseen direction to immediately begin design and pilot of the SCENICC. To be honest, he was relieved by the change in plans, as this was the one area he had left to chance in the unfolding plan. He feigned confidence in the cabin that last evening with John, noting that he had this under control--but of course that was a lie. John had given him a long skeptical look upon receiving this news, which took all of Joe's will to show no emotion. Inside, questions burned in his mind about if or how he could gain the technical knowledge that John had amassed over a decade. There was no choice at the time though, else John never would have accepted the plan if there had been doubt. One week to bridge the design gap with the currently undefined SCENICC is much better than no time to bridge the 5-year gap on an already functional design.

Joe's thoughts were interrupted by a knock at his office door.

"Come in," Joe replied.

The door knob slowly rotated, and in peeked the face of Randy. Holding the door open enough to just slide her head into the office, she asked, "Can I come in?"

You've got to be kidding, thought Joe to himself. What did I do to deserve this, he asked himself. Wind the clock, he told himself, wind the clock. Joe remained silent.

Randy opened the door and slid into the office, asking "Do you mind?" as she pointed to the chair.

"No, not at all. Now that you've invited yourself in," Joe said, "Grab a seat."

"Thanks," Randy replied. "About that conversation we had this morning." She paused.

"The one about SCENICC, I assume?" smartly replied Joe.

"No the other one," she replied.

"Which other one?"

"The one about New Year's," she replied.

"Oh yes, that discussion. What about it?"

"I didn't remember it that way," Randy replied.

Joe instantly felt as if he was being psychoanalyzed, but said, "OK then, how do you remember it?"

"I think there was more to it than that," she stated. "Didn't you?"

"Nope, and I'm actually more interested in discussing your thoughts on the SCENICC guidance delivered 15 minutes ago."

"So there's nothing between us?" she asked once more.

"Zip," replied Joe.

"Oh, OK." Randy paused for a painstaking 10 seconds and looked down, her eyes focused on the front of Joe's desk.

"So, uh, my thoughts on the meeting today. Well, both you and John have been pushing for SCENICC for over a year. It's the right thing to do--You know it, and Jim knows it. It's our future, despite the associated financial outlay and uncertainty."

"Uncertainty. Hmmmm. So what do you think is our largest hurdle?" Joe asked, still trying to keep her focused on anything other than the turn of events on New Year's Eve, which he of course did not know first-hand.

"From an intelligence perspective, I expect our partnership with the yet-to-be-named Pharma Company for 19 CFR device registration will be our weakest link, with FDA approval being a distant second. Pharma guys think differently than we do, and get mired in the details. Just be glad that we're pursuing design and registration of a surficial device versus an implantable. If the latter design was the case, the clinical trials alone could take three years, or more. Even with our surficial device, we can expect a minimum of one year of trials."

"But this should be no different than a glass or plastic contact, which is existing technology with existing FDA registration," noted John.

"Yes, but we're adding a new wrinkle with the embedded electronics, which I doubt can fall under a similarity exclusion."

"So you're not worried about the battery, which currently is over half the weight of the current goggle system," pointing backwards towards the unit on the credenza behind him.

"No, not so much. We already have NiCad technology that should be able to be packaged in a power pod no larger than a deck of cards," she replied.

"I like your confidence," replied Joe.

"It never pays to be negative. Even when others don't remember what happened less than a year ago." Randy's eyes met Joe's.

"OK, time for you to go now," Joe replied, standing up and pointing to the door.

Randy stood from her chair, turned and walked to the door, then stopped.

"So nothing, huh?" with a curt smile.

"Nada," replied Joe. No smile.

Then she left the office.

Chapter **31**

John awoke to the noise of passing footsteps outside his apartment door. They continued down the hallway and eventually to the stairway located one door down from his apartment. After a few seconds, silence returned to non-existent apartment 310.

John checked his watch which read 3:05 pm, amazed that he had been asleep for over five hours. He stood up, stretched and walked over to one of the two windows in his living room. From this vantage point, similar to the window at the end of the outer hallway, he had an excellent view of Rue Daguerre, and the nearby park to the west. The local Parisians were in the midst of their Sunday routines, with numerous families and their pets out for a mid-afternoon walk to the market. John had heard that over half of the populace living in Europe owned at least one dog, and the current sight confirmed this, with every other walker sporting a leash-connected-dog in their hands. Between the individuals walking the streets and the cars zipping back and forth interspersed by a surprisingly large number of mopeds, it was quite a commotion for a lazy Sunday afternoon. Farther to the left of his view, John noticed a line already snaking into the Paris Catacomb exhibit, which Joe had explained was strategically located across the street.

John retreated back to the living room. It was clear that one or a Team of Joe's many associates had done a meticulous job of selecting and setting up the apartment. All of the accoutrements of home had been tirelessly selected and placed in the apartment. It looked well lived in, as if he had been living here for years.

Unbeknownst to anyone other than John though, Joe had a calling card. Specifically, in all of Joe's safe houses he would select and purposefully stage a single out-of-the-ordinary decoration or piece of furniture. To most people, this item would never be noticed. Hidden inside this item though, would be a clue to next steps, or a message describing Joe's whereabouts, status, and in rare instances, how he could be contacted. John's experience with this process originated during their assignments in the Persian Gulf, whereby Joe would secretly let John know his condition and whereabouts, much to the chagrin of the military, who frowned on such leaks of intelligence.

John moved to the center of the living room, just in front of the couch. He began rotating his body to enable a 360-degree panoramic view of the entire room, noting each individual piece of furniture and decorations that were arranged in the room.

The room was adorned by contemporary styled furniture, sporting the bright primary and rather loud colors of red and blue, with a common herringbone pattern. Not exactly John's first choice, but no one asked his opinion. The decorative accents ranged from small pictures on mini-easels, to abstractly shaped pieces of artwork that were no more than sculptured clods of clay painted with solid glossy colors. He had no idea who was included in the pictures, nor did he really care, fully knowing that they were props. The sculptured clods of artwork would provide excellent projectiles, if needed, but were not the items that John was looking for. As a final detail, small vases lined the six-level bookshelves that occupied each corner of the room. The bookshelves were a nice use of empty space, but again, not of interest at this time.

Then he saw it. A simple, nondescript utilitarian device located to the left of the television--that being a retro battery-operated AM transistor radio. It was a device that operated on electronics of yesteryear, circa 1970s to be exact. Although solid state electronics were less than a few decades old, the transistor first replaced the vacuum tube in 1947 when Bell Labs demonstrated the first prototype.

Seven years later, the transistor radio entered the market, culminating in billions manufactured by the mid-1970s. And now, a silver and black Sanyo 8S-P3 radio stared John in the face--a clear candidate for Joe's calling card.

John walked to the radio, reaching out his right hand to lift it from the table. As John rotated it in his hands, he noticed slight rust on the bottom, assumed to be a result of leaking batteries or from prolonged sitting upon a wet surface. John looked for screws that would enable entry into the antiquated device, and located four barely visible screws at the corners of the rear cover on the radio. It would be a chore to find a screw driver small enough to fit these barely visible screws. In fact, they were so small, it was difficult to see whether they were normal or Phillips head type. John also knew that locating a screw driver in this apartment that fit these screws would validate he had indeed found Joe's intended device.

John brought the radio with him into the kitchen to search for a screwdriver that would fit these screws. After a few checks of cabinets and drawers, the matching tool was located visibly stored in the silverware drawer. A small metallic gold-colored screwdriver, one that might have been used by an optometrist to fix reading glasses, was in the leftmost section of the silverware tray amongst the table knives.

He removed the screwdriver from the utensil tray, noting it was a Phillips head type that he could now see aligned perfectly with the size of the four screws on the back of the radio. He inserted the screwdriver into each screw, rotating each 720-degrees counterclockwise until they fell to the tabletop, making a metallic "ting" as they bounced upon impact.

The back cover was easily removed, with an aided pry from the screwdriver. Inside the radio were the typical components that included two ferrite antennas, audio transformers, a volume control dial, a loudspeaker, transistors, and the battery compartment with battery. All of the components were rusted and dusty, with the exception of the battery, which shined like it was brand new-- because it was.

John removed the battery, which revealed what he had been looking for--a small slip of paper, completely hidden from view by the battery. John removed the neatly folded slip of paper, and opened it to reveal the following message:

Hello Bro--Good job finding my outdated electronic gadget. By now, you've adjusted to your new surroundings--hope you like Brenda's taste in interior decorating. I pray that you are doing well. Do not worry about me, as I am smarter than you and thus am doing equally as well. I will be in touch, but as we discussed in the cabin, you MUST plan an escape route via the Catacombs across the street as soon as you are able. The time will inevitably come when you will need to move on. This may be a week, or it could be years, but we both know it will someday occur. You will constantly remain in my thoughts and prayers. Take care. Joe.

John walked over to the kitchen sink, located a matchbox in the cabinet, removed and lit one match and proceeded to burn the letter, letting it drop into the sink to burn to ashes. Activation of the water stream eliminated all traces of the message, diminishing it to no more than a few gray ashes swirling down the drain.

"Thanks Joe," whispered John to himself. "I'll keep you in my prayers as well." No worries, John thought to himself, I'll check out the Catacombs in the morning. He opened a few cabinets in search of food, and was pleasantly surprised by the selection that had been provided. Likewise, every type of plate and utensil lined the cabinets—thanks, Brenda. Time for a quick meal and a quiet evening. John had much to think about and welcomed the solitude.

Chapter **32**

The Catacombs were located directly across the street from John's new apartment, which was not by accident. Many locations in Paris afforded the ability for a fast get-away, but none had the options that the Catacombs provided, or at least that was Joe's opinion, which John was about to verify.

John proceeded down the stairway in the front of his apartment complex, and headed to the corner to safely cross the street. As the entrance door to the Paris Catacombs attraction neared, he could see a line of customers already waiting to enter the attraction. Clearly all of those in line were tourists, some with young children, and others with their partners, but no locals. John joined the end of the line, behind an Asian couple talking in what he recognized as Mandarin. They both wore matching Lucky Brand jeans and solid colored polo knit shirts; the kind with the grossly oversized polo horse and jockey on the left chest. Personally, John found this style of shirts rather obnoxious, which he assumed was the desire for most Polo customers.

A hand unexpectedly grabbed John's left shoulder from behind, startling him. He spun around to assess the situation to see a middle-aged man with his partner, asking a question.

"Have you been here before?" the man asked John in a quieted French vernacular.

"Uh, no, not yet," stammered John. "Why are you asking?"

"We've been through the Catacombs many times. You're rather tall, and not exactly on the small side," replied the man. "You will need to be careful when you get to the bottom of the stairs, as I've seen many first-time visitors scrape the top of their heads on the low ceilings. One poor soul actually knocked himself out. Since I'm on the tall side, I have learned to crouch and walk through the very long tunnel. Neat, huh?"

Yeah, neat, thought John to himself.

"Ok, thanks for the heads up," said John.

"No, you need to keep your head down," noted the man, his partner rotating her head from side to side in a "no" fashion, silently reiterating her friend's comment.

Attack of my Tarzan French strikes again, thought John.

"I mean, thank you for the advance notice. I will be very careful once I get into the tunnel," John stated, in much clearer French, avoiding the slang and speaking much more slowly.

"That will be 20 Euros," noted the attraction attendant, a welcomed sight at this point in his current conversation, her hand out in expectation of payment. She was a rather scary sight, with jet black hair that fell over half of her sickly pale face, adorned with glossy black lipstick and too much white makeup.

Yikes, John thought to himself, consciously holding back a surprised gasp. He was wondering what he was about to get himself into, considering his newfound friend in line and the rather absurdly decorated attendant. Maybe that's the expected employee attire, considering the venue, he thought.

John tried not to stare at or count the row of loop earrings that pierced her bottom lip, and reached into his rear pocket to remove a blue 20 Euro note, handing the attendant the payment, with a forced smile.

"Watch your head on the way down," she noted without looking up. "The circular stairs can also be a problem. Please sign the release on the line at the bottom of the page."

As John signed his name, he was beginning to get a complex that he must look like some kind of basketball player to these guys. He slid the executed agreement back to Goth Girl and quickly turned to enter the attraction, which at this point was a dark spiral staircase that descended to the depths of who knows where.

All that John knew about the Paris Catacombs was what Joe had told him. Specifically, the Catacombs housed the exhumed remains of the Parisians that were once buried where the larger edifices such as Notre Dame now stood. Apparently, in the early 1800s, when the foundations for these structures were being excavated, they encountered the original remains for Parisians buried during the late 10th century, which required relocation to this current exhibit. In total, remains from 17 cemeteries, 145 monasteries and 160 religious areas with proper burial grounds were moved to their final resting place in the Paris Catacombs. Apparently, there were many more miles of original catacomb tunnels beneath the City, with most prohibiting public access. As was hard to fathom, this 2 kilometer tourist-permitted path represents only 1/800th of the total tunnel network under Paris. John suspected that inherent hazards existing in the real Parisian Catacombs were much more serious than just receiving a bumped head.

The entry to the attraction was exactly as the attendant warned, with an extremely narrow cylindrical stone staircase that wound downwards into the darkness. John hugged the outside wall of the staircase with his hands extended upwards to contact the underside of the stairs above. He carefully placed his size thirteen shoes on the size eight outer stair steps--one misstep and he would plummet on top of the individual descending directly ahead, and below him.

The seemingly endless winding continued, with John losing his sense of perspective and depth to which he was proceeding below ground--almost to the point of dizziness. Luckily, after 130 steps which he estimated as being 50 feet below street level, the steps ended and he was once again on level ground.

A long dark tunnel lay ahead, lit only by hanging light bulbs spaced too far apart to produce useable light, but enough to provide a target for your next destination. As John took his first step, his head scraped the ceiling of the concrete-and-brick-lined tunnel, which must have been no more than five feet in height and three feet wide. The comments of his nameless friend were instantly resurrected in John's mind. He smiled to himself, and stooped down further as he walked onward.

The voices of those stumbling farther down the tunnel echoed forward, not recognizable, but with a noticeable heightened sense of excitement. John felt the friend behind him occasionally touching his back in the darkness--apparently his pronounced experience didn't help in this situation. John plodded along, with his arms extended, keeping his focus on the next light bulb. Over the next 75 yards, this process continued, until the group entered a larger room, with numerous hallways leading in three different directions, only one of which was not cordoned off by a wrought iron gate.

From out of nowhere, a tour guide slid into the dim light, holding a flashlight. The beam of light darted around the room, casting shadows of each of the visitors now lining the room.

"Welcome to the Paris Catacombs," the guide said. "We're glad to have you visit one of the most unique and comfortably gruesome exhibits that you will ever experience. For your safety, I recommend that you remain with our group, else suffer the consequences of being lost forever in the mazes that lie beneath the City. We actually don't mind if you get lost as you've each signed our waiver, but we more so don't care for the smell if you do get lost and get eaten alive by the rats that frequent these tunnels."

The guide let out a maniacal laugh, which was well rehearsed and probably the most exciting part of their extremely monotonous role.

John took in the scene, looking at his surroundings with a completely strategic focus, already beginning to understand Joe's previous comment on the benefit of this odd attraction.

As the group continued down the only unblocked tunnel of the three, the strangest sight became visible in the distance. Specifically, a tight spotlight was focused on the lower leftmost wall of the tunnel. The line ahead of him slowed to a stop, as each person took a look at the oddly placed relics. As John approached, he could see an assortment of skulls and femurs, carefully and rather artistically arranged to form the leftmost wall of the tunnel. An assortment of femurs, probably numbering in the thousands, were piled behind this wall, which was stained light brown and then shellacked to protect the ancient bones. The tour guide noted that over 6 million people were reinterred in this exhibit.

John noticed words neatly engraved into the stone facade above the first tunnel, stating "Stop! The empire of death is here," as the warning of Jacques Delille at the entry to the ossuary of the Catacombs. How comfortably gruesome, John noted to himself.

The next 45-minute walk was more of the same, from vestibule to tunnel filled with bones arranged in various patterns. John estimated that he easily traversed the entire 2 kilometers in the process, never doubling back on the same path, with countless other paths that were never entered. Who knows how large the maze of tunnels must have been--a perfect place to escape any foe, once familiarity with the layout was gained, as John's new objective over the short-term.

A final spiral stone staircase was located at the far end of the tunnel system, but not as tall as the first. John ascended the staircase, in a shorter 83 steps. The most unexpected result upon surfacing was that the exit at street level was nowhere near the entrance, with John completely unaware of where he was in the City. From the signage at the corner of the nearest building, he was located to the far south of the entry at the corner of Rue Rémy Dumoncel. He looked for the closest Metro station, as the most recognizable landmark, and easiest means to return to his apartment.

After a short two block walk, the Metro was located, which after a 10 minute trip, brought John back to his apartment. His objective over the next few weeks, was to gain familiarity with the maze system, at 20 Euro a pop.

Chapter 33

John was awakened at the normal 6:00 a.m. hour by the alarm clock sitting next to his bed. It was shocking how quickly five years had passed since he first moved to Paris, and how comfortable he felt as a true resident, even more so than when he lived in the States.

As he did every morning, he performed 600 sit-ups while still in bed, starting with the oblique crunches, then progressing to the floor for 100 push-ups followed by 25 pull-ups via the pull-up bar installed in the doorway. This routine was the best way to get the blood flowing in the morning.

John slid on a T-shirt, a pair of Nike shorts, socks and his running shoes and stopped by the kitchen for whey protein powder mixed in water, as his normal pre-run snack. A quick stop by the bathroom finished his morning routine. Jeanette's toiletries lined the edges of his bathroom sink, alongside her hair brush visibly filled with strands of her fiery red hair. Her toothbrush leaned next to his, in a cup located to the right of the cold water faucet.

Although a known weak link in his secret life, John had contacted Jeanette shortly after their unexpected meeting on his Air France flight to Paris. Her perfume was too intoxicating and her long flowing red hair too enticing to resist, plus there was no substitute for companionship when you are instantly thrown into a new country and culture. She had a positive impact on his psyche, and certainly enhanced his renewed French vocabulary, amongst other things a man needs.

She clearly made John happy, and kept him generally distracted from his distant memories of his previous life. He found himself having to wind the clock less these days—which, for his Obsessive Compulsive mindset, was a good thing. John wondered how Joe was doing, but knew that the lack of contact was a good thing, as continued validation of their best kept secret.

Today, he would run by Cafe Marin after his daily three mile jaunt, to meet up with Jeanette for a Cafe-au-lait. Typically she would join him on his morning run, but she was just returning home from a two-week international flight throughout North and South America. He was glad she was finally back in town, as she was really his only friend in the City, and in all of Europe for that matter.

John grabbed his key, iPhone and earbuds, and walked out into the hall. It was quiet as normal, with an occasional "yip" from the Jack Russell terrier next door--named "Rosco." He headed down the two flights of stairs, two steps at a time, and bounced past the mailboxes on his right. Other than a few magazines and advertisements, Mr. Jean Pascual intentionally did not receive much mail -- with the exception of a few postcards from Jeanette when she was traveling. John knew that he could not fly with her, in an effort to prevent close inspection of his Passport -- the incident five years ago at Charles de Gaulle was enough for him. Jeanette had yet to question his response that he was scared to fly, and seemed satisfied for the day trips they took, driving to their favorite secluded spots across Europe. She also considered flying as part of her job, which it was, and enjoyed the break from what she called the "office." Don't question a good thing, John would tell himself, but it still stuck in his mind as odd.

The morning dew was visible on the many fragrant plants that decorated the front porches and balconies that bordered the sidewalk that John traversed every day. Even though he knew better than to take the same route every day, as advice received from Joe a half-decade ago, John felt comfortable and took more liberties with every passing year. The original plan discussed with Joe was to move every other year, to maintain his anonymity. John was a home body though, and now that Jeanette was in the picture, moving and starting again was far from his mind.

An early morning three-mile run always set John's mind at ease. It was the only time when he really had nothing else to do but think and listen to music--there were no interruptions, no phone calls or texts (or at least ones that required immediate attention); only a repetitious up and down bounce that provided the runner's high that so many athletes strived for. John's father called exercise "cleaning the spleen," which made perfect sense. When Jeanette ran with him, it was even more enjoyable. He missed her when he ran alone, but knew that she would soon be with him at the Cafe.

Chapter 34

Just as Mick alluded, Joe knew what had to be done. The ride in the Black Crown Vic limo occurring just minutes ago was an indication that John's time was very limited--their five-year secret had unfortunately come to an end.

The 48-hour head start, as the curious man in the Crown Vic called it, was a gracious lead, but also a treacherous path--one that would either aid Joe in alerting John of impending danger, or lead his assailants directly to him. For all Joe knew, they were already on John's path. If only they had known that they had their intended target (that being Joe), fully in their clutches while they were riding in the limo. If Joe executed the next steps properly, they might still never know.

"Where do you want to start?" Joe verbalized into the fEP.

No answer.

"Mick, are you there?" Joe repeated.

"I'm here," came Mick's reply through his earpiece. "Just thinking."

"I'll need more than that," noted Joe.

"I know," replied Mick. "Get your Passport. I will see you in the Frankfurt Airport promptly at 8 o'clock a.m. tomorrow. Let's plan to meet at the sushi restaurant at the entrance into Terminal D."

"I hate sushi," replied Joe.

"As you should, since it's not even on the top 20 for local German food, but the bar is located in an open and well trafficked area. I'll stake it out and clear the area before I grab a table. You know the drill. Safe travels."

"Yes, and remember that I taught you 'the drill.' See you there," replied Joe.

Chapter 35

John turned the final corner that led to Cafe Marin, and could see Jeanette already sitting at a table, her hair partially covering her face as she peered into what he assumed was a book. She was the ultimate anti-social person, after getting hit on for years in her role as an airline stewardess--odd that she hit on him five years ago while she was in that same role, but he was glad that she did.

She looked up, just as John passed through the wrought-iron gate that surrounded the outside seating area of the Cafe. They caught eye contact and she immediately smiled, rose from her chair and walked towards him, giving him a warm hug and kiss on the cheek. She had already changed into her running gear, sporting all pink hues, from her New Balance shoes to her no-name cap, through which her hair was bound into a single strand that extended out the hole in the back. Her pony tail was the epitome of the descriptor.

"Mon Cherie," she said, still smiling, "How was your week?"

"Boring and lonely," John replied. "Not as exciting as yours, for sure. How was São Paulo?"

"Of all of the cities I fly to, São Paulo is one of the most stressful. It's a beautiful country when you're outside of the airports, taxis and hotels, but the over-population and snarled traffic of the city mask the intrigue," she replied. "I've also always been amazed how the graffiti reaches the top of most of the buildings downtown-- how do they do that?"

"Good question," responded John. "I haven't been there for many years, but from what I remember, the coastal beaches such as Santos and Guarujá are breathtaking, and amazingly secluded."

"So true--but this time I wasn't able to get away, as we we did the round-trip between Miami and São Paulo two times in succession. It always surprises me how far south São Paulo is--12 hours, yet still in a similar time zone."

Jeanette paused, then looked into John's eyes and said, "Maybe my next flight there, you'll come with me?"

John tried to look unfazed, knowing that his preference, even after five years in Paris, was to avoid venturing into an airport anytime soon.

John played along, "When might your next Brazilian tour occur?" not really interested in the answer, unless it was within the next few weeks, which would force a near term diversion.

"About six months from now. Can you wait that long?" she asked.

Perfect, John thought to himself, but replied, "Rather than wait, why don't we take another drive to Geneva, and stay in Le Montreux overlooking the Lake, just as we did last summer?"

"The Grand Hotel Suisse Majestic was very nice," Jeanette suggested.

"A bit stuffy, but I agree," added John. Actually, really stuffy, John thought. He was surprised that such a stately establishment existed in Montreux, resembling a plantation home more so than a Swiss mountain retreat.

"Being there during the Montreux Jazz Festival was perfect--let's try for that same week."

"I'll ask for some time off from work," John said in jest, with Jeanette knowing that he was independently wealthy, and did not have a daily job. With the exception of the time he spent as a tour guide at the Catacombs, he was fully unemployed. Jeanette had never asked about this apparent fetish with the macabre. He explained it away by noting his fascination with French history--the Catacombs certainly met this interest, as the age of the remnants of the inhabitants spanned much of Paris' colorful history. John's mind many times drifted off into the mazes and hiding places that he now knew so well, almost to the degree of being able to draw them from memory.

Jeanette's cell phone buzzed from within her arm band--a single vibration as an alert of a text message or email, but probably the former as she did not keep the e-mail alerts active. She looked down to see the message, her brow wrinkling in recognition of the words that spanned the screen.

Jeanette clicked the phone back to a black screen, and asked, "Can we run back to your place?"

"Not fair--I thought it was coffee time. I've already run my three miles, and now you want to double that?" John replied, knowing full well that he could easily run four times that. Jeanette knew it too.

John's comment didn't faze her, as she waited without response or visible expression on her face for his answer--one that he could not recall that he had seen before. He also noted her eyes darting out towards the street, as if she wanted to look, but restrained herself.

"Sure. Did you pay yet?" John asked.

"I just did," with Jeanette plopping down a 10 Euro Note on the table. She was already standing next to the table no more than five seconds later.

Let's see how quickly she runs, as an indication of what's up, John thought. Excitement always makes one run faster, especially Jeanette.

Jeanette was already through the gate, looking back towards John with the "What are you waiting for?" look. OK, just go with it,-- "Coming," he noted.

They ran the same route that brought John to the Cafe, with the exception that the speed was a minute per mile faster, as confirmed by John's Run Keeper App on his iPhone. Something was clearly awry, as Jeanette was leading the pace, which was out of character, as he would typically do so. At one point, she was actually pulling away, slowly adding distance between the two of them.

John caught up to her and asked, "Everything OK? You seem distracted, or focused. I cannot tell which."

"Yes, I am both," she replied in between breaths, clearly pushing the envelope past her normal running pace. "I just need to run to the restroom."

"OK--but we've passed quite a few," so what's so special about the one at my apartment?"

"It's a woman thing. You know what I mean--I need my thing," Jeannette quipped.

"Oh, that thing." John now knew exactly what Jeanette meant, as apparently Jeanette was without "the thing"--the thing associated with a woman issue that men don't like to discuss at length, especially whenever a woman mentions it. John had made that mistake only once, about five years ago, when he commented on the "thing." He asked one of his close friends at the Pentagon why she didn't carry a spare "thing" when that time of the month neared. It made perfect sense to John to be prepared, so when a woman needed the "thing," it was readily available. John suspected that if it was a man "thing," that men would hide the "thing" at numerous locations, so it would be easily found--one in the car, one in the wallet, one in the desk drawer at work, etc. To say John's advice was not well received by his friend, was an understatement. Lesson No. 1--don't ever discuss "the thing," or make suggestions on how to be more effective with "the thing."

Jeanette was nearing the last curve before Rue Daguerre, when she slowed down.

"Tired?" John asked.

"Yes, but glad that I made it. Let's walk the rest of the way."

"Um, Ok. That's fine. Are you sure you're ok?"

"Yes, just in a pinch. I should have planned better." .

Wow, John thought. Maybe she's the type of woman that I could have the "thing" discussion with--or then again, maybe not.

John and Jeanette reached his apartment and climbed the stairs. The front door to the building still opened without a key, and they stepped inside the corridor. Jeanette was still acting oddly. John sensed something was wrong, although it may have been further enhanced by "the thing." John's previous trained CIA subconscious was coming back--indicating that Jeannette was on guard, looking for something, or someone. Or then again, maybe John was just being paranoid.

As they walked past the mailboxes on the left, Jeanette stopped, looking towards mail box 310.

"Pascual, when did you get your mail last?" she asked.

"A few days ago."

"So should mail still be in there?"

"Yes--I'm getting lazy and only remove it every two or three days."

"Is your box damaged?"

"No, why do you ask?"

"Because there is mail in the box, which appears normal, but it appears the lock has been damaged."

John looked closer at the box, and noticed that she was correct. The mail box keyhole looked as if it had been widened, similar to the effect a screw driver might cause if jammed into the keyhole and forcibly turned. John's mail was still in the box.

Jeanette turned and headed to the stairs, bounding upwards two steps at a time. John followed behind her, tracing her footsteps on every other stair. She stopped at the top, at a point where John's apartment door was visible. John almost ran into her back. She put her index finger to her lips, making the universal "be quiet" sign.

She turned to John, pointing to his apartment door, and asked. "Did you by chance leave your door unlocked when you left this morning? I suspect your answer is 'No,' but as you can see, your apartment door is slightly open."

"No--I locked it. I am completely sure of that."

"Well, it's open now."

John could now see that, and was completely taken by surprise, the questions spinning inside his head. Who was there, were they still there, what did they steal...
"Pascual, concentrate!" Jeanette whispered. "Stay with me--I'm going closer."

And then it happened. Jeanette reached inside her belly pack and removed a Sig Sauer P238, turning to look at John as she did, and aiming it at the partially opened door.

"Follow closely behind me."

John did so, not fully comprehending what was unfolding before his eyes. They walked towards the door, with Jeanette's outstretched arm, and Sig leading the way.

As they moved within a few feet of the door, men's voices could be heard from within his apartment, along with the occasional ransacking of contents in between the chatter.

"We're done here--let's get out," Jeanette whispered, as they backtracked to the stairs.

John stopped. "What's all this about and since when did you become a gun slinger?"

"Trust me, we don't have time for this."

"I'm not sure who to trust," replied John.

"Not now--just follow me out, and I'll explain."

"No--I need to know what or who we're running from."

"You really don't need to know," Jeanette replied, still walking backward with the Sig pointed up the stairs. "I'll explain when we're in the Catacombs--we must follow the plan."

"The plan? How do you know about the plan? I'm not moving until I understand what's going on."

Jeanette stopped, and looked sternly into John's eyes. Her disposition very serious and words deliberate, saying, "I will explain later, but if you want to live, you will follow the plan that you and Joe developed five years ago. Lead me into the Catacombs, John--it's our only option."

John stood motionless, and didn't speak. This was the first time Jeanette had ever called him by his real name. So many thoughts ran through his mind, none of which made sense.

It immediately dawned on John that the needed return to his apartment was never about the woman "thing"--instead, the text that Jeanette received at the Cafe must have been a warning, resurrecting that fateful day five years ago.

The day that Joe had predicted and that he and John had planned for, had finally come. And somehow, Jeanette was part of the plan.

Chapter **36**

The Frankfurt Airport is a familiar arrival point for many a European traveler, especially when traversing the Atlantic from the United States. Even though Joe was a world traveler, Frankfurt was always difficult to navigate due to its numerous levels and confusing signage, apparently even for the locals who called it home. It seemed to change every time Joe was there, with seemingly continuous construction occurring in every terminal. Surprisingly enough, the only constant was the sushi bar located in the entry hallway prior to security control in Terminal 2.

Joe's plane landed 30 minutes ahead of schedule, touching down at 6:30 am, vs. the projected 7:00 am. Joe considering John in this similar scenario, almost five years earlier, arriving into Paris via Charles de Gaulle.

Orchestrating the purely coincidental meeting between Jeanette and John was no easy task, but worthwhile considering that she was his only conduit to reach John in the event of emergency. Hopefully, they were on their way to Kaysersberg, France, where they would meet to strategize next steps.

Jeanette had been one of Joe's most talented operatives during a Romanian human trafficking sting occurring in early 1991. Originally educated in International Relations from Columbia University, her keen aptitude for foreign languages and her calm demeanor made her a perfect candidate for spy-school. When they first met, Joe had remarked on just that, more so of a pick-up line than a formal invitation. Little did Joe know that Jeanette was fluent in French, Russian, German and Italian, as well as English. When she responded with piqued interest, Joe headed her in the right direction by contacting the then Director of the Central Intelligence Agency, Robert Gates, who quickly opened the doors to the contacts and training offered only to the CIA Elite. Jeanette quickly rose through the ranks in a short two years, with Robert as her mentor until he left his role in 1993.

One of Jeanette's trademarks was her unbridled confidence when confronted with hazardous situations--her hand-to-hand combat capabilities were exceptional, as well as her marksmanship. She had placed in the top five shooters in her graduating class at the Academy, which is nothing short of incredible for an individual who had never shot a handgun until four years earlier. She was a natural, to say the least.

Joe had texted Jeanette four simple letters to alert her to drop everything, gather John, and immediately abscond from Paris--They were K-A-Y-S. This message was one which they had used numerous times in the past, as their favorite meeting place for relaxation more so than escape. Kaysersberg was a sleepy French town nestled in the lower Alsace Valley, well known for the vineyards that lined the local countryside. The town was named after Kaysersberg Castle that still stood amongst the vineyards guarding the town. Other than the summertime when tourists and wine enthusiasts freely roamed the town, there was little activity, which made it a perfect spot to meet for a long weekend or temporary hiding place for those on the run. Joe's French and German were rusty so he was glad that Jeanette would be with them. If he and Mick could stay quiet, they should be able to avoid being pegged as tourists.

Joe grabbed his duffle bag from the overhead compartment, and deplaned with the others passengers. Nothing during the flight indicated that he had been followed, which was one reason that Mick had suggested Frankfurt as their entry to Paris, with Kaysersberg as a midway point between Paris and Frankfurt--facilitating the arrival of both teams within a few hours from each other.

The line of exiting passengers stopped, as a small child slowed in the Business Class section to retrieve the ear buds that were discarded by already deplaned passengers. They were probably worth less than a dollar each, but passengers were willing to pay upwards of five times that to bide the time watching movies or listening to the radio during the 12-hour flight. John wondered why anyone would pay this, considering that every human on earth owned a cellphone that came with free earbuds.

The child had apparently obtained his fill, with a visibly tangled ball of wires and buds dangling from both hands--which assumedly would take him an hour to unravel. The line resumed movement, past the waiting stewardesses and pilots, who repeated the "Baa-bye" mantra over and over, just as in the Seinfeld episode that revisited the same humorous tradition associated with deplaning an aircraft. It was interesting how decades old Seinfeld clips still corresponded to current events.

Joe continued down the square corridor towards Passport Control, reaching into his front pocket to assure it was still there. It was. He reached into his pocket and removed the thin rectangular black booklet, with the words "DIPLOMATIC PASSPORT" and the seal of the United States of America blazing across the front. As Joe was a long-time military employee, he was provided the Black Passport, vs. the standard issue blue passport for most U.S. civilians.

Joe successfully answered the few questions from the Passport Control Officer and proceeded towards the sky link train to transfer to Terminal 2. As if the airport wasn't difficult enough to navigate, knowing where to board and when to exit the Sky-link was another chore.

Direct signage was posted, but it did not do justice--nor did the German voice that incessantly repeated the exit instructions, or at least that was what Joe assumed was being repeated. Joe's trick when traveling overseas was to always look like you knew where you are going--even if you were completely lost, and people would assume the same.

The Sky Link slowed upon approach to Terminal 2, applying the brakes in a rather haphazardly inconsistent fashion, atypical for supposed German Engineering. Nevertheless, the train stopped exactly aligned with the outside door, which opened after a five second delay. All passengers exited, some slowing to first assess where they were, causing a minor traffic delay for those still exiting. Others, more familiar with these surroundings, patiently waited. Finally, Joe could extricate himself from the line, taking a deep breath once he was free and able to walk at his own pace.

Joe quickly traversed the corridor that led to escalators towards the entry to Terminal 2, continually scanning the crowd for any passengers who seemed to be more interested in him, more so than their next destination. Joe's training had sharpened this sense of self awareness, allowing him to identify such out of the ordinary activity. Ironically, it was the person that was most uninterested who many times was the target, versus the one staring straight at you. In this scenario where they are the hunter, it was almost written all over their faces.

Joe had taken note of each passenger and traveler that even remotely met these characteristics, from the moment he entered the airport, throughout the flight and to this point in his journey. So far, no one was fitting the part, which was comforting to Joe. He would intentionally pause to tie his shoes, delay to check his phone, or whatever it took to be the last person in the queue. His frequent check of the fEp, that he was still wearing, was extra insurance except that it was now running low on battery power. As a last resort, Joe had used the backward-facing camera to look behind at times when he feigned texting, just to be sure.

At this point, Joe was confident that he had not been followed. As he would not physically leave the confines of the airport, he now had to be aware of potential adversaries already in place ahead of him, hence the very visible meeting space at the sushi bar. Joe knew that Mick had entered the Terminal hours ago, and had scoped out the area, assuring all was in order prior to their impromptu meeting. Just as in Red's a few days ago, Mick would either visibly be at the sushi bar if all was in order, with a napkin on the table. No napkin meant that there was an issue, and to just pass by and await further contact via the fEP.

Joe passed the many duty-free shops common to International Terminals, where passengers wait for hours until they are summoned to their flights. Unlike the International terminals in the states, passengers in many of the larger foreign airports are not alerted of their gates until roughly an hour ahead of time, and are forced to wait aimlessly in the Terminals. Joe considered this a sales technique, as the only thing to do to pass the time until their gates are announced is shop, or eat. Once the gates show on the schedule board, there is a mad dash for the noted gate, which many times can be upwards of 30-minutes away. This would not be the plan for Joe and Mick, who would be renting a car for the 300 kilometer drive south to Kaysersberg. If they were to take the A35, they could arrive in less than three hours.

Joe entered the crowds wandering through the mall, the walls lined with shops named Monte Blanc, Benetton, Boggi Milano, TUMI, BOSS, Bvlgari, Omega and Swarovski, with the sushi bar located near the Starbucks, in the center of the massive room. Not surprisingly, there were very few customers interested in dining on sushi at such an early hour, with the exception of an elderly Asian couple and a brunette wearing jeans and a blue t-shirt. Joe circled the room one more time, scanning for any followers, before seating himself on a stool a few seats to the right of the couple and an equal number to the left of the brunette, neither of whom paid him the slightest attention; the couple still eating, and the brunette burying her face into a paperback book.

"What you want to eat?" the sushi chef asked, in broken English. "Good sashimi today, fresh," he added.

Fresh from where, thought Joe, not comforted by the thought of sushi for breakfast, or eating at an airport sushi bar.

"I'll have a California roll," noted Joe, as the safest choice that did not include raw anything other than processed crab meat.

"Ok--that all for you?" asked the chef.

"How about a bottled water—still," replied Joe.

"You mean no bubbly?" asked the chef.

"Correct, no bubbly. Still water," replied Joe with a smirk.

He watched as the chef created his roll, placing it in front of Joe within four minutes from his order. Two chopsticks and a teaspoon of wasabi were perched on the edge of the plate. Not Joe's preferred early morning staple.

To Joe's left, the Asian couple was readying their bags for their upcoming flight, as Joe assumed their gate had just been announced. When he looked to his right, the brunette stopped reading, took out a pen from her backpack, and wrote something on her napkin and slid it over to Joe.

The words, "What took you so long?" were visible across the top edge of the napkin. The brunette's face was again buried in her book.

John took a pen from the counter and wrote in reply, "I was dreading a breakfast of sushi. Couldn't stomach the thought, so I delayed," and slid it back.

The brunette turned towards Joe with a half-smile, saying in a hushed tone, "Good to see you too."

"Ditto, Mick," quietly replied Joe, continuing his gaze forward. "You ready to go?"

"Have been for an hour. Meet me in the Hertz rental car garage. I got a Land Rover". Then she grabbed her backpack and left, without ever granting Joe eye-to-eye contact.

Chapter 37

"I don't have time to explain, so stop delaying or trying to ask," snapped Jeanette. "Just get us into and out of the Catacombs and we can discuss this--just not right now."

"Ok--I can do that," replied John. "Where are we going?"

"You're not listening. Right now, into the Catacombs."

John and Jeanette quietly sprinted two steps at a time down the staircase, expecting to see a lookout at the bottom, but surprisingly there was none, which simplified their undetected escape from the apartment building. They slowed at the row of mailboxes, in efforts to detect a sentry at the front door. None was visible, but assuming that the individuals already in John's apartment arrived via car, their driver was most probably armed and waiting within view of the entry.

"No, can't chance it--is there a back door?" asked Jeanette.

"That would be the second place they would watch," noted John. "My guess is that they watched me exit for my run this morning."

"I suspect not, as they would have grabbed you then. Was there anything out of the ordinary about your run this morning?"

"Not that I am aware, although I have become comfortable in my daily routine so my Spiderman senses are rather dull."

"So there's a possibility that they may have followed you to the Cafe. I doubt that, as again, we have the element of surprise in that they don't know we're on to them."

"Who is this 'they' you keep referring to?" asked John.

"Joe is working on that," replied Jeanette.

"That's actually rather comforting to hear, considering the issues he's 'dealt' with in his career."

"As have I," added Jeanette. "You're in good hands, assuming we make it to the Catacombs. About that back door--where is it?"

"Follow me."

John backtracked past the mailboxes and passed to the left of the staircase, where the ground floor, zero-floor to be exact, apartments were located. After walking past two apartment doors, another door could be seen located at the far end of the hallway. It was seldom used, as it was dedicated as a fire escape in the event the front entry to the building was blocked. It also exited to a rather dark and sketchy alley, in which many interesting characters could be found. John made this discovery when he first moved to the apartment building, to include a stark realization that the door locked behind him when exiting. There was no doorknob on the outside, with an oddly placed trestle that was covered with by an overgrowth of vines. Once closed, the door was completely unidentifiable, which was perfect for their exit, as any bystander looking for a back door, would assume there was none. That is, if they only searched from the outside.

Jeanette opened the door just a crack to assess the situation, then kicked it wide open with her foot, the trestle on the back of the door making a metallic clang as it struck the opposing pieces of vine flying everywhere. Jeanette exited, gun first, sweeping the alley, which luckily was empty.

"Nothing like broadcasting that we're coming," noted John.

"Shock and awe, shock and awe," replied Jeanette. "Better to take the offensive and surprise them, than to be too cautious and take a bullet in the head."

"Now I know why Joe assigned you to this role. You are as aggressive as he is."

"More aggressive actually--he's a pussy cat."

"Yeah, ok, right," replied John. "So, crazy lady, just for your information, I can get us to the Catacombs from this alley, but we'll need to cross a few streets down and double back. You might want to holster your Sig once we get outside--you might attract attention."

"Roger," replied Jeanette, sounding just like Joe did the last time John and Joe were together.

John led Jeanette down the alley, which eventually led to the street almost directly across from the Catacombs. From their vantage point, there was no car with a sinister driver waiting out. Assumedly, they were dropped off and the driver was parked within direct view, which may become problematic.

John and Jeanette walked one block away from the alley, and mixed in with the crowds on the sidewalk in attempts to shield themselves. As they walked past the parked cars on the side of the road, none appeared to have anyone inside them with the sole exception of a black BMW parked 40 feet ahead, to their left.

"Do you see him?" Jeanette asked.

"I do, at 10 o'clock. Black BMW, one driver," replied John.

"That's the one. We don't have a choice but to pass him on the side in order to get to the Catacombs, which are only 100 feet past him."

"It might be nothing," commented John.

"Maybe. As we pass, I'll turn to see if he or she appears interested in us. From here, they are looking towards your apartment."

"Not a good sign," John added.

"Nope, but again, we have the offensive."

"You gonna shoot him?"

"Do you want me to shoot him?"

"No, I'm just being funny."

"I'm being funnier," quipped Jeanette.

"We're the perfect couple," noted John.

"That's what I was thinking," Jeanette replied, which brought a smile to her face. "Focus, John, focus."

As they approached, the driver remained motionless, continuing his gaze towards John's apartment. This was clearly not a good sign, but it validated that John and Jeanette had the offensive.

"We're about out of time," noted Jeanette, as they kept walking; the crowd now dispersed leaving them fully exposed.

"What does that mean?" asked John.

"In about 10 feet, we will be visible to the driver from the side view mirror. Apparently the driver isn't watching his rear view mirror, but will certainly catch motion in his right side mirror as we approach."

"Ok, and then what?" asked John.

"From that point, we run to the Catacombs. Got it?"

"Got it."

When they were within 10 feet of the parked car, Jeanette could see the driver's body in the side view mirror. After four more steps, she could see his torso, then two more, his face--his eyes were now clearly focused on them, and he immediately reached down for what Jeanette hoped was a cell phone and not a gun. She clutched her Sig just in case, as she and John took off running. In mid-stride, Jeanette looked back--the driver was still in the car, dialing his phone. Within seconds, he would exit the car and be only a few feet behind them.

"Don't stop. Don't look. Just get inside the Catacombs," Jeanette screamed.

John obeyed, and within 30 steps they were inside the entrance, after pushing past the early morning visitors, still sipping their morning coffee as they waited in line. The attendant at the counter, and the tour guide that John recognized from his frequent visits initially attempted to stop them, but seeing Jeanette's gun, decided it was a bad decision. They moved out of the way as oil spreads on the surface of water, providing a open pathway to the downward spiraling stairway.

"We'll need to slow down, or we'll break our legs going down the staircase," John advised Jeanette.

"What is our alternative?" asked Jeanette. "Can we slide down on our butts?"

"No--I'm going first. Just follow me and don't fall on top of me. We need to descend the stairs and pass completely through the entry tunnel before they arrive, else one ricocheting shot down the corridor will tag us."

Surprisingly, Jeanette had only visited the Catacombs once with John, so she was aware of the hazards and the benefits of the attraction. Once inside, she knew John would lead them through. One unknown was if their assailants knew where the exit was.

John entered the spiral staircase, and hugged the outside wall while placing his feet one after the other, sideways onto each narrow step. His hands pressed against the roof above. He looked up to see that Jeanette was having an easier time, most probably due to her smaller feet. Concentrating intently, they reached the bottom without incident. Then John stopped.

"Why are you stopping?" asked Jeanette.

"Let's listen to see if our friends are following," replied John. "The acoustics are excellent due to the stone walls. From here, we should be able to tell how many are pursuing us."

Within 20 seconds, a scuffle could be heard at the ground, with men's voices recognizable above the scuffle; what sounded like three men to be exact.

"Ok--that's enough delay. Let's go!" John whispered as he turned and began down the long corridor. Jeanette followed directly behind. No sounds could be heard from the stairway, indicating that they were still in the clear. It would only be a few more seconds before this was no longer the case, the long stone corridor providing an advantage for any shooter. They continued to semi-run in a crouched position, stumbling at times due to the uneven rock pathway, their hands raised to avoid scraping their heads on the uneven stone ceiling.

Via the discontinued light provided by the incandescent lamps secured to the roof of the tunnel, John and Jeanette could see the end of the tunnel only 30 feet away, after which the tunnel opened into the first cavern. The unexpected sound of the gunshot deafened them, masking the subsequent sound of the bullet ricocheting and tumbling through the tunnel, breaking the third to the last lightbulb on the ceiling.

Jeanette and John instinctively dropped to the floor, hugging the corners of the tunnel in hopes to avoid additional shots. At this point, the tunnel had taken a slight turn, so they were not visible to their assailants, who were literally firing blindly into the tunnel.

The sound must have been deafening adjacent to the shooter, which was clearly the case as there was a pause before additional shots were fired, with a clearly agitated voice discernible above the ringing in their ears. John and Jeanette continued to army crawl towards the opening, as two more shots flew over their heads.

"You ok?" John asked, trying to look back at Jeanette, but unable to see no more than a shadow still following close behind.

"Yes, no damage, but just a little pissed off," replied Jeanette in a hushed voice. "Keep moving--almost there."

Within 20 additional steps, John and Jeanette reached the end of the tunnel, taking a sharp turn to the left to avoid further direct hits. They stood next to each other, both looking at their scratched up hands.

"Where is your Sig?" John asked.

"Back pocket."

"I suggest that you shoot them now," noted John, still panting from the recent maneuvers.

"No, never shoot unless you have a target in sight. We may need the entire clip in a few minutes."

"I'm not arguing."

"Then don't," replied Jeanette, "just pick a tunnel and get us out."

At that point, another gun shot was heard, but coming from the opposite side of the cavern.

"Was that an echo, or did that shot come from the tunnel to the left?" Jeanette asked.

Just as John replied, "We're boxed in, if so," another shot came from the leftmost tunnel.

"That would be a positive. I assume they came through the exit, or were already in the Catacombs, which would be highly improbable."

"But possible," noted John. "Come with me, as I know how we might still get out in one piece."

John led Jeanette into the middle tunnel, and around a gate meant to prevent access to the general public. Behind this gate, as was typical of much of the Catacombs, was another path that reconnected into the Sanctuary Cavern in the middle of the maze that comprised the Catacombs. These tunnels used to be available to the public, but were discontinued since visitors would become infinitely lost, circling the tunnels looking for a way out. John had purposefully educated himself in these paths, more so out of curiosity, than strategy.

"John, these tunnels are completely dark. Any idea where we're going?"

"Yes. Place your hand on my back, stop talking and follow me. We can only hope that they do not have night vision goggles, otherwise we're toast."

John led Jeanette down the dark tunnel, moving surprisingly fast along its length. Luckily these tunnels were almost seven feet high, else it would have slowed their movement down significantly, in addition to a thoroughly scratched and scraped head.

Voices and movement could be heard echoing from all directions, from the assailants closing in from both sides.

"Do you think they know where we are?" Jeanette whispered as she continued to hold onto John's belt from behind.

"I doubt it, as this tunnel is not on any maps that you can find on the Internet. I assume they are simply following their tunnel, hoping to box us in. The fact that they stopped shooting indicates they cannot see us, or their partners."

At this point, beams of light could be seen from behind them, flickering back and forth in search mode.

"Not good. They are either in the tunnel with us, or directly next to us," whispered John. "We're at a point where we may need to stop and hide, as at some point, one of them will intersect at our location. We can assume they've split up by now, which puts us in a bind."

"Ok--what are our options?" asked Jeanette.

"We actually have quite a few, if you don't mind covering yourself up with thousands of years of bones."

"At this point, I don't care," replied Jeanette.

"There are plans to open an additional 200 yards of tunnels, directly to our left. Piles of bones have been collected and stored in piles amongst the trails, for eventual stacking and shellacking, to match the decor of the established tunnels. We could bury ourselves up to our eyeballs very easily, with the piles currently stored there. It won't taste good, but we'll be almost completely hidden as long as we can stand it."

"I'll keep my mouth closed," suggested Jeanette.

"It's our only option."

In the dark, it seemed that John took a left off the current tunnel, passing through another wrought iron gate that creaked ever so slightly when moved.

"One concern is that we're heading into a dead end, no pun intended. Once the coast is clear, we'll need to re-trace our steps to get to this tunnel, and eventually exit."

"We'll make do. Get us the pile, and start digging."

John led Jeanette approximately 30 yards down the tunnel, and stopped.

"We're here," he said. "Reach downwards, to our left, and you'll feel the bones piled up against the wall. All in all, they are about 10 feet deep, with the femurs and skulls mostly located to the right side. Smaller parts to the left. Our best bet is to dive into the smaller parts, as far as we can go, then pull the heavier bones on top of us."

"You go first, since I have the gun."

As John pushed his body into the pile, feet and legs first, Jeanette could hear his progression, accompanied by a crunching sound similar to walking into a pile of sticks and leaves. These sounds continued as John entered further into the pile, with some of the larger skulls now falling to the ground and audibly bouncing. Those that didn't bounce, assumedly broke. In the dark, the sounds continued, soon followed by a very dry dusty odor that seemed to permeate Jeanette's nose and mouth, with a most unappealing taste.

"So far so good," replied John. "All I want to do is sneeze. I'm up to my chest in this mess, and will need your help to cover me up. Back yourself into the same path that I made, and come to my left, so you can reach the bigger bones to my left."

Silence.

"Ok, Jeanette?" John asked.

"Um, yes. I'm ok. Knowing that many of these people died of plagues and other epidemics, are we going to be infected?"

"I would assume that the pathogens are long gone, but if we don't ingest this stuff, we should be ok."

"That's not very reassuring, as I feel as if I've already got a mouthful."

"Just think of this as a pirate horror movie. Didn't you always want to be a pirate?"

"No, not so much. Pirates were pretty low on aspiration list," replied Jeanette, trying to gain her courage to begin digging her hands into the pile to cover up John.

"Just be glad that it's dark," noted John. "It's pretty gruesome when illuminated."

"You're not helping."

"I'm being serious," replied John. "Hurry up and start digging. I'm not sure how much more time we'll have."

Jeanette reached into the darkness to the right of John's voice, her hands almost immediately touching the remnants of previous ancestors. It was almost like being in a haunted house, with bones and cobwebs strewn everywhere, except in this case, these were not props. She repetitively piled each piece towards John's voice, eventually reaching the level that she assumed covered him to head's depth.

"Ouch, that would be my eye," reported John from the darkness.

"Sorry, why didn't you bring me a SCCENIC to wear? I could have been much more caring in my work of covering you with dead people."

"I'm sure, and to be frank, I have my second unit securely hidden near the exit stair."

"Oh, really? That's great, except that we may never get there."

"Be positive. I know this place like the back of my hand. Start walking backwards into the pile next to me, start covering, then crouch down into the pile to hide yourself. I'll shift some of my pile on top of you."

"This is nuts, but ok," noted Jeanette, as she turned and began wiggling herself into the pile.

Lights could be seen from both sides of the tunnel that connected perpendicularly to the one they were in.

"No more chitchat," noted Joe.

It surprised Jeanette how quickly she was able to conceal herself in the pile, as the bone fragments would fall directly in front of her as she backed adjacent to Joe. Once she stopped moving, she could feel Joe shifting to one side, immediately followed by the feeling of light sticks quickly shifting around her head. Dust, or at least that's what Jeanette forced herself to think, encroached every orifice on her head, so she held her breath to limit the entry, eventually breathing out of her mouth to lessen the temptation to sneeze. Her head was now fully covered, and hopefully fully indiscernible by a quick swipe of light from a flashlight.

John stopped moving completely, mere seconds before light entered their tunnel. Jeanette did not have direct view from beneath the bone fragments, but the flashlight beam was easily visible as it bounced between the bones blocking her direct line of sight.

The lights became brighter--the voices increasing louder, as an unknown number of men entered the tunnel. They were speaking a language unfamiliar to Jeannette, but Arabic in origin. Four different tones were evident, which assumedly correlated to four individuals. They must have been no more than a few feet from their hiding place, as heavy breathing could now be detected, in between uninterpretable conversation.

At this point, they stopped, one of the men sneezing two times in succession. Jeanette slowed her mouth breathing, to avoid any further shifting of bones, and hopefully her blood pressure.

John was in a similar state, controlling his breathing also through his mouth. He too could detect the light flashes in between the bones that covered his face. Due to his tours in Palestine and Iraq, he could also detect the Israeli dialect, and was able to catch the gist of their conversation.

The first man who had just sneezed, was noting how dusty the Catacombs were, stating that he needed some fresh air. Comments from another man mentioned that the taste and smell was nauseating. If only they knew, thought John.

One man began to mention the higher amount of dust in this particular tunnel, an issue which John considered as they were shifting into the pile. He could imagine that the dust was very heavy due to their actions, much more so than any of the other tunnels. If the men were science-minded, they would be quickly aware that the increased dust was no accident. Joe suspected that they were not, as the run-of-the-mill assassin was typically not the sharpest knife in the drawer, or at least he hoped not.

The men remained in the tunnel, mostly talking about how this attraction was the one of the oddest they had seen. Another began to sneeze, followed by a raspy cough. It was a different sneeze than the first sneeze heard.

John could detect conversation shifting to the topic of eyes, with one man commenting that his eyes were burning. These unexpected ill effects might just work in their favor, with all men beginning to comment on same. Another, or the same man, coughing.

The last clearly detectable word was clearly "Kaysersberg," to the complete surprise of John. All men quieted, as one individual instructed the others that their immediate orders had changed, with Kaysersberg as their next destination.

Jeanette heard the same mention of "Kaysersberg" at the same instant that John did. This either meant that Joe had been located, or was already in their control. Either way, it was not a good sign, and made Jeanette wonder how this could have so quickly become apparent.

The men, with their new orders began to direct their flashlights away from John's and Jeanette's location, as they turned to exit the tunnel. It wasn't until the flashlight beams were imperceptible that John and Jeanette took a breath from their noses. Jeanette shifting to her left leg, as it began to fall asleep in the position she had assumed. She could feel John moving slightly as well, and was the first to break the silence.

"Did you get that?" he asked.

"Other than the word 'Kaysersberg,' no, I could not understand them," Jeanette replied.

"They were Israeli. I could only pick out a few words, but their plans have been changed and they are on their way to Kaysersberg."

"How could they know, I mean we only received Joe's email 30 minutes ago," queried Jeanette.

"True, but we also were well within their detection range, and they could have very easily been scanning all cellphones in the area. Our SCCENIC could have done the same, if we had narrowed the reception range down to 100 feet. We would have had to sift through thousands of texts, which I assume they did."

"But would four letters give that away?"

"Apparently, yes. They clearly couldn't locate us, but the four letters of KAYS were descriptive enough to tip them off. We need to get above ground to inform Joe that we're not coming, and establish another text that is less meaningful, considering that your phone may also be tagged as a source. Where is it, by the way?"

"I removed the battery and dropped it down the sewer when we exited the alley behind your apartment."

"That was good thinking. And the SIM card?" John asked, referring to the card that stored pertinent information such as contacts, saved phone numbers, etc. on every cell phone.

"Got it right here," replied Jeanette.

"Good girl. We'll need to wait a few more minutes to assure no stragglers remained behind, but we need to get above ground as soon as possible, and beforehand, pick up the other SCCENIC near the exit."

John and Jeanette stood motionless without talking for what seemed like an eternity. They both assumed that one or more of the men probably remained in the Catacombs, in the event they were to surface. Oddly enough, if Joe was the target, why would they have been so focused on heading to Kaysersberg, to chase who they thought was John? Was their clever cover somehow compromised by a single four-letter text, or had something else tipped them off? No matter the explanation, they needed to get above ground as soon as possible, else Joe would be a sitting duck.

Chapter **38**

The rental car garage in the Frankfurt Airport was nothing less than gargantuan, housing over 2,000 cars, as one of the largest in the world, second only to Heathrow. Understandably, locating your assigned car in the cavern was no easy feat. Joe had been to this edifice many times yet always experienced difficulty in finding his car--this time was no exception.

Each rental car company had its own section in the garage, with cars located in numbered spaces in each section--no surprise for a German-engineered process. The problem that Joe had run into is that after the lengthy walk to the section, his numbered space would be empty, requiring a return trek to the counter, to discuss the issue with the attendant, who fully believed they were infallible. Never a fun process when you're exhausted and ready to get to your hotel after a 12-hour flight. Hopefully this would not be the case today.

Joe and Mick proceeded from the secure confine of the airport and headed to the car rental counter, with the bright green Hertz logo. The German attendant began to speak in German, which was always a compliment to those traveling in that they dressed themselves appropriately, to appear as a local. Within seconds of Joe's lack of response, and five seconds later after the male attendant had looked Mick's shapely body up and down, he replied in English.

"Name?" he asked, turning his gaze back to Joe.

Mick replied, "Lambleau," semi-surprising the attendant, who was pleased to be given the opportunity to look back at Mick, without upsetting his male customer.

"OK, I see that. You have our second best car, a Range Rover four-wheel drive."

"What is the first best?" asked Joe.

"Mercedes, of course. German engineering," he replied with smug look.

"Oh, of course," replied Joe. "But do you have an SUV, because we need the room?"

"No; no German SUVs here, but I could have gotten you one if you had asked."

"I just asked," replied Joe, being the smart-ass he was.

"I mean, if you had asked before now," externally controlling his emotions, but not so much on the inside.

"That's fine," interrupted Mick. "We'll take the Range Rover," as she looked at Joe in disbelief that he was randomly causing a raucous with the attendant.

"Do you need a GPS?" asked the attendant, intentionally avoiding eye contact with Joe.

Joe commented before Mick could reply, "No, I have my iPhone. A non-German invention that will save me the 20-Euro per day fee, for your antiquated German GPS innovation."

The attendant continued to look down, wanting this to be over.

"OK, no navigation."

He punched a few keys on his keyboard, reached behind him for the keys, tucked them into the rental agreement, and handed the envelope to Mick, that had 'parking space 42E' emblazed on the front in large block print.

He turned to Mick and said, "Your friend is the sole driver. If you want to drive, then you must pay me an additional 50-Euro per day."

"No, first of all, I would pay Hertz, and second, when I am out of your sight I can drive all day long and you will never know."

"Um, yes, I guess you can," noted the attendant. "Is there anything else I can help you with, Madame?" looking back to Mick.

Mick smiled, looked at Joe, and then back to the attendant, "No, all is good," and turned and walked away from both testosterone fueled humans, still staring each other down.

Mick stopped about 10 feet later, and said, "Coming Dear?"

"Yup, right behind you," replied Joe.

They took the elevator to lowest floor, which was in itself four stories below ground, and began the walk to the Hertz level and their Range Rover

"Why do you do that?" asked Mick, staring at Joe with her head at an angle as she waited for his reply.

"What, that? He was cocky. I don't like cocky."

"You just don't like people in general," replied Mick. "If our car is not down here, I will go back to the counter, and you stay down here."

"I don't like cocky," Joe repeated.

"I heard you the first time. Do you think that you can change them? Is that why you do that?"

"No, I just like to put folks in their place."

"That's sweet. You realize that this may be the underlying cause for your bad experiences whenever you travel to Europe."

"You think?" Joe smirked. "I was just having fun, to see if I could get a rise out of the guy."

"Consider that one a success, 'Mr. I Hate Cocky,'" replied Mick. "Personally, I think it's a man thing."

"How's that?"

"Because when a woman is around, men get their feathers all ruffled trying to show who the alpha dog is."

"So now you are comparing me to a dog?" asked Joe, with an over emphasized dog-like tilted slant of the head.

"Can we change the subject?" asked Mick,

"Wow--where's your sense of humor," said Joe.

"I left it at the rental car desk."

"Ok. Got it. So what's the plan?"

"Drive to Kaysersberg, meet John and Jeannette, and then disappear."

"I'll drive," said Joe, with a smirk. "Did you get the attendant's number?"

"And why would I have done that?" asked Jeannette.

"So I could text him a picture of 'me' driving, just to get a rise out of him, of course."

"This is me not listening to you," Mick replied indignantly, as she turned away and walked ahead of Joe to the shiny grey Land Rover, now within sight in Hertz parking spot 42E.

The driver and passenger doors were unlocked. Both Joe and Jeannette raised the handles on the respective sides, swung the doors open and lifted themselves up into the Land Rover, grabbing the handles that were located inside the door panel to do so. They nestled into their respective seats, which enveloped them like the massage chairs commonly seen in the showroom of the Brookstone Company.

"Nice seats," noted Joe.

"Still not listening," replied Mick.

"Roger that," noted Joe. "Should make for a quiet ride--until you need to go to the bathroom."

"Shut-up and drive," replied Mick.

Joe placed his foot on the brake and started the car with a push of a recessed button labeled "Start," to the right side of the steering wheel, and replied, "Driving."

Chapter 39

Just from the few words that were spoken, John and Jeanette knew that the game had immediately changed. Something had tipped off their assailants that Kaysersberg was a destination of interest, and were most probably on their way there now. This completely changed the plan of approach, with an alternative rendezvous, point needed, and a secondary and more pressing issue of how to communicate same to Joe and Mick, who were most probably en route, that moment. Nevertheless, the first need was to extricate themselves from underneath the piles of bones, and exit the Catacombs.

After an additional ten minutes in silence, John could feel Jeanette shifting in her crouched position.

"Time to get out of here," she whispered, "We'll have to chance that there is at least one of their agents still down here, so we'll need to proceed carefully."

"I know a direct and unmarked passage to the exit. Consider though that there is only one exit, with a spiral rock staircase similar to the entry," noted John.

"We'll need to take our chances," replied Jeanette, "unless you have another idea."

"I looked for alternative exits, such as one that could allow exit from visitors in the event of an emergency. The only other options are complete dead-ends, no pun intended."

"Ok, let's stay close then. I'll lead," replied Jeanette.

John and Jeanette slowly twisted themselves from the dried bone pile, accompanied by the low pitched clinks as the falling clavicles and femurs collided. Within minutes, they were free, both fighting back the urge to sneeze due to the overwhelming particle count that was now floating in the air of the passage they had chosen. With John's hand on Jeanette's shoulder they slowly crept along the left wall of the tunnel, listening for any sounds or apparent movement within the tunnel. At the end of each passage, they would stop, with John silently tapping Jeannette's shoulder to indicate the direction to take that would eventually lead to the exit.

After what seemed like an eternity, a dimly lit passage lay ahead of them, with a grey, or possibly white-colored arrow painted on the wall at eye-level, indicating the 'EXIT' ahead. In the distance, a light could be seen that led to the winding stone staircase that lead to the street above.

Within 75 steps, they had reached the base of the stairs.

"OK, that was easy," noted John. In the dim light, he could detect the ashen color of Jeanette's face, and whole torso, as a remnant of their previous cover. "You look dirty," he whispered to Jeanette.

"Thanks genius," she replied. "We'll be quite a sight once we get to the surface, just like the living dead."

"I was just thinking the same, so--what are our options? We do not have time for a shower or a change of clothes."

"Let's take one thing at a time. First we get out, then we work on our appearance."

"OK--right behind you. Watch your head on the way up. I have hit my head many a time on the underside of the stairs, as it's significantly shorter than the entry stair."

"Will do. Keep listening for our friends on the way up. I still have my Glock, if we run into issues," replied Jeanette.

John counted each of the 135 steps on the ascent towards the Catacomb exit, pausing along the way to assure his footing on the very thin ledges that made up the winding staircase.

After a 15 minute period, John and Jeanette reached the ground surface, which led to a white door, with a brass handle and a large sign with black lettering stating "Sortie / EXIT." What was on the other side of the door, was a complete unknown, and could very possibly be a quick ending to their escape plan. Noting the urgency of the conversation overheard while deep in the Catacombs, there was a glimmer of hope that the entire team had departed.

Jeanette drew her Glock from within her belt, pulling back the handle to allow a single round to enter the chamber.

"Ready?" she asked.

"Yes," replied John.

Jeanette reached down and grabbed the door handle, turned it slowly counterclockwise, and pushed the door open just a sliver. No sounds were detected, from either the door or anything on the other side.

As their eyes adjusted from the darkness of the Catacombs, it was clear that there was no visible threat awaiting them outside of the Catacombs exit on Rue Remy-Dumoncel, which to the surprise of most visitors was located 10 city blocks away from the entrance.

On the streets, numerous local residents could be seen walking their dogs, and minding their own business.

They had no obvious interest in two would-be tourists exiting from the well-known attraction--an occurrence that happened every five minutes, from 11 am to 5 pm, Tuesday through Sunday.

Both John and Jeanette were surprised that the exit was clear. They walked calmly from the nondescript white exit door, continually looking over their shoulders for adversaries. They circled the block, watching the exit from a distance to assess any overly interested parties. There were none.

The nearest metro was approximately a half mile from the Catacombs exit, which was another surprise for visiting tourists. Taking a right from the exit, they turned left towards Metro Alesia, instead of a right towards Mouton-Duvernet, which was closer to John's apartment, which was a destination they were now unable to to return to.

The couple remained silent until they were seated in the silver commuter car, when John spoke.

"Where to now?"

"Not Kaysersberg," noted Jeannette. "By their conversation, that is their next destination. I can only assume our text was intercepted."

"Now we need to alert Joe and Mick," noted John.

"Yes, but that may be problematic, as the second they receive our text, our friends could triangulate their location."

"Possibly, but better to have a warning, than send them blindly into a firefight."

The metro slowed as it approached the next stop. John and Jeanette's senses peaked, expecting that any new rider could be searching for them. Jeannette silently motioned her head towards the door, indicating that it was time to depart. They stood simultaneously, and moved towards the still sealed doors, reaching for the looped plastic handles that hung from the car ceiling as they walked.

They waited adjacent to the door without saying a word, standing slightly behind a young woman with a small leashed dog, until the car came to a complete stop. The dog was clearly a regular on these trips, as he appeared completely disinterested in the goings-on that surrounded him or her.

The car doors opened, and John and Jeanette slid out, almost stepping on the dog as they focused on the eyes of the row of customers waiting to board. They blended into the other departing passengers and mixed into the crowd as it funneled towards the exit, or Sortie, identified by a white figure walking toward a white rectangle. They continued through the exit tunnels toward stairs that would eventually return them to the surface. Upon reaching the street, they slowed their pace, John speaking first.

"Do you see something?"

"No, but I couldn't guarantee that one of our friends was already on the metro with us; not fun to get boxed in. Plus, if one of them noticed us, it would have been a matter of time before a call could be made to intercept us at a later stop. At least this way, the next stop didn't provide enough time for them to notify and gather."

"Ok--makes sense. So it's time for us to notify Joe and Mick, right?" asked Joe.

"Yes, I've been thinking of our best approach. We need a throwaway phone though."

"Good plan," responded John. "Any of these street shops will suffice," as he pointed to a storefront that had a red strobe light in the front window, yielding hand-written signs. John and Jeanette crossed the street and entered the shop, wincing as they passed the blinding flashing strobe. The lights inside the store were almost as brilliant, and equally annoying.

"I might get an aneurism in this place," smirked John. "I'll never understand the curb appeal of such a display. Plus it has nothing to do with what they sell."

"But it worked," answered Jeanette. "We're here, aren't we?"

"Oddly enough, you're right."

"Are you saying it's odd that I'm right?" asked Jeanette.

"No, odd that the dazzling display was an effective attraction," replied John. "You can be right every now and then."

"Thanks for that. Now choose a phone and let's get out of here."

Directly to the left of the entry was a display of phones, some with talk and data contracts, and others that could be paid month-to-month or via the purchase of more minutes.

"Get the cheap blue one, to your right. We only need enough time to send a quick text. Then we throw it away."

John saw the one Jeanette suggested, reached out and loosened it from the metal post to which it was attached. It was a pay-as-you-go unit, which could be loaded with minutes by the cashier at the front of the store.

"So what code do you suggest, as apparently our friends are craftier than expected," noted John.

"First, we need to alert them to divert from Kaysersberg, and direct them to our next destination."

"Which is exactly where?"

The cashier asked, "How many minutes do you want to load?"

"100 please," replied Jeanette, which seemed excessive to John, for just one text.

The cashier nodded his head in agreement, and began processing the minutes, for pre-load into the phone. The process couldn't have taken more than 60 seconds, as he connected the phone into a cord connected to his computer.

"How would you like to pay?" asked the cashier. "We take credit as well as cash. If you use credit, I can set up an auto refresh of your minutes, and have it charged to your card. That way you won't lose service in the middle of a call, such as would occur if you pay with cash."

"Let's go the cash route, please," replied Jeanette. "I don't like to spend money that we don't already have."

"Cash it is, then. The total will be 50 Euro, which includes the phone, activation and the 100 minutes."

"Texting is included?" asked John,

"Yes. 100 minutes includes 150 texts, for no additional cost. The 150 is divided between texts received and texts sent, just to be clear."

"OK. Makes sense." replied John.

John paid the bill with a single 50 Euro note, took the phone presented to them, and he and Jeanette left the store. Once outside, they continued their discussion as they walked away from the store.

"So what key word can we text to alert Joe and Mick, which will not tip off our foes."

"We also need to define a location for us to rendezvous," Jeanette added. "We need to stay one step ahead of the Massad, which at this point is questionable."

"Ok, one option that comes to mind is the train station in Basel, or the Schweizerische Bundesbahnen in German. Since the SBB is the national railway company of Switzerland, they will know that our destination is somewhere in Switzerland, but not the exact station."

"Except that the Basel SBB is the closest station to our current location."

"True, but the station is the size of a small airport, and is well known to all of us. The Basel Hilton is also located right across the tracks, and is one of our common stopping points."

"So, how about police codes, with a destination?"

"Like 10-19, SBB?"

"What's 10-19?"

"Return to, and then list SBB."

"The Massad would figure that out too," noted John.

"Assuming they are still monitoring the texts, and if they are, they should be delayed, we can add, 'Floor 9,'" explained Jeanette.

"Yes, I am assuming you're referring to the unadvertised 9th floor of the neighboring Basel Hilton Hotel, which is not advertised, and is only accessible via stairs from the 8th floor."

"True--there is not even a 9th floor button in the elevator. Will Joe understand?"

"Absolutely, as will Mick."

"Ok--that works. So we'll text '10-19, SBB, 9th floor,'" restated John.

"Yes, let's do it now," stated Jeanette.

"Ok," replied John, and entered the text message into the new phone, and pressed "Send."

"Sent. Now let's get to the airport. We'll probably arrive in Basel a few hours behind Joe and Mick, assuming they receive the text message in time."

"Let's hope so."

Chapter 40

Joe had been driving for about two hours after leaving the Frankfurt airport, when the first sign for Kaysersberg appeared, indicating that it was 30 kilometers away. Driving distances were deceiving in France, due to the many small towns with 15 kilometer per hour speed limits, and the ease of getting off the beaten path. Joe could remember numerous times when he had unknowingly taken an incorrect road, and ended up in a quaint but historic town reminiscent of World War II movies the he had seen when he was a child. Amazingly enough, the towns looked exactly as they did almost one-half decade ago, with many residents still living in the town, which in itself made for fascinating discussion when visiting the local pubs.

In the distance, other artifacts of the war could be seen, as large rock edifices dotted the now farming landscape, once French strongholds against the attacking German army. Joe was imagining what this now peaceful view must have been like during that time, when Mick interrupted him.

"Le Chambard, I assume, off the Rue du Général de Gaulle?"

"Yes, that's the one," replied Joe. "I've always enjoyed that hotel, and their restaurant, La Gastronomique. We'll arrive well before John and Jeanette, so let's get our rooms and take a walk to the castle."

Kaysersberg Castle was one of many castles that could be seen across the Alsace Valley, and was the name behind the town. The castle was an impressive structure, located amongst the vineyards that overlooked the town. It was never impacted by the war, and had been well preserved and cared for by the local town.

"So, what is the plan?" asked Mick, "I mean, after our hike."

"At best, we wait until John and Jeanette arrive, and then stay ahead of the Massad."

"At best, yes, but what if we have already lagged behind?"

"Always the pessimist, aren't you," replied Joe.

"I instead prefer to be labeled as a Realist, versus a pessimist."

"OK, Ms. Realist, what are your thoughts?"

"How will we know if we're ahead?"

"You already asked that," noted Joe. "If they don't show within six hours, we'll have an idea. They should be flying into Basel-Mulhouse within the next three to four hours. After a 45 minute drive, we can expect to gain contact."

"Do they have the SCENNIC?" asked Mick.

"I would assume not, as remember that we've not seen or heard from them for almost five years. I certainly didn't send one, so I'm not sure how it could have been sent."

"True," answered Mick. "So, we know that they received the KAYS text, due to the receipt signal we received, but since then, it's been radio silence. This concerns me."

"As does me, but John is smart enough to know that text messages and calls can be easily intercepted, so I can only assume he's playing it safe. He's much smarter than both of us combined."

"No argument there," replied Mick. "By the way, did he ever figure out that I was a woman?"

"Was? Is there something you need to tell me?"

"No, I mean 'am.'"

"Oh, yes, and I do not think so. When you first met him in that wooden shed on the lake, I called you Brenda. My guess is that he would never put two-and-two together, or that we were using voice transformation on the SCENNIC."

"He knows that SCENNIC has that capability, though."

"One of many capabilities. John did only have exposure to the prototype. The current unit is 10 versions past that. I guess that it wouldn't have ever passed his mind."

"OK--that should make it interesting when we see them later this evening, especially since Jeanette's been in the know since we brought her into the picture as a flight attendant on John's initial fight to Paris."

"Yes, she's been doing a great job. I'm confident that John is still alive, due to her extensive training and day-to-day oversight."

"She's a keeper," replied Mick. "This may sound like a woman thing, but do you think that John feels duped, as he is now well aware that she's been his handler for the past five years, and one of your colleagues. I mean, what if he really fell for her."

"From what I've heard, it's mutual, so no harm, no foul. Plus, at this point, having a hot body guard is not a bad thing."

"I guess," replied Mick. "Pretty impressive planning on your part."

"It has worked out well, thus far. We're not out of the woods yet."

The entry to Kaysersberg neared in the distance, with a small brick sign alerting them of their arrival. After a number of turns and small hills, the road thinned and turned to cobblestone. Within 100 feet, Le Chambard was to their left. Joe pulled into a small portico to the left of the hotel, and parked the Land Rover under a small cover area adjacent to the entry to the check-in desk. A bellman came to Mick's door first, opening it, coincident to a second bellman circling towards Joe's door.

"Checking in?" asked the bellman.

"Yes," replied Joe. "I am here with my wife for a relaxing weekend of hiking in the Alsace Valley."

"Fabulous. The weather should be perfect this week. No rain, with temperatures around 20C," replied the bellman. "Shall I park your car?"

"No, thank you. I know where to go."

"Very good. Please feel free to leave your car here while you check in, and let me know if you need assistance with your bags or advice on hiking trails. My name is Etienne, and I am the concierge, as well."

"Will do," replied Joe.

Joe and Mick exited the vehicle and walked into the entry door on the left that led to the front desk. A young brunette woman was standing behind a waist high desk that included an ornate flower arrangement to the left. She looked up when Joe and Mick entered, giving an extended up-and-down stare to Mick, as was the norm when she entered a room.

"Welcome to Le Chambard. What name is on your reservation?" she asked.

"Petit. Jean and Michaela Petit."

"Is this your first visit to Kaysersberg?" asked the woman, unable to keep her eyes off Joe, and ignoring Mick as if she was not present.

"No, we've been here a number of times, and look forward to another wonderful stay."

"I welcome you back, Monsieur Petit, and offer you my personal assistance for any matter that arises. Here is the key to your room on the second floor, overlooking the vineyards that line the hills below Kaysersberg Castle."

The woman continued to lock eyes with Joe, and slowly extended her hand holding the key to Joe. In an unexpected move, Mick quickly reached her hand out and took the key from the woman, before Joe knew what was happening.

"Thank you so much," Mick replied and turning towards Joe said, "Let's go Sweetie," and gave a scowl at the young woman as she turned towards the staircase that led to the second floor.

The woman at the front desk reacted similarly, acting as if she didn't care. Joe followed behind Mick, not wanted to get in the middle of the cat fight.

"And you say I was being obnoxious to the guy at the rental car place. What was that all about?"

"Men are so oblivious, but she was coming on to you."

"Um, and what's wrong with that? It's not every day that I have a young French woman after me."

"And in front of your wife, Mrs. Petit? This isn't ladies night you know. You're forgetting that we're married and must play the part."

"Oh, yeah. Then there's that," replied Joe. "I forgot."

"OK--let's get serious here. I'm still not comfortable with all going on here. We're still not out of the woods and until I see John and Jeanette in person, I'll remain on alert."

"Agreed."

Joe and Mick continued to the room, using the metal key to open the door to Room 206. The room was larger than the European norm, with a King sized bed in the center of the room, a reasonably sized flat-screen television on a table in the corner and the large bathroom to the left. The windows of both rooms were fully open, the curtains bellowing inward from the wind, overlooking the beautiful countryside covered in vineyards.

"Incredible view, as usual," noted Jeanette. "It's a shame we're not staying this evening."

"True, but at least you won't keep me up snoring."

"This is me pretending I can't hear you. Let's take that walk you mentioned."

Joe smiled, and threw their luggage onto the bed, keeping the car keys in his hand.

"I'll meet you at the edge of the path that passes through the vineyards, as I need to move the car from outside the front lobby."

"Oh--I forgot about the car. Yes, I'll see you there."

Joe and Mick exited the room, closed the door behind them, and took opposite directions down the hallway. Joe reached the front desk, and intentionally did not connect the gaze of the woman at the front desk, and passed through the exit to the Land Rover. He slid behind the wheel, started the car, and drove it to the far back corner of the parking lot located behind the hotel. As he exited the SUV, he could see Mick crossing the parking lot from the rear exit of the hotel, directly below their room, where he could see the curtains still bellowing into the room.

"You ready?" Joe asked as Mick approached.

"Yup," replied Mick. "This town is one of the prettiest in all of Europe, especially from the top of the castle."

Joe and Mick began their trek, starting at the base of the dirt path at the parking lot, and quickly wound their way through the vineyards that surrounded the castle located at the top of the hillside. With each step, the couple gained altitude revealing the stoic town beneath them. Within a quarter mile, they had reached the base of Kaysersberg Castle, providing a brilliant view of the town below. They turned and stood at the entrance to the castle.

"Spectacular," Joe noted, as he and Mick gazed at the rooftops below.

"Yes it is, Mr. Stone," a man's voice unexpectedly replied from the shadows of the door of the castle. Joe and Mick turned as the same man from the limousine that picked up Joe just two days earlier, stepped from inside the door. Behind him were two of his henchmen, each sporting a .22 LRS, pointed directly at Joe and Mick, respectively.

Chapter **41**

John and Jeanette arrived at Charles de Gaulle, after a quick trip to a clothing store to purchase and change into new clothing to replace the centuries-old crushed bone attire they generated in the Catacombs. Luckily there was a store adjacent to the metro station, two blocks from the exit of the Catacombs, so they did not have to venture far to do so, or ride the metro in that condition.

Charles de Gaulle was crowded as usual, with the typical business travelers intermixed with hordes of tourists, visibly sleepy from their cross continental flights. John was slightly nervous about airline travel and having to use his passport, considering his experiences entering into Paris just five years ago. Jeanette reminded John that inter-European customs and passport control are much less intense, and that he had nothing to worry about. In addition, the Basel-Mulhouse airport was still in the country of France, and they would intentionally exit the Mulhouse (France) side of the airport, and drive across the border to Switzerland.

The ticket counter was not crowded, as most if not all current day travelers arrive with tickets in hand. As not to attract attention, John and Jeanette acted as if they had last second plans, and chose to fly instead of drive. They approached the woman seated behind the counter and John stated:

"Hello. My friend and I were going to drive to St. Aubin, Switzerland, but are now considering a flight instead. What is the closest airport to St. Aubin that has a direct flight from Charles de Gaulle?"

"You have a few options, but I suggest flying into Basel-Mulhouse, which is located on the France and Switzerland border. It's the cheapest flight and available every few hours. In fact, the next flight leaves in one hour. Are you interested in a round trip, or one-way?"

"Round trip please, and yes, the flight in one hour works well," replied John.

"OK, that will be 70 Euro please. What name will that be under?"

"Jean Pascal and Jeanette Thomas," John replied, as he reached out to pay with a 100 and a 40 Euro note.

"Very good. This will work well."

"Passports, please," asked the woman behind the counter.

John's heart rate began to rise, even though he knew this was a formality, but the fact that he was about to be brought back onto the grid made him nervous. Even though he had a fake name, it was still disconcerting after being off any lists for so long.

John and Jeanette plunked their passports onto the counter. The woman reached for them, opening each and placing them flat on the counter top in front of her. She scanned each with a barcode reader of some type and then under an ultraviolet light, that John assumed enabled visibility to an identifying symbol that hoped his fake passport had.

The attendant looked up at John, and asked, "Do you travel, as your passport has not been stamped in 5 years?"

"I do enjoy travel, but very seldom do I fly as it scares me. Driving is certainly my preference."

"Well you have nothing to worry about. Our planes are very safe, and you will forget that you ever left the ground."

"I believe you, but I would much rather drive."

"I see that your friend is a flight attendant. Has she tried to convince you of the joys of flying?"

"Not so much," replied Jeanette, "as it's just work to me. I also cannot relax when I fly, as I feel I should be serving the passengers."

"Well, I wish you the best on this flight. Here are your tickets. Enjoy the flight."

John and Jeanette turned from the counter and walked towards a line snaking towards the security entrance.

"See, that wasn't so bad," noted Jeanette.

"No - but now I'm back on the grid," replied John.

"In a few hours, it won't matter."

"Maybe, but what if our text did not make it, or what if it arrived too late? You would think they would have texted back."

"No, they wouldn't have texted - it would have broken protocol. Joe knows better than that. We just need to continue with the plan, and meet at the Hilton Basel."

Passage through the Security line was uneventful, and within minutes, John and Jeanette were sitting on the plane, waiting for takeoff. They were only an hour away from landing at Basel-Mulhouse, and near term reunion with Joe and Mick. At least that was their hope.

Chapter **42**

Joe and Mick had no choice but to stand still. They had no weapons, and were still reeling from the surprise that had just occurred. They were also not the targets, which ironically was not the case, but hopefully was still the belief of their captors.

Slyly, Joe stated, "Twice in two days. We need to stop meeting like this -- people will talk."

"Mr. Stone, we've been through this before. I'm tired of your silly commentary."

"Actually, I'm really feeling like we're getting to know each other. Feel free to call me 'John.'"

Joe added this comment on purpose, which in itself was a risky move, as his captor may have already figured out his real identity. Joe could see the tension in Mick's eyes when he said this, as they both stared at the man trying to gauge his response.

This was actually an approach that Joe and Mick had planned for. Specifically, if they were captured, Joe would continue to follow the guise of John, and note that they had the wrong guy, which would work well if their captors did not realize their mistake.

"Mr. Stone, if I had known better, I would have kept hold of you when I had you in my limo."

Both Joe and Mick tried to remain emotionless, as it appeared that Joe's real identity was known. Nevertheless, Joe replied, "How would that have benefited you?"

The man stood speechless, a smile growing on his face.

"We know now," he replied.

"What exactly do you know? I'm kind of slow, so you'll need to help me out."

Joe and Mick knew that they were in a bad situation, which required a hand versus gun fight. They instinctively turned their bodies slowly sideways, perpendicular to the two men with handguns, to lessen the size of the target. Within a few steps was a 20-foot drop to the path below that entered the castle, otherwise there was no other exit, or other escape options. This was not a situation that either Joe or Mick were used to - and they were individually wondered why they had let their guard down.

"Well, Mr. Stone. It's come to our attention that we should have approached this differently. Any ideas how?"
"No idea -- Surprise me, then," replied Joe.

"When I had you in my car, I should never have let you go."

"OK - now you are repeating yourself," stated Joe. "Get to the point, or just let us go, as you now know that I'm trying to find my brother."

"Yes, we knew that you would try, which is why we gave you 48-hours' notice."

"Cut to the chase. So what?"

"So, Mr. Stone, we know that you are in contact with your brother."

At this point, both John and Mick realized that their guise was still a secret, but just to confirm, Joe stated,

"How would you know that I am in contact with Joe?"

"We intercepted your simple four-letter text, which sent us here."

"You guys are very perceptive -- but just lucky in that everyone takes a walk to the castle while in Kaysersberg."

"Yes, hence this little meeting that we are now enjoying."

Joe asked again, "So our text message tipped you off. So why do you still need me, such as when we were in the limo?"

"Mr. Stone, I knew that you would lead us to Joe. In fact, if I had been smarter, we would have kept you in our control to do so."

"That would not have been good for your health."

"That, we too, realized. We also knew that if Joe was indeed dead, you wouldn't be here right now. So you have confirmed our guess that he is still alive."

"Wow - you guys are geniuses. My friend and I will see you guys later. We are leaving now."

"No, you're not. We will be keeping you and your friend in our control, so we can find your brother together. He surely received the Kaysersberg text, and will eventually be on his way here."

As a positive, Joe and Mick now knew that Joe's disguise was still intact. Clearly their captor did not know that they already had Joe in their control, for the second time.

The negative was that John was still their target. Little did they know that he was not on his way to Kaysersberg, or at least that was the hope. This left them with two unfavorable options, considering that escape was not feasible. Either spend time with these individuals until it was clear that John was not coming, or alert them that John had moved on, and guide them to Basel.

This choice was about to be made for them, as Joe's cell phone made a muffled ding from his front left pocket, attracting the downward gaze of all. Both henchmen directed their LS's towards John, moving in behind their leader.

"Are you expecting a text or email, Mr. Stone?"

"No, now that you're here, I cannot imagine who else would call."

"I am becoming impatient with your humor. Slowly raise your hands above your head, turn your back to me, and place your raised hands on the wall above you."

What Joe would soon realize was that the ding was an incoming text message, with the text "10-19 SBB 9th," from an unknown source. Unfortunately, the original text that was sent by John's new cell phone did not process until the phone re-established local access upon landing at Basel-Mulhouse airport.

"Just so you are not surprised, one of my men will reach into your pocket to retrieve your phone. I suggest that you remain still, else we will execute your brunette friend."

Joe looked at Mick, and gave a slight nod for her to follow this command. She nodded ever so slightly in acknowledgement, knowing that the cards had turned from their favor.

Joe turned as instructed and raised his hands, attempting to keep the man in his vision. He felt the butt of the gun pressing into his lower spine.

"Look at your raised hands, Mr. Stone."

Joe tilted his chin upwards, as he felt a hand reach into his left front pocket. He resisted every instinct he had to break free and stood motionless as his phone was carefully lifted from his pocket. He was not about to provide his password, but knew a preview of the sender along with the email or text message, would be visible on the screen.

Joe tried to look down to achieve a glimpse of the sender or message. He saw that the sender was unidentified, with a short text following. Joe could see Mick a few feet away, the gun now redirected from her, back to himself. Joe's phone was now in the palm of the leader, who was looking down at the locked screen.

"Mr. Stone, I do not expect that you will provide me with your password, nor will I ask. Given your experience and level of caution, I also expect that multiple tries at your password will clear your phone, thus all that I have is this rather cryptic text message from an unknown sender."

Joe looked back at the leader, awaiting his next response. Still no way out, for him or Mick.

"Mr. Stone, now that we're friends, I'm asking for your help in deciphering the text showing on your iPhone. What exactly does '10-19 SBB 9th' mean to you, and is it worth your friend's life?"

Joe and Mick exchanged glances, not yet sure what the text message meant, or if it was from John. After a few seconds, Joe could see in Mick's eyes that she had figured it out. She was always the first one who came up with the more obscure solutions, and in this case, he believed she had the answer. The problem was, how would they be able to discuss, in privacy?

Joe asked the lead man, "Can you be more specific in your question, as you are the one holding the phone, remember?"

The lead man threw Joe's phone back to him. Joe entered his password and could see the odd text, "10-19 SBB 9th," still unable to understand its meaning.

"We have a dilemma, Mr. Stone. You and your partner need time to decide your next step, added to the fact that we are both on the heels of your brother. I also suspect that the text message is from your brother."

Joe worked hard to maintain his composure, despite the thoughts spinning in his mind.

"So, Mr. Stone, I have the choice of either letting you go and following you again, or just hanging onto you and your girlfriend, and having you lead us to Joe. I choose the latter, but will give you a few minutes with your friend before we head to our next destination."

"So that's it?" asked Joe. "You want us to lead you to Joe? What benefit does this provide us?"

"Well, we could just shoot you both, right here, right now, as we're about as close to Joe as we have ever been."

Joe thought silently to himself, if you only knew how close you were.

"Joe is probably on his way here right now, or certainly within a hour or two. At some point, he will text you again. I am confident that not hearing from you will cause Joe to make another mistake."

"Joe isn't known for making mistakes. I have known him for many years, and can attest to that."

"But he already has, Mr. Stone. His first mistake was sending that text."

"Why are you so sure it was from him?"

"Let's just say it is a hunch. Now, this is against my best judgement, but let's proceed to the top courtyard of the castle, where we can allow you and your friend to discuss next steps, in an area where you are easily shot. Sound good to you?"

Joe and Mick looked at each other. They knew they were the underdogs in this fight. They also knew that the sooner they could partner on a plan, the better off they would be, with the secondary result of reaching out to support John and Jeanette. Mick let Joe know via a simple nod that this made sense.

Joe replied, "Ok, we need a few minutes together to discuss. I am not making promises that we will proceed, and need to discuss first."

"Excellent, Mr. Stone. Lead the way up the stairs, to the courtyard. I assume you know the way."

"Yes, we know the way. Let's go."

Chapter 43

The small dual engine Embraer turbo-prop noisily descended and landed at Basel-Mulhouse after a few rebounds of the landing gear onto the runway. The flight had been uneventful, short of a few elevation swings due to side winds affecting the yaw of the plane.

The flight attendant's voice came over the loudspeaker. "Welcome to Basel-Mulhouse airport. Please stay seated as we taxi to the gate. You will deplane away from the terminal, so please be careful descending the stairs and follow the yellow path to the terminal. If you checked luggage, it will be returned in baggage area 2. Thank you for flying Lufthansa Airlines."

John and Jeanette grabbed their backpacks from the overhead bin, which was barely a few inches above their heads in the cramped quarters of the 40 seat plane, and joined the exit line from the plane with the other passengers. Upon exit from the rickety stairway, they could see luggage being removed from by the airline attendants; their only luggage was the backpacks they now carried, that now contained their sole belongings.

"Nice to travel light for a change, huh?" asked John.

"It has its advantages, but in this case, I miss my stuff. For once, it paid off to carry our passports, as this is really all we need from this point forward," replied Jeanette.

John and Jeanette walked from the plane, staying in between the yellow lines painted on the ground that led to the terminal ahead of them. Basel-Mulhouse was a small airport that oddly straddled the French and Switzerland borders, half in one country, and half in the other. The outside was covered in glass panels, slightly tinted to reflect the sun that shined less than half of the year. As they neared the terminal, the yellow lines disappeared as they entered into a small alcove that snaked around the base of the terminal. Within 100 feet they found themselves entering a door that led into the terminal. As they had not left France, there was no passport control, as Jeanette noted to John earlier. He breathed an audible sigh of relief.

To exit the Basel-Mulhouse airport, passengers originating from within France pass into a central baggage claim area, that is followed by two exits, one to France, and a second adjacent exit to Switzerland. These exits lead through a small customs area, where Jeanette had yet to see an agent working there, and then outside of the terminal area into a single hallway, divided by a glass wall. Passengers visiting France exit to the right side of the glass divider, and visitors to Switzerland are shuffled to the left, at which point passengers are picked up, or they proceed to parking or the rental car desks. Oddly enough, there is duplicity in all of these areas, whether that be parking, rental locations, etc., as a result of the country-specific ownership.

"This is still one of the strangest airports, considering its location," noted John. "I'll never forget one visit where I rented a car on the France side of the airport, visited Switzerland and without thinking, returned the car to the Switzerland AVIS rental on the Swiss side of the airport."

"And they made you leave the AVIS parking lot, drive out the airport, enter France via the adjacent highway, and re-enter the same AVIS parking lot for the France side, to return the car, right?" interrupted Jeanette.

"Yes, exactly!" replied John. "Have you done the same?"

"I have. The funny thing was that I was literally in the same parking lot, but on the other side of the concrete divider of the parking area."

"Wow, and I thought the AVIS attendant was just kidding when he noted that I needed to park on the other side of the divider."

"Won't be an issue this time, as we'll exit on the French side, and drive to Switzerland. Basel is only a 30 minute drive."

John and Jeanette walked up to the AVIS desk as a young male attendant entered from an office behind the desk, wearing a sweater hung loosely from his shoulders as if it was a scarf; very French-like. John guessed that he was no older than 22.

"Welcome to France. May I see your passport please?"

Jeanette handed her black passport to the attendant that identified her as U.S. Military; an issue that John had never witnessed, but now made sense.

"Thank you. Do you plan to drive to other countries while visiting Europe?" asked the attendant.

"Possibly, as we're here on a sight-seeing week. Let's say, Germany, Belgium, in addition to France."

"OK. Here are your keys. Please be sure to return the car to the French side of the airport."

That would have been useful years ago, thought Jeanette and John to themselves.

John followed Jeanette to the French exit side of the airport, passed through the sliding doors, and walked through the line of cars until they arrived at a mid-size Mercedes. The doors unlocked with a thud, upon pressing the unlock button on the key fob, and they both hopped in, throwing their backpacks into the rear seats.

"I'll drive," noted Jeanette.

"Do you remember the way?" asked John.

"Even though it's been a year, I actually do. Signage to Basel is surprisingly good."

The key word being "signage," was at practically every corner from the airport, there were signs that clearly identified the city name, with an arrow. In this instance, leaving from the French side of the Basel-Mulhouse airport meant they would need to drive across Border Control, from France into Switzerland. This was nothing more than having a Border Control agent look at the driver, and ask where they are going and possibly why. So many people are in the line, that the process is similar to a U.S. toll booth, except no toll is taken. Not very secure in Jeanette's opinion, but it was the norm for many European countries.

After a 3 mile snaking drive from the airport, they entered the highway and quickly assembled in the Border Control line. After 3 minutes they reached the control agent, who gave Jeanette a wave through with his right hand, without even asking for any information.

"Typical response, and much easier than a customs discussion at the airport," noted Jeanette. John nodded.

The drive to Basel took less than 15 minutes, with traffic being very light. The weather was cloudy as usual, with slight drizzle, as the norm. Jeanette remembered one of the locals describing Basel's weather as primarily rainy in January, February, March, April, May, June, July, August, September, October, November and December; or in other words, year-round. On average though, it actually was overcast only 20 days each month, with some very beautiful scenery once outside of the bustling city,

Within minutes, the Basel Hilton appeared on their left, located directly across the street from Bahnhof Basel SBB, the largest train station in Basel, and in all of Europe. From the outside, the station looks deceivingly small, but once inside the station, visitors will find restaurants, pharmacies, services and a multitude of shops spanning an area of almost 16,000 cubic meters, or 4 acres in total, operating 365 days per year. It offered the perfect location to become quickly lost in the multitudes of passengers traversing Germany, France and Switzerland. Jeanette and John selected this location for this very reason, and had already prepared their meeting plan with Joe and Mick.

Jeanette took an immediate right in between the SBB and the Hilton, and entered the ramp to the underground parking facility for the Hilton. As was common for many buildings in Europe, underground parking garages sometimes extended the same number of floors below ground, as the building was tall. The ironic thing was that cell service strength, even at these depths, was stronger than most surface locations in the U.S.

Jeanette parked and then the couple collected their backpacks, locked the car, and headed towards the central elevator, which was already open. They walked in and pushed the button labeled with an "L," for "lobby." The doors closed slowly, and the elevator began its ascent.

"Being back in Basel brings back fond memories of our drives throughout Europe, especially this hotel," noted John.

So true, and unbeknownst to you, Joe has been a frequent visitor as well."

"What do you mean?" questioned John.

"Well, now that you know that I am more than just an American Airlines flight attendant, it's important that you know that I've kept in touch with Joe."

"Why?"

"Joe was concerned about you, so I was enlisted to keep tabs on you."

"Like, from the beginning, when I first flew to France?"

"Uh, yeah, from then, and even before," replied Jeanette. "Joe has told me stories about you for years. I was intrigued, and volunteered."

"So this was just work," stated John. He turned to face Jeanette to read her expression.

She looked John straight in the eye, and said, "It was, but then it changed. It didn't take long for me to realize how special a person you are. You are intelligent, thoughtful, and a perfect gentleman."

"I'm really glad to hear that," replied John. "For a second there, I was concerned."

"No need for concern. I believe things happen for a reason, no matter the circumstances or environment. I see a great future for us."

"Even considering the situation we're in, I agree."

The elevator door opened with a "ding." The hotel check-in desk could be seen directly outside the now open door. John and Jeannette walked up to the desk, and remained quiet, as a common game they would play to see which language the attendant would start with. For some reason, locals would assume John was Austrian and Jeanette, German. Jeanette was fluent in German, French, Italian, Danish and English, which covered most of the local languages. Whichever language they started with, she would continue, as if they had correctly guessed. This was the polite thing to do, but was confusing when she would leave speaking English.

John was fluent in French and English, although could understand many others. Living in Europe makes this possible.

This time, the attendant began by welcoming Jeanette and John in French, which worked well for both. They were assigned a room on the 9th floor, which along with the 8th floor, was the only other true Executive Floor in the hotel. Jeanette accepted the plastic credit-card shaped key, and turned to head back to the elevators that proceeded to the rooms. John followed.

To reach the 9th floor, which did not have a dedicated button in the elevator, guests must go to the eighth floor and take the stairs. This was a surprise for first time visitors, especially those with luggage, which must be hand carried up the double flight of stairs. The Hilton Executive Club was also located on the 8th floor, which behind-locked key, provided unlimited drinks and food, during the morning, lunch and evening meal times. The food was reasonably good, with ample supply of Belgian chocolates a known favorite. Another convenience was the concierge, who was present from 9:00am to 5:00pm, to provide 1:1 support with any hotel, airline or dinner needs, from any guest. Jeanette was continually amazed at the number of languages the concierge could speak fluently, as they addressed questions from visiting travelers, on a minute-to-minute basis.

"What's the plan?" asked John.

"Drop off our luggage and head to the lounge for a drink," replied Jeanette. "Do you remember the view from the lounge?" she asked.

"Not so much, so please remind me," said John.

"Let's go there first then," noted Jeanette.

They exited the elevator, and walked approximately 30 feet down the eighth floor hallway. A glass door stood to their left, with the concierge visibly seated just inside the door, to the right. She looked their way, and clicked the door release, allowing them to enter.

In French, she welcomed them to the club, and asked for their names as a double-check that they actually were staying at the hotel. John replied with their room number, and Hilton Honors number.

John and Jeanette entered the club, when John noted, "Ok, how could I forget the view from here?"

John was referring to the view of the outdoor boarding area for the metro below. Even though they were 8 floors above the street, they had a direct view to the entry and exit of the SBB train station below; a perfect location for remote reconnaissance, in addition to the unlimited liquor and food behind them.

"Joe will enter through the station, to let us know when he's here," replied Jeanette. "He will give us every opportunity to warn him of adversaries, and likewise, we'll be aware if he's being followed."

"Makes sense," replied Joe. "How much longer before they arrive, as we better drop off our luggage in anticipation of their arrival?"

By this time, the concierge was paying a bit too much attention to their conversation. She asked, "Is everything in order?"

"Yes, just reminiscing," replied Joe.

"Is this a special occasion?" asked the concierge.

"No, not really. This view of the SBB always brings back memories of previous travels to Basel," replied Jeanette.

"It is a grand view," replied the concierge. "Please let me know if I can be of assistance. I'm here during the daylight hours."

"Thank you. We'll keep that in mind," replied Jeanette. She turned towards John, "Hon, please go drop our bags in the room. I want to stay here and enjoy the view."

"Ok, I'll be back shortly."

John grabbed their backpacks and exited the club, leaving Jeanette and the concierge to continue their discussions. As John took the stairs back to the 9th floor, he was wondering what his brother was doing at that minute. Did he receive their text? If yes, was he on his way? If no, and hopefully that was not the case, but what situation was he in the midst of? Wind the clock, John told himself, and have faith.

Chapter 44

Joe and Mick ascended the rotating stone steps that led to the plateau courtyard located on the top of Kaysersberg Castle. Thousands of years ago, during the Renaissance, this courtyard was crawling with activity, from inhabitants selling their wares, to the guards that patrolled the town. The circular courtyard was surprisingly large, with a diameter in excess of 30 yards. Surrounding the courtyard was a parapet wall, from behind which the castle archers could easily pick off their prey from their precarious perch. There was literally no escape from these walls, unless one was a professional climber, which was certainly not an option for either Joe or Mick. These same thoughts passed through their minds, making both Joe and Mick perplexed as to their next steps. At least they would be afforded a minute to strategize, even if escape seemed futile in the near term.

When Mick knew they were out of ear-shot, she stated, "I know where they are."

"What?" asked Joe.

"I know where they are, or at least where we are supposed to meet them."

"Just from the text on my phone?" asked Joe.

He looked down at his locked cell phone and speedily entered his password with his right thumb. The home screen appeared, with a small red number "1" superimposed over the text icon, signaling the presence of an unread text message. Joe clicked the icon with his other thumb, which activated the text message screen. Centered in the screen was the text that originally appeared on the preview screen, 10-19 SBB 9th.

"Ok, what does it mean?"

"It's the Basel Hilton," suggested Mick. "Joe is telling us to go to the Hilton, using 10-19 as return to station, and the Basel SBB as the landmark."

Joe continued to walk towards the center of the courtyard, turning to assure they were still outside of hearing range.

"I think you are right, but what about the 9th?"

"It's got to be the Hilton Honors club in the Hilton."

"But that's on the 8th floor," noted Joe.

"It is, but John was being cryptic."

"You are assuming this came from John, as the phone number is not one I recognize."

"It's got to be a throw-away," suggested Mick.

"Ok, assuming it is, how will we get there, considering our current situation. I mean, we're in a much compromised situation, the last I checked."

"'Compromised' is an understatement. There is only one route that exits from this courtyard, and our friends are blocking it. We cannot go over the edge, as we're looking at a minimum 50 foot sheer drop. We cannot climb farther into the tower, with the queen's bedroom the only room at the top."

"Plus, it's the wrong direction."

"Yeah, I get that."

"So why are they allowing us this private discussion?" asked Jeanette.

"I'm still trying to figure that one out. But no matter the reasoning, we only have a short window to devise a plan."

"If they keep us together, we have a chance while we descend the stairs. You can draw from your par-core training."

"The training I had almost five years ago? I think not. That tool left the tool chest when my body aged past 40. I'm not as limber as I used to be, or capable of unlimited summersaults."

"OK. No matter, as whatever chance we have to escape is out the window until we get off of the castle. They build them to avoid entry and exit for a reason."

"So we wing it, and then what? Can we get to John and Jeanette before our captors?" asked Mick.

"Yes, and if we do not, we know Basel very well, which we can use to our advantage," replied Joe. "I am also hesitant to reply to the cryptic text, in the event the signal could somehow lead to John."

"I Agree." replied Mick. She froze for a second, her head slowly turning 15-degrees clockwise, towards the vineyards that lined the mountainside.

"Do you hear that?" she asked, from the position.

"No, what do you mean?"

"It's a low frequency hum, coming from the west." Mick motioned with her chin in the same direction. "You really don't hear anything?"

"Not yet," replied Joe.

At this point, both Joe and Mick were looking in the same direction, when they saw it. Approximately 300 yards to the west, a white helicopter could be seen gliding over the terrain, it's rotating blades completely invisible, but causing the chop-chop-chop sound that increasingly reverberated as the craft approached.

"Good or bad -- any ideas?" asked Mick.

"I didn't call them, nor does anyone know we're here."

"You're not answering my question," repeated Mick.

"I'm not able to. I'm guessing not-good, and suggest that we move from the center of the courtyard, as we're either about to get shot at, or rescued."

"Hmmmm. Would be a shame to have the chopper land on top of us."

"Yes, let's not have that happen," suggested Joe, as he began to shift to walk towards the edge of the courtyard. Mick followed, trying to read the posture of their assailants.

"They don't look nervous, do they?" commented Mick.

"No, I'm noticing that too. The chopper is expected."

"I have a very bad feeling about this," noted Mick. "I'll be careening down the side of the castle before I get inside that thing."

"Wind the clock. We don't know what's in store. We've been in worse situations."

The helicopter continued its glide path, now within 100 yards, and dropping in elevation. It was clearly targeting the castle. Their assailants were approaching their location, in efforts to intersect their location, towards the edge of the courtyard. Their LRS handguns were now holstered, as they watched the helicopter's descent.

"We could try to dash," suggested Joe.

"Except that would be futile. Would be tough to outrun a chopper, even if we were able to get off the castle."

"At least we're not a target, and I plan to stay close enough to our friends to prevent a clear shot."

"Same here. I may go for one of the LRS's, if the option arises."

"Just wait. Let's see this out."

"You got it," replied Mick. "I'll follow your lead."

The helicopter was now within 20 yards of the edge of the courtyard wall, approximately 50 feet above them; the turbulence from the rotating blades now detectable. The chopper stopped its descent, and rotated two full rotations, righting itself while the pilot decided where he or she was going to land. Everyone's eyes remained glued on the craft, with Mick and Joe aware that the LRS's were still in ready position, available if needed. Not an option, at this time of distraction.

The pilot had made the decision, choosing the direct center of the courtyard as the landing target. Through the gray tinted windows, a single pilot could be seen, with two figures visible in the seats behind him or her.

Within 15 seconds, the helicopter had landed, the blades already slowing in speed as the engines were throttled back.

The lead individual spoke, "We have someone who wants to meet you."

"That's comforting. If I had known, I would have dressed differently."

The man just rolled his eyes, clearly unimpressed with the situation, and more so focused on the arriving guests. He walked towards the chopper, blades now barely spinning, and reached for the door handle to extricate the passengers. Movement was noticeable through the windows, as the passengers were removing headphones and moving towards the doors. The first to exit was a young man, closely resembling the three armed monsters who surprised Joe and Mick no more than a few minutes ago. The second man to exit was much older than the first, probably in his early sixties. He was wearing a button-down white shirt, and a matching khaki suit jacket and pants. He wore a pair of dark sunglasses that matched his slicked back, black hair.

John and Mick remained motionless, off to the side of the courtyard.

"Let him come to us," whispered Joe.

"My sentiments exactly," replied Mick. "I don't like the looks of this."

"We'll be alright. We would already be dead if they wanted us to be."

Mick very slightly shook her head in agreement, keeping her eyes focused on the approaching man, who was now within 20 feet of their location, his bodyguard 5 steps behind.

As the man neared, the man slid his sunglasses up past his forehead, pressing the hair flat to his head. Joe recognized him immediately, as the Israeli General from almost a decade ago -- the same General who lost his only son as a result of Joe's apparent actions. This was actually not the case, but was the story that initiated the events leading to the current situation.

Joe turned to see Mick's expression, which was one of utter surprise, as she too recognized the General. She unconsciously turned her body sideways, making for a smaller target in anticipation of a potential gun fight.

"Relax, Mick. I have an idea. Do not do anything you might regret."

"This could be very bad," replied Mick.

"No, I don't think so."

The man stared straight at Joe as he approached, to the point of making Joe uncomfortable. Joe kept his composure, but was concerned that the General had recognized him. That would be the worst case scenario, and would not lead to anything good.

"Hello Mr. Stone -- it's been a long time."

"Has it?" answered Joe, feigning ignorance.

"Actually, yes. About 10 years in fact, when I lost my only son."

"I'm sorry to hear that, but what does this have to do with me?" replied Joe.

The man looked closely into Joe's eyes, for what seemed like an eternity, then he spoke.

"I actually do not know exactly what happened that sad day occurring one decade ago. In fact, there is only one person who knows the truth. That would be your brother Joe, which is why I am here today. You see, I am asking for your help."
"Your gun brandishing colleagues over there made me assume otherwise," replied Joe.

"That was just a precaution, to assure you would stay until I arrived. It worked, by the way."

"Yeah, I see that," replied Joe. "So are we done here?"

"No, I need you to lead me to Joe."

"And exactly why would I do that?" asked Joe.

"As you will soon find out, I am a gaming man. I have everything I could possibly want in life. Money, women, fame, and everything else money can buy."

"That's nice. I'm very happy for you."

The General ignored Joe's remark, and continued.

"My true loves are gambling and hunting. Even the rich are not guaranteed to win at either, hence it gives me a "rush," quoting your American term."

"Ok, where are you going with this, and how am I involved?"

"I need you to lead me to your brother, as he has the answers behind my son's early death. I just want time with Joe to understand what really happened."

"And if I don't assist?"

"Then you, your pretty girlfriend, your brother, and many others close to you will die, as collateral damage."

"You're not necessarily going to obtain the desired rush, by controlling the odds," noted Joe. "Especially if you are such the gamer."

"This is true, hence this proposition to you. As a hunter, I enjoy the chase, so if you agree to lead me to Joe, and you get to him first, then you will live."

"Live indefinitely, or get shot the next time I turn my back on you?"

"Forever, until you die of old age, get hit by a bus, or whatever you American's are plagued by these days," replied the General. "With one condition that I have time with Joe to understand what led to my son's demise."

Oddly enough, Joe thought to himself, the General was having the requested time with Joe, at that very moment.

"So what's the catch?"

"You leave now, we chase after you. It's that simple."

"So, let me repeat my understanding of your proposal. You let us go, and you chase us en route to us locating Joe. If you don't catch us en route to Joe, we arrange a meeting. You meet with Joe to get the inside story, then we're all free."

"Yes, that's the deal. To summarize, the first one to get to Joe, wins."

"Why should I trust you?"

"You have no choice, that's why."

"There is always a choice," replied Joe. "And I need some flexibility in the process."

"How so?"

"I want to predefine where we will meet, assuming we get to Joe first."

"So you want to change my plan? What authority do you have to do this, and what benefit is there to me in this change?"

"No benefit per se, but an increase in the difficulty of the game," replied Joe. "You said you were a gamer. I'm offering you a challenge."

Mick looked at Joe, a slight smile showing from the corner of her mouth. Joe was an expert at manipulation, and this was an opportune time to even the odds. Joe concentrated his gaze at the Israeli General, knowing by his prolonged silence that he was hitting a sensitive area.

"So, do we have a deal?" asked Joe.

More pensive silence, as the General's face remained motionless.

Finally, the silence broke. "What location did you have in mind?" asked the General.

Joe was already five steps ahead in his thinking, knowing the one area, short of the U.S. Embassy, that would afford difficult entry for the General and his team, and an easy exit for Joe, John, Mick and Jeanette, if and when the need arose. The location that he had in mind was well known to Joe and Jeanette, most recently as Joe's primary research donor for the SCENICC platform.

"Are you familiar with the Headquarters for Transivo Pharmaceuticals, in Basel?"

"I am very familiar. It is one of the most opulent headquarters in the world, rightly so for one of the largest pharmaceutical giants in the industry."

The General was evidently well aware of the Transivo Campus in Basel that included buildings designed by architects the likes of Frank Gehry; Studio di Architettura; Rafael Moneo and Adolf Krischanitz. The Campus had been transformed from a 51-acre industrial site beside the Rhine River into a modern research and administrative headquarters comprised of outdoor parks, greens, and large-scale art, for enjoyment by the 5,500 employees that call it home. Oddly enough, the Campus straddles the French and Swiss borders.

One of the more recent constructions is the visitor's center, designed by Peter Markli. The building's front facade is decorated with a massive LED scroll marquee created by the artist Jenny Holzer that displays the oddest of sayings, 24-7.

"You are quite an assuming and pompous man, typical of so many Americans. Do you think that I am foolish enough to accept this ridiculous proposal?" boomed the General.

"To answer your question, no, I do not think that you are foolish, and yes, I do think you will accept this challenge. By making this offer, I am complimenting you and your capabilities. Only you and your team could pull off such a feat as to covertly enter and navigate the confines of the Transivo Campus."

The General remained silent, continuing his gaze at Joe.

"So do we have a deal?" asked Joe.

"Your compliments will get you nowhere, and your lies everywhere," replied the General. "The idea is so ludicrous that I like it. You realize though, that if I do not gain face-to-face contact with your brother, then there is nowhere you can hide. By me entering the Transivo Campus, this will be evident. I can find you anywhere, and will not stop searching until I find out the answers about my son. I think you know what I am saying."

"Yes, I completely understand," replied Joe. "I doubt even you can circumvent the security of the Transivo Campus. So we have a deal?"

"Yes, we have a deal."

"We will be on our way then," replied Joe, as he turned away from the General, and began walking towards the initial two bodyguards, who still had the LRS's raised. Mick followed close behind.

As Joe neared the bodyguards, he turned towards the General and stated, "Any reason why your henchmen still have the guns drawn?"

The General caught the eye of the larger of the two men, and gave a slight head nod indicating that they should lower their weapons, which they did.

"Thank you, General. I will see you inside the Transivo Campus."

The General asked, "Transivo is a very large Campus. Assuming that you get there first, when and where should I meet you, and more importantly, your brother Joe?"

"Do you like Italian?" responded Joe.

"Italian what?" asked the General.

"Food. Italian food," replied Joe.

"Not particularly. Why do you ask?"

"Because that is what we will be eating, and where we will have the discussion with Joe."

"Inside the Campus?"

"Appears that you do not know the Transivo Campus," replied Joe, as he kept walking towards the stairs from the courtyard. "The Transivo campus has numerous restaurants, some of the best in Basel, so we will plan to meet you at one of my favorites, named Dodici. As you enter the restaurant, the tables are situated to the right side. We will be seated in the table farthest from the entry."

"How exactly will I find this location, considering that I may have security following me."

"You're a smart guy. I expect that you can figure out a plan. I will text you when we need to meet."

"But you don't have my cellphone number."

"Clearly, you have mine, else you wouldn't have been able to find me at this location."

"This is true," replied the General.

"We will wait for one hour after I text you. If you cannot get to us by then, then we're gone, and I can guarantee you that it will take more than the 10 years it took you to find us this time. "

"Understood," noted the General, "and good luck."

Joe and Mick had already turned and began walking away. The General waited and watched as they traversed the courtyard, and disappeared into the doorway that led to the stairs, knowing that they would soon meet again. He turned, summoning his four guards, and walked towards the waiting helicopter. With the gesturing twirl of his hand, he instructed the pilot to start up the engine, for immediate departure. They would fly to Basel immediately, to wait to intercept the next cell phone call from Mr. Stone, to his brother.

As Joe and Mick entered the stairwell, Joe said, "Stay inside the cover of the castle when we reach the bottom of the stairs. We don't want to become targets if the General changes his mind."

"True," replied Mick. "I'm actually surprised that he accepted your offer. I mean, why take the risk of losing us. He could have just captured us and held us as collateral to attract you, or I mean, John."

"Possibly, but I suspect that there is more to this story that we realize. His primary goal appears to be a 1:1 discussion with me. Since the bombing, I've heard rumors that he has paid millions to find out what actually happened. I never gave a thought to these, until now. This meeting may actually bring us closer to the underlying answer."

As they reached the bottom stair, the helicopter could be heard whirling above the courtyard, as it slowly lifted and turned away from the castle. Joe and Mick patiently waited until no further sounds could be heard. Then they stepped out into the open.

Chapter 45

"That was fun," noted Mick, her eyes squinting as they adjusted to the sunlight.

"Actually, it turned out better than I could have expected. And so ironic that I've been right under their nose, the whole time."

"Twice, to be exact," said Mick.

"Three times may be our last."

"How so?" asked Mick.

"An issue that has come to my mind during these meetings is the possibility that our assailant, whether that be the General or whomever, actually knows that I am Joe. The General paused for quite a while when we first locked eyes. I was sure that he recognized me."

"It's been 10 years. That would be quite a memory."

"Yes, but if he was able to see me and John at the same time, such as next to each other at Dodici, the difference might become evident. We may look similar, but it's our mannerisms that make us different. The second issue is that John doesn't have any idea of the events that occurred the night of the bombing -- only I do."

"So?"

"So," Joe replied, "I'll need to educate John on every detail, to predict any question that the General may ask. This will not be easy."

"I thought that John knew most of the story?"

"Only the high level details. I intentionally kept him in the dark to protect him. The more that he knows, the more vulnerable it makes him."

Joe and Mick continued to the winding path that led back to their hotel.

"So why not play the part of Joe, when we meet at Transivo? This will eliminate the need for divulging additional details to John."

"That's actually a very good idea as there is no way possible to train John on the details from a decade ago; too much Intel and too little time. I'm not even sure that I can remember."

"True. One slip-up in the recount of the story, and it could be disastrous."

Mick stopped walking and turned to Joe, "Have you considered that he wants you both. I mean, maybe you're correct in that he recognizes you, but is feigning innocence until he gets both of you together."

"That has crossed my mind, but I cannot decide how or why this would be the case. There really is no benefit to having us both together, unless he wants to assure that I, or John, or whomever we pretend to be, is dead."

"So more of a 'If I have both, then I cannot be deceived into missing one' idea. That actually makes perfect sense."

"It's what I would do if I were in his shoes. It solves the issue he's been dealing with over the past decade, never knowing, always second guessing if he had the correct brother."

"So that changes things a bit."

"Yes, it does, as we cannot be visible at the same time, or certainly present at the same table, just to assure we keep the advantage on our side."

"I'll bet you wish you were triplets now," joked Mick. Although two is enough in my opinion."

"Again, you come up with another brilliant comment," replied Joe, winking back to Mick.

Mick was used to this behavior from Joe. She knew he had already decided the path forward in his mind, as was commonly the case after years of similar partnerships on the battlefield.

They kept walking along the path that led back to the hotel, silently this time, as mere suggestions became formal strategies in Joe's mind. Mick knew that by the time they traversed the entire path, Joe would unveil his plan that they would bring to execution. The only worrisome unknown was John. Had he become soft in the few years since he left the service? Had living in Europe lessened his instinct and technique? Luckily Jeannette had been posted at his side, since day one, so there was added opportunity for success. Should make for an interesting 24 to 48 hours.

After the final mile, Joe stopped walking, the small castle behind the hotel now visible.

"We'll need to make a few changes to the plan we discussed, but this is doable. The outcome easier controlled and less prone to error. Let's grab our backpacks and discuss on the ride over."

"And our friends?" asked Mick. "Should we expect some trouble in route to Basel?"

"I doubt it. If the General's intent was to have John and me together then preventing us from ever getting to Basel would be counterintuitive, and would end our game before it ever started."

"Assuming your intuition is correct."

"That's where Plan B will come in. We still have the element of surprise. The key is that we control the implementation, to maintain the advantage."

"What are our chances?" asked Mick.

"Pretty good, actually. We just need to get to Basel as quickly as possible, as I suspect that the General and his team are already there, preparing for our arrival. Let's go over the plan, and then get on the road."

"We can also discuss during the drive over," noted Mick.

"We're not driving," noted Joe, who kept walking ahead of Mick. "We'll fly."

"Wait, what?" asked Mick as she caught up to Joe's stride.

"We're flying," replied Joe. "I suspect that the rental may be an easy trace, so we'll start the deception there, with the help of a yet-to-be-defined friend."

Don't ask, Mick thought to herself. The plan will be unfolded soon enough.

Chapter **46**

An hour had passed since the 10-19 SBB 9th text was sent by John, to Joe's cell phone. With local roaming in Switzerland, there was no way to define if the text was ever delivered, or formally received, as when connected in the States. It gave John a sinking feeling in his stomach, as he could never remember a time when there wasn't some type of response from his brother. This time was a bit different, in that there was no advance notice, no cryptic messages hidden in the hotel room, or any other direction to follow. From Jeanette's body language, it was clear that even she was unclear of next steps, frequently checking her cell for instruction that never came. Something had to be wrong, or maybe no news was good news; but unfortunately pessimism clouded John's thoughts.

Jeanette returned to the Hilton Executive club, sliding her key to gain access to the room. Others had entered since her earlier departure and had assumed their respective seats spread throughout the comfortable chairs in the room. Most were from the U.S., obvious from their accents and avid and sometimes loud discussions of political issues occurring across the pond that many internationals would not have knowledge of or care to discuss. There was one German speaking man who went to the far corner of the room, to talk on his cell phone. He seemed disinterested in anyone there, and was even very cold to the attendant who greeted him when he entered, refusing to acknowledge her cordial greeting in his German vernacular.

Jeanette smiled to the attendant as she entered the club, a few of the men's eyes involuntarily turning to her direction, but returning back to their business as she approached John and sat down.

"Any news?" She asked John, as she sank into the lounge chair next to him.

"Nothing. Any clues or messages hidden in the hotel room?" John asked in return.

"No, not that I could find," she replied. "Plus, it appears the maid just cleaned the room, as I saw her exit just as we arrived."

"So, you had no idea today was the day?"

"If by 'the day,' you mean expecting that we would abscond unexpectedly from Paris, and then to Basel. No -- I had no idea that today was the day."

"So this excursion was a complete surprise?"

"Yes, I knew that the day might come where we would be exposed, but after almost a decade, I thought we were in the clear. Almost to the point of letting my guard down. I've failed you -- I've failed Joe."

"No reason to apologize. Considering your quite innovative efforts to get us safely out of Paris, and to the apparent safe haven where we now, I do not feel that you've lost your edge."

"I guess -- and thanks," replied Jeanette, as she turned her eyes to look down towards the bustle of the people outside the SBB eight stories below them. "I would have liked this to turn out differently, with advance notice or at least a formal plan. Right now, we're running blind."

"At least Joe had enough foresight to prepare us for a safe exit from Paris. We wouldn't have made it here if we were not so familiar with the Catacombs."

"This is true. We were almost out of luck, if not for the text received by our assailants that allowed us to tip off Joe and Mick. I'm still amazed that we all had cell service down there."

"We're assuming that our tip-off text to Joe had a positive effect. At this point, I'm not so sure. Plus, Joe has always been very deliberate and thorough with his plans -- this feels different, as if even he was also surprised."

"I'm thinking the same, but he's very creative and has lived through many of these scenarios," replied Jeanette. I suspect that no news is good news, as he crafts our next steps."

"So, at what point do we act on our own, as no news is only good news, for a short time? How long do we wait?"

"48 hours is my suggestion; we stay put until then."

"And then what?"

"Then we backtrack to Kaysersberg, to see what clues we can find," replied Jeanette. "Right now, patience and faith are our friends."

"Ok -- but you know I'm short on patience, but will follow your lead. You've been spot-on since I met you five years ago," noted John, winking to Jeanette.

Jeanette was about to respond, when her cellphone made a distinct "ding," alerting her that a new text had arrived. She hastily reached down to unlock the screen, anxiously typing in the incorrect password.

"Frustrating piece of junk," she declared, and tried entering the password again. The second time it worked, showing the text from an anonymous source.

The text read, 'I need to add to my collection.'

By then, John had moved to view the screen, which forced a puzzled look on his face. "What?" he said.

Jeanette replied, "It's not from John's cellphone number that we sent our message to. Which either means that that cellphone number has been compromised," then John interrupted, "or the text could be from someone else."

"Yes -- then there's that," replied Jeanette. "So we need to be clever in how we respond -- which must be via text to avoid triangulation?"

"With current technology, text blips can also be co-located."

"Which is why we'll text from the train."

"Ok -- but what about our reply. We must send something that validates that Joe or whoever received our earlier text, while also not giving away who or where we are."

"So we'll ask the right questions, so we're sure he is the sender."

"But I still do know what the original text means. What 'collection' does the sender 'need to add to'?"

"Which makes me think that this is Joe's way of identifying himself, all the while preventing whoever may be intercepting these texts, from knowing our plan."

"That makes sense, especially if the sender is Joe. Are you ready to get out of this hotel?"

"Yes, and on our way, I need to pick up a few toys from a local friend."

"I can only imagine the toys you play with -- just don't get us killed."

"Just the opposite, as these toys are the kind that will protect us."

"I feel better already, although I am curious about the friends you refer to -- will we meet them?"

"Trust me -- my friends are not your type; they don't like people in general."

"Ok -- maybe next time," replied John. "Let's go."

John and Jeanette stood from their chairs, and headed single file out the door, each of them thinking of options for the reply text that they would soon send. They turned right and walked down from the club entry. Jeanette reached out first and pushed the single down arrow button, since the elevator did not go to the ninth floor. After a painstakingly long time, the rightmost elevator arrived and opened with a ding, the green down arrow illuminating on the wall beside it. It was empty, which was not a surprise as elevator access to the eighth floor required room card key access. Jeanette and John entered, and turned 180-degrees to face the door as it slid shut behind them. Jeanette punched the '1' button for the first floor, which was actually counter to the European norm of the ground floor being the '0' button on the elevator, since they were in an American-style hotel. The elevator hung for a second, then descended with a whir.

John immediately re-started the conversation.

"Before we disclose anything about who or where we are, we need confirmation that we're actually in contact with Joe. We also need to know that he is alone, and not telling someone else what to type."

"That's not too hard," replied Jeanette. "Joe and I knew a cryptographer at Langley that taught us a few tricks. The simplest is to use certain letters of each word to spell out the desired message. Joe will be expecting this, and whoever is with him, friend or foe, won't have any idea."

"So give me an example."

"Alright. Grab me a piece of paper, and I'll scribble as we walk to the train."

The elevator opened with another ding upon arrival at the ground floor, the doors sliding open directly ahead of the front desk. The attendant at the front desk looked up, as they exited towards her. Jeanette walked ahead of John, and asked for a pen, this time in Russian. The attendant looked confused, so Jeanette made the universal sign for a writing instrument, with her right index finger. The woman behind the desk nodded, and reached for a Hilton Basel branded pen from behind the desk, and handed it to Jeanette. Jeanette again spoke a guttural phrase in Russian and pointed to herself, indicating if she could keep the pen. The front desk attendant understood and replied 'yes' with a silent up and down head nod. Jeanette smiled and rushed to the rotating door to the right of the front desk, grabbing a small map from the counter of the Concierge desk before exiting the hotel.

"Was that really necessary?" asked John, after they mixed into the crowds that lined both sides of the streets, "I mean, all we needed was a pen. Not to confuse the poor woman at front desk."

"No, we needed obscurity. Anyone could ask, 'Have you seen an English speaking couple here'? -- which would be too memorable." John and Jeanette crossed the street to the four outdoor train platforms across from the Hilton.

"I would think just the opposite that a strange-speaking woman and her confused-looking male accomplice, would be a worse give-away."

"Maybe in the U.S., but not here."

They arrived at the third to the rightmost platform, just as the No. 1 train was approaching. Jeanette finished scribbling two sentences on the corner of the map, and handed the map to John just as they stepped aboard. The sentences read,

'Many slight roaming-only fees?'

Followed by:

'Swell destinations east are really affected nine and ten times.'

John focused silently on the sentences for at least five minutes, as the train rocked back and forth as it slid in between the traffic. At the third train station, John looked up at Jeanette. "Not bad for a first try. I would have used a different approach, but the focus on cellular messaging is rather clever, and timely. The word 'swell' needs to change to something else -- it's too casual."

What John had quickly figured out was that the message was hidden in the second letter of each word. The first sentence asked if Joe was 'alone' and the second advised that 'we are fine,' with an extra 't' at the end to make the sentence more readable.

"It's all I could do on short notice," replied Jeanette. "I considered the advancing letter method, with progressive letters in each word, but wasn't sure if John had the time to figure this out. In efforts of time, let's just send this thing. Either way, even if he's alone, it will not alert anyone tapping his phone with useful information."

"OK -- I'm good with the message. Type it in and send it."

Jeanette typed in the first sentence only, and hit 'Send,' and waited.

Chapter 47

The unexpected ding from Joe's cellphone made both he and Mick jump, as they were approaching Basel via a roundabout route driven from Kaysersberg. Not knowing if the General's henchmen were following close behind, Joe intentionally chose a route through the French countryside, that included multiple twists and turns through quaint towns, making following very difficult due to the very short site distance. Anyone who was able to follow them would have to follow so closely, that it would be obvious. Overhead surveillance via helicopter would also be immediately obvious. The drive had been uneventful thus far, with Joe and Mick wondering if John had received their cryptic text request to 'add to their collection.'   First and foremost of the text was to confirm if communication was possible, and secondly, to establish a meeting point that was not easily decipherable for anyone intercepting the text. Clearly this was a previous error that they did not want to repeat.

Joe slowed the car down to retrieve his cellphone from his front right pants pocket. The second he saw the sentence, he smiled.

"It's John, thank goodness. He's sending using one of ole' Raymond's tricks, back from Langley."

"Raymond Combs?" asked Mick. "I haven't worked with Ray for almost three years."

"Yes -- good ole' Ray Combs. Mr. Cryptic himself."

"He's dead, you know. Got mixed up with the Columbian Cartel, and took the fall when they cracked one of his codes."

"Yea, I heard. Ray's son Barry is now following in his footsteps."

"Can you figure this out while I continue driving?" asked Joe.

"Sure -- but what am I looking for?"

"Look for patterns, grouped letters, capital letters, etc. John would have made it easy to decipher for a quick turn, knowing that by the time anyone figures out the code, we'll have moved on."

Over the next few minutes, Mick methodically proceeded through the simplest tricks that were part of every CIA cipher 101 class. Within 5 minutes, the code was cracked.

"Wow -- couldn't be easier. It was the second letter option."

"And?" asked Joe, as he tried to concentrate on the road, but also see the text,

"John is asking if we're alone, which we can assume translates to no captors."

"Great -- reply with a 3rd letter 'Yes.' Once confirmed, we can expect more from a second letter perspective, specific to their condition."

Mick thought quickly, and typed in 'Try wrestling -- it's a kick.'

Within seconds, the text reply, 'Swell destinations east are really affected nine and ten times.'

"They are fine," replied Mick. Now we need to set up the meeting point."

"Just in case the General has figured out the Basel SBB, let's get them to another meeting place, that being the watch shop one block off of the Messeplatz, so they can add to my collection. Jeanette knows the shop well, as I am their favorite customer."

Mick typed, 'Buy a blue-Lumi.'

The reply text was, 'To match the white, black-out and orange?', referring to Joe's increasing collection of Luminox Navy Seal composite watches, more specifically the colors purchased over years of visiting Switzerland.

Mick read the text to Joe and let out a sigh of relief. "I'm feeling a bit better about things right now -- not great, but better than an hour ago."

"You and me both." agreed Joe. "If all goes well, we'll soon all be together for the first time in over five years. You'll remember John from the boat house spectacle we staged a few years back. Don't be surprised when he calls you Brenda, or asks where your bikini is."

"For Jeanette's sake, I hope he doesn't."

Chapter 48

"So his collection that he referred to are watches?" John asked Jeanette. "When did he start collecting watches?"

"Long story, but yes, watches plus other things. Your brother has become a collector of sorts, just like your father."

"Maybe our Father's 'wind the clock' has another hidden meaning," replied John with a smile.

"I hadn't thought of it that way, but very possibly."

"So where do we buy the blue watch?" asked John. "And more importantly, when we arrived in Basel, you also noted that Joe had been a frequent visitor to Basel over the past few years. You never expanded on the 'why' behind this statement."

John was referring to the recent conversation that focused on why Jeanette had been assigned to watch John, which never progressed to the reason behind Joe's frequent visits to Basel."

"Yes, as I mentioned earlier, Joe and your previous partners at EXos have progressed the design of the SCENICC Prototype far over the past five years since you left the U.S. The prototype is now named the fEP, which is short for 'femto Eye Phone.' Right after your orchestrated departure, Joe was assigned to lead the expedited research and development, and create a prototype of the fEP, in a short five years."

Jeanette took a breath and looked back at John, who was stunned by this news.

"In five years, with clinical trials and all. That's ludicrous. Without the technical knowledge that supported development of the SCENICC, that mostly being me, and a few hundred million dollars of support, there is no way this could occur."

"Well, you're exactly correct, but if you think about it, a complete redesign was the only way that this option could work, since Joe did not have your brains to run the program, and further enhance the SCENICC design to a field-ready state that could effectively function on the battlefield, or any other environment where small size and long battery life were essential. With the Pentagon giving the go-ahead, Joe could use the knowledge that he and the EXos team had, to pursue an alternative design. The fEP was the outcome."

"And funding? How much was given to support this effort?"

"300 million U.S dollars, plus another 200 million, upon successful completion of the trials," replied Jeanette.

"Wow -- that would just about do it. Clearly the team has been cost conscious, but with that amount of funding and a full five years there was a small chance for success, with the sole exception being FDA approval. EXos has minimal experience with 19 CFR requirements and clinical trials. We were concerned with this exact issue on the front-end of the SCENICC design, especially since the unit would become an implantable design."

"Not really, as the fEP is not implanted -- it's more closely aligned to a contact lens, not an implantable device like an intraocular lens. Trials and validation to support 19 CFR requirements are much simpler as a result."

"Yes, but we're not a pharmaceutical company, with years of experience and hundreds of PhDs who can support thousands of pages of medical device registration applications under 13485."

"No, we're not, but the Pentagon realized this, and brought on a partner for EXos."

"What type of partner?"

"A pharma powerhouse that you know well, one that is located in Basel," mentioned Jeanette. "Any guesses?"

"There's only one big player in Basel, which explains why Joe would be a frequent visitor – Transivo."

"Bingo," replied Jeanette. "The biggest in Europe, much the less in Basel."

"So how do you know so much about this, considering that you've been a stewardess for many years? Or is this your real job, with stewardess as your cover?"

"Well, that's complicated. We really need to get to the watch shop, but yes, I've worked at Langley since I graduated college, and have held many types of positions all over the world. You would be amazed how creative the U.S. Intelligence agencies can be when assigned their operatives. I actually chose this assignment, especially considering the reputation that you and Joe have developed since you entered the scene."

"This is nothing less than incredible, and impressive that Joe has led EXos and the SCENICC to this point. Back to the issue of Transivo. Did they purchase us, I mean, did they buy-out EXos?"

"No, it's purely a joint venture. They are being paid separately to lead the registration, which has proceeded well thus far. The registration has already been submitted, with trials initiated. They're estimating less than one year for the actual approval, which is rather fast, even for a pharma giant like Transivo."

By this time, John and Jeanette had made their way from the No. 1 to the No. 6 train that passed through the Messeplatz.

"This is our stop," noted Jeanette. "We'll be walking two blocks to the watch shop."

John and Jeanette rose from their backwards facing seats and grabbed the plastic loop handles that hung along the length of a metal bar that ran the length of the train car. A female voice came across the loudspeaker announcing the station name in an unintelligible language, which John knew was a mix between German and Swiss. He assumed that Jeanette could understand, still amazed at how his world had changed over the past 12 hours.

The train stopped rather abruptly, and the doors slid apart to expose the street below. Jeanette led the way, and exited through the middle of the awaiting passengers waiting anxiously to board the train before the doors closed. John followed, enthused that he would soon see his brother Joe for the first time in more than five years. He also knew that there was much more to the few-minute historical Cliff Notes summary that Jeanette had just given him. There were clearly many positives that had occurred over the past five years, but he knew the story was also filled with negatives, which could be lurking around the next corner.

Just then Jeanette reaffirmed his thought with a "Stay right behind me, as we have a slight detour to take before we just walk unprepared into a watch shop per the direction from a potentially unknown text."

John and Jeanette parted the crowds that passed by them in every direction. There was no pattern to who walked on the right or left side of the street, such as occurs in the United States where people drive on the right side of the street, and walk on the right as well. Since the EU was such a mix of cultures, driving occurred on the left or right side was a function of which member state you were driving in. As a result, people walked sidewalks in the same fashion, without consistency.

John watched Jeanette pass amongst the crowded sidewalks like a shark through the sea, weaving from side to side, but evading collision with any passers-by. John, on the other hand, felt as if he was continually in everyone's path, even though he was attempting to follow in Jeanette's lead.

Jeanette was heading towards the street corner, when she took a quick left into a clothing store. John followed her into the shop a mere 10 seconds later, and noticed her in the corner speaking to another woman who appeared to be admiring a black dress that was on a nearby manikin. The one woman pointed towards the racks of dresses, where John assumed that subject dress was available. Jeanette headed that way, looked through a few sizes, and then with a disappointed expression, turned towards John who was still standing close to the front entrance. She passed the front desk, nodded a polite thank you, and headed past John and out the door. John followed quickly, trying to keep up as Jeanette sped away. After a quick sprint, John was next to Jeanette.

"Didn't like the dress?" asked John.

"I was not shopping for a dress," replied Jeanette. "Although I did find this." Jeanette nonchalantly reached behind her back to reveal a black handgun of a brand John didn't recognize.

"Does it make my butt look big?" asked Jeanette.

"What? Where did that come from?"

"I just picked it up in the dress shop," replied Jeanette. "Do you like it?"

"Um, yes, but how did you ..."

"You don't want to know." interrupted Jeanette.

"Yes, I guess not."

John and Jeanette rounded the second street off of the Messeplatz, from which point John could see a watch shop, Bucherer AG, about half way down the street.

"Is that the one, I mean, the Lumi-shop?" asked John.

"That's the one, which is why I'm going to go in first in the event we're walking into a trap. Right now, I need you to double back to the Messeplatz, then come in from the opposite side of the street. If I'm in the front of the shop looking out the front window to the street, then the coast is clear. If I'm not visible, or looking towards the back wall of the shop, then keep walking past the shop and take the No. 3 back to the Hilton, and disappear. Understood?"

"Disappear — for how long? You know how I like specifics."

"Forever, as if your life depends upon it." Jeanette looked him in the eye, in a serious yet sad look, that he had never seen from her.

John was quiet, maintaining the gaze.

"Do you understand?" repeated Jeanette.

"Understood," replied John. Jeanette turned and walked away.

John never liked good-byes, and this was about as abrupt a good-bye as possible. He really wanted to be reunited with his brother Joe, and continue this beautiful relationship with Jeanette to grow. Following instructions, he slowly turned and headed back to the Messeplatz. Within 100 steps, he reached the square, waited a few minutes there, then doubled back towards the shop. 200 steps later he approached the shop, this time from the opposite direction, and could see people moving about the store, but not Jeanette. He approached the shop slowly from across the street, and could see other customers milling around the show cases near the front of the store. He ventured closer. When within a mere 10 feet from the storefront, he saw Jeanette, looking out of the window. The coast was clear, and John made a bee line for the front door, trying not to look too anxious, but knowing that he couldn't control himself.

Chapter 49

Joe and Mick had arrived approximately 20 minutes before, and had carefully and repeatedly scanned the surrounding blocks and shoppers, in efforts to locate any overly interested bystanders or customers. Once they were confident that they had not been followed, or that any observers had entered the shop before them, they waited outside the door to be beeped inside.

As was the case for many high end jewelry and watch shops in Europe, the sales personnel inside had to remotely unlock the doors, holding down an unlock button until the patron successfully pulled the door open. The intent of this process provided the patrons with comfort that they were safe, more so than it was to protect the shop from robbery, which unknown to the general public, was a growing issue across the region.

Joe and Mick knew the drill. They stood outside the thick glass entry door, looking inward towards the salespersons behind the clear glass cases of watches of every type and make. After the salespersons felt comfortable, which took them approximately 10 seconds, a loud click then extended buzzing sound could be heard as their button was depressed. Joe reached for the door handle and pulled the door towards him, which opened with little effort. Joe held the door open allowing Mick to walk in, then followed behind her. All salespersons watched intently, ready to sound the alarm, and remained staring until the door closed securely with a thud.

Once inside, the din from the outside traffic and passers-by was silenced, due to the double-paned windows that surrounded the room. The store room was very cool, with countless clear glass countertops that reflected the fluorescent lights that hung from the ceiling above.

"Can I help you?" asked the male salesperson behind the watch case to their right.

"Just admiring your collection," replied Joe. "My friend and I are looking for an IWC watch."

"IWC -- an excellent time piece, painstakingly hand made in northern Switzerland. One of the best you can buy, and one of the most expensive."

Both Joe and Mick were well aware of the International Watch Company, or IWC, located in a small town north of Zurich, named Schaffhausen. Transivo operated a surgical device manufacturing facility in the same town that they had toured during their first year of the joint partnership. The town was on the border of Germany, with spectacular views of the mountains and pastures filled with sheep.

"We are familiar with IWC, and have actually toured the shop in Schaffhausen just a few months ago. We expected that they would have an on-site store, but quickly learned that they only sell via professional shops, not from the manufacturing site. The tour is quite worthwhile, nonetheless."

IWC watches prices started in the range of five to six thousand Euros, and seemingly had no upper limit of cost. Joe specifically remembered admiring one piece that had an asking price of 30,000 Euro, the cost of a European car.

Just as they were speaking, Jeanette walked up behind them from her lookout position from the front window of the store, where she had successfully alerted John that the coast was clear.

"I'm more of a utilitarian watch wearer, and prefer the much more durable Luminox brand," she said. Joe gave her a wink of his eye, acting coy as if he didn't know who she was.

"Do you have any with a blue watch face?" Jeanette asked the salesperson.

"Why yes, we have two actually, one with and one without the chronograph. Which is your preference?"

"Actually, it's for my friend who is on his way here, as we speak. I know he prefers the non-chronograph version. Would you mind opening the door for him, as I see him crossing the street right now?"

All four turned their heads in the direction of the front door to the shop. John could be seen walking towards the door, with his eyes locked on Joe, who was now clearly visible to John.

The salesperson reached behind the desk, to depress the entry button. The same buzzing sound occurred as John reached for the door handle, pulled the door open, and entered the shop. He walked four feet into the room, and stopped, clearly shocked but enthused to see his brother whom he had not seen for the past five years.

"They have the blue Lumi that you were looking for, Dear," stated Jeanette.

John approached the clear glass cabinet, but never once looked down at the watches. Joe was also equally enthused to see his long lost brother, telegraphed by the smile running ear to ear on his face.

"I'll take it," replied John to the salesperson. "Just ring it up and I'll wear it out."

"Very good, Sir. My, you two look amazingly similar," the salesperson commented, as she stared back and forth at the brothers.

"Folks have a tendency to say that," replied Joe, breaking his stare at his twin for the first time since entering the store. "You could almost say we look like brothers."

"Mick and I will head outside while you guys talk," said Jeanette. "We'll see you soon," as she and Mick turned to leave the shop. "Don't forget we have dinner planned at Schifflande, so don't take too long."

"We won't," replied John. "We'll pay and be right there."

The salesperson opened the glass display case, drawing the Luminox with the navy blue face from its stand. "I'll need to find the box, so I'll be right back. Will this be credit?"

"No, I'll pay cash," replied John.

The salesperson left to search for the watch box, and John and Joe were left alone in the shop now that the other two customers had just exited.

John was the first to speak. "You look great, Joe. You don't look any different than you did five years ago. You actually look better than you've looked in a long time."

"As do you," replied Joe. "Looks like life has been treating you well, too."

"I cannot complain. Things have actually been a bit boring, until about 12 hours ago," replied John. "Jeannette has been an amazing partner, but I guess that you know the whole story, from that end."

"A bit of the story, yes, as we've kept in touch over the past 5 years for business purposes, and personal as well. She's one of the best operatives I know, which is why I placed her on this assignment — your assignment."

"To watch over me?" asked John.

"Yes, initially, but I know how things have changed since the beginning of her assignment. She's very fond of you, you know."

"So it's real then. Since this morning, I assumed she was just playing a part just to keep me engaged."

"Yes, it's real -- but do not let her know I'm telling you this. Even though she violated Rule No.1 of surveillance by getting personally involved, she's been able to successfully balance the risk and attachment that causes many to fail."

"Not that I expected that to be the first discussion we would have when we reconnected, but it's been on my mind since she leveled with me on this whole issue."

"Yeah, then there's that," replied Joe. "We really don't have much time to discuss at this point. To sum up our real issue in 20 words, you may remember Prince Hassan. Well, he's pissed, and is looking for you, I mean me, but he thinks it's you."

"So he thinks I am you. I've got that. So why are you here in Basel? Is he far behind?"

"Unfortunately, much more than that. He's already here, or at least in Basel somewhere, awaiting my text."

"OK -- so let's hightail it out of here. Why deal with him at all?" asked John.

"As we discussed in the cabin our last evening five years ago, he is a patient and devious man. He gets what he wants, and whomever he wants, no matter the cost. He won't give up trying to find you, I mean me. If we hit the road, we will spend the remainder of our lives looking over our shoulders -- which I do not recommend, and cannot live with."

Joe's phone made a ding, alerting him that a text had arrived. He looked down, to see Mick's text to hurry up. Mick was beginning to get nervous, and was ready to move to a safer location.

John sent the reply, "Messeplatz, in 10. Sweep, per protocol."

"10-4. Already in work. All clear thus far," replied Mick. "Alert me when you're leaving. I'll be with J near the food tents."

"KO" texted Joe, and returned to his discussion with John. The salesperson returned at the same time, with a box and a blank Bill of Sale. "That will be 255 Euros, including VAT," she replied to John -- who was already placing five 50-Euro notes on the display cabinet.

"Round it to 250 please, just to simplify things."

"I can do that," she said, and began to fill out the Bill of Sale and warranty card.

"We have much to discuss, John, to include a suggested plan of approach to end this once and for all. Let's meet up with the girls, as they will play a large part in the plan."

The salesperson completed the sale, John placed the watch on his wrist, and they exited the store, walking in tandem a few feet apart, so as not to attract unwanted attention as two very extremely similar looking men.

Chapter 50

It took the four approximately 10 minutes for the four to meet at the Messeplatz, as they slinked into a nearby bar, away from the crowds. Once a back door had been confirmed, they sat at a booth in the back that provided a clear view of the entry.

"Our plan is simple," explained Joe. "Get into Dodici, undetected, and sit with the Israeli General."

"What exactly does that mean?" asked John. Joe spent the next 15 minutes explaining his and Mick's adventure over the past 12 hours, and the so-called gentlemen's agreement that he and the General discussed. Knowing that the General had access to one or both of their texts, he would by now know that the brothers had connected, which was the first part of the deal. That being that if they connected before his team intercepted Joe (actually John), then they would be alerted via text with a day and time to meet at Transivo. The day would be today, and the time was to be decided.

"Wow, this reads like a spy novel," replied John, after fully comprehending Joe's recount. "It is actually rather ingenious, with my first reservation being how to successfully get me into Transivo. Both you and Mick, or Brenda, or whoever you are, already have security clearance, I assume due to your dealings with the Pharma Giant."

"Yes, that's the easy part -- since Jeanette has the same access card. Although the site is a fortress, it's very unlike the U.S. Government sites that we're used to. They don't have any redundancy of facial recognizes, or IR tracers. It's purely a non-RFID access card. And you really don't even need that."

"OK, I'm listening," replied John.

"One of Transivo's vulnerabilities is the front security guard house."

"The Main entrance, where every visitor must check in and provide their identification? Wouldn't a secluded rear entry gate be a bit easier?"

"No, all of the side and rear entry gates are all single-person full length rotating turnstiles, and we're not going to be scaling any walls. The front entrance through is your best way in."

"What if you just accompanied me to the main security gate, and sign me in?"

"And you passport is where?"

"Good point -- I don't have any identification"

"And exactly how are you suggesting to get me through the front gate?" asked John.

"Simple -- We'll ride right in, and no one will ever notice," replied Joe. Both Mick and Jeanette looked at each other, smiling slightly, clearly aware of Joe's proposal.

"I cannot see how driving up in a vehicle is going to work." I'll be a sitting duck in the back seat, still with no identification."

"Nope -- I didn't say we were driving, I said 'riding' -- on a bicycle." Hundreds of employees ride their bicycles to work in Basel, with the critical mass riding through Transivo's security gate between 7:30 to 7:50 am. It's the perfect storm — hundreds of bike riders, with you in the middle."

"Hmmmm. Didn't see that one coming. Don't they check employee badges, or other identification?"

"They do, but as the crowd of riders all pass through at about the same time, all the security guards can do is get a half second glimpse at their employee badges. A color photo copy of my badge will suffice."

"Or I could just use a copy of your badge, and walk right in. Remember, we do look exactly alike."

"Good point, but Transivo has recently implemented facial scanning software, which has an iris reader. Not exactly high tech, but could present a factor we just don't need to deal with. Better to go with the bicycle option."

"I see your point," replied John. "So when are we doing this?"

"First, we head back to the Hilton to discuss specific details of the plan, shoot for tomorrow morning for the entry, with a lunch meeting at Dodici when it's most crowded. I've been thinking about this since this afternoon."

"Oh good, a plan that was just derived over the past few hours. I'm not feeling the love here."

"Hang tight John -- it only gets better! Let's pay the bill and get back to the hotel."

"I'll take point," suggested Mick. "Jeanette takes the rear."

"That works," replied Joe. "Additionally, John and I will need to stay separated by at least 20 feet, for the reasons I noted before."

The four stood, and aligned themselves as noted, Joe placing a 20 Euro note on the table for the waitress. Mick led the way, followed by Joe, then John, with Jeanette close behind. Each of them knowing that they were not in the clear, but also confident in each other's capabilities. The next 24 hours would be the last step in a long saga, if things went as planned. But of course, no plan ever does.

Chapter **51**

"They found him," replied the General's Central Intelligence advisor.

"What -- how could they have done this so quickly? We just let the two go only a few hours ago. Have you not received their intercepted texts?"

"Yes," replied the advisor. "We saw a few odd texts that were clearly in code. About an hour later, there were simple back and forth texts, describing a 'Lumi,' among other comments. The more recent texts place them at the Messeplatz."

"And you've sent my men there?"

"Yes, immediately, but we also know that they are long gone, since they know we're receiving the texts."

"So why would they be so open as to their whereabouts?"

"Simply because that was part of our agreement -- if they got to Joe first, we wait until they communicate the day and time when we meet."

"Inside the Dodici restaurant on the Transivo Campus," noted the General.

"Exactly," replied his advisor. "Now we wait for the call or text."

No more than a matter of seconds later, the General's phone beeped, announcing the receipt of a new text. He knew who the text was from, and smiled as he looked down to confirm that it was John.

The text was simple: "6pm."

"Mr. Stone -- you never cease to amaze me," the General repeated out loud. "I just hope you come with the answers I'm looking for, else our dinner will be one of your last dining experiences in the world we know."

Chapter **52**

"Do you think he got the text?" asked John.

"No doubt in my mind. Plus I think he's rather perturbed that we connected so quickly."

"So, what if you had texted without finding me first, to get them off of our trail and gain additional time to find me?"

"I thought about that," stated Joe. "The problem being that the added time is insignificant, and sending the General into the Transivo Campus, would have been problematic without us being there. He would have gone berserk once he realized he was duped, and would take on the hunt for us as a lifetime vendetta."

"Or he would have been caught at the front gate, and sent away. A simple advance phone call could have made this happen."

"The fact that Mick and I are here now, makes me believe that the General just wants answers. I'm not fully comfortable with this assumption, but enough to follow through with the meeting, with a few back-up scenarios."

"I'm all ears."

"Mick and I were discussing this earlier, but the worst case scenario, and one we must avoid, is for both of us to meet in person with the General. Clearly this is what he desires, but this is problematic, since I'm confident that he will be unable to tell us apart, and could take us both out."

"By eliminating us both, he's assured to get one."

"Correct," replied Joe. "We don't want to make this too easy."

"So does only one of us go to the meeting?"

"In a perfect world, yes, but we're dealing with a complete unknown, and the one who goes could be kidnapped."

"Ok, so what are our options?"

"Neither of us goes," suggested Joe.

John asked, "But we promised him that we would discuss the events leading up the bombing, and unfortunate death of his son?"

"True, but we never said that this would occur 'in person' — hence we have an option. Let's get back to the hotel to discuss. We can assume that the General's team is on their way here, so we need to leave now."

The four headed to and boarded the nearest train, and remained silent for the entire ride. John knew that Joe was in his mental zone, planning and executing in his mind, every minute over the next few hours. Slowly winding the clock.

Chapter 53

"Any ideas how we'll enter the Campus, in time for a 6pm dinner?" asked the Advisor of the General.

The young man, barely a third of the General's age replied, "Yes, but I'm yet undecided on the best means to do so."

The General's grandson, Ammon, entered the room. Ammon had a striking resemblance to his grandfather. Matching the same height, with the same chiseled facial features, and wavy dark hair. He could have passed for the 20-year younger version of his grandfather.

"Why not try the direct approach, Sir? Just drop us onto the roof top, and then we make our way to Dodici?"

"Remember that Transivo has radar stations spread across the perimeter of their Basel Campus, with snipers available within minutes across multiple positions behind parapet walls, for just this reason. I've heard that they have Patriot Missiles and Phalanx silos spread equally across the rooftops. Even if we assumed a low altitude approach, we would never get out again. There are better ways to get inside."

"Such as?"

"Just walk in the front door," replied the young Advisor.

"You've got to be kidding," Ammon replied in surprise.

"No, I'm serious; they will not expect the unexpected," replied the General.

"Yes, truly an unorthodox approach. And if they do expect this, certainly we're not the first to try this?"

"We'll improvise. We'll need a distraction that will allow you, me, and two of my best, to gain entry. Once past the outermost security walls, we'll have easy access to the entire Campus. Amazingly enough, Transivo does not have building security once Campus access is gained, with the exception of the Human Resource building where personnel files are maintained. We will need personal identification badges, as the lack of these may alert passers-by."

"Not a problem," stated the Advisor, "I already have these in work, in expectation of our dinner plans. The only roadblock that I see is gaining Campus access -- no need for a distraction. Once inside, the ID badges will only keep others from questioning your presence on-campus."

"OK, but we only have a few hours to make a plan, to arrive by 6pm."

"What about driving in through the underground parking garage? Once inside, a simple swipe of the badges will gain us less noticeable access," suggested Ammon.

"I was thinking exactly the same thing; a very feasible solution," replied the Advisor.

"So about those badges?"

"Easier to accomplish than you would imagine. Transivo employees don't realize how valuable their badges are in protecting Campus security. I know a small restaurant two blocks from the first train station, where many employees gather for drinks at the end of the workday. Most do not remove their badges, and if they do, they simply place them inconspicuously in their jackets or backpacks."

"And thus readily available for the taking," noted the General.

"Exactly," noted the Advisor. "We'll only need four badges. I'll arrive at the establishment at 4pm, and meet you at the southwest corner at 5pm, with badges in hand. You pick me up, and we'll head straight to the parking garage."

"Will you search for employees that look like us?" asked the General.

"I won't go as far as acquiring women's badges, but no, it really doesn't matter what the employees look like. You see, once we're in the underground parking structure, the only use for the badges will be to gain entry through the turnstiles that enter the Campus from the parking area. Once you're past those, you're in and free to roam the Campus."

"What if the badges are reported stolen?"

"Exactly the reason for entering the Campus as soon as possible from the time the badges are listed from the employees. Most will return home after the evening, and most probably won't realize their badges are missing until the next day."

"But what if they do, and the badges are deactivated?"

"Again, we're looking at a period of less than one hour from physically acquiring the badges, to using them to gain access to the Campus, barring any delays of course. Once we're past the turnstiles, it's less important if or when the badges are reported stolen."

"Can we expect extra scrutiny by the Campus Security Team when one of the badges is reported stolen?" asked the General.

"Respectfully Sir, you are being overly paranoid. From our intelligence reports, the Transivo Security Team receives over 100 lost badge reports each month. Even if they are reported, a badge or two lost at an after work party will not raise an eyebrow. If it does over the following day, we'll be long gone."

The Advisor could still see the perplexed look on the General's face, and made a suggestion to appease him. "To allow for unexpected events, I'll be sure to acquire a few extra badges, just in case," and looked back at the General.

"Better. Much better," replied the General, his brow visibly loosening ever so slightly. "Also, grab a few that at least look similar to the four of us. Let's get this going. We only have a few hours."

Chapter 54

John, Joe, Mick and Jeanette's train pulled into the SBB depot a mere 20 minutes after boarding the No. 6 at the Messeplatz. They exited single file and began the short walk across the rail platforms, towards the Hilton Basel.

John broke the silence. "I have confidence in your plan, but am a bit concerned about getting past the Transivo Security guards. It's easy for you guys as approved contract employees, but I'm kind of on my own, if things go south."

"That's not part of my plan," replied Joe, smiling.

"I'm sure, but what's the Cliff's Notes version, just to humor me?"

"Can you ride a bike?" Asked Joe.

"Um, Yeah. But so what?"

"Can you ride a bike past the guards?"

"OK, now there's a genius plan that's doomed to fail," answered John, obviously displeased with the approach. "What's the back-up plan?"

"No back up plan needed," replied Joe with a smile, turning to Jeannette who was also looking a bit perplexed. "As you know, Basel in particular is filled with avid cyclists, who would rather ride than drive. In fact, some say that a car is not needed to live in the City."

"Great info, but I'm still not sold."

"So every day, first thing in the morning and at the end of the day, literally hundreds of Transivo employees traverse past the front gate on their bikes, adjacent to the main Security building. They enter in droves, and it's the role of a single guard to manage the wave of folks entering and exiting the facility. He clearly cannot validate that all entrants have badges, and much the less, that they are the person shown on the badge."

"OK, I feel bad for that guy, but consider that I'll be coming through shortly before our dinner reservation — in the wrong direction from those exiting at the end of the day. Also, I'm surprised by this lack of security for a Corporation of such sophistication."

"This was clearly a known vulnerability for decades. So much so, that Transivo implemented a facial recognition system at this lone entry point to prevent improper entry."

"Smart. So how does the system work?" asked Joe.

"It's rather clever, yet simplistic. The system reads and analyzes unique facial features of each rider almost 20 yards upstream from the main entry point, and compares them to the Transivo employee database. If they're on the database, no issue. If they're not in the system, then the single guard I mentioned earlier is automatically alerted through his earpiece of the intruder, and nonchalantly detains the rider. From that point, the rider is taken behind the main security entrance, where it is unclear what happens next."

"That's a slightly better plan, except as I noted earlier, I'll be going to be riding the opposite direction from the mass exodus of employees, and most concerning is that I'm not in their database."

"The directional issue is accurate, although you actually are in the database — or at least your picture is, since you and I look identical. Consider also that the facial readers will be consumed with those exiting the Campus, so a lone entrant will not be so significant."

"So what is the downside?" asked John.

"There are always unforeseen risks, such as if the system somehow knows that you are not actually me, or that it knows that I am already on the Campus. The latter issue is why I must not enter the campus before you ride in."

"But if the system is operating correctly, you'll be unable to enter after me, either, since it will have me already logged in as an entrant."

"Correct — except that surprisingly, the system only red-flags repeat entrants that occur within 30 minutes of each other, to prevent folks from piggy-backing in by handing their badges through the turnstiles to let others follow behind them."

"So the system has a flaw?"

"Yes, you might say that. Plus the facial recognition system only monitors the main security entrance, as the only location where employee can enter on bicycles."

"Ok, I feel a bit better about this," replied John, as they entered the Basel Hilton lobby, and proceeded to the elevators past the registration desk. Joe pushed the button to summon the elevator.

"Let's meet here in 30 minutes," said Joe. "We've got quite an evening ahead of us, and I still have much to relay to you specific to the remainder of the plan. If all goes to plan, we'll be in two hours before the General and his entourage."

John replied, "Looking forward to it". Although he had the ultimate confidence in his brother's capabilities, not to mention those of his formidable two female partners, the meeting was well outside his level of comfort. There was no choice at this point, but to go along and listen as Joe unfolded the plan. Joe had led much more intense scenarios than this, but not with John as a key target. John considered himself as the weak link, which was more so what was redirecting his ability to focus. Wind the clock … just wind the clock.

Chapter 55

"We're in," **replied the General under his breath, spoken just** loud enough for his grandson, Ammon, and two of his best bodyguards, to hear.

The Advisor came through with his end of the deal, expertly stealing five identification badges from unsuspecting Transivo employees in a nearby restaurant, a mere 30 minutes ago. After picking the Advisor up from the closest corner to the establishment, the General's limo proceeded to the below-ground Transivo parking garage. The car was granted entry using one of the ID badges, from a man named Matthew DeSault. As the knife gate raised to allow their vehicle entry, the General knew the first test had been passed, with the turnstiles as the final roadblock for entry. The Advisor swapped seats with Arlo, the most senior of the General's personal bodyguards, and drove to the closet turnstile, where each of the four nonchalantly exited the vehicle and used the stolen badge to rotate the 8-foot tall metal turnstile, the type with rotating bars every 8 inches from ground level to the top. Not knowing if proximity metal detectors or X-ray machines were in use past this entry point, none of the four carried guns or any other weapon, so as not to alert Transivo's expected Security forces. The General was sure to use the same badge taken from Mr. DeSault to enter the turnstiles, to avoid the artificial intelligence detection of the access system that was expecting his entry after driving into the garage.

Per the General's request, the stolen ID badges reasonably matched their faces, which took a bit more time, but was good insurance in the end. They wouldn't pass facial recognition software, but from a longer distance video perspective, was adequate. The Advisor drove slowly from the garage, intentionally exiting from a different gate, in the event cameras monitored incoming, and immediately outgoing, vehicles. Little was left to chance, with this meeting a long-awaited and pivotal event in the life of the General, and his grandson Ammon.

"As we discussed, keep walking and focus forward, knowing that we're on camera since the minute we arrived," noted the General to his team of three, as they approached the parking structure stairs that exited the garage to the ground floor.

At that moment, Transivo Security Special Agent Alexander was alerted by the security system to review the video feed from the camera from the parking garage turnstile; the location where the General and his team just entered. Agent Alexander was used to receiving these alerts, which were triggered by the system as potential threats, this one due to the off-hour re-entry of four of the Information Technology, or IT, team members. Transivo's access control system recorded and analyzed the entrance and exit history of every employee on the Campus, comparing access events to the norm for each employee dating back to their first day on the job. In this case, the historical data indicated that the subject four TS employees seldom returned to Campus after the work day was over. Except for today, where they just re-entered via the parking structure.

"Got an alert on parking turnstile B2L," noted Agent Alexander to the shift supervisor. "Four IT guys; I'm reviewing the video feed now."

Agent Alexander's screen reverted to a black and white image from the video taken less than one minute ago, clearly showing four male employees entering the Campus, via the parking structure two levels below ground surface. The picture looked similar to every other entrance that occurred thousands of times each day, but for some reason, the security system thought otherwise.

"No obvious signs of broken protocol," replied Alexander. By then his supervisor, Sr. Agent Hamilton" was viewing the same video over Alexander's right shoulder.

"What was the trigger?" Sr. Agent Hamilton asked.

"After hours return, less than an hour after they all left for the day."

"Not uncommon," noted Hamilton, who continued to watch the four men ascend the stairs to the ground floor. "Keep following their progress, cameras V2 through V4, just to see where they're headed."

"Yes, ma'am," replied Alexander, his screen rolling to the consecutive video feeds that sequentially followed the General and his men. "They stopped in the main quad, past the corporate building. We can probably look down and see them out the window right about now."

Sr. Agent Hamilton moved to the window. "Yes, I see them. They are still right now, staring at the Visitor's Center. Send an Agent to check them out. Better yet, you go."

Unknowingly, below their gaze, the General, his grandson, and his two bodyguards were directly visible staring at the Visitor Center, enthralled as many first time Visitors to the Transivo Campus are, by the massive LED scrolling marquee that adorned the Visitors Center.

"What do these mean?" asked Ammon, as he and the others were captivated by the moving LED marquee scrolling slowly along the base of the Transivo Visitors Center: "SLIPPING INTO MADNESS IS GOOD FOR THE SAKE OF COMPARISON," and then followed by "YOU ARE A VICTIM OF THE RULES YOU LIVE BY," and then "ALWAYS ..."

"Quite interesting aren't they?" interrupted a young man who appeared without warning directly behind them. The General knew the look, instantly identifying the man as one of Transivo's private security team. He caught the still unsettled gaze of his bodyguards, letting them know that he would handle the issue.

"Yes, even though we read these daily, they never seem to repeat themselves, nor do they actually make sense all of the time."

The agent had also silently assessed the four, without any instinctive feeling that something was out of the ordinary, other than the fact that one of the larger men looked familiar. Per protocol, he asked "Where are you headed to?"

The General replied, "We're returning to Campus for an after-hours dinner, to review our management strategy as we approach the New Year," Ammon nodded in agreement, impressed by his Grandfather's impromptu response, aligning with their actual return to the Campus.

The Agent knew this, which collaborated with the recent re-entry, yet replied, "Which restaurant are you planning to dine at?"

"We're meeting at Dodici, at 6pm," replied the General, remaining silent after the reply.

After the second response, and the alignment with their re-entry to Campus, Agent Alexander felt comfortable that this was an honest response. He knew that his supervisor had by this time zoomed closely into the conversation, and could hear all accounts through his lapel microphone. Through his earpiece, Sr. Agent Hamilton replied, "No additional concern here, let return to base. I've got clear video. Pull facial recognition after shift change, just to assure we have them on record." Alexander looked upward towards the Security office window, and nodded, as affirmation.

"Very good. Enjoy the evening" replied Agent Alexander, remaining in place to see in which direction the party of four moved.

"Thank you," replied the General, quickly turning and heading towards the Visitor's Center, which was also the correct direction for Dodici. This was noticed by Agent Alexander, further confirmation that the response was legit.

As the foursome walked out of hearing distance, Ammon replied, "Well done. Not sure that I could have kept so calm and collected if I was in that position."

"Comes with years of practice, but don't be fooled by the apparent lack of concern by the Agent. We can assume that they've been analyzing our every step since we entered Campus, and it's a guarantee that he is still second guessing everything I've said, and will perform a deep dive into the background and habits of these four employees. This encounter will severely limit the amount of time we have on Campus, as they will find a gap somewhere in our story, and will personally return to address the shortcomings."

The foursome continued walking straight towards the Dodici entrance, which was now about 20 yards away.

"I'm surprised by your pessimism," replied Ammon to his Grandfather. "We've been very careful, and I am confident that we will remain below their radar."

"Your immaturity will fail you someday, with this exact instance an example of your foolishness. We are working with a $60+ billion organization with operations and associates worldwide, many of which are located in the most intensively radical countries in the world. The building that this gentleman came from houses their Security Operations Center, staffed by Ex-MI3, CIA, and other intelligence personnel recruited from across the globe. These specialists are supported by intelligence systems unlike any that we have seen, or can afford. As I stated before, we'll be lucky to have 30 minutes before they're back."

"Alright. So what's our exit plan?" Asked Ammon. The two bodyguards remaining silent.

"It is all worked out. You will know when the time is right," replied the General.

By this time, they had reached the entry door to Dodici. It was exactly 6:00 pm.

Stopping at the door, the General turned and addressed the two bodyguards. "Gentlemen, you occupy one of the tables in the front, while Ammon and I proceed to the rear of the restaurant to meet Mr. Stone. I will text you any new instructions. We will leave in exactly 20 minutes, and meet in the courtyard."

The two men nodded in agreement. One reached out to grab the door handle, and pulled, allowing the General and Ammon to enter, the smell of Italian sauces wafting out from the open door. Dodici's was well illuminated by individual incandescent lights at each table. There were wooden booths along both sides of the path that cut through the center of the room. Even though it was after hours, the popularity of the establishment was evident, with almost every booth filled with patrons, clearly enjoying the food and drink of the day. With each passing table, different languages were being spoken, indicative of Transivo's global culture.

The hostess was returning towards her station at the front, and met them as they neared the wooden podium from which she operated.

"Do you have a reservation, as we're completely booked until 7:30pm," she responded. "The bar has a few seats open though."

The General replied, "My colleagues and I are meeting a party of two, who have already arrived and are sitting at the last table on the right. We can also grab two seats at the bar, since you're so busy."

"Sounds great," the hostess replied. "You guys know the drill. Beer and wine are two-for-one until 7pm. Appetizers are half off until the same time. I suggest the Chicken Parmesan. It's on special this week."

"Thank you for the suggestion," replied Ammon, who was visibly anxious to reach the table, and walked ahead of the General who indiscreetly grabbed his shoulder to slow his pace.

As they continued down the aisle, the General scolded Ammon, speaking in a low tone, "Slow down and keep your head on straight. Despite my better judgement, I brought you along for a reason, so be respectful of this privilege I have granted, as I could very well have left you back in the car. Do you understand?"

"Yes, Sir. You know how important this moment is, especially for me," replied Ammon.

"I do, but let's control the emotions and remain calm, to allow the truth to be told."

By this time they had almost reached the end of the aisle, with the last booth quickly approaching on their right side that would contain the two Stone brothers. Ammon arrived first, and stopped abruptly; the General almost colliding into his back.

"What the?" replied the General, unable to see past Ammon, who just stood motionless at the edge of the table. The General came around Ammon's left side, and understood the hesitation now that the table was visible.

Chapter 56

The booth was empty.

With the exception of two iPad devices sitting on the table, tilted on a 45-degree angle, facing the rightmost empty bench seat. The device on the left portrayed a video close-up face of John Stone; one device 18-inches to the right, was a similar video close-up, but projected the face of Joe Stone. The brothers looked so amazingly similar, making the definition of their identity practically impossible. As they appeared as live video feeds, it was evident that they were not the same person.

"Sit down," said the man on the screen to the left. "And close your mouth. It's still hanging wide open, in what I can only imagine as amazement."

"Or it could be shock," said the man on the screen to the right. Both screens emitting the sound of laughter.

Ammon slid into the bench seat first; the General next. He was the first to speak.

"This is rather unexpected. I was under the impression we were meeting in person."

"General, my apologies," said the face on the left screen. "I am Joe Stone, and my brother John and I agreed to have a discussion with you, but not necessarily in person with you."

"Again, this is not what I expected," replied the General.

"Nor I," interrupted Ammon. "This is crap."

"I'm sorry you feel slighted," replied John, this time. "We were told that you wanted to discuss an issue. Your disdain makes me believe that information wasn't your first priority."

What the brothers could not see from their remote FaceTime positions, was the General texted his bodyguards at the front of the restaurant:

TEXT — *The Stone brothers are not here* —

TEXT — *They are both FaceTiming us via two iPads left in the booth* —

TEXT — *Dropping you a pin now* —

TEXT — *Use the pin and CO-LOCATOR to triangulate the location where they are FaceTiming us* —

TEXT — *Go there. Find them. Need them alive. We still need info from them.* —

TEXT— *I will keep them talking until you text me back* —

Triangulation between three communicating devices is a simple trick that every iPhone is capable of. Each device produces a circular radio frequency field that pinpoints its central location. If the chosen circular frequency band of two devices overlap, there are only two points that intersect along the overlapping circles. Adding a third device, and thus a third circle, will show the common location of the third unit. This is analogous to seismic soundings used to identify the epicenter of an earthquake.

The two bodyguards knew exactly what to do, having used CO-LOCATOR numerous times. Within seconds, a third dot showed on their iPhone screens, identifying the location where at least one of the brothers was using FaceTime to connect through the iPads left in the restaurant. Surprisingly, the location was in the building literally 50 yards away, that being the Transivo Visitor's Center, the same building with the massive scrolling LED marquee, where they had entranced them earlier.

The two bodyguards rose from the bar, focused on the mission at hand. Find one brother, or hopefully both brothers, and text the General. They knew that they had the element of surprise, and expected this to be an easy feat.

Chapter **57**

"The two bigger guys are leaving," noted Agent Alexander to Sr. Agent Hamilton.

"What?" replied Hamilton, as she walked over to view video surveillance from inside the restaurant.

"The party split up. Two went to the bar, and two are sitting at the back table. The two guys at the bar are leaving, the other two are still eating."

Sr. Agent Hamilton was watching the video feeds, as they subsequently followed the movement of the two men leaving Dodici.

"Let's not jump to conclusions. Let's see where they go. Switch to high-resolution; take facial close ups, for comparison to their personal photos on their badges."

"Yes, ma'am. This may take a few minutes."

"We have time. It appears that they just entered the Visitor's Center. Tonight is the Employee Awards celebration, so the ground floor and basement are already packed. See how the video looks from VC-1 and VC-5. It may be tough to find them in the crowd, but at least the lighting is good, and with the limited distance, the resolution should be high. Keep me posted. We have a BOLO just coming to the front gate."

"Running the traps now. Which BOLO? The guy that was fired last week from HR?"

"Yes, the same one. I would Ike to keep an eye on him, more so than the two guys now in the Visitor's Center."

"I'll work the first one."

"Thanks."

Chapter **58**

"I'm still not amused by your trickery," stated the General.

"Trickery?" Questioned Ammon. "It's pure dishonesty. We let one of you and your girlfriend free in Kaysersberg, under a gentlemen's agreement that you would lead us to Joe. Instead, we're talking to you via a stupid video chat, and we are no closer to answers or resolution."

Joe responded, "As I asked before, what resolution are you expecting? Our intent was to hold a candid discussion. If you truly want information, then we could have done this over the phone," replied Joe. "Or is there something more?"

"Nothing more," replied the General. "Just try to place yourself in our shoes. We come from a very social culture, built upon trust. We make decisions based upon collaboration and personal connection, not simply via phone or video calls. My grandson, although immature at times, is wired the same way as I am. He cannot help but be very disappointed in how this meeting is progressing."

"So what do you want us to do?"

The General paused, knowing that he had to continue talking, as no text had been received from his bodyguards. "We want to meet in person."

Chapter 59

The two bodyguards entered the ground floor of the Visitor's Center, and were immediately engulfed in a sea of employees enjoying a party of some type. The iPhone still showed the illuminated red dot, seemingly right on top of them, but clearly they could not be transmitting from the midst of this crowd. Nor did they see anyone talking into the camera lens of their iPad or iPhone. Turning to their right, 10 feet away from where the dot was emanating, was a stairwell to the lower level.

"It's got to be coming from the lower level. We must be right above them," replied one bodyguard, who instinctively headed to the stairwell, his partner following right behind him. It was a matter of seconds before they both darted down the stairs, opened the door, and entered yet another group of employees, overflow from the party on the ground floor.

"It's still strong," noted the lead bodyguard as he zeroed in on the location. Then he stopped.

"What now?" Asked the other.

"It's coming from behind the door. Right there!"

"Time to crash the party then," noted the other bodyguard. "Are you ready?"

"Yes," as he reached cautiously towards the doorknob, turning it slightly, and opening it with a slow movement.

From their vantage point, they could see approximately 10 cubicles in the room, all about 48-inches in height. The area probably served as temporary office space for visiting employees. There were no other doors, so cornering the brother or brothers would be easy if they were in this room. As the overhead lighting had been turned off, the only light in the room came from the far most cubicle. And then they heard it.

"We want to meet in person." It was the General's voice. They had found the transmitting location. Now how best to approach, without giving away their presence.

The first bodyguard silently used his hands to gesture to his partner how they would split up and approach from two different directions, to allow capture of their foe. They knew one brother had special hand-to-hand combat training, with the other having close to none. They also had former advantage, and were confident in their skills.

They slowly advanced towards the illuminated rear cubicle, and once they were within a few feet, simultaneously jumped around the corner.

Chapter 60

"Uh oh," replied Special Agent Alexander. "We have an issue."

"What this time?"

"V-1 gave me a clear shot of man number one. He's not a match to the badge owner, Mr. Carvalo."

Sr. Agent Hamilton came running over, "Are you sure?"

"Unfortunately, yes. You take a look, just to double check. Sometimes our badge photos can be a bit old, even though employees are supposed to update their photos annually, but this one is way off."

"You're right. Where are they now?"

"The foursome entered Dodici about 10 minutes ago. Remember that we do not have video inside the restaurant, since the renovation last month. The inside cameras have yet to be replaced. We're blind inside."

"Wait," interrupted Alexander. "Time lapse on external video shows the two larger men coming out and walking into the Visitor's Center. The other two must still be inside."

"We need to get eyes on both of these guys. The problem is that there are almost 1,000 employees and guests inside the Visitor's Center for the President's club appreciation dinner. We'll have a tough time finding them on video. Who's assigned to the party, from the Team?"

"Agents Whitaker and Trumble are inside. Whitaker on the ground floor, and Trumble in the basement."

"Radio them," commanded Sr. Agent Hamilton. "Now!"

Chapter 61

The two bodyguards were amazed by what they saw.

The cubicle farthest from the door contained a desk, with an illuminated work light. On the desk were two sets of iPads, facing towards each other. The face of the Stone brothers could be seen on the first set of iPads, which was projected onto the second adjacent set of iPads. This explained why CO-LOCATOR brought them to this location, but did not give away the brothers' exact location.

"Odd," said the first man. "Why go to the trouble, when a simple FaceTime would suffice. Why have this second set of iPads?" They could hear the conversation continuing between the General and the Stone brothers. From behind them, at the doorway, came a woman's voice.

"Not really that odd," she said. It was Mick, who had silently entered the room. She stood just within the doorway and continued.

"You see, the dot on CO-LOCATOR led you here, which is where you must stay for a little while. It's not that we don't trust you, but we thought it best to keep you out of the picture while the others talked. Just relax, and I'll be back in a few minutes."

"Wait," said the first man, trying to stall. "Can we talk through this first?" He started to move away from the cubicle, towards the door, which was still 30-feet away.

"No need to try to come over here. I'll lock the door after I leave." While she stated this, Mick backed out of the room, shut the door behind her, and locked it. The two men had been tricked. They were now trapped, with no way out, short of knocking a hole in the wall, which was not an option given the party that was occurring outside the room.

Both men traversed the room, just to check the door. The larger beady guard arrived first, reached down, and turned the doorknob. The door was locked, and they were staying put until they thought of an alternative exit plan.

Chapter 62

Mick passed through the crowd of people in the basement, exited the Visitor's Center, and returned to Dodici. As she passed the front desk, she grabbed a pad and menus, and walked to the back table where the General and Ammon were seated. By this time, the bodyguards were relaying the story of the aligned iPads, and the events that led to their current predicament, being locked within a room in the basement of the Visitor's Center.

"So, what would you like for dinner this evening?" interrupted Mick, as she stood at the end of their booth. They turned with a startled look, still bewildered by the events that were unfolding with their partners.

"Um, we're not really ready yet," replied the General. "Can you leave the menus, and return in a few minutes?" Both the General and Ammon returned their gazes to the iPad screens.

"No, I cannot, actually," responded Mick. "I need you to follow me, please. And bring the iPads."

"What?" Asked Ammon.

"Didn't you say that you wanted to meet Joe and John in person, to continue your discussion? They are not patient types. If you delay any longer, I can guarantee that you will lose the opportunity."

Both men looked at each other, and pieced together what was happening. Mick confirmed it, stating "Yes, this was their doing. They may be impatient, but they are very careful. Your bodyguards are safely detained, as I'm sure they have explained to you. I personally locked them in the basement, and will let them out after the meeting with John and Joe has concluded." She turned and walked briskly down the aisle, towards the entrance.

The General and Ammon slid out of the booth, to catch up with her. They exited the restaurant and turned towards the Visitor's Center, which was visibly full of people through the floor to ceiling windows.

"Can I ask exactly where we're going," asked Ammon. "I mean, since you kidnapped our bodyguards, how do we know we're not being led into a similar situation?"

"You don't know, that's the fun part," Mick replied as they entered the building. "Stop asking questions, and try to keep up. By now, we've been identified by the Security Team, and they know that you're not who you say that you are. This is where it gets interesting."

Mick expertly maneuvered through the crowds, and the General and Ammon squeezed behind her, almost losing her multiple times in the crowd. They continued through the first floor, to a set of stairs, that led upwards and down.

"Your friends are enjoying themselves downstairs in the basement, but we will be going in the opposite direction and will eventually be located directly above them, on the roof. As you may have figured out, the location dot that your friends followed is aligned through all floors of the building; Joe and John were Face Timing from their iPads on the roof, to the iPads in the basement, then to the iPads in Dodici. We intentionally drew your friends to the basement, to assure their isolation, before we approached you two. Pretty clever, huh?"

The General and Ammon remained silent, trying to act unimpressed, all the while wondering if the brothers were actually on the roof at all.

At the top of the stairs was a door labeled with the words "ROOF ACCESS." It appears that the woman they were following had been truthful about the roof. She stopped at the door, stating, "Remember that you do not have much time. Although renovations of this building have conveniently disabled much of the video surveillance, we can assume that the Security Team is on its way. I will handle this, but I can only temporarily delay them. Make the best of your time together, and see you soon."

Mick opened the door to the roof, gestured for them to pass, then turned and retreated down the stairs.

The General and Ammon remained standing at the door as she left, and ventured out onto the roof. The roof was immense and was covered with small grey and black gravel, spread evenly to the edges. They could see construction equipment of every type spaced randomly across the roof, as well as boxes that they assumed contained materials for use in the renovation. A garbage shoot was visible on the far side just off one of the edges, made of bright orange corrugated plastic. Then the metallic door creaked closed behind them with a bang.

They spun around, in surprised response to the sound of a man's voice, "Ok - we're meeting in person. What do you want to discuss?"

Directly behind them was not one, but both of the Stone brothers, and a woman with strawberry blonde hair.

The resemblance of the brothers was uncanny. Even at this close distance, they were difficult to tell apart. They had the same build, hair style, and dark brown eyes. The only visible difference was their clothing, with one of the brothers wearing a grey denim jacket Ammon was one to recognize, voices though, which he remembered from the remote conversation at Dodici.

The deeper voice being the brother with the denim jacket, which was the brother who spoke next.

"We have five minutes at most. The video on this roof has been inactivated due to the construction, but we're now live from every other rooftop, including the tall building to our left. I suspect I know your personal interest in meeting."

The General replied, "Yes, I'm sure you do. It's about my son, and your involvement in your country's operations almost a decade ago. Which of you was there that day, and what happened?"

"That would have been me," replied the brother wearing the denim jacket. "I am Joe Stone, and I was there during that unfortunate event. We were on a surveillance run through Pakistan. That morning, our recon indicated a cell of insurgents had holed up just over the border, with indication that they had captured three local informants that we had been partnering with. The three were just young men who simply wanted to enter in international relations, eventually showing their proficiency in intelligence, leading to their appointments as information specialists. They were our assets that we were to recover. Nothing more than that."

"And then?" Asked Ammon.

"We dropped into the area by chute, in the early dawn. What we didn't realize was that there was a fourth. One of yours."

"That would have been one of my sons," replied the General.

"Yes, I was made aware of that, after the fact," replied Joe. He continued.

"So when we approached the camp before dawn, we were focused on recovering three men, not four. We came into the camp on night vision, and were easily able to find and recover our three packages. Our recon never showed the fourth, so we left him."

"But that wasn't the end of the story," noted the General. "You would have thought that they would have been together."

"Yes, that would have been expected, but when we came in, there were only three. We came in silent, and he had to leave as quietly. We never gave our guys the chance to explain that there could have been a fourth.

"And then?" asked Ammon.

"We retreated from the facility heading towards the original drop point, undetected. We were one click out, and we saw a single person, running after us. From a distance, night vision binoculars showed that it was a man, running towards us, unarmed. That was when our men told us that there was another."

"A bit late for the notice," replied Ammon.

"Yes, for some reason, it was late notice. Our three men were mostly in shock, still groggy from being pulled out alive from their expected final demise. They wanted to get as far away as possible, at all cost."

"I can relate," replied the General, Ammon's face displaying an unsympathetic gaze at his Grandfather.

"Then everything went south," replied Joe. "Our chopper was coming into view in the light of the dawn, and at the same time. The Camp lit up, as the escaping prisoners became known. Your son was still within 100 yards from the camp; he had no chance at this point. There was nothing we could do to help him."

The General and his son were silent; they both locked eyes for a full 10 seconds, as they fully processed Joe's testimony. Until this moment, the death of the General's son had been a mystery. He had just vanished, with a unsubstantiated report that he had been killed. As with any story without closure, there remained the option that he would return someday, dispelling the story that in their conscience, they knew was true.

The General released a deep sigh, which clearly was a sign of his despair, but maybe an equal showing of relief, finally knowing the truth.

"Not that it may matter at this point, but our men reported that your son was a good man. Truthful, smart and dedicated to the cause. I know that you are proud of him, and I am sorry for your loss."

"Thank you, Joe," replied the General. "It was our agreement to release you from this indirect bond, and I appreciate your candid testimony. We are out of time, and must go now."

Jeanette spoke up, "Guys, look below — we have Visitors."

Chapter 63

"Whitaker or Trumble, report your locations," radioed Agent Alexander, which was received on their in-ear headsets.

"Whitaker on the ground floor," shortly followed by "Trumble in the basement. What's the issue?"

"We have two identified BOLOs in the building. I am forwarding their photos to you now."

"Wait," shouted Alexander. "The other two from the foursome just left Dodici's, trailing behind a woman. Looks like they're also heading for the Visitor's Center." Alexander paused. "Yup, entering now."

"Whitaker. Can you get to the west entrance? We've got four BOLOs now, being led in by a brunette, wearing jeans and a light grey jacket."

Whitaker replied, "This room is packed. I'm next to the east entrance. Trumble, come upstairs. Need some support."

"Roger that," replied Trumble. "May be a few minutes. The basement and the stairs are filled with folks."

Alexander located Whitaker on video, and panned the room to locate any of the foursome. The view was a sea of people, wall to wall faces, making identification near impossible.

Alexander replied to Hamilton, "We need more guys on the ground. We're gridlocked inside the building."

"Assigned Agents as we speak. I'm going down myself," replied Hamilton.

Before Hamilton could turn to leave, a red-tinted visible alarm came across all video screens.

"Incoming chopper from the west," reported Hamilton. "Who called them? Have we received any emergency medical calls?"

"That's a negative. Go to our Emergency Channel." The emergency Channel was that which is used by outside agencies, for direct communications with the Transivo Security Team."

"Control, this is Swiss Air-Ambulance. Repeat, Swiss Air-Ambulance."

"Go ahead Swiss Air," replied Hamilton, looking at Alexander, who gave a confused shrug of his shoulders.

"Swiss Air-Ambulance requesting clearance to land at the heliport on top of building 17, for medi-evac."

Hamilton turned off the microphone, looking towards Alexander. "I have no idea what's going on. I have no request for Swiss-Air".

"Not seeing any issues on the video from inside, although we would never see anyone drop in such a large crowd. Could have been an internal call, direct to the hospital."

"Trumble or Whitaker. We've got a medi-evac request from Swiss Air. Any visible trouble in your vicinity?"

"Negative, but again, we've overloaded this building, so it could be anywhere. We're both on the ground floor now, but I'll head to the roof. May be 10 minutes before I can break through this crowd."

"10-4, proceed," instructed Hamilton. She looked over at Alexander. "Not good. This is not good. Grant landing privilege to Swiss-Air. I am going over there." She grabbed her jacket and raced out of the control room to join Trumble and Whitaker, grabbing Agent Savoir to accompany her as back-up.

Chapter 64

"Hi guys. Time to go," replied Mick, peeking her head into the now unlocked door that contained the two bodyguards. They were both sitting in chairs in the middle of the room, quickly stood up and were bolting across the room towards Mick, who expertly slid her jacket to the side to display her Glock, hidden in her left hand.

The men immediately slowed their pace, as she entered the room and closed the door behind her, drawing her weapon, now pointed in their direction.

"Relax gentlemen. You may remember me from the Castle in Kaysersberg, but if not, then I'm now the one with the gun, and you are not, so I suggest that you stay put until I explain what's going to happen."

Both men stopped mid stride, looking at Mick with ill intent.

"You see, I'm actually here to help you, so don't do anything stupid. I'm also an excellent shot, and have no issue in taking either you out, just because. Do you both understand?"

Both men looked at each other, and shook their heads up and down in agreement.

"Ok – good," replied Mick. Then she continued. "I am going to let you go, and you have one opportunity to get off this Campus, as I'm sure by now you and your friends are a hot item with the Security Force on this Campus."

Both men continued to listen, both coming to terms that they had few alternative options to escape outside of the plan Mick was presenting.

"I am going to bring you to the General, who is now located on the roof. The issue is that once we step outside of this office space, we'll be on camera, which will attract the Security Team that is now looking for all of us. So you'll need to follow me directly up the nearby stairs. You will both go first, and I will follow a few yards behind you. Once we're on the roof, we'll be outside of Security's visibility, since the cameras on the roof are off due to the construction in this building. Got the plan, guys?"

Both men hesitated, the larger speaking first. "Then what happens when we get to the roof?"

Mick replied, "Not my problem. I'm just returning you to your friends. That's all."

"Fair enough. We really don't like you, by the way," replied the second bodyguard.

"I get that a lot. Join the club. I'm just doing my job, just like you guys are. In time, I'll hear I'm very likable. Enough chit-chat guys. Let's go -- you first, and don't delay, no matter what happens."

Mick stepped back to the left wall of the office area, motioning with her Glock that they exit, which they did, all the while cautiously staring at Mick from a distance. As soon as they exited, Mick followed close behind, as they weaved through the mass of employees towards the stairs. They took the stairs from the basement, slowed by the upwards and downwards passage of people, looking for an open spot to stand and continue their conversations. The upper level seemed a mile away at this pace.

Chapter **65**

"Targets located on the lower level - two men, one woman," announced Alexander into his mic. "Trumble and Whitaker, do you have a visual, they are just coming up the stairwell to the ground floor?"

"The stairs are packed, but I do see the two men that appear to match the photos, followed by a brunette female, climbing the stairs to the upper level. We're 100 feet away, but heading in that direction. We'll need support, as the female appears to have identified us."

"Hamilton and Savoir are in route, and should be entering the building in a few seconds."

"10-4. We can get to them quickly once we make it through the crowds. There is no other way down once they get to the upper level, as the far stairwell is closed due to the construction."

"Convenient for us, not for them. Keep me posted. I'll be watching on video."

Alexander lost visibility as the three climbed past the first floor, but was able to pick them up on the upper floor. Unexpectedly, they continued past the mass of employees on that floor, and continued up the stairwell. Alexander reported this to the Team.

"Targets bypassing the upper floor, and continuing up the stairwell. Nothing left up there but roof access."

Mick and the two men were clearly visible on the video portrayed on Alexander's screen. Then the woman trailing the men stopped, and began to descend the stairs, back to the second floor.

"Change of plans. The woman now coming back down the stairs. The two men are out of sight. Assume they are exiting at the rooftop. She's coming towards you — take caution!"

"We're closing in, and approaching the stairwell. Should have visual in less than 1 minute."

Alexander could see Trumble and Whitaker on the ground floor video, pushing their way through the thick crowd towards the stairwell. They were not hiding their sense of urgency, not caring if they collided with their guests, or spilling their drinks.

Alexander watched Mick arrive at the upper floor. He was unsure why she would have returned. Did she forget something, or someone? Did she just realize that the other direction had no escape? It made no sense. And then, it did. The woman knew exactly what she was doing.

Mick continued with determination towards the back side of the stairwell that led back to the ground floor. Reaching up with her hand, she broke the glass pane on the panel next to the stairs, and pulled the lever that activated the fire alarm. Strobe lights and sirens were immediately activated through the building, drowning out the din of employee conversations. Within seconds, there was mass pandemonium, as each guest realized what the alarms meant, and they each focused on one thing: exiting the building.

Alexander watched the hysteria that quickly elevated as the crowd dropped their plates and glasses, and tried to reach the exits. People were literally crawling over those slower than themselves, once they realized that the building was filled above capacity. Trumble and Whitaker could be seen stuck in the wave of fearful people, moving backwards towards the exits. They could do nothing at this point. Moving forward towards the now congested stairwells was impossible. Hamilton and Savoir were also visible, being pushed out of the exit doors, before they ever had a chance to enter.

"Trumble to Control. Trumble to Control. Can you see this?!?" Trumble screamed over his microphone.

Alexander replied, "Yes, just grab a wall. Once the building dumps, you can proceed."

"Might be a while. We've got two floors of employees and guests. Visible injuries too, as the exits are incapable of allowing this volume of egress. Where are our targets?"

"No visibility," replied Alexander, who lost the woman in the commotion, assuming she probably mixed in with the exodus of employees. "The men continued up the stairs, but I'm guessing the woman is coming your way. Keep an eye out for her."

"Roger that," replied Trumble. "I'm here with Whitaker near the east exit. Will alert you if we see her."

Mick had already identified and passed Trumble and Whitaker near the exit, moving with the wave of frantic people, out into the growing frenzy that had since moved outside. She was outside the building within a few more seconds, walking slowly away from the commotion towards one of the side exits from the Campus. She looked up. A Swiss-Air Ambulance was already landing on the roof-top, throwing loose construction debris consisting mostly of paper and plastic wrapping from stored materials amongst the crowd below.

Transivo Security could be seen everywhere, talking loudly into their radios in a futile attempt to understand the situation and control the chaos that now enveloped the Campus. Employees were coming out of every building, as well as from the Visitor's Center, some trying to see what was going on and others realizing it was best to get off Campus. It was utter chaos — Mick smiled as she exited the Campus via one of the turnstiles. Her job had been completed, and exceeded expectations.

Chapter **66**

The door to the roof swung open with ease. With the alarms and sirens piercing the stairwell, it was good to get outside. From the two bodyguards' location, they could see the General, Ammon, and the two Stone brothers, and a woman they did not recognize, a mere 20 feet away. As soon as the General saw his team, he put his hand up to motion them over. They approached cautiously, still expecting another surprise, which came immediately as a Swiss-Air Ambulance helicopter circled into view behind them. It was expertly guided by the pilot and abruptly landed on the pad on the far side of the roof, exactly inside the circle with the large red 'H' inside it, the blades causing a whirlwind of dust, paper and plastic, that proceeded over the edges of the building, and rained on the crowds below.

"Gentlemen, meet Joe and John Stone," exclaimed the General as they approached. "I see that their associate was able to successfully gain your escape. Now we must depart, via the copter that I summoned."

Both John and Joe feigned nonchalance, but were impressed by the General's creativity. A helicopter would be the only exit means possible from such a spectacle. To use an Air Ambulance was also genius, as one of the few entities that would immediately shed concern, and not get shot out of the air by local defenses.

The brothers knew that it was only a matter of time before Transivo Security figured out the ploy, but by that time, the General would most probably be long gone. The doors to the Air-Ambulance opened, with both bodyguards and Ammon running towards the chopper. The General stayed with John and Joe, leaning closer to them stating, "I do appreciate your candor. It's been over a decade since I lost my son, and as sad as I am, I have closure for the first time."

"Yes, Sir," replied Joe. "Again, my condolences."

The General turned, and walked towards the only open door of the helicopter, ducking his head slightly and shielding his eyes, as he passed beneath the blades, that had only just slowed slightly to facilitate their entry. The door remained open, as the helicopter blades increased speed, slowing taking flight from the helipad. John, Joe and Jeanette turned and began to walk away, knowing that they had very limited time to complete their escape. The path would lead them straight to the construction debris chute, providing a gradual drop to the dumpster below that had been prepared for their exit.

"Ladies first," noted John to Jeannette. Knowing their limited timeframe, Jeanette was quick to comply, jumping into the chute. Within five seconds, she could be seen safely waving from within the dumpster.

"Your turn," noted Joe.

"Sounds good," replied John.

And then it happened. A shot rang out, and Joe slumped over, blood running out seemingly everywhere from his jacket. As John looked for the source, he could see Ammon retreating into the helicopter, the gun still in his hand, as the helicopter lifted away from view.

Chapter 67

Joe lay motionless on the roof, the blood beginning to pool below him, discoloring the gravel surface in a growing dark round circle. John knelt down beside Joe, who remained face down, and rotated him to his side, blood sputtering from his lips as he gasped for breath.

"What happened?" stammered Joe, his eyes now wide open. He was trying to lift himself, which produced more blood from his mouth.

"Stay down, Joe," replied John. "You've been shot. I'm not sure how bad, but you've already lost a lot of blood."

"How? Where did it come from?" asked Joe.

"It was Ammon. I saw the gun in his hand as they took off in the chopper. He must have grabbed it when he got in. He shot you in the back as we were walking away, once, maybe twice."

"Makes sense why he was in a straight-out run to the chopper," said Joe, laying his head back down on the roof. "I've been shot a few times. I'm feeling different about this one. Must be the blood loss."

"Just take it easy," replied John. He really didn't know what he was going to do. He was alone, Jeanette was already on the ground waiting for them, and everyone on the Transivo Security Team was in route to their location.

"Come closer, John," whispered Joe. John moved nearer, to hear above the droning sirens and alarms going off from every direction.

"I'm not good. I feel it, bro. I'm not good. I need you to listen to me."

"I'm listening," replied John.

"One of us needs to make it out of here; they cannot find us both when they finally get up here. I've thought about this day for many years. Ten years ago, I took your life away." Joe's head fell back to the roof, silent, his eyes still slightly open, but fading.

"I took your life away for a decade. Everything you knew, everyone you had, was ripped away when you were forced to live in France," Joe said, at a much quieter whisper. "It's time for you to take your life back. Take it back and enjoy what you should have had."

"Hold on, Joe. You're not going anywhere. We can do this together, just like we did back at Langley."

"Maybe we will, but right now, you need to go. Join Jeanette, and assume the life that I have had. She can lead you through the process. I knew that you love her, and she loves you. See where fate takes you. But you have to let me go."

John thought through what Joe was instructing him to do. In his heart he wanted to stay; he also knew that Joe was right. He looked down at Joe. His head resting on the roof, laying in the center of the red pool that stained an area three feet across.

"Joe -- I understand, and know in my heart that you're guidance is correct."

Joe was no longer moving, his eyes now fully closed, his breathing shallow at best.

"Joe -- do you hear me?" John moved his ear as close as possible to Joe's mouth. No sound of any type was detectable. He placed his finger on his wrist, to detect a pulse, but could hear men ascending the stairs behind him, screaming commands to their team, as they neared the door to the roof. John placed Joe's arm back on the roof next to him; it was completely limp, as was his entire frame, now drenched in blood that had stained his grey denim jacket, coloring it black, versus red.

John stood, and walked backwards towards the trash chute, watching Joe's curled motionless body. John turned, and entered the construction chute, and descended to the roll-off dumpster below. Jeanette met him at the bottom.

"I heard two shots as the helicopter was pulling away. What happened?" She asked.

"Joe was hit, as we were walking away. It was Ammon. There's nothing I could do. He told me to go with you, and assume his life as my own. It's just not right."

Jeannette remained silent, as she processed what had happened, looking back up at the roof, at the crowd spinning around the dumpster in which she and John were located, and then back at John. "We cannot just leave him there."

"What choice do we have," replied John. "He's gone. It looked like he bled out in a matter of minutes. The bullet must have severed an artery — I've never see so much blood in such a short time."

Jeanette looked back intently, trying to determine alternative scenarios other than just walking away. She knew that they still had a very probable chance to escape from the Campus, once they mixed into the crowd. They could leave and return in the future. Just like every other Transivo employee, they had badges, and identities as contractors.

No one would ever know the difference between John and Joe; they looked practically identical. Jeanette assumed that Joe had left his passport, wallet, and personal items all back at the hotel. Leaving now made sense, with the chance for success dwindling as the minutes ticked away. She was interrupted from her deep pensive thought, by John's voice.

"Jeanette. We need to get into the crowd, and get off the Campus. I could hear the Security Team coming up the stairs — they're probably already to the roof by now. Our escape route will become quickly obvious."

Jeanette knew that John was right, nodded in agreement, and headed towards the wall of the dumpster closest to the building. John followed her and steadied her climb over the edge, and followed. They both fell to a crouching position at the edge, which was now surrounded by fleeing employees. Only a few noticed them, amongst the commotion that continued around the building. They easily mixed in with the crowd, and shuffled with the masses towards the front of the Campus, exiting the front security gate as local Swiss police units were entering. They continued walking across the front entry to the Campus, towards the crowds that collected near the train platform. Knowing that there were cameras everywhere that would eventually be scoured for clues, they focused forward to align with the other fleeing employees, else risk easy identification. They both knew that for this guise to be successful, they would have to return someday. Not soon, but someday.

After 15 minutes, enough trains had processed through the platform to allow their boarding. It wasn't until they were approaching the SBB that Jeanette spoke.

"I'm so sorry, John. I'll help you through this."

"Thank you, Jeanette," John replied. "I cannot do it without you." John was still in shock, everything which just occurred spinning through his thoughts. He was about to assume the identity of his brother. No, actually, he was going to reassume his own identity, and as Joe stated, take back his life.

Chapter 68

Six months has passed since John and Jeanette returned to the United States. John was just beginning to feel comfortable with his current role at EXos, as the co-lead for the fEP Project, which had been renamed to Project "I." Jeannette had been a key player in making this possible, just as she stated while in Basel. Upon their return, John moved her to the office next to his, concurrent to her promotion to Project co-lead, as his advisor, of sorts. She had quickly brought John up to speed on the technical side of the fEP, as well as clandestinely reintroducing John to his Staff and coworkers. She and John had also spent a significant amount of time with the U.S.-based Transivo team, in the past six months, both knowing that at some point they would soon need to travel back to Basel to meet with their European counterparts.

Jeanette poked her head into John's office doorway, which he always kept open.

"Hey. You good?" she asked.

"Yes, was just thinking," John replied.

"I had a feeling that was the case. I just didn't want for you to forget that we have a ten o'clock meeting on the Project, with another prospective client. Amazing how news of our partnership with Transivo travels so quickly. The Team is receiving calls almost daily now."

"We are very fortunate," replied John. "You go meet the client. I'm right behind you."

"OK. We're meeting them in the Boardroom. The first floor Boardroom. Remember?"

"Yes," John smiled, remembering how he spent the first few weeks walking circles around the building trying to locate conference rooms. "I'll be there in a few minutes."

Jeanette returned the smile, turned, and walked down the hallway.

John still had times when he lost focus, as memories of only six months ago were resurrected. Handling these events was getting easier, but he dreaded the near-term visit to the Transivo Campus. He was unsure if he would be able to keep his composure when this time came, and he stood yards away from where Joe had died. He knew that Jeanette would be there with him, helping him identify the many colleagues that Joe had grown to know over six months of conference calls. She would also be there to silently console him.

"Well, I'll deal with that when that time comes," he said to himself. He rose from his desk chair, grabbed the folder labeled "Project I," and headed down the hall to the Boardroom. As she approached the closed Boardroom door, he could hear that Jeanette had begun the presentation, as she was a stickler for punctuality; a trait that he was battling since his return to the U.S.

John grabbed the handle, turned it, and opened the door.

Chapter 69

As John entered the Boardroom, he noticed that the first gentleman sitting at the table to his immediate right looked familiar. Within seconds, John clearly remembered the man from six months ago on the roof of the Transivo Visitor's Center, as the Mossad General's bodyguard. John turned quickly to his left to see Jeanette already sitting at the table, being held at gunpoint by the other bodyguard. The General, hidden behind the still open door, closed the door behind him.

Before John could respond, the General already had his index finger to his lips, motioning for John to be quiet. Then he spoke.

"Mr. Stone ... Mr. John Stone, to be more exact," he stated slowly.

John remained motionless, still utterly surprised and yet undecided if he should fight or listen. The latter being his second choice, considering the events in Basel.

The General continued. "John, I need you to sit down, please." He walked over to the conference room table, pulled out the chair next to Jeanette, and motioned for John to sit down.

As he walked to the head of the table, he continued, "Please don't do anything stupid. My friends here are not your fans, but are under my orders to restrain themselves. For now."

John walked slowly over to the open chair next to Jeanette, who looked absolutely petrified. Her body visibly shaking as she unsuccessfully tried to maintain her composure. He sat down, poised at the edge of his seat.

"Do I get to ask a few questions?" asked John.

"No, no questions. Your job is to listen. Do you both understand?"

John and Jeanette looked at each other, then nodded slowly.

"First of all, I am not here to cause you any harm," spoke the General.

"At this point, I'm having a hard time believing you, given the surprise visit, and the state that we're being addressed," replied John.

"I tend to agree that this is not the friendliest of reunions, but I need you to hear me out. Very specifically, I am here to ask for your help."

He stopped speaking, and stared directly into John's eyes. John was skeptical, but intrigued. He thought to himself, why would the General consider such an absurd request, given the fact that he was responsible for the murder of his twin brother, Joe?

"You've got to be kidding," John quipped. "I have no desire to assist you, given the turn of events just a few months ago. The fact that you are here today absolutely confounds me."

"Yes, it should. But consider, am I that stupid to personally return to this country, come into your office, and not have a truly valid reason. I am taking a huge personal risk, for myself, and my men."

John thought for a few seconds, deciding that the General had a valid point.

"Possibly, or there is more to your story. Continue."

"Thank you, please keep an open mind," replied the General, by this time pulling up a chair, directly across from John and Jeanette, and sitting down.

"This is about my son, Ammon, and his twin sister Allete. They have both been kidnapped during a recent trip to Los Angeles."

"Not my problem. Good luck with that," replied John. "Are we done?"

"I understand your distaste for me and my family, but there is something more to this story."

"There always is. I'm truthfully not interested in learning any more of your issues."

The General continued as if John had said nothing. "You see, Ammon and Allete were the twin son and daughter of my son, who perished in Pakistan. The fourth man that Joe and his team didn't know about. The man that died that fateful day."

"You know that this was not Joe's fault. He would have done all he could to rescue your son, if he had known. He is that type of man, or, at least he was, until Ammon executed him."

"I realize that now, but until our conversation in Basel, I only could assume what may have happened that day. Let me continue. I did expect that Ammon would be infuriated when he learned of the exact details of his father's death. When Joe confirmed that he was indirectly involved, Ammon reacted."

"So if you expected this, why were you not more careful to control Ammon's response? You allowed him to commit murder, as revenge for his father's death. That I cannot accept, and now you come to me with a request for help. It's purely incomprehensible to me why I would help you, much the less help with an issue that includes my brother's murderer."

"Don't Americans have a saying, 'Turn the other cheek'?"

"Yes, but in this instance, 'An eye for an eye' more so comes to mind," replied John. "At this point, I really don't care about your situation. You had my brother killed. You may not have physically pulled the trigger, but you willfully enabled your son to do so."

"Yes, I can understand how this looks, but it was not I who conceived the scenario, and outcome." He stopped.

"So if not, you, then whose plan was this?" asked John.

The General paused, stared deeply into John's eyes, and without blinking, stated "This was Joe's plan."

Chapter 70

John was stunned. The General was implying that Joe was the driver behind his own death. That was so unlike him, but in his dying breath, he stated that he was giving John his life back. Was this an eye for an eye, or more simply, a life for a death? John looked over at Jeanette, who had transitioned from her original state of fear, now joining him in a state of confusion.

John sank backwards into his chair, staring past the General through the windows that lined the far wall. Questions with seemingly improbable answers filled John's head. He remembered Joe's dying request that he fully live his life, after so abruptly being forced to live a decade of his youth, hiding in a foreign country. John believed to his core that Joe was regretful for having chosen John's life path; one that John had zero input into. In other words, what the General was suggesting, made sense, with the exception of a few details that John needed to uncover.

John began, "So you are alleging that Joe committed suicide, in effect."

"For you to regain your true identity, yes," replied the General. He motioned to his bodyguards to holster their weapons. They immediately complied.

John continued, "Despite his gruff exterior, Joe was an empathetic man. I could see this scenario as his plan, but I also know that he is a survivor, and not one to allow loss of life or the damaging impact on others for the loss of his own. It just isn't the way he is wired. The bottom line is that he would not have included his own death in the scenario, unless something went wrong."

The General nodded. "I never implied or stated that something went wrong. In fact, it all went perfectly to plan."

"You're not listening to me. Joe would have had an alternate plan. Suicide would never have been an option."

"Actually, no he did not have an alternate plan. Everything went as he directed, and the outcome of suicide never entered the discussion."

John was growing tired of this back and forth discussion. "OK-- It appears that you know all of the details, but continue to be less than transparent. If you want to gain our trust, or our help with your son and daughter, I need to understand why Joe would have allowed himself to be killed?"

The General paused, and moved in towards John's seated position at the table.

"I never stated that Joe allowed himself to be killed, and this is why I risked coming here to relay this in person." Then he said slowly, "Joe — is — alive — and — well."

John and Jeanette bolted upright in their chairs, looked at each other, and then back at the General.

"What? I saw Joe get shot multiple times, and pass away in my very arms!" exclaimed John.

The General continued, "Not only did Joe plan the entire scenario, he proposed the entire plan to me months ago."

"This is so ridiculous and completely impossible — why would I believe such a story?"

"Think about it," stated the General. "Joe knew that my son would never stop until he succeeded in achieving vengeance for his father's death. Joe also knew that you would always be in danger, as eventually we would land in another 'eye for an eye' scenario. Joe contacted me with this plan, which would, if correctly executed, provide closure for my son Ammon and allow you to return to a normal, and safe, existence in the United States. It was genius."

John remained silent, processing the information, but still questioning its validity. This was the type of scenario that Joe was capable of creating, and executing. It made much more sense that the suicidal option.

Jeanette spoke up for the first time, "So what proof do we have of this? I mean, you could have concocted the entire story, to coerce us to help you."

"Yes, but first answer your cellphone, Mr. Stone," replied the General.

"My what?" asked John.

"Answer your cellphone," repeated the General.

"It's not ringing, so why would I ..." John was interrupted the chiming alarm of his cellphone. He looked down and saw 'Unknown Caller' on the screen.

"Answer it, before it goes to voicemail," repeated the General. "Do us all a favor, and place it on speaker, so we can all hear."

John raised his cellphone, pushed the green button, switched the call to speaker, and placed the phone on the table directly in front of him.

"Hello?" John sheepishly replied.

There was a long pause, and then a voice. "Hey John." It was Joe's voice. "I have a lot of explaining to do."

John's emotions ranged from excitement, to fear, to confusion. He remained silent.

From the cell phone, Joe repeated, "Hello? Are you pissed, or what?"

"Oh my God, I cannot believe this," John finally replied. He looked over at Jeanette, who already had tears welling up in her eyes. "Where are you … what is this about … I mean, what is going on here?"

Joe continued, "Wow, long story, but I expect that the General has given you an overview. Will take a while to describe the events that led up to this unpredictable outcome, but I hope you understand my good intentions. I never meant to hurt you and Jeanette, but this was the only option given the conditions."

"Yes, as I think about it, this plan has your name all over it. Where are you?"

"That's not important right now. I'll get to that later, when we see each other in person. I do want to inform you that if it wasn't for the General, my plan never would have succeeded. We both owe him our lives."

John was silent again, for a few seconds, then he asked.

"And I expect that we consequently owe him our support, as a result?"

"Yes, we do," replied Joe, "and I'm asking for your help. I need you, and Jeanette, to help me find Ammon and Allete."

John was still reeling from the realization that Joe was alive, and now from this unexpected request for support for the man who was originally thought to be the villain.

"Um," John looked at Jeanette, tears streaming down her face, as she nodded her head, "Yes."

"Yes, whatever you say, Joe — we're in! So when do we start?" Asked John.

"We already have," replied Joe. As soon as the words came from the speaker of the cellphone, the door opened behind them. It was Mick, sporting a grand smile. She nonchalantly stood in the doorway.

Joe continued, "Your driver just arrived; who you may remember well from our recent escapades across the pond."

"Yes, fond memories," replied John, standing from his chair to give Mick an extended hug.

"Let's go guys," Mick said. "Everything we need is in my car. The General's jet awaits us."

"On to our next adventure," replied John, not exactly comfortable with the situation, but more so excited by the opportunity to again partner with his amazing twin brother, Mick and Jeanette.

Over the phone, Joe replied, "Yes, the story is just unfolding. How's your Russian, John?"

"Russian, it's been a while," said John.

"Great," replied Joe. "You'll have time to brush up on the flight over. See you tomorrow! I have someone else from our distant past, who is very interested in reuniting with you."

About the Author

DAVID SMAT is an Engineer who enjoys dabbling in writing in between family activities with his wife and four sons.

Double Take is David's first novel, following publication of his first book *The Playground Principle*, in 2012. Three decades of global travels provide the backdrop for the adventures in *Double Take*, as well as in the sequel, *Triple Take*, planned for publication in 2020.

Originally a Chicago native, David and his family now reside in Fort Worth, Texas.

For more information:

Twitter @David_Smat

www.ThePlaygroundPrinciple.com